Also available from Amanda Weaver and Carina Press

The Romano Sisters series

The One I Love to Hate
Love Around the Corner

The Grantham Girls series

A Duchess in Name
A Common Scandal
A Reluctant Betrothal

Also available from Amanda Weaver

This Book Will Change Your Life
Always
Sky High
The Notorious Lady Grantham:
A Grantham Girls Companion Novella

LOVE AND THE LAWS OF MOTION

AMANDA WEAVER

carina
press

**carina
press®**

Recycling programs
for this product may
not exist in your area.

ISBN-13: 978-1-335-89588-2

Love and the Laws of Motion

First published in 2019. This edition published in 2024.

Copyright © 2019 by Amanda Weaver

For questions and comments about the quality of this book,
please contact us at CustomerService@Harlequin.com.

® is a trademark of Harlequin Enterprises ULC.

Carina Press
22 Adelaide St. West, 41st Floor
Toronto, Ontario M5H 4E3, Canada
www.CarinaPress.com

Printed in U.S.A.

To scientists everywhere who dedicate their lives to unlocking the mysteries of the universe, just to enlighten mankind.

Chapter One

There was only one thing about Brooklyn that Livie Romano didn't love: there were never any stars out at night. Most of the time, when you looked up, you saw... nothing. Just a flat rust-colored glow as the streetlights reflected off the clouds. The light pollution was so powerful that it managed to blot out the entirety of the universe overhead, which was saying something.

The first time she'd seen stars—actual stars, not the random sighting of Venus that managed to puncture New York's omnipresent glow—she'd been six. Vacations had been nearly nonexistent when they were kids. There was always too much work at the family bar and too little money. But one year Uncle Vincent had rented a cabin upstate on Lake George and invited them up for the weekend. Her parents—that was back when her mother was still alive—had piled the kids into the family car and off they went.

The first night, her sisters and cousins had shrieked and laughed as they chased fireflies in the woods. Livie had wandered to the end of the dock, lay down on the worn wood, still warm from the day's sun, and stared up at the sky, at the overwhelming sight of thousands of stars. Even the Milky Way was visible—a magical, cloudy sweep across the sky, looking just like it did in books. It was like peeking into a world that had been hidden in plain sight all her life—a world that stretched into infinity.

These days, as she pursued her PhD in astrophysics, she was no longer dependent on a clear night sky. She stargazed through computers, with a telescope orbiting thousands of miles above tiny earthbound complications like clouds and light pollution. But there was still something special about just looking up and seeing the stars, silently burning away for millennia.

Livie glanced up when she reached the street corner. Nothing but a low-hanging wall of clouds tonight. You'd hardly even know the universe was up there. But it was, waiting for her with its mysteries to be unraveled, if only she could figure out how.

She dropped her eyes from the blank sky to a more comforting glow—the golden light of the front window of Romano's Bar, and the electric Michelob sign that was older than she was. Just like the Milky Way, Romano's lights seemed to burn on for eons.

The poorly oiled hinges on the front door shrieked to announce her as she entered. Her older sister, Gemma, glanced up from a stack of credit card receipts.

"Livie, you're ten minutes late. Were you mugged? Kidnapped? Did you fall into an open manhole? You're never late."

She hurried across the bar and ducked under the pass-through, banging her elbow on the edge of the bar as she did. "Sorry, slow train." She hated being late, and anything less than ten minutes early counted as late.

"Ugh, don't get me started on the MTA," her younger sister, Jessica, growled from behind her laptop.

"What are you doing here, Jess? I thought I was covering Dad tonight."

"You are. I'm filing the quarterly taxes."

Thank God Jess handled that odious task. Gemma was hopeless at math and Livie hated accounting. She could use numbers to explain the bending of time and space, but forget about finance.

"How was the first day of classes?" Gemma asked. "You're teaching this semester, right?"

"Campus opened this week, but classes don't officially start until next week. My section of Astronomy 200 starts next Tuesday."

Hard to say who was less enthusiastic about starting classes, Livie or her incoming students. Standing up in front of a room full of undergrads was her worst nightmare come to life. But since it was required as part of her grad student stipend, she was just going to have to suck it up and do her best to avoid eye contact.

"Why were you at school all day if there were no classes?"

Livie turned to face her sisters with a triumphant smile. "Because I have big news."

Jess and Gemma both looked up expectantly. Livie had been bursting to share this with someone—anyone—since she'd left campus an hour ago. And the fact was, she didn't have many people besides her sisters to share good news with.

"We got the Skylight grant. Well, Finch got the grant. Which, since I'm working on her research for my dissertation, is like *me* getting the grant."

Jess grinned. "That's awesome, Livie!"

"The what grant? You're getting money?"

"I told you about it, Gem."

"Livie, I love you, but you know I don't understand half of what you tell me." Gem waved her hand, miming information flying over her head. Livie wished she wouldn't do that—that flippant dismissal of her lack of education. Gemma might not have gone to college like her younger sisters, but she was one of the smartest people Livie knew.

"Professor Finch—"

"Your thesis advisor," Gemma said. "See? I remember some things!"

"Anyway, Janet applied for this big grant from Skylight last year. You know, the telecommunications company?"

"I remember you helped her with the grant application," Jess said. "It took you forever."

"Thanks for proofreading it, by the way."

"Anytime."

"Well, she found out over the summer that she got it. Which means her research is fully funded. Which means I can work on it with her for my dissertation. Working on this with her is the whole reason I chose Adams. And now we've got the money to do it."

"I can't wait to see how her research pans out. It's amazing that you get to be a part of it, Livie." Jess was the only person in the family who understood even half of what Livie's work entailed. Everybody supported her, but Jess really *got* it.

"It is, but it means I've got a lot of work to do. Janet wants to start purchasing as soon as possible, which means I've got to start pulling together ordering info." She sighed. "I love research, but this administrative stuff is so boring."

"Agreed," Gemma said. "Why do you think I make Jess do the bookkeeping?"

Jess made a face at her.

"I also need to find a programmer, and I have no idea where to start with that one."

Gemma held her hands up. "Don't look at me. You know I can't even reboot the cable box."

"But, Livie," Jess said, "I thought you had a programmer listed as part of the grant proposal."

"We just included a line item for it. Janet had someone in mind when we drew up the budget. The guy is good. One of the best. But he's *so* expensive. It's going to eat up a huge chunk of the money before we even get started. If I can find someone to do it for less, then the grant money will go so much further."

"Isn't there someone at Adams who can do it?" Gemma asked. "They must have a computer department. Then it'd be free."

Livie didn't say so, but she doubted anyone in Adams's computer science department could program their own smartphones. There were a few academic bright stars at Adams, like Janet, but it was not a powerhouse university.

"This is beyond some college programmer. This is like, NASA-level coding. People who can program at that level aren't just wandering around looking for a part-time gig."

"You need help with your computer, Livie?" Frank, one of Romano's die-hard regulars, had been listening in on their conversation, as usual. Outside of football season, Mondays were quiet at the bar. Romano's was mostly empty, just the handful of regulars, like Frank. "Dennis, you remember that DeSantis kid? Gloria DeSantis's nephew? He was some kinda computer whiz, wasn't he?"

Dennis Mulchahey, another old-timer, rolled his eyes and set his beer down. "A troublemaker, that's what that kid was. But yeah, he was all into computers and stuff."

"No offense, Frank, but a kid who's good at video

games isn't what I need." Although that's what she loved about their regulars. They felt like family, and, like family, were always ready to pitch in when there was a problem.

Frank ignored her, because, well, he was like family. "He went to some fancy college, didn't he?"

"He went to *Jess's* college," Dennis confirmed. "When he was just sixteen. Full ride, too. Those De-Witt guys were desperate to get him in there."

"He went to DeWitt at sixteen?" Jess interjected. "He's gotta have something going on if he graduated from DeWitt, Livie."

DeWitt was Ivy League, one of the best universities in the Northeast. A computer programmer who went to DeWitt sounded promising.

"Don't think he graduated, though," Dennis said. "He got into some trouble."

"Trouble?" Gemma asked. "What kind of trouble?"

Dennis and Frank looked at each other as they searched their memories. "He got mixed up with the law, I remember that," Frank finally said.

"What, like a drug bust or something?" Gemma, ever protective of her younger sisters, had taken over the interrogation.

If he was some drug dealer, then Livie wasn't interested, computer genius or not. This research was too important to risk that way.

"Nah, not NYPD," Dennis replied. Dennis and Frank, like many of Romano's patrons, were both retired cops. "This was FBI, I think. The kid was mixed up in some serious stuff. Left college and disappeared."

"Disappeared?" Livie's tiny spark of hope snuffed out. It sounded like the guy was a dead end.

Frank turned to Livie. "You want me to get his number from Gloria for you?"

She didn't have the smallest hope that Gloria DeSantis's nephew was the person for this project, but if what Dennis said was right, and he worked in computers at that level, then he might be able to help her find the right person. And a tiny lead was better than no lead at all.

"Sure. Thanks, Frank."

Chapter Two

The address was in DUMBO, almost to the water. At the end of the cobblestone street, Livie could see the Manhattan Bridge, arching away into the city. This guy must be doing pretty well for himself, because real estate in this neighborhood was not cheap.

It might be a warning sign, though, one to add to all the others. Gloria DeSantis had been able to provide her nephew's name, but she didn't have a clue where he was, because in her words, "there was bad blood," whatever that meant. When Livie tried to find him online, she'd hit another dead end. There were mentions of him from his teenage years—stuff about his early acceptance to DeWitt, listings in the student directory, but nothing recent. No Facebook, no Twitter, no Instagram. What kind of twenty-something had zero social media presence? Well, *she* didn't, but Jess had informed her in no uncertain terms that it made her a freak.

In the end, Gemma had asked their uncle Robert, an NYPD detective, to dig up a phone number for the guy. Livie had protested at the ethics of it, but Uncle Robert had produced a number, so despite her misgivings, she'd used it. Despite the mysterious Mr. DeSantis's incognito existence, he'd replied instantly to a texted inquiry from a complete stranger about a freelance project. There was definitely something sketchy about this whole situation.

When Livie pressed the button by his name, someone buzzed her in without even asking who she was. *Okay.* She took the elevator to the fourteenth floor, which turned out to be the top one. It opened onto a small vestibule, and there was only one door. Meaning he had the whole floor.

She knocked and had just glanced down to double-check the info in his text, when the door opened in front of her. Livie's eyes flew up and she froze.

Oh.

Whatever she'd been expecting, it was certainly not this. He was incredibly, *unbelievably* good-looking. Tall, with messy dark brown hair and riveting dark eyes that made her feel pinned in place. He had one hand braced on the door frame, making his biceps flex and his tight gray T-shirt stretch across his broad shoulders.

This couldn't be right. There was no way this was Gloria DeSantis's computer geek nephew. He had to be his hot, soccer-player roommate or something, right?

"Um… Nicholas DeSantis?"

A tiny line formed between his heavy, dark brows. "It's Nick. You Olivia?"

"It's Livie."

The corner of his mouth twitched—almost a smile—and she melted inside. There was no other way to describe it. Her insides had gone all warm and golden and glowing. An absolutely ridiculous physical response to have to another human being.

"Okay," he said, backing away from the door. "We cleared that up. Come on in."

So he *was* Gloria DeSantis's computer geek nephew. And he was also spectacularly hot. Livie rarely noticed such things, and she'd never, *ever* been so rattled by a guy's appearance before. They hadn't gotten past exchanging names and she was almost too flustered to speak.

He turned and walked away, leaving Livie to come in and close the door behind herself. "How'd you get my name again?" he asked over his shoulder. There was a restless energy in his body, evident even as he casually walked across a room, like he was a steel spring, tightly wound and ready to explode. He seemed like he might already be in the middle of a hundred other things. Why had he even bothered replying to her text?

Livie hurried after him. "Gloria DeSantis, your aunt."

The sudden appearance of the Manhattan Bridge looming just on the other side of a wall of glass stopped her in her tracks. His apartment was huge, with floor-to-ceiling windows overlooking the bridge, the East River, and the Manhattan skyline. The furniture was all that low, sleek, leather stuff you only see in magazines. There were no family photos on the walls, no opened mail scattered across the coffee table, no shoes kicked off in a pile by the door. It barely looked like anyone lived there.

He stopped and turned back to look at her. "But Aunt Gloria doesn't have my number. Nobody in my family has my number."

"I know." She swallowed thickly. "I got your number from a cop. He tracked you down."

Nick's expression shifted, like he was really seeing her for the first time since he'd opened the door. "Okay, that's interesting and also a little bit alarming."

"Sorry. I tried to find you online first, but you're not really online anywhere."

He waved away her apology. "You wouldn't be online either, if you'd seen what I've seen. So, Livie—you said it's Livie, right?—you know my aunt Gloria?"

"She's my neighbor."

Those thick, expressive eyebrows lifted in surprise. "You're from the neighborhood?"

"Yeah. I grew up there. Romano's Bar? That's my family's place."

Nick let out a surprised huff of laughter. "Romano's? That place is still around?"

Hey. The Romanos might complain about the lousy business, but she wasn't about to let someone else slag on the bar.

"Since 1933, and still going strong." *Limping along* was perhaps more accurate, but he didn't have to know that.

"I haven't seen that place since I was a kid."

"It's three subway stops away." How could he be this close to home and yet his own aunt didn't have a clue how to reach him? Her sisters could track her phone's location at this very moment.

The little line between his eyebrows came back. "I don't get home much."

He turned and kept walking across the very large open-plan living area, passing through a door on the far wall, which led to a smaller room. This one, obviously his office, was tucked into the corner of the building, with walls of windows on two sides and the same spectacular view of the bridge. Up against the windows were two long black tables, meeting at right angles in the corner. And every square inch of their surface was covered with computer equipment. Livie counted four jumbo displays and at least three CPU towers buried in a snaking nest of cables and peripherals. Maybe this guy was good enough to tackle the project after all.

Nick dropped into a black office chair and swiveled around to face her.

"So what are you looking for?"

Her eyes were still busy cataloging his setup. Top-notch research labs didn't have this much computer equipment. There were pieces of hardware she didn't even recognize. It must have cost him a fortune.

"I'm looking for some help with a computer program."

Nick sighed. "I don't know what you might have heard about me, but I don't do tech support. Call Geek Squad."

She turned back to face him. Okay, he was extremely attractive and obviously successful, but did he have to be so arrogant? "It's a little more complicated than that. I need to write a new program for my dissertation."

Nick leaned back in his chair, stretching his legs out and crossing them at the ankles. Threading his fingers together, he rested his hands on his abdomen—which looked like it would be firm to the touch. If she were to touch it. How did this computer geek have a body that was so hard and sculpted and distracting?

"Okay, pitch me."

Livie blinked, embarrassed that he might have caught her staring. "Excuse me?"

"Tell me why I should take on your project."

"Um, well, I can pay you, of course." Although she had the sinking feeling that Nick was a long way from the budget-friendly alternative she was looking for.

Nick scoffed. "I don't work for money. I've done that already."

What a ridiculous thing to say. "And, what, you

earned money once and now you have all you'll ever need?"

Nick said nothing—he just hiked an eyebrow and smiled—a slow, crooked curling of his lips that had Livie's toes curling inside her shoes in response. Butterflies set up a flutter in her stomach. Oh, he was way too attractive for his own good.

It was too bad she was never going to see him again.

"Okay, so you're not interested." She turned toward the door. "Thanks for your time. I'll just—"

"I didn't say that," he interjected. "I don't know if I'm interested until you tell me what it is."

Taking a deep breath to marshal her thoughts, Livie turned back. "It's for my dissertation."

"You said that."

"I'm getting there. We're going to be receiving a lot of data."

"Who's 'we'?"

"Me and my thesis advisor, Dr. Janet Finch. She's brilliant. It's her theory we're attempting to prove."

"Okay, you're going to be receiving a lot of data. What kind of data? From where?"

"I'm getting to that." Did he ever let anybody finish their train of thought? "There's already a set of standard routines to sift through Hubble data. But what we're looking for, what we hope to find, won't show up in any of the standard analysis tools—"

"Hold up." Nick's feet hit the floor hard as he sat up abruptly. "The Hubble? Like the space telescope?"

"Yes. Did I mention I'm an astrophysicist?"

Again, the corner of his mouth twitched with that toe-curling smile. "No, you didn't. You're going to get to *use* the Hubble telescope?"

"We'll need to submit a proposal, but that shouldn't

be a problem. We probably won't get an observing time until next spring, so between now and then, I need to write this program. Do you know anything about astronomy?"

"Not a thing. I'm in."

"Wait…you'll do it? I haven't even told you how much the budget is." There was cheap and then there was what she'd been planning to offer him.

"Don't know. Don't care. Writing new code for Hubble data…see, *that's* interesting. I'm in. That's the pitch I was looking for."

"We can't afford to pay you what you're obviously used to." Well, they *could*, but then they might as well go with the guy they'd already scoped out and blow half the grant money on *him*. The whole point of this was to find a cheaper alternative.

"I told you, I don't work for the money. I mean, yes, people pay me, but the money doesn't determine what jobs I take on."

Who *was* this guy? How did he start where she started and end up here, having built this life for himself?

"What *does* determine it? I mean, what kind of jobs do you usually take?"

He shrugged before leaning forward and hooking his ankle around another office chair and pulling it closer. "Have a seat. I do whatever appeals to me. A little banking, although not as much of that as I did in the past. Some government work, a lot of consulting. Whatever I'm interested in, really. And only what I'm interested in. I have no interest in doing some tedious corporate gig, no matter how fat the paycheck."

Taking the offered chair, she fiddled with the strap of her messenger bag and debated asking him any one of the hundreds of questions swirling around in her head. "I've heard some things about you."

Leaning back in his chair again, Nick smiled— a full-on grin this time—and his eyes sparked with amusement. His voice dropped into a lower register, something flirty and sexy. "Oh, really? Like what?"

"You got kicked out of DeWitt."

If she'd expected him to get defensive, she was mistaken. His expression didn't shift in the slightest. "Kicked out, quit—it's all in your perspective. DeWitt and I chose to part ways."

"And you got arrested."

Again, not even a ripple of a response in his eyes. She envied his confidence, even if it scared her a little bit.

"Unindicted," he said with a careless shrug. "The government and I reached a mutually beneficial agreement."

"Which is?"

"They didn't file charges and in return, I did some work on their systems, to make sure nobody else can do what I did."

"Which was?"

"I hacked into the Department of Defense."

"You hacked the *government*?" That was *not* what she'd expected to hear.

Another shrug. "It wasn't that hard. Which is why they needed me. I made it hard."

Well, he sure was confident in his own abilities.

"So you're a hacker." Which was super illegal, when the hackee was the federal government. Growing up surrounded by the *other* side of law enforcement, she hadn't so much as been chastised for jaywalking, never mind crimes of that level.

"Only theoretically now, to keep my skills sharp."

"Because it's illegal." Surely he'd learned his lesson now, right? Figured out the difference between right and wrong?

Nick scoffed, swiveling back and forth in his chair. "Legal, illegal. What does that even mean?"

Apparently not. "Um, one is right and one is wrong."

He spun back to face her. "Right and wrong? Right and wrong has nothing to do with what's legal or illegal. Everything in this world, every person you meet, every choice they make, is all a murky shade of gray. You figure out right and wrong for yourself, Livie." The way he said her name was like he'd just whispered it in her ear, followed by something dirty.

"I'm not sure I believe that."

He chuckled, and the sound sent a shiver down her spine. "I'm sure you don't. And that is the difference between me and you."

That was far from the only difference between them. Maybe Nick came from the same neighborhood as her, and he had an Italian last name, but the similarities began and ended there.

He was so...she couldn't even come up with the right words to describe him. Good-looking for sure, but there was something more, some undeniable presence, something that pulled her in—enthralled her—in spite of his annoying arrogance. Charisma? That hinted at his power, but it didn't fully explain it.

She didn't know what to do with all this nervous, humming awareness, as it had literally never happened to her before. Men—they were definitely out of her area of expertise. She wasn't even casually familiar with the whole men/dating/sex thing. She hadn't avoided men and sex on purpose, but she'd never felt compelled to explore it with anyone she'd met. And she wasn't going to do anything just to say she did it. Now here she was, twenty-five and completely inexperienced with men. That had never once bothered her—until now.

How did you talk to a guy like Nick? Oh, they were already talking—about her work and his life. But how did she *talk* to him? How did she—as a woman—engage with a guy like Nick—as a man? If there was an instruction manual on flirting with the opposite sex, Livie's had gone missing the day they handed them out.

Now, after all these years, she finally liked a guy and she had absolutely no idea what to do about it. Why did she like him anyway? Sure, he was attractive, but he was also practically a felon—arrogant, cocky—and then there was his alarming moral flexibility. But despite all that, she did like him. To a dangerous degree.

And now they'd be working together, for who knew how long. She suspected he was way out of her league, but she couldn't help the tiny spark of excitement—hope—that flamed to life in her chest.

"So you'll help me with my coding?"

"Can't wait to get started." His grin turned that spark into a bonfire. He was talking about the computer program, but it felt like he could be alluding to so much more. "So tell me what you're looking for out there in the stars, Livie."

She could feel herself smiling back at him, feel her body beginning to lean toward him. She might not have a clue what to do next, but she was definitely going to grill Jess tonight to find out. "Well—"

Out in the other room, a door opened and closed, and a voice called out, "Hello?"

A high, lilting voice.

In moments, the owner of the voice appeared in the doorway to Nick's office. She was tall, impossibly skinny, and stunning, with long, pin-straight silky dark blond hair and large blue eyes.

"Oh, hello," she said in surprise when she spotted Livie. "I didn't know Nick was working."

She was British, too. Of course. Her accent was like something from *Masterpiece Theatre*.

Nick hopped up out of his chair, practically sprinting across the room to the willowy goddess. If Livie had a single doubt left about who she was, the next moments crushed that. He leaned down to kiss her cheek before turning to Livie with a smile that lit him up from the inside. "Livie, this is Poppy, my fiancée."

Chapter Three

The halls of the Astronomy building were barely controlled chaos on the first official day of classes. Undergrads wandered slowly, scanning room numbers looking for the correct classrooms, or they sprinted, desperate to be the first to throw themselves on a professor's mercy and beg to be let in to an already full section. Livie neatly sidestepped one after another as she made her way to Janet Finch's office.

Her door was cracked open when she reached it, but Livie rapped lightly, out of politeness. "Janet?"

"Livie?" she called out. "Come in! Come in!"

Her heart sank as she stepped inside and looked around. Janet's office looked like a bomb had gone off in it. She'd had this whole place organized and perfectly clean at the beginning of summer. All of Janet's notes scanned and filed, all the books back on the shelves, organized first by subject, then alphabetically by author. Everything had been ready for their return to classes this fall, so they could dive right into Janet's research without delay.

Now she couldn't even see her behind all the clutter.

"Janet?" As the chair of the Astronomy department, the professor had one of the bigger offices in the building, but still, it shouldn't be possible to *lose* her in it.

Then Livie spotted her light brown flyaway hair, streaked with gray, behind a stack of books and a second later she popped up from behind her paper-strewn desk. "Livie! Sorry, I dropped my pen and then I couldn't seem to find it." Janet looked around as if she'd just noticed the mess.

She seemed to exist on another plane for 99 percent of her life, which was why, Livie suspected, she was so brilliant. It was like she had some direct connection to the stars, seeing the universe with her naked eyes while everybody else had to guess at its shape by the tiny clues it left behind.

During her senior year, she'd attended a lecture Dr. Janet Finch had given about her new line of research, and her imagination had been captured by all the potential. Livie had stayed behind afterward to ask some questions, and she'd liked Janet right from the start. When the offer came from Adams—delivered by Janet personally—Livie hadn't been able to say no.

There had been other offers, but shouldn't you be passionate about the work, first and foremost? In the end, Livie had followed her heart and Janet and she'd chosen Adams. And now that they had the Skylight grant, it felt as if her gamble had paid off.

"It does seem to have gotten a little cluttered in here," Janet murmured, as if the papers mysteriously flung themselves around the room. "And after you had everything tidied up."

"No problem. I'll get it sorted out." *Again.* "You wanted me to stop by?"

Janet looked down at the papers strewn around her desk and then back up at Livie. "I did?"

"You did." Livie bit back a smile. "Did you want to talk about the undergrad lab assignments?"

That had to be it, even if she'd forgotten.

"Undergrad labs? Yes...ah, yes." She sifted through the papers on her desk and came up with a spreadsheet, peering closely at it. "Section two. Tuesday evenings. Does that suit you?"

"Of course. Whatever you think is best."

"Section two is the good one," she said, finally coming fully back to Earth and all its mundane concerns. "The Monday night sessions are always overcrowded and no one shows up for the Friday night ones. That Friday night slot is a waste of a perfectly good graduate student."

"Then section two is perfect. Have you checked your email yet?"

Again, Janet glanced down at her desk, as if she'd just remembered email existed. "Not yet. I got a little sidetracked this morning."

Janet's "sidetrack" could possibly end up changing human beings' understanding of time and space, so Livie was happy to overlook the small annoyances.

"I emailed you an initial purchasing proposal. Let me know what you think."

Again, Janet briefly returned to Earth. "Oh, wonderful. I'd love to get started on purchasing equipment as soon as possible."

Livie took a deep breath before mentioning her other bit of good news. "And I may have found someone to write our program."

Finch looked up in surprise. Her wide, pale blue eyes were magnified by her oversized tortoiseshell glasses. With her tiny willowy frame and the dandelion fluff hair, she sometimes looked like a baby bird in a nest. But it was a mistake to underestimate the razor-sharp intelligence hiding behind her unassuming appearance.

"Someone in the computer department?"

Livie scoffed. "No, that was a dead end. If I wanted a first-person shooter game developed, they'd have been perfect, but analyzing Hubble data? Not a chance."

"First-person shooter?"

"Never mind. Anyway, I asked this guy to come in tomorrow during your office hours to meet with you. I hope that's okay?" She skated right past Nick's unconventional résumé, hoping that he would so impress Finch at their meeting that she wouldn't care about his qualifications. Or his police record.

"Of course, of course." Janet's attention had been snagged by something in a report she'd unearthed from her desk, which meant the useful conversation was over for today.

"Okay, I'm taking off."

"Good, good. Nice to have you back, Livie," she muttered, already lost in the sheet of numbers she was examining.

Livie paused at the door, glancing back at Janet, absorbed in the universe inside her head. Her advisor was going to be laser-focused during tomorrow's meeting with Nick, though. He'd better be able to withstand the scrutiny.

Chapter Four

With her undergrad lab assignment sorted, Livie's next stop was the department office to get her office assignment. After two years of storing all her stuff in a tiny little grad carrel no bigger than a closet, she was finally getting a real office. With a desk. And a chair.

"These kids," Anita sighed when the scrum of frantic undergrads finally cleared out. "I tell them they gotta talk to the professor to add a class, but do they listen? No, they come in here and insist on telling me all their sad stories. Bet you weren't like that in undergrad, were you, Livie?"

"Hmm, not exactly." She was always first off the mark at registration, completing it before most other students had even logged on. Not getting into a class she wanted wasn't something that happened to her very often.

"How was your summer, Livie?"

She'd worked straight through her brief summer hiatus, plowing through all the published research she didn't have time for during the school year. "Nothing special. How was yours?"

"We redid the kitchen this summer, so it was hell on earth. You're here for your office assignment?"

"Are they ready?"

Anita fished through a drawer in her desk. "They are, and I made sure you got a good one." She handed over a set of keys. "406. It's closest to the copier and farthest from the lecture halls. Nice and quiet." She leaned forward, her voice dropping to a whisper. "This one has a *window*."

"Thanks, Anita."

Peter Hockman burst into the office and lumbered noisily over to Anita's desk, crowding Livie out of the way. "Anita, I need my office assignment."

Peter had started the PhD program at the same time as Livie, here to work with Dr. Langley on his interstellar medium research. Better Peter than her. She couldn't imagine a more boring way to earn her PhD. Generally, she did her best to avoid him. Now that they were through the classroom portions of their PhD and onto their dissertation research, hopefully their paths wouldn't cross much.

Anita's face was stony as she wordlessly handed Peter's keys across her desk.

"412?" Peter said as he checked the number on the keys. "That one's right next to the bathrooms! It's noisy as hell and it smells."

Next, Anita handed across a lengthy form. "If there's a building issue, submit a request to Maintenance. They'll come check it out. In a semester or two."

"Come on, Anita. Let me switch with someone."

Livie curled her hand around her keys. No way was she giving up her office assignment.

Anita shrugged, shuffling files on her desk. "All the offices are already assigned, Peter."

"But—"

"Hey, Peter, if you're done, I need my office assignment." Peter's massive frame completely blocked

Michiko Satsuma, who was standing behind him. When Peter moved to the side, Michiko flashed a sunny smile at Livie. "Hey, Livie. Good summer?"

"Um, yeah, it was fine."

Michiko was tiny, barely five feet, with a long glossy black ponytail and little wire-rimmed glasses. She'd started her PhD at the same time as Livie and Peter, and had been in nearly all of Livie's classes for the past two years. Despite crossing paths with her almost daily, Livie knew next to nothing about her. That probably had more to do with Livie than Michiko, though. Waiting on Romano's regulars was one thing—she'd known most of them her whole life—but casual interactions with people her own age were a different thing altogether. If the subject wasn't astronomy, her mind went utterly blank.

Peter turned on Michiko. "Hey, Michiko, switch office assignments with me."

"Not a chance, Hockman," Michiko scoffed, not the least bit intimidated by Peter's size. Where did she get all that confidence? When Peter started blustering and taking up too much space, Livie's instinct was to make herself smaller, while Michiko seemed to double in size.

Leaving them to their standoff, she quietly slipped away to her departmental cubby on the other side of the office. It was stuffed full with beginning-of-the-semester info. Nothing important, since all that came through her school email. This was all flyers for the departmental potluck and sign-up sheets for the grad student softball league. She flipped through it over the recycling bin, dumping as she went. None of it had anything to do with her.

"So, Livie." She did her best not to lean away as

Peter came to lean on the mailboxes next to her. "How was your summer?"

"Fine." He'd pestered her a lot when they'd first started at Adams, always wanting to get coffee and hang out. She'd always declined, usually because she was busy, but also because Peter Hockman wasn't interesting. He only ever talked about himself.

"Guess you're going to be pretty busy this year, huh?"

She didn't look up from her stack of papers. "We're all going to be busy. It's a PhD program."

"I meant you and Finch. You got the Skylight grant."

"We did."

"Lucky you. Funding like that isn't falling from trees these days."

"It wasn't luck and it didn't fall from a tree. Dr. Finch spent a year putting together the grant proposal. I helped." That was an understatement. She'd spent countless hours last year helping Janet ready the grant application.

"Sure, sure," Peter said quickly. "Of course she did. Well, good luck with it. We'll muddle along with our old computers for another year, I guess."

"All the departmental equipment is old." The entire Astronomy building and all the equipment in it was held together with duct tape and optimism.

"But you're going to get new stuff."

"Yes, with our grant money."

Peter floundered for a moment. "I'm just saying, it would be nice to get new equipment, too."

She turned to face him. "Then you should apply for a grant."

Peter's mouth fell open. "Sure, sure," he said after a moment. "Langley's got big plans for that."

Yeah, sure he did. Langley wasn't exactly setting the research world on fire. As far as she knew, he hadn't published a major piece of research in years. Just endlessly slogging through his interstellar medium work, which nobody cared about anyway. If he ever got around to publishing his research, six other people would have probably beaten him to it.

"Sure thing. Hey, you get your undergrad lab assignment yet?"

"Section two."

Peter's face fell. "Fuck. That's the good section."

Livie bit back a reply, simply shrugging instead, like that was news to her.

"Finch had better not shaft me with that shitty Friday night slot."

She kept her eyes on her stack of paper and said nothing, as she suspected that's exactly what Finch would do. Peter was by far the weakest candidate in their program.

Peter's big meaty hand suddenly came down on her shoulder and Livie stiffened. "Congrats again on the grant. I know you guys will do great things with it."

Ugh. He was standing too close, and *touching* her, and just…no.

"Hey, Peter, move. I need to get to my cubby and you're literally blocking, like, the *whole* thing." Michiko had once again silently popped up behind Livie.

Peter swung around to glare at her—thankfully removing his hand from Livie's shoulder in the process. "Satsuma, how many people have told you you're a pain in the ass?"

"How many have told you that you're one of the greatest minds working in astronomy today? Because it's that many. Now move."

Livie watched in disbelief as Peter—big, huge Peter who didn't pick up on a single one of Livie's hints—moved out of tiny Michiko's way just because she told him to. It was like she had magical powers.

"You chicks all on your periods or something?"

"Yes!" Michiko grinned, her eyes lighting up with glee. "And you know three menstruating women together can form a wicked cabal with the power to rob you of your manhood. Hands over your junk, Peter. Can't be too careful."

He looked alarmed for a millisecond before sneering down at Michiko. "Very funny, Satsuma. Whatever, I'm going to get my lab assignment."

Still scowling, he thundered out of the office.

"Stupid little asshole," Anita muttered as soon as the door closed behind him, and Michiko burst out laughing.

"What a total dickwad," Michiko said, clearing out her own cubby. "You should come."

"What?" When Livie looked up, Michiko pointed to a flyer still clutched in Livie's hand.

"The departmental potluck next Sunday. You should come. It would be nice to have somebody normal to talk to at one of those things." Michiko waved over her shoulder as she hurried out of the office. "See you around, Livie."

Livie stared at the flyer for another moment, imagining clutching a soda, trying to look relaxed while making small talk with strangers. Her stomach roiled at the thought of it. Besides, next Sunday was family dinner day, and she might have just hired a felon to work on the most important project of her academic career. She had plenty on her plate already. She dropped the flyer into the recycling. "See you later, Anita."

Chapter Five

It was entirely possible that Janet's meeting with Nick DeSantis would be a disaster. He didn't exactly match one's mental image of an expert computer programmer, and his résumé was unorthodox, to say the least. What if Janet asked him where he went to college? What if he *told* her? Janet was hardly going to be impressed by a dropout felon. Well, nearly a felon. His actual legal status was a little unclear. But he was brilliant, and full of enthusiasm about the project, which counted for something. She just hoped it counted enough to convince Janet.

As Janet typed away on her computer, Livie worked through the heaps of papers and books littering her office and checked the time every two minutes, alternately eager for, then dreading, Nick's arrival.

Nothing of a romantic nature was ever going to happen between them, of course. He was practically *married*. She just wished she could turn off these inconvenient feelings now that she knew that. It was tremendously frustrating that the first time she ever felt this zing of interest in someone, he turned out to be completely out of reach. But she needed him for this project, so she couldn't let her inconvenient "zing" get in the way of her work.

As she moved on to reshelving books, she took to checking her phone every minute. It was nearly time. Then it was past time. Because he was late. Lateness made her crazy. Of course, Nick had no regard for laws. Why on earth would he have any regard for punctuality?

After ten minutes, she began a whole new line of worry. What if he never showed? He seemed mercurial, easily engaged and perhaps just as easily disengaged. Sure, he'd seemed completely fascinated by her research when she'd met him, but maybe in the two days since then, some more interesting project had come his way and he'd forgotten all about the awkward grad student with the cool astronomy project. Who cared if he was a genius if he turned out to be a flake she couldn't rely on?

She'd all but resigned herself to starting her search for a programmer all over again when there was a knock at the office door. She startled and dropped the book she was shelving, yelping in pain when the corner of it hit the top of her foot.

"Oh, dear, have you hurt yourself, Livie?" Janet asked.

"Um, no. It's okay. That must be Nick DeSantis. I'll, um, I'll let him in."

Janet blinked at her when she made no move to actually do that. "You'll have to open the door to let him in."

"Oh! Right." She hobbled over to the door and threw it open.

Once again, she was completely unprepared for the sight of Nick. Her chest flooded with heat, and her tongue suddenly felt too big for her mouth. This was even worse than the first time she'd met him. This feeling was supposed to go away now that she knew he was off limits. *Danger, Livie, danger.*

He looked at her expectantly, and, after several excruciating moments of silence, his mouth quirked with a smile.

"You okay, Livie?"

"Errrr." Coughing, she swallowed and tried again. "Fine. Yes, I'm fine. You're late."

Nick absorbed the accusation with a casual shrug. "Got distracted," he said by way of explanation, even though it explained nothing.

She scowled in disapproval, but he didn't seem to notice. "Um, come in. This is Dr. Janet Finch. Janet, this is Nick DeSantis."

"Nice to meet you," Nick said. Then he strode into her office, grabbed a chair, and dragged it around to Janet's side of her desk, throwing himself into it. "Now tell me about your research."

Oh no. He did *not* waltz into Janet's office, make himself right at home, and then demand that she explain her work to him. Livie's heart sank. Janet was going to toss him out of her office. She'd think Livie was out of her mind for suggesting *this* guy to design a key component of her research. And she'd be right. This was a *disaster*. She was definitely going to have to find another programmer. If Janet even let her after she'd presented *Nick* as a possibility.

Livie braced herself for Janet to politely but firmly tell him he was not what they were looking for after all. But to her astonishment, Janet turned to her computer and began to do as he asked, as if strange men invading her office and demanding a walk-through of her research was an everyday occurrence.

The breath Livie had been holding left her in a shaky exhale. Apparently that charm that had so discombobulated her worked on *all* women. Good to know.

Since Livie knew this part of Janet's walk-through like

the back of her hand, she took the chair still remaining— on the *correct* side of the desk—and watched in silence as Janet explained her theory to Nick. He was fully engaged, his gaze alert and focused as she explained the work she'd done so far. Janet was a brilliant scientist, but she often forgot that not everyone around her was as sharp as she was. More than one student had been reduced to tears as they frantically took notes in her class, unable to keep up with her lightning-fast mind. That wasn't a problem for Nick. Every now and then he'd ask a question that would prove how closely he'd been listening. He might not know anything about astronomy, but that didn't seem to be slowing him down at all.

With his early admittance to DeWitt and his success in his field, she'd assumed he was intelligent, but she hadn't been prepared for this level of brilliance, this kind of agile, expansive mind. Of course, that only served to make him more appealing to her. Why couldn't he be smart and capable, but utterly boring? Or an obnoxious ox like Peter Hockman? Why did he have to be hot *and* brilliant? It just wasn't fair.

"This is amazing," Nick said, when Janet finished explaining what they would be looking for. "You could change telecommunications forever. This could be how we finally make transporters work."

"Transporters?" Janet asked.

"*Star Trek.* You know, where they stand on the platform and the transporter turns them into an energy pattern and then beams them to another location?"

"Well, beaming an object to another location is outside the laws of physics—"

"As far as you know right now."

Livie bit back a gasp. *Nobody* knew the laws of astrophysics better than Janet.

But Janet shocked her again by letting out a laugh. "You're right. Perhaps we'll have to rewrite the laws of physics by the time we're done."

"I'm all for breaking a few laws."

Then he glanced at Livie and winked. *Winked.* She'd be furious if she wasn't too busy being flustered.

"Can I take it you're interested in working with us, Mr. DeSantis?"

"Oh, yeah, I already told Livie I'm in. I just wanted to hear more about it. When do we start?"

Janet clapped her hands. "Wonderful! Why don't you get started with Livie? She's got all the Hubble data and knows the parameters of what we're looking for."

Nick shifted his attention to Livie and grinned. "Can't wait to get started." Her stomach flip-flopped dramatically. *Stupid, stupid stomach.*

He glanced down at his phone. "I gotta run. Walk me out and we'll figure out a time to start."

Livie slowly rose to her feet, in no rush to face Nick one-on-one. His effect on her was bad enough when he was paying attention to someone else. It was pathetic.

She waited by the door as Nick made his goodbyes to Janet. "Welcome to the team, Mr. DeSantis."

"It's Nick. And are you kidding me? This is the coolest thing I've worked on in months."

Janet looked pleased and flattered as they left her office. He really could charm anyone, even Janet. Well, she wasn't going to let him charm her anymore. She was putting a stop to that as of right now. It would only get in the way of the work they had to do together, and she couldn't afford that kind of distraction.

As they left the office, Nick grasped Livie's elbow and steered her to the left. "This way."

It was the first time he'd touched her, and every

nerve ending in Livie's left arm recorded the moment for posterity. It was like she'd been reduced down to that single point of contact, the only important part of her body being the one he had his hand on. But if that were true, then why did she feel his innocent touch in a dozen other embarrassing places? While her body had come to pulsating life, her brain, usually the most reliable part of her, shut down entirely. If Nick had asked her her name, she wasn't sure she could answer him. So much for putting a stop to her inappropriate feelings. That had lasted all of thirty seconds.

She still couldn't find her tongue, but Nick didn't seem to need other people to help carry on a conversation. He could do it all by himself.

"I think we should work at my place."

"*Your* place?" Her voice was a breathy squeak. "Not here?"

"I'm going to need some serious computer power and storage and frankly..." He cast a look around at the scuffed linoleum, chipped paint, and flickering fluorescent overhead lights of Simmons Hall. "I doubt the departmental computers have the muscle to handle it."

Well, he was probably right about that. Eventually they'd have all new computers for Janet's research, but university purchasing could be painfully slow, and in the meantime, all Adams U had to offer were crummy budget-priced desktops five years out of date.

"I mean, honestly, we could probably do it all remotely," Nick continued. "But when I get on a roll, I like to keep going. It'll drive me crazy if I email you a question and I have to wait for your answer. Can you work at my place? Is that okay?"

He looked sideways at her and her throat closed up. Alone with Nick at his place? That was probably a bad idea, but she didn't really see a way around it. "Um, yeah, sure. We can work at your place. When do you want to start?"

"Can you come by tomorrow afternoon?"

She taught her class at noon. Just thinking about that was enough to give her hives. Teaching had turned out to be every bit as terrifying as she'd expected—a classroom full of undergrads, staring her down with judgment and disapproval in their eyes. And now she'd have to face Nick at the end of it.

She missed last year, where she could sit in the back of a classroom instead of standing in the front, and her out-of-class hours were spent in quiet solitude with a ream of research instead of with this hot computer genius who scrambled up her hormones and turned her brain inside out. Last year had been easier in a thousand ways.

"I think I can be there by two? Is that okay?"

"Two is perfect." He grinned, and she suffered through another wave of embarrassing tingles.

They'd reached the front doors of Simmons Hall. Nick spun around and walked backward toward the exit. The sun pouring in through the glass doors illuminated him from behind, almost like a halo. The muscles of his upper arms were picked out in sharp relief, making him look like one of those ancient Roman statues of conquering princes, and it lit up coppery highlights in his hair she hadn't noticed before. "I'll see you then. This is gonna be fun, Livie."

She watched him turn and push open the doors, disappearing into the bright white sunlight outside. "Yeah," she whispered to herself. "Fun."

This was going to be the absolute opposite of fun.

Chapter Six

When Livie texted Nick after class the next day to let him know she was on her way over, he replied with the code to his building, explaining that he was busy with something and might not hear the bell.

Letting herself into the lobby, she prayed that Poppy would be there. What she needed right now was a strong dose of reality to crush these stupid, inconvenient feelings, and a six-foot blonde goddess with Nick's ring on her finger was as real as it got.

In the vestibule upstairs, she tapped lightly on his front door and when she got no response, let herself in there, too.

"Nick?"

No answer. And no Poppy. *Damn.*

She made her way to Nick's office and found him scowling at one of his monitors, his cell phone pressed to his ear. He acknowledged her with a brief glance and motioned to the chair next to his.

"Hang on, I'm finishing this up."

She took a seat, then scooted back a bit when she noticed how close her knee was to his. Nick's one-sided conversation was a series of grunts and "okay"s to whoever was on the phone. When he finally hung up, he kept tapping on his keyboard, eyes still on the monitor. "Sorry, one more thing."

"Are you still working? We can reschedule." She wouldn't complain, actually. Maybe next time Poppy would be here. Maybe Livie could plant her squarely between her and Nick, just to be safe.

"No, this isn't work. Something came up. These little shits," he muttered under his breath.

"Is there a problem?" Livie asked cautiously.

"Not really a problem. An issue." Exasperated, he swiveled in his chair to face her. "Do you know what a DDoS attack is?"

"Sure. A Denial of Service attack launched by a hacker, right?"

"Yep. There's kind of a big one hitting Europe right now. Seems to be targeting airlines. It's a fucking mess. Usually these things are launched by some shady black hat operators looking to ransom the company to get them back online. Anyway, I started tracking these guys through the usual sources—"

"*You* started tracking them? I didn't realize you did that kind of work."

Nick shook his head. "It's not for a job. I try to shut stuff like this down when I can because it's a shitty thing to do. Yeah, maybe the guys doing it are just making a buck, but real people's lives are being fucked up by this. There are thousands of flights grounded right now. And we're not talking about people's vacations. I found out about it because there's someone in Edinburgh trying to fly into London for a kidney transplant and she's stuck. Her transplant window is narrowing while these assholes fuck with the system. That's not right."

Ah, hell. Like the looks and charm weren't already doing a number on her. Now he had to go and be *de-*

cent. "That's really nice of you, Nick. You're like a cyberspace Robin Hood, minus the tights."

"Don't make me out to be too noble," he warned. "You have to put these guys in their place. Maybe it's not affecting me or one of my clients this time, but next time it might."

Well, that's what he might be telling her, but his genuine concern was hard to hide. He might be wrapping it up as a sensible business decision, but he cared, whether he wanted to admit it or not. "It's still a nice thing to do."

"Thanks. But it doesn't matter. I hit a dead end. I tracked the attack back to the server, but it doesn't belong to the guys launching the attack. They're renting space and automated services from a third party. I can't shut them down at the source."

Livie thought about it for a minute. "Have you asked whoever owns the third party server?"

"It takes too long to get a cease and desist drawn up."

"No, not legally or officially or anything. Just *ask*. One person to another."

"What…just *ask* them nicely to shut these guys down?"

"Sure, why not? The anonymity of the internet makes people act like jerks. I bet if you put them on the spot about something specific, they'll choose to do the right thing."

Nick scoffed. "You are ridiculously optimistic, Livie. In my experience, people are generally assholes. They only respond to direct threats."

His dismissal made her bristle. "And in my experience, they're not. Just try it. What do you have to lose?"

He watched her for a moment, considering, before turning back to his keyboard and typing something.

"Okay," he said, sliding his keyboard over to her. "Give it a go."

"What, *me*?"

He smirked. "Ask. Nicely."

So what if he thought she was a starry-eyed Polly-anna? She wasn't going to give in to his cynical world-view. He'd opened a chat window, presumably with whoever owned the server. Livie considered for a moment, then started typing. She kept it brief and pain-fully polite, explaining the situation and asking them to intervene. She made sure to emphasize that the server owner probably had no idea what was happening, be-cause surely they'd *never* want to get involved in some-thing so illegal and immoral, but now that they'd been made aware of what was going on, she had no doubt they'd choose to do the right thing.

Nick, reading over her shoulder, snorted in laugh-ter. "That is the most passive-aggressive polite request I've ever read."

"Hush. Being hostile doesn't solve everything."

"It can solve an awful lot."

She hit Send on the message. "We'll see."

"Hang on." He took the keyboard back and typed something else.

"Now what?"

His eyes were busily scanning a screen full of code. "Now we wait and see what happens. Okay, let's get back to our programming—"

But at that moment, a ping indicated he had a new incoming message. "Holy shit."

"What?"

"They booted the hackers off the server."

"See?" Livie cried triumphantly. "I told you. People will usually do the right thing if you give them a chance."

"Well, I also informed them that they were in violation of the law in about four affected countries, even if they were only hosting."

"Nick!"

"Hey, you be nice if you want. I'll fight dirty."

"Now we'll never know who won."

One of his eyebrows hiked and the smile he gave her made her heart beat faster. "It was a competition?"

"Not a—a competition." His teasing was making her all flustered and tongue-tied again, just when she'd started to relax around him.

"Oh, yes, it was," he replied, nudging her knee with his. Their chairs had inched closer together while they'd been sharing his keyboard. She pushed hers back. "Admit it, Livie, you've got a competitive streak."

"No, I don't."

"Everybody has a competitive streak."

"Not in my experience."

"Because you're at Adams. You like it there?"

Wait...what? What did Adams have to do with anything? "Excuse me?"

"Adams. You like it?"

He was harder to keep up with than Janet when she was on a roll. "Sure. I mean, the research project with Janet—"

"Aside from the research, I mean. Surely you do stuff outside of class? Friends? Fun?"

"Oh. Not really."

"You don't have other astronomy geeks you hang out with? Talking about, I don't know, the Big Bang, or whatever?"

Her social awkwardness was bad enough to live

through. Trying to explain it to someone else was a whole other level of awful. "I don't really have too many friends." *Don't sugarcoat it, Livie.* "Um, none, really."

"Really? None?"

"I have my sisters."

"Family doesn't count. So no friends?"

"People find me..."

Nick nudged her foot with his and she startled. "What do people find you?"

Well, it wasn't as if she was ever going to fool him into thinking she was cool and sophisticated. Might as well admit the whole truth. "I heard some of the undergrads in the class I teach talking about me. They think I'm odd. They don't like me."

"Yeah, but they're undergrads." He rolled his eyes. "I'm sure they're terrified of you."

"I'm not terrifying." There was nothing even remotely scary about her. She couldn't even manage assertive.

"Intimidating, then."

"I just don't understand how you can text through a presentation on star nurseries. It's *fascinating.*"

"Don't take it personally. The average undergrad could probably text through their own funeral."

Okay, they'd talked more than enough about what a social defect she was. His turn. "I bet you weren't an average undergrad."

"You could say that. I was different in a lot of ways, starting with being sixteen."

"I forgot that. That you went to college at sixteen."

Nick tapped his temple. "On the academic fast track since birth. But even though I was younger than everybody I went to school with, I still managed to have fun."

"Right. By hacking into the Department of Defense."

"No. I mean, yes, that was fun. But I had regular college fun, too. Parties. Girls. Three a.m. pizza. Didn't you?"

"No, but I also didn't get kicked out of school at eighteen and arrested for a federal crime."

He burst into laughter and held up his hands. "Okay, okay, if this is gonna get dirty, we should just focus on work. I thought we'd get started by looking at the existing Hubble data protocols."

She sat back in her chair and watched him as he downloaded the info she'd emailed and started opening files. After that conversation, he probably thought she was nothing but an optimistic do-gooder with no social life—astronomy's hall monitor. But she'd also figured out something about Nick that he'd probably rather her not know. For all the law-breaking and big talk about moral gray areas, he was a good guy, an honorable guy. She almost wished she didn't know that about him, because resisting him was going to be harder than ever now.

Chapter Seven

"Okay, this stuff that's recorded right here, isn't that what Finch is looking for?" Nick rubbed his thumb across his eyebrow as he squinted at his principal desktop monitor. The first few times he and Livie had worked together, it was all about learning the digital layout of Hubble, how it recorded data, and what kind of pipeline processing was added before the data could be downloaded. Livie was giving him a crash course in modern astronomical optical technology. Nick had spent years up to his neck in some of the densest coding out there, but this was different. And different was good. Different was exciting.

Different could also make your brain hurt.

Hubble was a masterpiece, but it was a decades-old masterpiece, so while some of what he was learning was brand new, some of it required understanding technology that was as old as he was.

Livie shook her head. "No, those are gamma ray bursts. That's established. What we're looking for is, at least right now, theoretical."

"And we can't observe it the same way Hubble observed these gamma ray things?"

Livie scowled at the same screen, carefully puzzling through coding so dense, some of the guys he knew in

Silicon Valley would be lost. Livie Romano was turning out to be a real surprise, and Nick was rarely surprised by people. She was scary-smart, probably smarter than anyone at that back-bench school she was at, including a big chunk of the faculty.

"Well, Hubble's already observing it. See?" He moved behind her, to see what she was pointing at. "Here's Hubble observing a primordial black hole—"

"A what?"

Livie glanced over her shoulder and startled. He had to remember not to sneak up on her. She was one jumpy girl.

She cleared her throat and kept going. "Primordial black holes. They're micro black holes formed during the Big Bang. Some consume enough matter to grow, others wink out of existence. Those are the ones we want to observe. We just need to get Hubble pointed to the right spot in the sky at the right time."

"Oh. Fine. We need to figure out how to point Hubble at a micro black hole at the precise moment it ceases to exist. No problem."

"I thought you were supposed to be some kind of genius," she teased.

"I am, I am. Some things are challenging even for geniuses."

"Anyway," she continued. "Hubble sees everything, which means it sees this, too, but it doesn't know it. The only way we can find it is by sifting through years of data after the fact. We want to teach it to recognize it right away."

"Right. Hubble can't show us what it doesn't know it's seeing. And if we can't tell it what it looks like, we don't know what to tell it to look for."

"Right."

The information swirling in Nick's brain suddenly snapped into place, like puzzle pieces that had been thrown in the air coming down and landing perfectly assembled to form a picture. "I get it. We need to teach it to speak a new language when we don't speak it. When *no one* speaks it."

Livie's face lit up. "Exactly! So you know what to do?"

Nick surged to his feet. "Not at all. But at least now I know it'll involve some kind of machine learning, and that's more than I knew half an hour ago. And that means I can figure out the solution eventually. I'm getting a beer. Want one?"

"Why are you always so confident you can figure it out? And no, thank you. I don't drink."

"Because whenever I've tried to figure something out, I always do. Your family owns a bar and you don't drink?"

"Surely there's some problem out there you can't solve. There has to be. Alcohol makes my head feel fuzzy."

"I haven't found a problem yet that I can't solve, so I refuse to believe one exists. And it's supposed to make your head feel fuzzy. That's the point."

"I don't know if you're the most confident person I've ever met or just arrogant. I don't like it when my head feels fuzzy."

"I'm both. So no beer?"

"No beer."

Livie got up and followed him out of the office. Nick stretched his arms over his head as he made his way to the kitchen, the problem still ping-ponging around in his brain. It was a challenge, for sure, but he'd crack it eventually. He always did. That wasn't arrogance, that was a fact.

Livie trailed after him into the kitchen. "Your apartment is really nice."

"It's Poppy's. Well, it was Poppy's when I met her. Now it's ours, I guess." He glanced around the apartment briefly. He supposed it looked nice, although he had no sense about that kind of thing at all. He'd have been happy, though, if there was one comfortable place, outside of his office, to *sit down*. Poppy's designer furniture wasn't exactly soft and welcoming.

"How long have you lived here?"

Nick had to stop and think for a second. Common problem when his brain was busy wrestling with a problem. His mind was back there tangled up in Hubble coding, and real life tended to get forgotten. It drove Poppy crazy.

"Um, a year? Nearly a year. Since I met Poppy."

"Where'd you live before that?"

"Palo Alto."

"California? You lived in California?"

"Yeah. That's where I headed after—" He caught himself right before he veered into something too personal to share. "I headed out there after DeWitt."

"Were you working for one of those tech giants?"

"Nah. I told you, the corporate scene isn't for me, I don't care if they have an onsite acupuncturist and free catered lunches, or whatever. I worked with those guys occasionally, jobbing in for a specific project, but I was always more interested in the start-ups, figuring out something brand new. That's a lot more fun."

"I suppose it was hard, though, being out there."

"Why would it be hard?" Actually, his years in California had seemed to pass in the blink of an eye, a blur of freelance gigs and fun. One day, he looked up and seven years had gone by.

"Well, your family is here."

He let out a bark of laughter. "*That* was not why I moved back. I haven't even seen them since I moved to California."

Her eyes went wide. "Seriously? Not once in all those years?"

"Not once."

"But they're so close—"

Nope, not having this conversation. "I came back to New York for a long weekend," he explained, cutting her off. "Just hanging with a friend. We were in this bar in Williamsburg and I met Poppy. Never went back."

"You moved back here for her?"

"I can work anywhere, so why not? I didn't have much to keep me in California." He pulled open the fridge and retrieved a Lagunitas. "You want something else to drink? Soda? Water? One of these green smoothie things Poppy likes? I don't know what's in them, but she swears they'll burn off ten pounds in a week."

"Water, please. How can Poppy lose ten pounds? There's hardly any of her there as it is."

Nick chuckled as he passed her a bottle of water. Livie could be surprisingly funny. "Trust me, in Poppy's world, you can always lose ten more pounds. She's a model. They think differently about that stuff."

"Wow, she's a model. Not that it's surprising. She's very pretty."

"I happen to agree," he said, grinning at Livie, who looked down, fiddling with the cap of her water bottle. Her hair was so long and thick you couldn't see her face behind it when she hid herself like that. He suspected she did it on purpose, to hide what she was thinking, and Livie thought *a lot.*

On the surface, she was another socially awkward genius. He'd certainly been around enough of those growing up. But every now and then, he'd catch a look in her eyes and realize she was noting everything happening around her, even if she didn't comment on it. Sometimes he'd catch her watching *him* that way and he'd suddenly feel like she could see every one of his secrets and fears as clear as day. That was not a comfortable sensation.

The way she'd grabbed onto his family issues just now—how did she sniff that out? He didn't mention his family to *anyone*, not even Poppy. He shouldn't have snapped at her like that. She was just being kind, worrying because he was on his own.

He'd never met anyone so solidly *nice* before in his life. It was a novelty. Even her crazy sense of honor was growing on him. In his experience, the world was full of truly shitty human beings. As for himself, he'd always thought he was fairly morally neutral. Not the best person alive, but by no means the worst—certainly better than a lot of the borderline sociopath tech geniuses he knew back in Palo Alto. But that was before he met Livie. She made him feel like he lurked down in the worst muck of humanity. Who knows? Maybe she was right, and he did.

As disconcerting as her ethics and mind reading could be, he still liked hanging out with her. She was easy to be around. Smart enough to keep up with his own zigzagging train of thought, while still coming up with the odd observation or comment that would surprise him or make him see something in a new way. In Nick's life, very few people had proved any sort of intellectual challenge to him. It was criminal that she was being wasted at a place like Adams University.

"So you're smart."

"Um. Thank you? I guess?"

"No, more than usual. Smart even by Ivy League standards."

"Um…yes?"

"Why Adams? You could have gone anywhere."

"Dr. Finch was here."

"You came to Adams for her?"

"During my senior year of undergrad, I saw her give a lecture about her black hole theory. After that, there was nothing else I wanted to study, and nobody else I wanted to work with, so I came to Adams. Plus it's in Brooklyn, so I can live at home."

Nick let out a huff of laughter. "You live at home?"

He could almost see her prickle with defensiveness. "Sure. It's cheaper."

"You moved away for undergrad, though, right?"

"I went to Columbia. I commuted."

"You've seriously lived at home your whole life?"

More prickling. "I like it. My sisters live at home, too."

"How many sisters?"

"Two. And they're my best friends. So yeah, I like living at home. I know that's lame."

Ah, hell, he'd pushed too much and pissed her off. "No, it's not. Sorry, Livie, I can be a dick sometimes. It's great that you're close to your family. You're a much nicer person than me."

"You're nice," she said. "When you want to be."

He chuckled softly. "No, I'm really not."

"Cyberspace Robin Hood, remember?"

"You're the one who took down an international ring

of black hat hackers with a politely worded email. I think that makes you a *superhero* of niceness."

She lifted her head to look at him, her large dark eyes lighting up, and a brilliant smile spreading across her face. A revelation made itself known in Nick's brain. Livie was *pretty*. Very pretty. How had he missed that up until now? Those large, glittering dark eyes, that dazzling smile…they were surprisingly potent. It was like she hid them inside, along with most of what she was thinking and feeling. But when she unleashed it all…well, the effect was kind of a punch in the chest.

Suddenly—inexplicably—uncomfortable, Nick did what he always did when he felt out of his depth—he retreated back into his work.

"Okay, let's get back to our Hubble problem. How do we teach it to speak a language that doesn't exist yet?"

The sound of a key turning in the front door lock cut off Livie's response. Poppy came in, a clutch of shopping bags slung over one arm. Some part of him was still disbelieving every time he laid eyes on her. She was gorgeous, and sophisticated, and she was with *him*. Girls like Poppy and guys like him—it didn't add up. Sure, he'd dated pretty girls in the past, but Poppy was in a league of her own. And here she was, in all her stunning glory, coming home to him every night, wearing his ring on her finger. Nick's sixteen-year-old self would never have believed it. He might be fucked up in a million ways, but he must be doing something right to have landed a girl like Poppy.

"Hey, you," he said with a grin.

Poppy dropped her shopping bags inside the door and drifted across the room that long-legged natural grace of hers. Poppy didn't walk, she glided, like a feather drifting on a current of air.

"Hi." She rested a hand on his shoulder and leaned in to brush a kiss across his cheek with the easy elegance of a girl who'd spent her entire life surrounded by money and sophistication. He'd never known anyone as effortlessly classy as her.

Her eyes slid to Livie. "Hello again. Libby, right?"

"Livie," she corrected.

"Are you two still working? Nick, don't forget, we have Klaus's party tonight."

"Ah, geez, is that tonight?" He *had* forgotten, and was now internally groaning at the reminder. The last thing he wanted was to spend the night with that Eurotrash poser and his vapid friends. But Poppy would sulk for days if he even hinted at not going, and it really wasn't worth the drama.

She toyed with the zipper on his hoodie. "And please change into something a bit smarter?"

"What's wrong with what I'm wearing?" Nick protested.

"You'll look like you're working the door."

"The guy working the door is probably more interesting than half the people inside."

"Just because *you* don't find them interesting doesn't mean no one does. *I* do."

Livie silently watched them bantering—or were they arguing? It was hard to tell—and she wondered what it was that had made them fall in love with each other. Their lives seemed a little mismatched, Poppy's centered on the fashion world and clubs, and Nick's existing largely online. But they were engaged. There had to be something there connecting them, outside of physical attraction.

Even there, they seemed a little at odds. Poppy's

beauty was the kind you usually only saw in magazines, with her luminous, pale skin, ice-blue eyes, and flawless features. She had that kind of grace that made her look good no matter what she was wearing. Her shapeless light blue sundress should have looked like a piece of used Kleenex, but instead hung elegantly from her narrow shoulders and skimmed her angular body at all the perfect places. The hem brushed her upper thighs, leaving what looked like three full feet of her long thin legs exposed. And her hair. Poppy's hair was like something out of a shampoo commercial, a long, satiny golden-blond sheet, seemingly impervious to NYC's early September heat and humidity.

Nick was handsome, but in a much more real-life sort of way. Taken individually, his features were a little uneven, his eyes a bit too close together, his nose not perfectly straight. But there was a perpetual animation to his face that drew you in. It was like you could see his brilliant mind busily at work in his dark eyes.

He was in good shape, but he wasn't some ripped bodybuilder. Certain parts of him *were* oddly arresting, though. The sleeves of his black hoodie—the one Poppy was displeased with—were pushed up, and there was something about his smooth, tanned skin and the flex of the muscles in his forearms... Never in her life had Livie noticed a man's forearms. She'd certainly never found anybody's forearms sexy. How could forearms even *be* sexy? They seemed like a distinctly unsexual body part. And maybe that was true of every other man on the planet, but Nick's forearms were impossible to ignore. Nick definitely had sexy forearms.

And there she went again, having all kinds of wrong thoughts about him when he was standing five feet away with his *fiancée*. It didn't matter if she couldn't figure out what drew them together, because they *had* been. The ring on Poppy's finger proved it. She needed to get out of here and keep her mind on the work, where it belonged.

"I'd better get going," she said.

"Hey," Nick protested. "We're getting to the good parts now."

"You have plans—"

"Oh, don't break up the fun on my account," Poppy protested. "Klaus's party won't start for hours. But Nick, please don't get lost in that computer all afternoon. You were going to add those new portfolio shots to my website for me."

"Ah, hell, I forgot. I'll get it done today. Promise."

Poppy looked to Livie and winked conspiratorially. "Honestly, he's impossible."

She didn't seem to be looking for a response from Livie, so Livie didn't give one.

"That won't take me long. We still have time to work," Nick said to her.

"No, I really do need to go. I have quizzes to grade for my class."

"Livie's getting a PhD in astronomy," Nick said to Poppy.

"Really? Another genius like Nick?"

"I don't think anybody is as smart as Nick." He absorbed her teasing with a shrug and a smile.

"Too true. I don't even understand what he's talking about half the time." Poppy laughed self-deprecatingly, and Nick squeezed her hand.

Livie reached for her messenger bag, still hanging on the back of one of the chairs lining the kitchen island. As she started packing it up, Nick reached out and touched her arm. She shifted away as subtly as possible.

"I'll text you," he said. "We can do some more work later this week."

"Sure. Just let me know when."

"Brush up on your Klingon in the meantime."

"What?"

"The nonexistent language we have to teach Hubble? Never mind. It was a joke."

Now his smile was full-blown, and Livie couldn't help but return it, even though she had no idea what Klingon was.

"I guess I'll see you soon."

"Guess you will." He grinned.

And for a minute, it felt like every stern lecture she'd been giving herself about her stupid crush seemed utterly in vain, because his smile made her heart beat hard enough to explode. Maybe she'd be over it by the next time she saw him. It was very unlikely, but she would choose to live in hope.

Chapter Eight

It was Wednesday before Nick wanted to get together again, and not until early evening. He'd texted her at four p.m. promising to spring for the pizza if she was willing to work through dinner. He said he felt *inspired* and wanted to work while his juices were flowing. What did inspiration or juices have to do with science? And why did it have to happen with no warning? She almost wished she was busy, just so he'd plan better next time.

When the elevator opened into the little vestibule outside his door, she immediately knew something was wrong. The door was partially ajar, for one. And through it, she could hear Nick talking. No, not talking—shouting. And then she heard Poppy's voice, too, high and tense.

"Jesus, Poppy, I said I can't go out tonight. It's hardly cause for World War Three."

"Can't or won't, Nick?"

"I have plans. I'm *busy*."

"That science thing you're working on with that girl, Libby? Just reschedule. For me."

"It's Livie," he snapped. "And leave her out of this. It's between you and me."

"Exactly! Surely you can blow off work this once and come out with me to my friend's party."

"You've dragged me out to your stupid parties three nights this week."

"Oh, my friends are stupid now, are they?"

"Quit putting words in my mouth. That's not what I said."

"But it's what you meant! You hate my friends!"

Livie leaned back against the elevator doors. They were fighting. And it sounded bad. This was not something she should be witness to.

"This has nothing to do with your friends."

"You hate spending time with me."

"What are you talking about? You're my fiancée."

"Exactly. But I have to fight to get you to look up from your bloody computer screen."

"Because I love my work."

"And I love mine. It would be nice if you'd take an interest in it now and then."

"It's not like you're desperate to hear me talk coding over dinner, Poppy."

"See, that's exactly it."

"Exactly what?"

"What do we really have in common, Nick?"

Livie heard him scoff in disbelief. "You can't be serious."

"I am. Tell me one thing you like about me. Besides the way I look."

"That's not fair."

"Maybe not, but I'm not sure I can answer it either."

There was a loaded moment of silence. This was *definitely* something she shouldn't be hearing. Livie spun around, desperate to escape, but the elevator had already gone back down. She was trapped in the vestibule until it returned. She stabbed the button repeatedly, like somehow that would make the elevator understand it was an emergency.

Inside the apartment, Nick spoke again. "What are you saying, Poppy?"

"Look, Nick, I don't think we're all that compatible. Not in any of the ways that matter."

"Fashion industry parties? *That's* what matters?"

"*That* is a huge part of my life. The way yours is your computer. We're just too different."

"You *liked* that I was different."

"But our lives don't mesh."

"We've been *meshing* for a year."

"And now I can see the truth. We don't work. Not in the long term."

"Are you breaking up with me?" Nick's voice rang hollowly through the apartment.

No no no no, she didn't want to hear this. She shouldn't be here, but there was no escape. The elevator was coming back up, but stopping at nearly every floor.

Poppy's sigh was so heavy, Livie could hear it out in the vestibule.

"I don't know what we were thinking, getting engaged. This isn't going to work."

"Poppy, you don't mean that—"

"I do. We're finished, Nick. I think it's for the best. Here."

There was a pregnant silence from inside the apartment. Then Nick muttered an oath and something metal pinged off something hard. The ring, she realized. Poppy had given Nick back her engagement ring. Then there was a metallic ping—like a ring being thrown across the room, maybe.

"Go ahead and keep it," Nick snapped. "I know how much you wanted it."

Livie looked up frantically at the lighted floor numbers. It was on twelve. Two more floors to go. *Oh, please hurry!*

"I think you should go, Nick."

"You couldn't pay me to stay, Poppy."

Livie cringed, making herself as small as possible as the front door abruptly jerked open. But she forgot all her own discomfort the second she saw the look on Nick's face. He looked utterly wrecked.

"Livie," he muttered roughly. He didn't even seem surprised or shocked to see her there.

"I didn't mean to intrude. I was just leaving."

At that moment, the elevator—finally—opened behind her.

Nick let out a huff of humorless laughter. "Me, too."

Somehow Nick found himself down on the street with Livie. He couldn't be bothered to wonder at her presence. Not when his life had just been ripped in two.

Poppy broke up with him.

She gave back the ring.

Well, technically, she still had it, since he'd flung it across the room when she handed it over. Right now, it was lying forgotten in some corner of their apartment. How fitting.

"Are you okay?" Livie asked tentatively. Then she shook her head. "Sorry. Of course you're not. You must be devastated."

Was he? Right now, all he felt was numb. Hollowed out. Lost. Still simmering with leftover anger and adrenaline from the...what was that? Was it a fight? It felt more like a lightning-fast shiv attack. He hadn't even seen it coming, and now here he was, on the ground and bleeding out. He was still too much in shock to feel the hurt. The pain would come, though, he was sure of it.

He dragged in an unsteady breath. "Fuck." Then one overriding need made itself known. "I need to get out of here."

What he needed, right now in this moment, was to put as much physical distance between himself and Poppy as possible. Otherwise, he might go back upstairs and start fighting with her again. Or he'd start begging her to change her mind, and that was not going to happen.

"Um, okay. Hang on." Livie hurried to the curb and managed to flag down a passing green borough cab. Nick didn't stop to think anything through. There was a car here, waiting to take him away from the scene of the crime and he was going to go.

He climbed in behind Livie and fell back heavily on the seat, his unfocused eyes fixed on the ceiling. The cab pulled away from the curb, then stopped at a red light on the corner.

Livie was silent beside him. So quiet he almost forgot she was there.

The cab driver was the one to break the silence. "Where to?"

"Nick? Where do you want to go?"

Now there was a question. Where did he want to go? What did he want to do? A man could spend his whole fucking life working on that answer and never find it. He'd thought he had. Success, money, Poppy. It had seemed like he'd found all the answers he'd ever been looking for. But she'd slipped through his fingers, as insubstantial as sand.

It turned out he didn't know the answers to any of those questions. Okay, forget the big questions. All he had to do was answer a little one. Who cared what happened tomorrow, or next week, or next year? He only cared what happened in the next ten minutes.

"I need a drink," he muttered.

At his side, Livie took a deep breath. "Well, that's something I can fix."

Chapter Nine

Nick was utterly silent for the ride to Romano's, but he sat forward and looked around as the cab pulled up to the curb and Livie paid the fare.

"Are we in Carroll Gardens?"

"Yeah. We're at our bar. You said you wanted a drink."

Nick sighed heavily, but he didn't protest as he followed her out of the cab.

It was a typical quiet Wednesday night at Romano's. A few regulars nursed beers and watched ESPN on the flat screen while Clyde, their one part-time employee, dried and stacked a rack of glasses.

"Where's Gemma?"

"Emergency. She needed some fresh rosemary."

"Only Gemma would consider fresh rosemary an emergency," she muttered.

"She'll be back soon." Clyde's eyes cut to Nick, full of curiosity. Livie had never brought a guy to the bar. Or anyone else, come to think of it. There was no one to bring.

Livie nudged Nick toward the bar. "Have a seat."

He fell heavily onto a stool and planted his elbows on the bar, lowering his head into his hands.

"Your friend okay, Livie?" Clyde asked cautiously.

"Clyde, this is Nick. He's had a rough day. He needs a drink."

Clyde wiped his hands on his dish towel and threw it over his shoulder. "I think we can take care of that. What'll ya have, my man?"

Nick lifted his head enough to reply. "A beer. No, wait. Vodka. Straight up."

"Got a preference?"

"You have Tito's Handmade or Reyka?"

Clyde snorted. "We got Smirnoff's. Grey Goose, if you're feeling fancy."

"Grey Goose it is, then."

Clyde grabbed the bottle and poured several fingers of vodka into a glass in front of Nick. "Good for what ails you. Livie? Soda?"

"Thanks, Clyde."

When Clyde had left to get her drink, Nick lifted his glass in Livie's direction. "Here's to oblivion."

She watched in silence as he tossed it back, wincing only slightly. This might be a very long night.

Clyde slid a ginger ale in front of her and wordlessly refilled Nick's glass. He set the bottle in front of Livie. "I'll leave this here. You good, Liv?"

"We're fine."

When Clyde had moved down the bar to pour re-fills for Dennis and Frank, Livie turned to face Nick. "Maybe she'll change her mind."

She probably would, right? Relationships often got patched up after fights. By tomorrow, maybe Poppy would have rethought the whole thing. Which would be good, Livie told herself firmly. Look how miserable Nick was. Of course she hoped he'd get back together with Poppy. It would be selfish—and pointless—to wish for anything else.

Nick took a sip of his vodka this time, instead of slamming it all back, as he stared into the middle distance. "She wasn't wrong, you know."

"About what?"

"I *hate* her friends. All these fake-ass pretentious fashion people. She's a model. Did I tell you that?"

"Yeah, you did."

"She doesn't get a lot of work. It's hard to break in. And you need to start when you're, like, sixteen. It's creepy as fuck, that industry."

"How does she afford that amazing apartment?"

"Her dad." He downed the rest of his drink before swiping the vodka bottle from in front of her and refilling his glass. Moderation hadn't lasted long.

"Her father bought it for her?"

"Yep. She said she wanted to come to New York and try modeling, and no way was his kid going to slum it in an apartment share like everybody else. So he shelled out four mill for her own personal luxury crash pad."

"That place costs four million dollars?"

"Don't worry, he didn't miss it. He's big in finance in London. And buying her an apartment is easier than showing a little affection. They both got what they wanted."

Nick's glass was empty again. Was that two or three? If she was having a hard time keeping track when she was dead sober, he was going to end up burying himself before long.

"Go easy," she murmured, touching his arm. "You're going to get drunk."

"That's exactly the point," he said, pouring another refill before launching back in on the subject of the moment: Poppy. "She says it's all networking. Who you know. That's how you get gigs. I tag along with her to all these fashion industry parties in these ridiculous clubs, and end up spending the whole night on my phone in the corner while she chats up the important people. I swear, I get so bored at those things, my eyes bleed."

"What was it like when you first met?" Livie took a sip of her ginger ale, unsure if asking him that question would make things better or worse. It wasn't like he was going to be easily distracted if she tried to change the subject, right? Might as well let him get it all out of his system, like lancing a boil.

His eyes were on his hands, his fingers slowly tapping out an uneven rhythm on the bar. "She seemed cool. Nothing at all like the girls I usually met back in California. She knew about all this stuff, art and books and theatre... I thought she was different. Smarter. More sophisticated."

She could hear the "but" he hadn't spoken out loud. "Did she not turn out that way?" she asked cautiously.

His hand was decidedly less steady as he took another swig of vodka. "Oh, she's sophisticated, for sure. The world she grew up in, the money they have, you can't even imagine it." He paused and shook his head. "Maybe that was the problem. I can't imagine it. Her life, her world, it makes no sense to me. Mine doesn't make sense to her either."

"Computer programming? What's confusing about that?"

"When we met, she thought I was some internet start-up hotshot. She figured since I'd already hit the jackpot with stock options—"

"What stock options?"

"All those start-ups I worked on? Most of the time, I got paid in worthless stock options in some company nobody'd ever heard of."

Suddenly Nick's stunning wealth made more sense. "I'm guessing all that stock didn't stay worthless."

"Nope. She liked that about me, that I'd had all this success in tech when I was so young." He scoffed softly. "I think she thought she was getting herself her own personal Zuckerberg. I guess I didn't turn out to be what she expected either."

"But you're still successful."

"It's the work she doesn't get. She doesn't understand why I still work so much when I don't have to."

"You don't?" He had *that* much money?

"No, but I *want* to. I like what I do. I like the challenge. That's what Poppy doesn't get. She wants me to fly off to Ibiza or Aspen or Paris with her every other weekend."

"Have you been to all those places?" Livie's family trip to Lake George as a child was the sum total of her travels. Suddenly she felt very small and unsophisticated.

He splashed some more vodka into his glass. "A few. Poppy's spent her whole life running from one hot place to the next. I don't think she knows how to just…stay." He rubbed his hand over his face. "Fuck, it's not as if I do either. Guess two people who don't know how to commit to shit probably shouldn't get married. It was a dumb idea anyway."

"What was?"

"Getting married. I didn't even really ask her."

"Then how—"

"We were walking down the street and she stopped at this store window, oohing and aahing over the jewelry display. She went nuts for this ring they had." He lifted one shoulder. "So I bought it for her. And then while we're standing there in the store and they're ringing us up, I made some joke about us being engaged now that I'd bought her a ring. She said why not? I said why not? And we laughed and decided we'd get married."

Of all the flippant, insincere... Livie didn't consider herself a romantic, but she had a few ideas about how declarations of love should go, and making a joke of it over a credit card receipt definitely didn't cut it.

"Maybe you dodged a bullet, then," she observed.

Nick gave that a moment of drunken consideration. "Maybe."

The door of Romano's squeaked open. Gemma's eyes took in Livie and Nick and the vodka bottle in a flash.

"Hey, Livie," she said cautiously as she crossed to the bar and lifted the pass-under door. "Who's this?"

"This is Nick. He's doing the coding for my dissertation. Remember?"

"Right." Gemma's shrewd gaze made short work of Nick. "DeWitt."

"DeWitt and I broke up. Like me and Poppy broke up." He laughed at his own bad joke.

"Who's Poppy?" Gemma asked Livie as Nick tossed back the rest of his drink.

"His girlfriend. Well, his ex-girlfriend, I guess. She threw him out. He said he wanted a drink, so I brought him here."

Gemma looked back at Nick. "Looks like he's had half the bottle already. I'm Gemma, Livie's sister."

"Nice t'meet you."

"You hungry?" Gemma asked him.

He craned his head around in confusion. "This is a restaurant?"

"No, but I keep stuff cooking in the back for family. I'll make you a plate."

"I'm not really—"

"If you're gonna keep sucking on that bottle, you're gonna eat something."

Gemma turned and headed to the back before Nick could protest further.

"I don't need to eat," he said.

"She needs to feed you."

"But—"

"She's like the Pasta Whisperer. She'll just guilt you until you eat. Trust me on this."

Nick broke out in laughter.

"See, you're really funny, Livie."

"I am?" When people complimented her, they generally mentioned her intelligence, her dedication, her work ethic. Nobody had ever complimented her sense of humor. She hadn't been aware she had one.

Nick leaned closer. Despite the vodka fumes, her heart started pounding. His voice dropped to a whisper. "It's like *stealth* humor. I don't even get that you said something funny until it's over. Like…like a drive-by joke. That's it."

Gemma returned, saving Livie from forcing her frozen vocal cords to function. She set a bowl of pasta and sauce in front of Nick and left part of a loaf of Italian bread on a napkin next to it.

"Maria DiPaola brought me some leftover bread," she said.

"Who?" he asked in confusion, still staring at his food as if mystified by its existence.

"Maria DiPaola?" Livie said. "DiPaola's Bakery next door?"

"Oh, right. I forgot all about them. They're still open?"

"Toughing it out with the rest of us old-timers," Gemma said briskly. She pointed at Nick. "Eat that."

Then she turned to Livie. "Keep an eye on him. He's a mess."

"That's why I brought him here," she said, as Gemma left to relieve Clyde. Because when you were in trouble and needed looking after, Romano's Bar was the only place she knew to come to.

Despite saying he wasn't hungry, Nick dutifully picked up his fork and took a bite. Then another, and another. "This is amazing," he said, mouth stuffed.

"Gemma's a good cook."

"Serious understatement."

His bowl was empty in a matter of moments. Then he sat back and exhaled heavily. "I don't feel so good."

"You drank half a bottle of vodka."

"That might have been unwise. I should go."

"I'll call you a Lyft," Livie offered, pulling out her phone. "Where are you going?"

He rubbed at his eyebrow with his thumb, face screwing up as he attempted to concentrate. "Ummm, I don't know."

"Do you want to text a friend, see if you can crash with someone tonight?"

He looked lost as he thought about it. "There isn't really anybody I could ask."

"Surely you have friends." Someone like Nick couldn't possibly be friendless. He was too charismatic, too charming.

"I do. But not here. I know loads of people out in California. And there's Kurt, but he's in Berlin. And Mitul, but he's in New Delhi."

"You don't have any friends in the city?"

"I spend a lot of time online, okay? And since I moved back, I've been hanging out with Poppy's friends, mostly. I'm *not* calling one of them."

"But you're from Brooklyn. You could call your parents and—"

"No," he snapped. "I'm not calling them."

Okay... Livie carefully edged past that land mine. "You don't have any childhood friends from around here?"

"I kind of lost touch with everybody when I left for DeWitt. Not that I had a lot of close friends before that. Going to college at sixteen puts you in kind of rarefied company."

Well, she understood that well enough. She'd always been an odd duck, moving through the world in her own little bubble. Without her family, she'd have nobody, really.

Nick was alone. Losing Poppy was just the tip of the iceberg. He was *alone*. For all his charm and confidence, he didn't have anyone he could reach out to in a crisis. Her heart ached for him. Because despite her being a square peg, Livie's family and community had happily made room for her pointy edges. It didn't matter if they didn't understand her. They loved her anyway. She'd always have a place to come home to, people who would accept and love her, no questions asked. And Nick didn't.

"Why don't you stay with me?"

"You?"

"Our house is right around the corner, and we have a spare room."

"I don't want to impose."

"It's not an imposition."

"You sure?"

"Positive."

"Damn. Are you always this nice?" He was looking at her like she was some rare species of bird. Honestly, it was no wonder he had so few friends if a little kind-ness was such a shock to him.

"Um, I guess? It doesn't seem extraordinarily nice to me. You need someplace to stay. I have room. That's just basic decency."

"Huh. Decency. Haven't run into that one in a while."

"Maybe it's time to hang around new people, then. Now, come on. You need to sleep this off."

When he fumbled for his wallet, she stilled him with a hand on his arm. "It's on the house."

"Thanks, Liv. You're the best."

He slid off his bar stool and immediately stumbled. Livie lunged forward, catching his weight as he righted himself. But he kept an arm slung around her shoulders, his side pressed up against hers. He was heavy and un-gainly, but her body didn't care, lighting up with tingles anywhere he touched her.

She was pretty sure she'd just made a terrible mis-take.

Chapter Ten

Thank God it was a short walk home, because Nick seemed to be getting drunker by the second, and he was *heavy*. He was also taking a drunken stroll down memory lane as they navigated his old neighborhood.

"Aww, look, there's Russo's Pizza. I can't believe it's still here. I *lived* in that place when I was a kid. Do they still have that ancient Ms. Pac-Man game?"

"Yep, it's still there. It's probably fused to the linoleum at this point."

"I spent, like, *hours* playing that game when I was a kid. Got the high score once."

Livie paused, and Nick lurched to a stop beside her. "Wait…are *you* NADS?"

She had to scramble to support him as he burst into laughter and doubled over. "Oh my God, I forgot all about that."

"*You're* the high score on Russo's Ms. Pac-Man?"

"When I was, like…" His face screwed up as he thought. "Ten? Why, did you try to beat my score, Livie?"

She ignored his teasing grin, keeping her eyes focused on the sidewalk ahead of them so neither of them tripped. "I don't play video games, but I heard every boy in school joke about it often enough. Why are gonads so hilarious to prepubescent boys?"

"I wasn't even making a joke."

"What?"

"Those are my *initials*. Nicholas. Anthony. DeSantis. NADS."

"Well, intentional or not, you're a legend to every obnoxious boy in this neighborhood."

"Whaddaya know? I live on in Carroll Gardens."

"On a video game anyway." She hesitated, but in the end decided he probably wouldn't remember any of this tomorrow anyway, so she asked the question that had been eating at her. "Why haven't you been back? What happened with your parents?"

Nick scowled, rubbing his hand across the top of his hair until it was left standing on end. "We had a fight."

"Was it about you getting kicked out of DeWitt?"

He shook his head too vigorously and threw his balance off. They lurched to the side briefly before she was able to steady him. "It was after that. Something bad happened. It wasn't my fault, but they blamed me anyway. Which is fine. They've got their golden boy, all safe and sound. They don't need me."

"Golden boy?"

"My brother. Doesn't matter. I'm fine."

So fine that now, when his life was falling apart around him, there was no one he could reach out to for help except for some girl he barely knew. That seemed like the opposite of fine to her. She couldn't imagine being estranged from her family, living in the same borough and never seeing them. Everybody's family drove them crazy sometimes, but they were still *family*.

"Tell me about your brother," she said, trying to keep

him alert as she maneuvered him around the corner and onto her block. Not much farther now.

"Chris," he muttered.

"Okay, his name is Chris. What else? Older than you? Younger?"

"Older. By three years." He was quiet for a bit, then he spoke again. "He's a stockbroker. At least, I think he is. He was supposed to be one."

"My cousin James is a stockbroker."

"Is he perfect like Chris? Chris is *perfect*. They're proud as hell of *him*."

"Your parents aren't proud of you?"

"They think I'm a criminal."

"Well, you *did* hack the Department of Defense."

"You are *so* hung up on that. I did it for *fun*. I didn't make any money off of it. I told you, I don't do the illegal stuff anymore. Everything I do now is totally inside the law. Well, technically. Mostly."

"Why do they think you're a criminal?"

"It doesn't matter. Nothing matters." Nick sighed, his eyes drooping. She was about to lose him, but their house was just a little farther.

"Come on, we're here." She wrestled him through the wrought iron gate and up the front walk.

"Everybody wants me to be something I'm not."

Great. They'd entered the maudlin phase of his drunkenhood. Livie didn't drink, but having spent her life in a bar, she knew all the kinds of drunk there were under the sun.

"You're perfect just the way you are," she mumbled, shifting his weight. "Stairs. Step up."

They were staggering up the three shallow steps of the front stoop when she realized what she'd said. Ugh, had she told him he was *perfect*? But Nick didn't seem to notice and even if he had, wouldn't remember it to-morrow.

She fumbled with her keys and unlocked the front door, then wrestled him through it and into the front hall. There she was confronted with the flight of stairs that needed to be navigated to get him to the spare bed-room. Nope. Not happening. Instead, she swung him to the right, though the arched entrance to the living room. He'd have to sleep it off on the sofa.

His eyes were closed when she pivoted him around and lowered him down on the sofa. They stayed closed as she wrestled his sneakers off and hoisted his legs onto the cushions. But he opened them and gasped in surprise when their elderly dog, Spudge, lumbered his way over and stuck his cold nose against his cheek.

"Livie, what—"

"That's Spudge, my dog."

Despite being nearly unconscious, Nick raised his hand and found Spudge's head, rubbing it affection-ately. "Hey, Spudge."

Of course he was a dog person, too. Could he kick a puppy or steal a senior citizen's walker or something so she could get over this stupid crush already?

Spudge groaned in instant adoration, eyes closed, leaning into Nick's hand. *I know, Spudge. I know.*

She left Nick alone with Spudge for a moment to re-trieve a pillow and an old quilt from the linen closet up-stairs. When she came back down, Spudge was resting his head on Nick's chest as Nick continued to pet him.

"Well, Spudge likes you. See? You're not completely alone."

"Spudge is my man, right, Spudge? Spudge under-stands me."

"Spudge is very understanding." She lifted his head

to wedge a pillow under him, trying desperately not to notice how thick and silky his hair felt under her fingers. Now wasn't the time. Actually, there would *never* be a time, and she knew it. So she was absolutely *not* going to get hung up on the way his hair felt, or the way he smelled when she leaned over him to tuck the quilt around his body.

"You have a lot of hair," Nick muttered, and her face flamed. She'd been leaning over him, getting him settled, and her hair had been brushing him everywhere.

"Sorry," she whispered, jerking upright and dragging it back over her shoulders, twisting it into a thick rope. When she was thirteen, her cousin Kendra had talked her into doing something "fun and different" with her hair. The resulting disaster had kept Livie away from scissors ever since. She knew it was unfashionably long, without a single layer or highlight to bring it into the twenty-first century, but it was better than that pubescent monstrosity she'd spent forever growing back out.

"S'okay. S'nice. I like your hair."

She felt self-conscious and stupidly flattered all at once. Instead of responding, she grabbed the wastebasket from beside the armchair. "Here," she murmured, setting it beside the couch, next to his head. "If the worst happens, aim for this."

"S'not gonna happen."

She sat down on the very edge of the couch, next to his hip, tugging the quilt up over him. "Well, you did drink a lot of vodka tonight."

He groaned. "Don't say that word."

"Okay. I won't say it again. But aim there when the thing that's not going to happen happens."

Then, out of nowhere, his hand landed on her knee. "Thanks, Livie. You really are the nicest person I know."

She stared at his hand, unable to look up at his face. Her whole body felt electrified, every inch of her focused on that place where he touched her, the weight of his hand, the heat of his palm. Shocking images flooded her brain, all the other ways she was imagining him touching her. All from one hand on her knee.

She was frozen, not breathing, not even blinking. Nick turned his head on the pillow, his eyes still closed. "You're a really good friend," he said, and then his face went slack with unconsciousness and his hand slid off her leg.

Friend. You're just his friend. Don't forget it.

And while her head knew that beyond a shadow of a doubt, her traitorous body didn't want to believe it.

She stood, pausing a moment to gaze down at him. His face was in profile, turned into the pillow, his thick dark lashes making shadows in the dim light. His hair—that divinely silky hair—was a riotous mess against the white of the pillow. Her fingers itched to smooth it, to brush it off his forehead, but she didn't make a move to touch him.

Friends. That's all they were. And she was happy he considered her a friend, truly. The feelings she had for him—she absolutely could not indulge in them. He might not be engaged anymore, but that didn't make him any safer for her. He was unpredictable, flawed, and damaged in ways she didn't even fully understand. He had Danger: Do Not Enter practically stamped across his forehead. He was the kind of walking dating disaster she'd heard Gemma and Kendra complain about for years.

That was why, she decided as she fetched him a glass of water and a couple of aspirin from the kitchen, she was going to keep him as a friend, where he belonged.

She'd forget the way he turned her thoughts inside out and the way his hand on her knee had set her whole body on fire. She set the water and aspirin on the end table near his head, then watched his chest rise and fall slowly as he slept.

Yes, they were friends. And friends was exactly what they needed to stay.

Chapter Eleven

Consciousness crept back in slowly. The first thing Nick became aware of was the lumpy sofa underneath him. The second thing he became aware of was a warm weight pressing down solidly on his chest. He opened his eyes and found a pair of large, sorrowful brown ones staring back at him.

A dog. There was a dog here. He didn't have a dog.

The dog's head was lying on Nick's chest as it gazed up at him with its solemn, watery eyes.

He swallowed and instantly regretted it. His mouth tasted sour and felt mossy. Very shortly, he realized the rest of his body wasn't in any better shape. Hung over. Badly. Maybe still drunk.

And he had no idea where the fuck he was.

His eyes drifted upward. The white ceiling, under its cracking paint, had that fancy molding that reminded him of his aunt Gloria's house. But that was the only thing that looked familiar. Aside from the lumpy brown couch he'd apparently slept on, there were a couple of drooping armchairs, a coffee table half buried under open mail and magazines, and a large flat-screen against a wall. Someone had tucked a quilt, soft with age, around his body. And the dog was making sure it stayed there.

He glanced around the room for clues. On the far wall, there was a framed family photo of three girls, two teens and an older girl. He recognized one of the teens, because she didn't look all that different now, with her big, serious eyes and her long, dark hair.

Livie. Right. Livie's family's bar. Vodka. *So* much vodka. It was hazy after that, but there were flashes. Livie offering to let him crash at her place. Staggering down the street. Sinking back on the couch.

He was in Livie's house. Because Poppy had broken up with him.

Poppy.

That all came back in a rush, too. Poppy's flat, emotionless eyes as she told him to leave.

Last night's vodka made a brief attempt at a reappearance, but he fought it back.

He heard a hum of female voices in another room. Livie and her sisters. Right, she had two sisters, who'd probably come home and wondered who the hell that stranger was passed out on their couch. How fucking embarrassing. And he must look like shit.

Shifting the dog's weight off his chest, he silently got to his feet. There was a half bath tucked under the stairwell in the entryway, so he was able to splash some water on his face, and rinse out the worst of the cotton-mouth before he had to face the music. Following the voices, and the smell of something cooking—which his stomach was alternately utterly rejecting and begging for—he passed through the living room and dining room. The dog, who had followed him to the bathroom, was still trailing after him as he made his way to the kitchen at the back of the house.

Livie was sitting with one sister at the kitchen table while the other—a tall woman he vaguely remembered meeting at the bar—stood at the stove cooking something. Had she forced him to eat last night? He kind of remembered that.

The dog, who collapsed heavily against his feet, gave a soft *wuff*, as if to announce his arrival. All three women turned to look at him.

"He lives," the tall one said, hiking one eyebrow and looking him up and down in a way that spoke volumes without a word. That woman didn't trust him. Hell, he'd spent the night on her couch in a drunken stupor. He didn't blame her.

Self-consciously, he dragged a hand through his wrecked hair. "Uh, yeah. I was in rough shape last night. Thanks for letting me crash, Livie."

She shrugged and looked away, bashful. "No problem."

"Sit down and eat," the tall sister said.

"I don't think so—"

"Eat. Trust me."

Deciding not to piss her off any more than she already was, he quickly parked it at the table, between Livie and—

"Sorry, I must have missed meeting you in my state of total oblivion last night. I'm Nick."

She reached a hand across the table to shake his. "Jessica."

Jessica looked very like Livie—same long, dark brown hair, same large brown eyes, same heart-shaped face. She was smaller than either of her sisters, almost petite.

"And since you probably don't remember me, I'm Gemma."

"I remember." Even though he wasn't entirely sure that he did.

She tilted her chin at the dog, who was sitting on his foot, his chin resting on Nick's knee as he gazed up at him with sad adoration. "And your new bodyguard is named Spudge."

"Spudge. I think we met last night, buddy." He ran a hand over the dog's bony head and Spudge groaned in bliss. "Sorry I was such a mess last night, guys. I don't usually do that."

Jessica hid her grin behind the rim of her coffee mug. "That's okay. According to Livie, you earned it."

"Sorry," Livie said. "I probably shouldn't have said anything about your personal life."

"Your family has a right to know how I ended up passed out on your couch." He wasn't exactly in a position to be annoyed. When you did embarrassing shit like drink yourself into oblivion and pass out in strange houses, the people who lived in those houses were entitled to ask a few questions about how you got there.

"Coffee?" Jessica asked.

"God, yes."

She got up to pour a cup as Gemma turned from the stove with a plate of bacon and scrambled eggs. The vodka still currently comprising half his bloodstream rebelled at the very idea, but his stomach suddenly thought that plate looked pretty good. She slid the plate across the table to him and set another one in front of Livie.

Jess plunked a mug of coffee in front of him. "Okay, I gotta go."

"But breakfast—" Gemma protested.

"No time. The G is running with delays. Signal problems at Bergen Street *again*. It's the third time this week, and of course, the MTA can't come up with a single decent explanation. But I met this guy who works for the MTA and he's *this close* to giving me the inside story. I'm going to blow the lid off the failing subway system. Figuratively."

"Jess is a reporter," Livie explained to Nick.

"Really? Cool. *New York Times? Daily News?*"

"Brooklyn Daily Post."

"Do *not* say you've never heard of it," Gemma warned. "She'll tear your head off."

"If I wasn't already late, I'd argue with you," Jess sniffed.

"But you won't." Gemma passed her a travel mug. "Go. And don't skip lunch today."

"You're so annoying when you're bossy. By the way, I'm not home tonight."

"I thought Alex was still in Brazil with his father," Livie said.

"The big acquisition party was last night. He flies home today." Jessica's face was glowing, and she didn't even try to hide her giddy excitement. Whoever this Alex dude was, she was totally head over heels for him.

Had Poppy's eyes had ever lit up that way when she talked about him? Two days ago, he would have said absolutely yes. Of course. They were in love, right? But today, that felt a whole lot less clear.

"If Daddy Drake is flying home, too, maybe you guys can double date tonight," Gemma said with a smirk.

"Oh hush. This is already awkward enough."

Livie turned to Nick to explain again. "Alex is Jess's boyfriend, and his dad is dating her boss, the editor at the paper."

Nick felt like he'd been dumped headfirst into the deep end of the Romano family. "Oh. That would be weird."

"You're telling me." Jess rolled her eyes. "But no matter how much Dan scrambles Mariel's hormones, she's still going to give me grief if I'm late to the morning editorial meeting. Gotta go. Nick, nice to meet you. Even under these particular circumstances."

"Same," he lied. There was *nothing* nice about meeting a house full of strangers with a raging hangover.

After she'd hurried out and the front door had slammed behind her, Nick's vodka-numbed brain finally registered something from the past conversation. Dan. Drake. Acquisitions.

"Wait… Daddy *Drake*?"

"Dan Drake," Livie confirmed.

"*That* Dan Drake?"

"Media mogul Dan Drake?" Gemma said. "Yep."

He looked at Livie in shock. "Your sister is dating Dan Drake's son?"

"You know him?"

"I know *of* him. Most people do. He's pretty well-known. You Romano girls are full of surprises."

"And don't you forget it," Gemma muttered at the stove.

Livie leaned closer and murmured, "How are you feeling?"

"Like I've been turned inside out and steamrollered." Although breakfast was improving that situation marginally. Bacon was some sort of magical hangover cure, for sure. And the eggs were perfect, flecked with herbs, fluffy, and delicious.

"No, about…you know."

"Oh, right. Poppy." Nick dropped his eyes to the scuffed Formica tabletop as he poked at his eggs. Honestly, he'd barely begun to process what had happened yesterday. It hardly felt real. Were they really over?

Forever? Or had Poppy thought things through after he didn't come home last night and changed her mind? When he felt his pockets, his phone was missing.

"I plugged it in to charge last night." Livie slid it across the table to him.

"You're a lifesaver. Maybe she texted—"

She hadn't.

There were a whole lot of texts from people about the various projects he was working on, but not a single word from her.

Guess she hadn't changed her mind.

He put his hand over his eyes and leaned forward on the table, pushing back against the bleakness inside.

"Nick?"

Right. He wasn't alone.

He pushed back in his chair. "Looks like I'm apartment-hunting. Fun times."

She didn't buy his weak attempt at a joke, and a little frown line furrowed between her eyebrows. "I'm sorry."

He ran a hand through his hair. "It's fine. Really. I'll be fine. Um, I need to…" It was overwhelming. He had to find a new apartment. Even assuming he found something right away, he had to pack up all his gear and move. He could get a hotel room for a while, but that would only solve the problem of a place to crash. He'd also lost his home office, and he was in the middle of half a dozen projects on deadlines. For that, he needed his computer setup, space to work, and a better internet connection than he'd find in any hotel.

"Nick?" Livie asked, touching his arm gently.

He opened his eyes and lifted his head, which had drifted down until his face had been buried in his hands. "Sorry. Feeling a little overwhelmed. I'll get a hotel. It'll be fine."

"But what about your work?" Livie was always surprising him with her perceptiveness. She'd put it together that he was fucked in more ways than one.

"I'll, um, figure something out." Somehow.

"Maybe…" She glanced up at Gemma in question. Gemma met her gaze and some sort of unspoken communication passed between them.

Gemma sighed and rolled her eyes. "Yeah, of course," she said in answer to the question Livie had never asked out loud.

"You can stay here," Livie said to him. "Until you figure something out."

"Here?"

Livie shrugged. "Sure. You didn't get that far last night, but we *do* have a spare bedroom."

"Thanks, Livie, but you've seen my computer setup—"

"There's plenty of room for that, too. And we have 2 G's down and up."

"Really?" That was pretty fast internet access for a private home.

"I need fast internet for my research."

If he tinkered with some stuff, he could get it significantly faster. It was only a matter of working around the cable company's throttling software, which was a piece of cake. "Are you sure?"

"You'd have plenty of privacy to work. Gemma and Dad are at the bar most afternoons and evenings. Jess barely even lives here anymore when Alex is around. And I'm at school a lot."

He had to admit, it would solve a lot of his immediate problems with one fell swoop. He could be back up and running online by the end of the day, and it would buy him some time to come up with a better long-term solution. "That's really generous of you, Livie. You sure this is okay?" He directed the last part at Gemma, who seemed slightly less enthusiastic about the idea than Livie.

"Sure," Gemma replied. "We've got the space."

"But you don't even know me."

"Livie does, and I trust her. For now. Plus, you've earned a seal of approval from Spudge, so you must be an okay guy."

That meant she had him on probation and if he knew what was good for him, he would not fuck it up. He patted Spudge, who hadn't lifted his head from Nick's knee. "Thanks for vouching for me, buddy."

"Okay, let's go," Livie said. "We'll get your stuff."

"We?"

"I have some time today. I thought I could help you get some of your stuff."

"Oh. That's… You really are the nicest person I think I've ever met. Thanks."

Livie turned her face slightly away to hide her smile. A faint blush stained the tops of her cheekbones. He was reminded, suddenly, of that revelation he'd had a few days earlier, that Livie was pretty, when you stopped long enough to look carefully. Not that he would be looking. Because she was a good friend and valuable colleague. And he was with…well, he and Poppy were over, but that didn't mean he was ready to… Not that he would with Livie anyway, because… Well, she wasn't his type, and she was a *friend*, and she was being really kind letting him crash at her house. Which was why he was definitely going to avoid all thoughts about Livie's attractiveness. He wasn't sure how he'd managed to have them in the first place. Vodka was a bitch.

When he tore his eyes away from Livie, he found

Gemma watching him with an expression on her face that sent a chill down his spine. That woman was not a fan.

But she didn't call him out or rescind the offer to stay. She just dumped another couple of slices of bacon on his plate. "Okay, eat up and get out of here. And welcome to the Romanos', Nick." Despite the "welcome," he heard the warning in her words loud and clear. Stay away from her sister. Which was fine. Livie was a good friend and that was one relationship he had no intention of fucking up.

Chapter Twelve

It ended up taking half a day to retrieve Nick's computer equipment from his apartment. He was understandably picky about how it had to be dismantled and packed up, and he didn't trust movers, so Livie and Nick had to pack it and load it into a rented van themselves, then unpack it all once it was loaded into their spare room.

Half a dozen times during the course of the day, Livie asked herself what she'd been thinking when she offered to let him stay. Sure, he was in a bind and they were friends. But he already engendered a million uncomfortable, inconvenient feelings in her, and now he was going to be living in her *house*. Her safe space. What was *wrong* with her?

But it was too late now. His equipment was loaded into the spare room and he was already hard at work running cables and doing something to their internet connection that Livie didn't want to know too much about. If she kept it strictly business and steered clear of him as much as possible, she'd be fine.

The next morning, she left for school well before class, to avoid the awkwardness of running into him in the kitchen over coffee, and she stayed at school as long as she possibly could, finding one project after another to keep herself busy.

When she couldn't put it off any longer, she finally returned home, only to find the house quiet and dark. No sign of her father and sisters, which wasn't all that unusual. It was Friday. Dad and Gemma would be working at the bar. Jess was probably at Alex's place again. But where was Nick?

A quick peek into the guest room told her his stuff was all there. Not that he'd brought much. All the computer equipment, of course, but only a small bag of clothes. He'd said he'd get the rest of it later.

Maybe he'd gone out? He didn't seem to have any friends locally, but maybe he had a late work meeting?

Or maybe he was with Poppy.

Maybe she'd had second thoughts, and he was with her now as they patched up their relationship. It was entirely probable that they would, right?

But suddenly, standing in the doorway of his empty room and imagining Nick back at his old place with Poppy gave her an unexpected and brutal stab of pain. She was nearly breathless with it—nearly leveled by this sense of *loss*.

Ridiculous. He wasn't hers to lose. If Nick managed to patch things up with Poppy, she was going to be happy for him, like a friend should be.

Downstairs, she headed to the kitchen to feed Spudge, where she spotted a note in Gemma's handwriting, stickied to the table.

Cooked tonight. Dinner at the bar.

Gemma cooked something *every* night, even if it was no more than a pot of sauce and some pasta. If she was leaving notes, it was because she was trying something new and wanted everyone there to sample it.

Well, Nick was a grown-up, and she refused to dwell on where he might be, or who with. After she'd fed

Spudge, even though she suspected he'd already conned Gemma into feeding him, she headed over to the bar to see what Gemma had whipped up.

It was a Friday, so it was a bit more lively than the other night. Actually, it was a lot more lively, and not because of the Friday night crowd joining the Romano's regulars. The bar stools, she noticed, were almost full, and not just with patrons. Jess and Alex were here. And so was Nick.

He turned as she entered, gifting her with a glorious smile, and she felt a sudden, wholly inappropriate rush of relief that he wasn't off somewhere with Poppy. Oh, this was very bad. No matter how often her brain went over all the reasons she needed to stay away from him, the rest of her seemed determined to get closer, like a moth to a flame. And everybody knew how moths turned out in that scenario—burnt to a crisp.

"Hey, you're here," she said, trying to keep her tone as normal and disinterested as possible.

"Your sister lured me here with the promise of dinner, which was *unreal*, by the way."

"Right? I told you, man," Alex chimed in.

"You did not lie," Nick said to him.

Alex turned to Gemma, who was wiping down the bar. "Gemma, it's always good, but tonight, you outdid yourself."

Gemma twirled her bar towel in the air and gave a little curtsy. "Thank you, kind sir."

"And Gemma thought I should meet your dad, since I'm, you know, living in your house at the moment."

"You ready for a refill, Nick?" Livie's father called from the other end of the bar where he was turning the TV channel to ESPN.

Nick lifted his half-full beer glass to her father. "Not yet, but thanks, John."

"Sit, Livie," Gemma ordered. "I'll bring you a plate."

Livie dutifully sat down on the corner stool, on Jess's other side, as her father made his way down to their end of the bar. "I put the baseball game on for you, Alex."

"Thanks, John."

"Who's playing?" Nick asked.

"Mets versus Cubs," Alex replied.

Nick eyed him warily. "Who's your team?"

"The *Mets*," Alex declared.

Nick raised his beer in salute. "Good man."

Alex clinked it with his glass of scotch. "You said it."

"When did this happen?" Livie murmured to Jess.

"It was bromance at first sight," Jess murmured back.

It shouldn't be a surprise that Nick was settling right into her family. Everybody liked him—well, maybe not Gemma yet. But a charming, friendly guy like Nick would have no problem winning over the rest of them. Part of her liked it—liked that her family liked him, too. But it also felt a little strange, maybe slightly scary, because she could tell it would be very easy to get used to this, to think that it might last. And one thing she was sure of was that Nick's time with the Romanos was temporary. No matter how right his presence felt right now.

"Hey, you didn't tell me your computer genius was *this* computer genius," Jess said.

"Which computer genius?"

"The computer genius who hacked the Department of Defense when he was at DeWitt."

Livie felt her face flush. "Oh. That."

"Yes, *that*. He's famous at DeWitt."

"Famous? Really?"

"Well, more infamous, really," her sister conceded.

"Like Billy the Kid or D. B. Cooper. You should have seen Alex when he realized who he was. Instant fanboy."

"All because Nick hacked some computer when he was eighteen?"

Jess shook her head, smiling fondly. "Boys."

Gemma returned, sliding a plate of food across the bar to Livie.

"Mmm, smells good, Gem. What is it?"

"I was playing around with one of Grandma Romano's old recipes for chicken in a cream sauce," she said, waving a hand in the air. "I classed it up a little, and left the chicken breasts whole and pounded them flat, layered it with some parma ham, added some rosemary and shallots to the pan drippings, finished it with sherry..."

Livie stopped listening after the first few words and just ate. Gemma was always trying to interrogate her about her recipes. *"Is it too heavy on the tarragon? Maybe a little lemon zest for brightness?"* Livie was terrible at teasing out one flavor from another. She only knew what she liked, and this was *delicious*.

"It's really good, Gem," she muttered, her mouth full.

"That's a vast understatement," Nick said. "Gemma, it was magnificent."

Gemma gave him a grudging thanks. That was an improvement from all the distrustful glares she'd been shooting at him that she didn't think Livie had noticed. Seemed Nick might be winning her over, too.

"That's our Gemma," Dad said, squeezing her shoulder. "She's a miracle worker in the kitchen."

When her father was called away to refill another customer, Frank roped Alex and Nick into conversation.

Livie leaned in to Jess. "You think we should rescue them?"

"Nah, they're good."

"But Frank is talking about his ex-wife again. You know he never stops once he gets started on that."

"They haven't heard it a thousand times like us. Listen. They're actually giving Frank advice."

Nick leaned forward on his elbow. "You know what you need, Frank? You need to sign up to a dating site."

"What, on the internet?" Frank scoffed. "I'm too old for that nonsense. No woman out there is looking for a dried-up old relic like me."

"Frank," Alex said. "You own your own house, and in this neighborhood, that place is worth a fortune now. You've got your police department pension and most of your hair. You're a real catch."

Frank considered that for a minute. "You think?"

"I do," Alex said. "You know, Jess and I met online."

"I thought you went to college together."

"It was both. We had to meet twice to get it right. I'll help you get set up on Match. Jess'll work on your profile with you, won't you, Jess?"

"You will?"

"Sure," Jess said.

When Frank and Dennis started discussing dating profiles with Nick, Alex turned his attention back to Jess. They were whispering to each other about something, Jess's hand brushing lightly against Alex's. Alex slid his hand up under her hair, stroking the back of her neck. A moment later Jess cleared her throat. "I have some news."

Gemma finished topping off Frank's Michelob and turned away from the taps. "Did your MTA source finally give you the dirt?"

"It's not about a story."

John Romano, his paternal senses tingling, walked

over to their corner of the bar, tossing his bar towel over his shoulder. "Something wrong, Jess?"

Poor Dad. Losing Mom when they had, being left alone to raise three girls, had put such a burden on him. He worried about the three of them constantly, always concerned that they were missing out on something because they didn't have a mother. Really, their dad was the greatest, supporting everything they did, whether he understood it or not, and always wrapping them up in his quiet, unassuming love.

"Nothing's wrong, Dad." Jess and Alex exchanged another glance, a million unspoken words flying between them. She took a deep breath and turned back to them. "Alex and I are engaged."

For a moment, it felt like the world stopped turning. There was silence, and Livie examined that word as it made impact and sank in. *Engaged.* Jess. And Alex.

Gemma was the first one to speak, and when she did, she shrieked loud enough to rattle the liquor bottles on the shelf behind her. "Oh, my God, *Jess*! That's amazing! When? How? Tell me everything!"

"He asked me when he got back from Brazil. I'm not going to tell you how, because it's none of your business."

Color stained the tops of Alex's cheekbones as he stared down at the bar. Livie could guess that the "how" had probably happened in bed. Without clothes.

"Married?" their father asked, finally finding his voice. "Aren't you both a little young for that?"

"Dad." Jess scowled at him. "I'm twenty-four. Alex is twenty-five. Gemma was a toddler by the time you were my age."

"Things were different then."

Gemma swatted at him with her bar towel. "Dad, it was nineteen ninety, not eighteen ninety."

Jess fixed her wide brown eyes on their father. "Dad, aren't you happy for me?"

John relented, his shoulders dropping and his heavy dark eyebrows unfurrowing. "Course I am, kiddo. Alex, you know I think of you as one of the family. It's only…" He looked at Jess, his eyes turning glassy. "I guess I just wasn't ready to lose one of my girls."

"Aw, Dad, you'll never *lose* me." Jess's eyes began to water, too.

Jess was getting *married*. She was going to build a new life with Alex. For years, it had been the three Romano girls taking care of each other. And Gemma, older by several years, had been as much a mother as a sister. It had been Jess, not quite a year younger than Livie, who'd been her constant companion in everything. Their personalities had diverged in a hundred ways, but when it mattered, they'd thought and acted as one. It had been years since they slept in the same bed, comforting each other through thunderstorms and nightmares, but it didn't feel like the distant past, not when Jess was still right across the hall whenever Livie needed her. Now Jess was moving out, moving on. Jess was in love, and so happy. Livie wanted to be happy for her, too. But part of her felt like it was breaking inside.

Their father had come through the pass-through to embrace Jess, so Livie forced herself off her bar stool. As shell-shocked as she felt, she refused to let Jess see it. Tonight was her night. She deserved to see them all celebrating her good news. When their father finally released her, Livie was right there, ready to hug her little sister tight before she slipped away from them to head out into the big wide world.

"Congratulations, Jess," she whispered against Jess's dark hair. She was warm, and smelled so familiar.

"Thank you, Livie."

"When's the wedding?" Gemma pressed.

"Oh, not for ages," Jess scoffed. "We're too busy to even think about it yet."

Behind them, their father had grasped Alex by the hand, pumping it hard, before pulling him in roughly for a one-armed hug. "Welcome to the family, son," he murmured gruffly.

"Thank you, John. It's an honor. And I promise you, I'm going to spend the rest of my life making Jess happy."

Jess pulled away from Livie to beam up at Alex, her eyes full of so much happiness and love that it hurt to look at her.

"This calls for a toast," Dad said. "Let's open some champagne."

Gemma scoffed. "Champagne? What do you think this is, the Plaza? I think we have a couple of bottles of prosecco, though."

"Fine, that'll do."

Moments later, a cork popped and everyone cheered. Gemma had rustled up enough champagne flutes for everyone—Livie had no idea where she'd found them—and their father was pouring, grinning from ear to ear. Whatever reservations he'd expressed in the shock of the moment seemed completely forgotten. Livie hadn't seen him look this happy in years.

Her father passed around glasses, including Frank and Dennis, because, let's face it, the two of them spent so much time at the bar, they were practically family, too.

"A toast," he declared, raising his glass and addressing Jess and Alex. "To my baby girl, Jess, and her fiancé, Alex. Salute!"

The bar erupted in applause and cheers, everyone joining into Jess and Alex's celebration, even if they didn't know them. This is what Livie had always loved about Romano's. It turned strangers into family.

And if strangers could celebrate this news, then she would, too. She might be harboring her own bittersweet emotions about Jess's engagement, but tonight— somehow—she'd make herself be happy.

Chapter Thirteen

The Romano house had its own quiet symphony of noises at night, ones Livie had memorized through many nocturnal hours spent fruitlessly chasing sleep. The thunks of the old plumbing deep in the walls, the scrape of the branches of the linden tree across her window, the faint roar of a jet passing overhead on its way to LaGuardia airport, the occasional sound of voices outside on the sidewalk, or a car driving down their block—it was all as familiar to her as her own heartbeat.

Tonight, when Livie woke at two a.m., one sound was missing—the steady rumble of Spudge's snore from his usual post in the hallway, right between her room and Jess's at the top of the stairs—and right where you were sure to trip over him in the dark. Spudge was getting old, and she got a little nervous whenever he wasn't where she expected him to be.

Slipping out of bed, she made her way to the stairs. Jess's door stood open, her room dark. She'd gone home with Alex after the big announcement, as she usually did. She was already halfway out the door, starting her new life.

At the top of the stairs, Livie paused. The entire house was dark, except for the living room, lit up with the flickering blue glow of the TV. Someone else was up. No one else was *ever* up when Livie wandered through the house at this hour.

Downstairs, she found Spudge curled up next to Nick on the sofa, his head in his lap.

"Hey, did I wake you?"

She shook her head. "What are you doing up?"

"I don't sleep much."

"Me neither. What are you watching?" On TV, a spaceship careened through the stars.

"Some Japanese sci-fi thing. Have a seat."

She hesitated, tugging at the hem of her sleep shirt. She wasn't wearing a bra, because she hadn't expected to find anyone else up. Her hair was probably a haystack, too. Not that she thought he'd notice, but still, she wasn't used to being seen when she'd rolled out of bed in the middle of the night, especially not by him.

"Spudge is good company but you make better conversation," Nick said, as she was self-consciously running a hand down her hair to smooth the bedhead.

Giving in, she settled on the couch next to him, pulling her knees up to her chest and tucking her feet under one of the throw pillows. "Why do you have the sound turned off?"

Nick shrugged as two guys in futuristic uniforms argued on the screen in silence. "I'm always up at night and Poppy complained when the TV kept her awake. I got in the habit of watching foreign films with the sound off. They have subtitles, so you can still follow what's going on."

"You like space movies?"

"Ever since I watched *Star Trek* with my—when I was a kid."

"And what's going on?" Because even with subtitles, Livie was having a hard time making sense of the action.

"These guys are the good guys, and they're under attack by those aliens in that ship. See? But their plasma beam is off-line, so these two are going to climb down into the bowels of the ship to get it back online manually."

"Plasma beam," Livie muttered. "That is not a thing, scientifically speaking."

"Neither are aliens with octopus heads, but here we are."

"Why is that guy going into that tunnel? It keeps filling up with flames."

"Oh, he's gonna die for sure," Nick assured her.

"How do you know that?"

"Because he doesn't have a name. They just keep calling him 'Ensign,' unlike our hero here. He's a total redshirt."

"His shirt is gold."

"No, a redshirt. Like in *Star Trek*?"

Livie shook her head. "Never watched it."

Nick turned his head to gape at her. "Where have you *been*?"

"Probably in the library. Explain what redshirts are."

"Okay, a redshirt is a character who's only there to die. They're cannon fodder. They don't get a name or a backstory and they're not really integral to the hero's story. They tag along with the hero and bite it first, so you know how much danger the hero is in."

"Like that guy just did," Livie pointed out, as the redshirt in question writhed in a blast of exhaust flames before plummeting presumably to his death.

"Yep. See ya, Ensign Whatever. Now our hero is left on his own to complete the mission."

"With the *plasma beam*."

"That plasma beam is about to save the day." Nick shifted his weight under Spudge, sinking farther down into the squishy sofa. Maybe it wasn't so bad, she decided, having company other than Spudge when she was awake at night.

She snuck a look at him as he watched the battle scene unfolding on the screen. The blue light cast his features in stark contrast, highlighting the little bump in the bridge of his nose and the shape of his lips, the lower a little bit fuller than the upper. This late at night, his face had a shadow of stubble that wasn't there during the day. Staring at him, imagining how it would feel to touch it, made Livie's insides twist up with a sensation that she couldn't identify as good or bad.

"Okay, watch this." He nudged her with his elbow. She turned her attention away from him before he could catch her staring and tried to pay attention to the patently ridiculous space fight playing out on screen.

At the very last second, the hero managed to flip a big metal lever that allowed the plasma beam to power up and blast their enemy's ship into oblivion. A *lever*. Like it was some old Victorian steam engine.

"This explosion is ridiculous," she said as a massive fireball engulfed the enemy ship. "That ship is far too small to contain enough oxygen to fuel a fire that large. The combustion would only expand until the fuel source burned up. And there's no way the good guys would feel the blast on their ship. There's no atmosphere in space to get displaced by the shock waves—"

Nick lifted his hand and put his finger against her lips.

His finger. On her lips. She froze, her eyes locked on his. She couldn't even breathe, staring into his eyes, imagining that fingertip sliding across her cheek, and down her neck.

Nick blinked and his fingertip slid away from her lips, although they still tingled from the touch. "I am never watching another terrible Japanese sci-fi movie featuring octopus-headed aliens with you again." His teasing blew away every bit of the tension from a moment ago, which had undoubtedly all been in her head anyway.

"Sorry," she mumbled when her ability to speak had returned. "My sisters hate watching movies with me."

He chuckled, his shoulder jostling hers gently. "It's fine. It's not like I'm watching for the plot anyway, and I like listening to you think out loud. You're more interesting than the movie."

It was nothing but a silly, offhanded compliment, but her cheeks heated with pleasure. On screen, in the aftermath of his triumph, the hero was suddenly embroiled in some sort of romantic subplot, with a woman who hadn't appeared on screen at all during the big battle.

"So your sister's fiancé."

Livie choked on the breath she'd been taking. "Her *what*?"

"Alex. They're engaged."

"Yeah, I know. It's just weird, hearing him called that. I'm not used to it yet. Jess, engaged."

"Is he always so perfect?"

"What do you mean?"

"Don't get me wrong, I really like the guy. But he's like a movie hero, right? Good-looking, rich, nice, and he's a Mets fan. It's like they made him in a lab."

Alex *was* disturbingly flawless. It was a good thing he was nice or he'd be insufferable. "I see what you mean. And yes, Alex is pretty perfect. He can't help it."

"Are you happy for her?" he asked.

"Jess? Of course I am. Why?"

"Earlier tonight, you seemed a little bothered."

"What? Bothered?" It alarmed her, that Nick could read her so well, that he'd been watching her closely enough to notice anything was amiss.

"You just didn't look all that happy. Is it Alex? Do you not like him?"

"No," she answered firmly. "Alex is perfect, like you said. And he adores Jess. I'm happy for her."

Nick turned away from the movie, which seemed to have launched into some mystifying fourth act. "But?"

Livie considered brushing him off. Outside of her sisters, she didn't really share herself with other people. But Nick was beginning to feel different. Talking to him, telling him what she was really thinking, came strangely easily.

"Alex is great," she said slowly. "But his life is very different than Jess's. He's got all this money and power." It took a minute to herd her thoughts into the right order. "I like him, but he's nothing like who I thought Jess would pick. He's not the kind of guy I thought would make her happy."

Nick shrugged. "Who's right for you, who makes you happy…maybe it's not always who you think it should be. Ah, hell, don't listen to me. What do I know about relationships? I'm a disaster."

Well, he had a point there. "It's not Alex. It's Jess. She's leaving."

"What do you mean?"

Livie tugged the hem of her nightshirt down over her toes. "For years, it's been the four of us. And now Jess is leaving."

"You're not going to lose her. I've only spent a day

around your family and I can see how close you are. That's not going to disappear."

"I know. But it'll never be quite the same, you know?"

"Maybe it'll be better? Because—" he paused, thinking "—maybe they made it official tonight, but the guy is already part of your family. And that's a pretty great thing. He's a lucky man, in more ways than one."

There was a tiny hint of envy in his voice. Sure, sometimes people were estranged from their families for very good reasons. But if that was the case for Nick, why did that little bit of wistfulness creep in whenever he talked about hers?

Livie watched him in silence as he stared at the TV, seemingly a million miles away. She was glad he'd connected so quickly with her family, but none of them could fix what was missing in Nick's life. No matter how much she was starting to wish they could.

Chapter Fourteen

Livie blew a strand of hair out of her face. She'd been wrestling with the department's temperamental printer for forty minutes, trying to get her handouts printed out, and now it was jammed. The last of her worn-out patience expired when Peter Hockman showed up, leaning against the wall of the alcove where the printer lived, lurking, watching her in silence.

Finally, she snapped. "Do you need something, Peter?"

"Just wondering how much longer you're going to be. I've got to print some stuff for Langley."

"Can't you use Langley's office printer? This is still in the middle of the job and right now, it's jammed."

"Langley doesn't like me touching his computer equipment."

Langley didn't trust him with his printer? How was Peter ever going to get anything done on Langley's research? That required handling equipment a whole lot more valuable than a university-owned printer.

"Well, there are thirty copies of two more pages in queue still. I'm going to be a while."

"Jesus, how long is your handout?"

"Six pages."

Peter scoffed. "Your students must hate you."

That was probably true. Okay, it was definitely true. Maybe she wasn't the most popular teacher, but she felt strongly that students should be armed with as much information as possible. They didn't have to like her to learn something.

"Hasn't Finch bought you your own printer by now?"

"Why would she do that?"

"You guys have all that sweet grant money now."

"Yes, for the *research*. Not so I can have my own personal printer in my office."

Peter scoffed. "Then you're an idiot."

Ugh. Peter Hockman seemed to be determined to live out every misogynistic science bro horror story ever reported. He'd never hassle one of their male classmates like this. If Nick had ever condescended to her this way, she'd have kicked him off the project in a heartbeat, hot or not.

"I'm an idiot because I don't siphon off grant money for personal use? Aside from being unethical, that would violate university policy. But I'm sure you already know that."

Peter narrowed his eyes at her before straightening up. He was a really big guy. Not particularly muscular, but well over six feet and very broad—beefy. He seemed to take up far too much space in the tiny alcove, and she felt uncomfortably hemmed in.

"What I know is that you and Finch better not get too smug about your little windfall."

Livie leaned back against the printer, wishing he'd back up a step, or leave altogether. "It's not like we won the lottery, Peter. Janet's theory is soundly researched, and our grant application was exhaustive. It wasn't a gift, and it's not *ours*. The money is Skylight's. They're just allowing us to choose how it gets spent."

"On Finch's little black hole fantasy."

She flushed, unaccustomed to confrontation and totally tongue-tied, as always. Why couldn't she come up with a good response? Or any response at all? As she stood there, feeling furious, frustrated, and annoyed with both Peter and herself, another voice piped up from somewhere behind Peter's meaty shoulder.

"Finch's research could transform telecommunications. Tell me what exactly you guys are trying to do with Langley's tired old interstellar medium research?"

Peter spun around to glare down at Michiko, who was calmly gazing up at him. She'd handed him the scathing set-down Livie wished she'd been able to come up with, and she didn't look even a little flustered. How did she *do* that?

Of course, now that the moment of confrontation was past, Livie had a hundred things to say to Peter. But her mind had been a total blank in the heat of the moment. Nick probably would have had a thousand perfect zingers on the tip of his tongue. People like him always did.

"Langley's a genius," Peter said. "Nobody in this second-rate school appreciates his work."

"If you say so," Michiko said cheerfully. "Do you need some help with the printer, Livie? I'm pretty good with it at this point."

"Um, sure."

Michiko paused, staring pointedly up at Peter, who had to be easily twice her size. "Um, excuse me, Peter. Can I get by?"

Peter stood there, seething silently for another minute, but finally he stormed off noisily down the hall. Livie slowly let out her breath.

"Thanks, Michiko. I don't know what his problem is."

Michiko shrugged, opening the front panel of the

printer and flipping a few levers with practiced ease. "He's frustrated because you're working on something so much more interesting than him. Congrats on the Skylight grant, by the way."

"Thanks. Well, it's Janet's grant, not mine."

Michiko whipped a crumpled sheet of paper out of the printer before closing it back up with a snap. "But everybody knows you did most of the heavy lifting on the grant application. Good work."

"Um, thank you." Compliments tended to leave Livie as flustered as confrontations. What she wouldn't give for Nick's easy charm.

Michiko paused for a moment. Livie swallowed hard, once again, scrambling through her mind for something interesting to say.

"Thanks for your help with the printer. You're very proficient with it."

The corner of Michiko's mouth twitched, like she was suppressing a smile, and her dark eyes twinkled behind her glasses. "No problem. So, I guess I'll see you around?"

"Sure. See you."

Livie was disappointed in herself as she watched her leave. Michiko had gone out of her way to be helpful, intervening with Peter that way, then fixing the printer. And Livie couldn't manage to engage in conversation with her for more than a few awkward sentences. Had she come across as rude? Ungrateful? She wished, for the thousandth time, that she was better at this stuff. Next time, she'd make a point of saying hello to Michiko first, no matter how nervous it made her.

Thanks to Michiko's intervention, the printer spit out the rest of her handout in less than ten minutes. After she'd finished collating and stapling, she left them in her office, ready for class the next day, and made her way through the halls of the Astronomy building to Janet's office. She'd emailed Janet some purchasing info last night and wanted to see if she'd had time to look it over yet.

She was nearly to her office when she heard raised voices, which was pretty unusual for the Astronomy department. Peter Hockman's weirdness aside, confrontations were rare there. Livie was even more shocked when she realized one of the voices was Janet's. In all the time she'd known her, she'd never heard her raise her voice about anything.

"If we don't acquire the new software from Asid Tech, our whole line of research will be out of date inside of a year." That was Professor Langley. He was also shouting, which was less surprising. He was kind of a showman, always talking the longest and loudest, and frequently touting his own brilliance.

"*Your* research, William. Interstellar medium is your line of research, not mine."

"But the software will benefit the whole department."

"Come on, William," Janet chastised gently. "No one else will have any use for it. It's got absolutely nothing to do with my research proposal. You want it for your research."

"What if I do?" Langley shouted. Livie flinched, imagining Langley blustering at the unassuming, softspoken Janet Finch.

"Then you should have tried harder to secure grant money to pay for it. Now if you'll excuse me—"

"You've got plenty with the Skylight money. It's a single line item, Janet."

"A line item that has nothing to do with my work and is outside the parameters of my budget proposal."

"You know as well as I do that departments fudge the expenditures all the time. You're the department head. No one's going to question your expenditures."

"That may be your experience, William, but it's not mine, and I have no intention of spending a dime of Skylight's money on anything that's not directly related to my work."

You tell him, Livie thought proudly. Of course Janet would shut down Langley's completely unethical proposition.

"Because you're the fucking star of this department? Uptight fucking women."

Livie gasped in shock. How dare he speak to her that way? But Langley wasn't done.

"If it's not part of your brilliant line of research, then fuck it? Is that it? You arrogant little—"

She'd heard enough. Ordinarily, she'd never dream of interrupting, but she wasn't about to let Langley keep verbally abusing Janet that way.

"Knock knock. Hey, Janet, is this a bad time?"

She turned to look at Livie, and Livie's heart squeezed at the expression on her face—so haggard and pinched. And she was pale. Confrontations like this weren't in her nature, any more than they were in Livie's. Screw Langley for attacking her that way.

"No, Livie, it's fine. Professor Langley was just leaving."

Langley shot her one more filthy glare before turning toward the door. "We'll finish this later."

"It's already finished," Janet said, recovering some of her usual equilibrium. "I have nothing further to say on the matter."

"We'll see about that." Livie had to stumble out of the way to avoid being shoved by Langley as he stormed through the door. No wonder Peter Hockman was such a sexist douchebag. His mentor had trained him well.

Once he was gone, Livie turned back to Janet. Her back was turned, her hands rifling through a stack of papers on her desk in an aimless fashion. Livie could feel her discomfort coming off of her in waves. She was probably as shaken up as Livie would be in that situation, and she needed a moment to compose herself. She busied herself getting out her laptop, giving Janet the time she needed.

"Your purchasing proposals look good, Livie," she said at last, her voice tight and small. "I'll sign off on them and get them emailed to the dean for approval tomorrow." If she wanted to pretend that ugly scene hadn't happened, Livie was happy to let her.

"Thanks."

"Did you get the bid for the new monitors?"

"Yes, I did. Let me find it in my email."

Livie scrolled through her email looking for the bid she'd received the day before.

"Livie…"

"One second. Oh, here it is. Okay, I'm forwarding it to you."

Then Janet made a noise. All the little hairs on the back of Livie's neck stood up. That was not a noise people were supposed to make…*ever.*

She looked up just as Janet crumpled slowly to the floor.

"Janet!"

Panic flooded her body as she rushed to Janet. She was curled into an awkward heap on her side. Livie gently rolled her onto her back. She felt so small, so fragile. Her color was bad. Very bad. The last time she'd seen someone this washed out and gray—no, she wasn't going there.

Her heart hammering, she sought out Janet's pulse in her thin, bony wrist with one hand, as she frantically dialed 9-1-1 on her cell with the other hand. When she finally found Janet's pulse, it was hardly even there, nothing more than a barely perceptible flutter under her fingers.

The whole time, as she breathlessly explained everything to the dispatcher, she prayed. She hadn't prayed since she was eleven. It hadn't worked then, so she'd given it up. But now she prayed to anyone who might be listening that that fragile little flutter would keep going until help arrived.

Chapter Fifteen

Livie hadn't stepped foot in a hospital since she was eleven. That hadn't struck her as particularly odd—she hadn't felt as if she'd been purposefully avoiding them—until the ambulance had taken Janet away and Livie, faced with the prospect of following them to the hospital on her own, went weak-kneed with fear.

She had to go. In the chaos of the ambulance arrival, as the paramedics had worked to stabilize Janet and secure her on the gurney, she'd learned from Anita that Janet's husband was out of the country, and her son was in Chicago this week for work. She hadn't even known Janet had a family, but according to Anita, her husband, a classics professor at NYU, was at a conference in Vancouver. Someone had to go to the hospital, and Livie quickly realized, her heart sinking, that there was only her.

The thing was, she *wanted* to be there. Janet shouldn't be alone. And sure, their relationship thus far had been purely student/teacher, but she liked Janet and wanted to be with her in this crisis. But when she pulled out her phone intending to call for a Lyft, she froze. She couldn't face walking into that hospital, at least, not alone.

She typed out a text in the family group chat.

Finch just taken to the hospital. I need to go sit with her. Can't go alone.

Moments later, there was a reply, but it wasn't from Jess or Gemma. It was from Nick.

Oh no. She'd had the wrong group chat open, the one she'd started a few days ago, to make sure Nick had everyone's contact info.

Which hospital? Meet you there.

Oh, God, how embarrassing. Frantically, she typed out a response.

Sorry, typed in the wrong chat. Meant for Gemma and Jess. Don't worry about it.

A moment after she hit Send, her phone vibrated with an incoming call. It was Nick. He started talking the instant she accepted the call.

"Just tell me which hospital. I'm on my way."

"Really, Nick, you don't have to—"

He bulldozed right over her protests. "Livie. Which hospital?"

"Maimonides. It's at—"

"I know where it is. Wait for me outside the ER entrance."

"Okay. And thanks."

At Maimonides, facing the ER entrance, once again she froze. She should just walk in. Stop being a coward and go. Then she could text Nick and tell him she was fine. Nothing to worry about.

But her feet simply wouldn't move. All she could

do was stare in mute horror at the sliding doors, feeling vaguely queasy. She restlessly paced the stretch of sidewalk out front, keeping her eyes averted from the bank of waiting ambulances, and cursed her weakness.

A black car pulled up at the corner and Nick stepped out on the sidewalk. The rush of relief she felt at the sight of him was embarrassing. And scary. The last thing she should start doing was depending on him, at least for anything outside of computer help.

"Hey, are you okay?"

Her embarrassment ratcheted up another notch. She didn't want him seeing this side of her, too scared to walk through a stupid hospital door.

"Really, you didn't have to come. I'm fine." Which was a lie, since she'd spent the past five minutes staring at a set of sliding doors in terror.

"Stop. I'm here. Let's go see how she's doing."

She turned and braced herself. It had been fourteen years. She was an adult now. Surely she was making a big deal out of nothing. She was probably going to walk in and be perfectly fine, and all this drama would have been for nothing.

The sliding doors opened for them and Nick ushered her in ahead of him. Her sense memory was triggered immediately. The antiseptic smell, the overly bright fluorescent lights, the cacophony of beeps and bells and overhead announcements—in an instant, her throat felt tight and her heart began to pound. Nick gave her a quick, assessing once-over, then placed his hand on the small of her back, propelling her forward. Thank God he had, or she might have stopped right there and refused to take another step. But his brisk efficiency grounded her, focused her.

In another moment, she found herself at the information desk, asking the nurse for Janet's location. Then there was a map to consult, and elevators to find, and before she knew it, they'd made their way to the right floor.

"What happened to her?" he asked as they walked down the long, bright hallway toward the right wing.

"The paramedics said they thought it was a heart attack."

"Were you with her?"

"Yes. She just…" She stopped, swallowing hard. He laid his hand on her back again, the firm, warm pressure of it bringing her back to the moment. "She collapsed. Her skin was so pale and gray. And I could barely feel her heartbeat."

"Lots of people have heart attacks and they're fine."

"I know. But—" It was too hard to finish that thought. She didn't tell him that she'd seen death in someone's face once before, and she'd seen it again today in Janet's.

The nurse looked up as they approached.

"Hi, I'm looking for Doctor…um, Janet Finch. She was brought in by ambulance about an hour ago?"

The nurse typed her name into the computer. "It looks like she's still in surgery."

"Surgery?" Livie echoed. "What for?"

"Are you a family member?"

"I'm her graduate student."

"I'm afraid I can only give out patient information to family members."

"But her husband is in Vancouver, and her son is in Chicago."

"Hospital policy. Sorry."

Nick turned to Livie. "Can you call one of them? Her husband? Her son? They should know what's going on."

"Anita already called them. They're on their way. But I have their numbers."

"Call," Nick urged. "They'll want an update and it'll reassure them, knowing you're here with her."

They found the waiting room and Livie made the calls. Her husband's phone went straight to voice mail, but she reached Andy, her son. He was at O'Hare, trying to get on the next flight to New York. Nick was right. Andy thanked her profusely for being there when he couldn't be and he promised to call the hospital as soon as he hung up, so they'd give Livie updates until he could get there.

Within fifteen minutes, a physician's assistant had come out to fill them in on her situation. Yes, it had been a heart attack. Tests showed blockage in two arteries. She was in surgery now to clear the blockages. They'd know more when she was out.

"Is it…" Livie began, then paused, not sure if she should ask what she was thinking.

"Yes?" The physician's assistant was nice, a woman in her twenties with kind dark eyes and a brisk, but warm demeanor. "Do you have another question?"

"What caused it?"

"The blockages? Any number of factors can contribute to—"

"No, the actual attack. Why today? Could it be… would stress trigger it? Like, a fight?"

"A stressful situation can raise the blood pressure, and yes, it can precipitate an attack, if the underlying conditions are already present. Is that what you mean?"

"Yes, that's it."

"I'll come give you another update when she's out of surgery."

"Thank you."

So Janet's heart had already been in trouble. But there was that fight with Langley. In her gut, Livie knew that's what had brought this on. This was all his fault.

"What's going on?" Nick asked when the physician's assistant had left. "Why did you ask her that?"

Did she really want to tell Nick about this? If either of her sisters had been there—but they weren't and he was, and they *were* friends.

"I heard something. Right before she collapsed. She was having this terrible fight with Professor Langley. I've never heard her sound like that before."

"What were they fighting about?"

"Equipment. Langley wanted her to purchase some software for his research with the Skylight grant money."

"I'm guessing that's a violation of a hundred different policies."

"It is. That's what I told—"

"Who?" Nick urged when she trailed off.

"Peter Hockman."

"Who is that?"

"He's another PhD candidate in my class. He said something to me earlier today, about buying equipment. He seemed really angry about the grant. It was weird."

Nick's eyebrows furrowed in concern. "Weird how?"

"I'm sure it's nothing," she said, shaking her head. "Peter's frustrated because his research with Langley isn't getting as much attention as what I'm working on with Janet."

"Did this guy threaten you or something?"

"No, no, it wasn't like that." Except it had kind of felt like a threat, hadn't it? Peter had been trying to intimidate her before Michiko stepped in and put him in his place. It was odd, Peter making all those comments about their "windfall" at the same time Langley was pressuring Janet to buy him new equipment with her grant.

"Yeah, maybe, but you tell me if he hassles you again."

Despite the tension of the situation, his glower made her laugh. "What are you going to do, Nick, beat him up for me?"

He smiled, a wicked smile that made her heart flip over. "Like I'd need to do that when I can ruin his life much more effectively from my keyboard."

His criminal threats *really* shouldn't make her heart beat faster. "You wouldn't do that, though."

"I'm very resourceful. Promise me you'll tell me if the guy gives you a hard time again."

"Sure." Although she was certain there'd be nothing else to tell. Peter was harmless. Michiko was right. He was just frustrated that his academic career wasn't going as well as hers. She was sure of that.

Chapter Sixteen

Livie sank into one of her pensive silences. But the thing Nick was discovering with Livie was that her silences were never really quiet. She didn't say a word or fidget at all, but he could *sense* her brain busily at work. Livie's silences practically shouted.

Reaching out, he tugged gently on a lock of her hair. She jumped, swiveling around to look at him with those big brown eyes. She had Bambi eyelashes, long and curling. They were totally unexpected in her serious face.

"Want to tell me why I'm here?" he asked gently.

"You said you wanted to come. But you don't have to stay. You can go, I'll be fine."

Okay, maybe he hadn't been the kind of friend who offered emotional support before, but that didn't mean he was incapable of it. "No, Livie, stop. I do want to be here. I know Finch, too, remember? I like her. I want to be here for her with you. I meant hospitals. Why couldn't you come in here by yourself? It was the hospital that freaked you out, right?"

She hesitated, biting her bottom lip, but then nodded. "I haven't been in a hospital since my mom died," she said at last.

He'd noticed, of course, the absence of her mother,

but he hadn't wanted to pry. John Romano was a nice guy, and he didn't want to go asking the guy about his wife if the story was an abandonment or an ugly divorce. Now that he knew, it made a kind of sense. For all their cheerful, loving connection, something felt missing in the Romano house, like they were all actively working around a gaping hole in the middle of the room.

"I'm sorry, Livie. How old were you?"

"Eleven. It's been fourteen years. It's ridiculous that I still have this…" She shook her hands in frustration. "This stupid, irrational *thing*. I didn't even realize I couldn't do it until I had to do it. Then I pictured it… the lights, the beeps, the smell…and I froze."

"Hey, it's okay. Everybody's got stuff that gets to them."

"Why? Why do I still get so freaked out? I mean, I know she's gone. I know I'm not going to walk around the corner and see—" She stopped, fighting back tears. "What am I afraid of, if it's not that?"

Shit, she was going to cry. He'd never seen Livie cry before. He leaned in, until his shoulder touched hers. After a second of hesitation, she leaned back. "Human beings are weird, illogical machines. Computers I get. But people… We have all these funny twists and turns. Blind alleys. Malware that acts in random ways."

"Huh." With a sniff, she swiped at her eyes. "Malware. That's one way to think of it."

"Maybe, if it helps, think of it like a bad line of coding."

"How do I rewrite the code?" Because for Livie, every problem had a solution if you tried hard enough. Next she'd be doing her dissertation on *that*.

"Hell if I know. But hey, so you're carrying around

a little bad coding. It doesn't mean there's something wrong with you."

"Do you have some bad coding?"

Her question set off a well-worn alarm in his head. He was more than aware of his own malware, but he preferred to go through life pretending that it didn't exist. "Sure, I do. I mean, I haven't talked to my family since I was eighteen. Something's got to be fucked up with me, right?"

But Livie was watching him with those unsmiling Bambi eyes, and she wasn't letting him off the hook that easy. "That's really sad, Nick."

There he went again, baring his soul to Livie in ways he never did with anyone else. Or maybe she could just *see* it, whether he'd meant to bare it or not. "It is what it is," he said, maybe a little too shortly. "My point is, everybody's got something, right?"

"I guess."

She was staring into the middle distance, doing her loud thinking again. "Want to tell me what happened with your mom?"

After a long pause, she dropped her eyes to her hands, picking at her thumbnail. "She had pancreatic cancer. It happened really fast. There were—" She cleared her throat, blinked, and went on. "There were other issues, a fight with her insurance company and stuff. But yeah, she got sick and just kept getting sicker. I guess I should have known what was coming, but I didn't. Near the end, Dad would bring us to the hospital every day to see her, and every day she looked worse, she was weaker. That last day, she was gray. There's no other way to describe it. Like all that was left of her was a worn-out shell. The living, breathing part had been all used up. Turns out I was right. She died that night. Janet looked the same way today."

"Hey." He reached for her, sliding an arm around her shoulders and pulling her into his side. "That doesn't mean Finch's going to die. I told you, humans are complicated machines. They can surprise you all the time."

"I know. But I like her, Nick. She's only my professor, but I really like her."

"Me, too."

He leaned back on the sofa, bringing her with him, her head finding its way to his shoulder. Her hair brushed his chin, and he could smell it, a faint floral smell he wouldn't have expected from Livie. Not that he'd given much thought to what Livie smelled like. But he liked it. He liked *her*. He liked her fearsome intellect and her surprisingly tender heart. He liked her loyalty. He liked that she didn't try to hide who she was or apologize for it. He hadn't met anybody in a long time—most certainly not in real life—who he respected as much as her. He found himself almost embarrassingly grateful for her friendship, and he hoped—prayed, really—that he wouldn't do anything to fuck it up. Because he had a pretty good track record of fucking things up with people he cared about.

They sat together in silence for a while, and it was peaceful. A sort of easy, comforting closeness he hadn't experienced since he was a kid. He hadn't been lying. He was definitely running some fucked-up malware in his head. The difference was, Livie's wasn't her fault. It was a product of a tragedy no little kid should have to face. His? It was all of his own making.

Half an hour later, Gemma Romano burst through the waiting room door and made a beeline for her sister.

"Sorry, my phone was under the bar. I just got your text. How is she?"

Nick disentangled himself from Livie as she got to her feet. "We don't know yet. She's still in surgery."

Gemma took a step closer and reached out to squeeze her shoulder. "You doing okay? You haven't been back here since—"

Livie cut her off. "I'm fine. Nick came to sit with me."

Gemma glanced over at him, something new and assessing in her eyes. Nick lifted a hand in greeting. He hadn't stopped to think when he got Livie's message, he just came right away. Was that weird, though? They were friends, but only for a few weeks. With something this personal, maybe he should have stayed out of it and left it to her sisters to support her.

But after today, their friendship didn't feel all that casual. He hadn't talked with someone the way he'd talked with Livie since…well, he wasn't sure he ever had. Being here with her when she needed someone felt right. Which is why he decided to stay, even though Gemma was there now. He did make himself useful, though, going for coffee and bringing back snacks to sustain them while they waited.

An hour later, Janet's son arrived. Nick was sure that's who the windblown guy in jeans and a rumpled oxford shirt was the minute he stepped into the waiting room, his frantic eyes darting from person to person.

"Are you Livie?"

She jumped to her feet. "Andy?"

"How is she?"

"Still in surgery." She filled him in on the last update from the nurse, which hadn't been terribly informative.

Andy was pale with worry. "Thank you for being

here, Livie. She'll be so grateful to hear you stayed. She talks about you all the time, you know."

"Me?"

"She said she hasn't had a graduate student in years with your kind of potential. This black hole thing she's doing is the most important research of her career. She's so excited that you're here to work on it with her."

Livie's eyes went glassy again. "She's brilliant. It's an honor to be working with her. Do you mind if I stay until she's out of surgery?"

"Of course not."

They all settled back in on the uncomfortable sofas, flipping through outdated gossip magazines or staring at the TV with unseeing eyes, waiting for word. It didn't take long. Fifteen minutes later, the doctor finally came to find them. He was small and wiry with a wizened face and glasses, and still in scrubs, his face mask hanging loose around his neck.

"Mr. Finch? I'm Dr. Singh."

They all scrambled to their feet and Andy crossed to shake the doctor's hand. "How is my mother?"

Singh didn't smile reassuringly, Nick noted. He didn't smile at all. "We've successfully cleared the blockages in both arteries."

"That's good news, right?" Livie asked.

"Yes," the doctor replied, still grim-faced. "However, there is more damage to her heart muscle than we like to see in someone her age and in her state of health."

"Damage?" Andy pressed. "What kind of damage?"

"The heart muscle is always damaged by an incident like this. Many factors contribute to the severity."

"And you're saying her damage is severe?"

"At this time, yes. But as she recovers, the damaged

muscle may recover as well. It's impossible to say how much at this point. Only time will tell."

Livie and Andy exchanged an anxious look. Neither one looked at all relieved. Nick didn't blame them. None of this sounded like good news.

Andy rubbed his hand across his mouth. "Can I see her?"

"She's still in post-op, under sedation, but yes, you can see her."

"How long until she's awake?"

Singh hesitated in a way Nick didn't like. "The anesthesia will have worn off completely by morning."

That wasn't exactly what Andy was asking.

"Are you saying she might not wake up?" Andy asked, his voice strained.

Now Singh did smile, but that only made it worse, because it was small and sad, and not the least bit encouraging. "Time will tell."

Andy exhaled, his eyes on the floor. Then he turned to Livie. "Why don't you guys go home? I'll text you if there's any change."

"Are you sure? I hate to leave you here alone."

"My father's flight lands in an hour. He'll be here soon."

Livie still looked like she wanted to protest, but Nick laid his hand on her shoulder. Finch's family was going to be here for her, as they should be. "Okay, but let me know if you need anything. Anything at all."

"I will. And thank you again, Livie. I'm glad you were with her when she—"

Andy trailed off, unwilling to give voice to what they were all thinking—that Livie might have been the last person Finch would ever speak to or see.

Chapter Seventeen

Janet didn't wake up by morning. Instead, Livie got a call from Andy. She'd had a stroke during the night, immeasurably complicating her situation. A full recovery still wasn't out of the realm of possibility, but the chances were much slimmer, and the timeline much longer, if it happened at all. Livie offered to come back to the hospital, but Andy declined. She wasn't conscious and probably wouldn't be for some time. He promised to call her if anything changed.

It didn't bear thinking about, Janet not fully recovering, so Livie tried her best not to think about it. She *would* come back, but it might take some time.

Outside of her very personal grief over Janet, her advisor's heart attack left Livie in a strange no-man's-land at school. Without Janet there, she was left spinning her wheels. Janet had some data analysis she'd wanted to explore in conjunction with the big black hole project. Livie pursued that on her own, waiting and hoping that Janet would be back at work soon.

At least the work on the Hubble program wasn't dependent on Janet's presence. She and Nick could move ahead on that on their own, and having him in her house had turned out to be good for that, although not always in a way Livie would have preferred to work.

Nick tended to work in fits and starts on whatever happened to capture his imagination, whenever it happened to occur. It wasn't uncommon for him to bang on her door at midnight or later because he'd suddenly had an idea and he wanted her to come work on it with him. It drove her crazy, but they were making good progress so she kept her complaints to herself.

But being around him so much was wreaking havoc on her peace of mind. She'd thought maybe familiarity would help dispel her stupid crush. Living twenty-four seven with his infuriating quirks should have killed her infatuation dead. Frustratingly, it didn't seem to be working that way. He was mercurial, sometimes hopping between five projects in an hour and sometimes closing himself away with an almost obsessive single-mindedness. He ran hot and cold, one minute happily embracing her entire family in a way sure to win her heart, the next throwing up his walls and refusing to talk about anything personal. He was, in short, everything she was not, and nothing she wanted to be. Nothing about him should have appealed to her. And yet he haunted her, and nothing she did—nothing *he* did— seemed to exorcize him. She was beginning to think nothing ever would.

The Lyft let them out in DUMBO in front of the building and they retrieved the flattened boxes from the trunk. It was Saturday, and nearly dark outside, the streetlights flickering on. Nick paused, staring up at the facade of the building. Two weeks after his breakup with Poppy, he'd decided to come get the rest of his stuff. Livie could see in his face that this wouldn't be easy for him.

"Are you going to be okay?"

His smile wasn't as reassuring as he meant it to be. "Sure. I'm fine."

"Are you worried about running into her? Should we have called first?"

"Don't sweat it. It's Saturday night. She's going to be out until three a.m. at least." Then, taking a deep breath, he produced his keys and let them into the lobby. "Let's go get this over with."

Upstairs, everything looked much as it had all the other times Livie had been there. Everything was sleek and orderly, no sign that Nick had ever lived there, and no sign of his absence. Shouldn't a place bear some imprint of the two people who'd lived in it? Shouldn't you have been able to see signs of the life they'd been building here? The absence when one of them left?

"There's no stuff here," she said, without meaning to.

Nick glanced over at her as he assembled a box. "What do you mean?"

"You can't even tell anyone lives here. There's no *stuff.* How do you do that?"

"Poppy likes minimalism. She read some book about it and decided her personal shit was crowding her psychic energy or something. She hates clutter."

Livie snorted in laughter. "You don't, though." It was amazing to her that someone with so few belongings could create such chaos with them. Nick was forever losing his keys, his phone…anything he owned was at risk of being sucked into his personal maelstrom of mess.

He chuckled, too. "True enough." He stopped and looked around. "It kind of feels like I was just passing through here, doesn't it?"

"That's what I was thinking."

"Funny," he said, shaking his head. "The shit you

see in hindsight. Anyway, that bottom shelf of books is mine. Can you pack them up while I get the rest of my clothes?"

"Sure."

Nick grabbed a box and started toward the bedroom, but before he reached it, the door opened. The rest felt like it happened in slow motion. Poppy stepped through the door, stopping abruptly when she caught sight of Nick.

"Nick—"

Nick's entire body went rigid. Livie could see the tension in his shoulders from across the room. His eyes flicked over Poppy briefly. "Sorry," he bit out. "I figured you'd be out."

"I was just leaving." Poppy gestured toward the front door. "If you come back in ten minutes—"

"What did you say, Poppy?" A man stepped up behind Poppy, laying a hand on her waist. His body had a lanky sort of elegance to it, and his narrow black pants and gold printed silk shirt made him resemble a guy in a cologne commercial. His choppy blond hair was artfully styled to one side, raking across his forehead. The accent sounded European, but Livie couldn't place it.

Poppy froze. Nick's gaze raked over the newcomer. A muscle in his jaw twitched as he ground his teeth together.

"Hey, Klaus." His voice was low, cold, and hard as steel. Livie had never heard him sound that way before. *Klaus?* The name rang a bell, and a moment later it came back to her. The party Poppy had been nagging him about—Klaus, the Eurotrash poser.

Klaus's eyes flicked over Nick in barely concealed disdain. "Hello, again, Nick."

"Nick—" Poppy began, but Nick cut her off.

"It's none of my fucking business. None of this is *any* of my fucking business. Not anymore."

Poppy took one step toward him. "Klaus was here to—"

"I said it's none of my fucking business, Poppy!" His shout bounced off the glass walls, echoing in the sparsely furnished room. Poppy jumped. Livie flinched. Klaus barely reacted at all.

She'd never seen Nick this angry. "Who you fuck is none of my business. Although I suppose it might be my business, depending on *when* you started fucking him. Right, Klaus?"

Klaus shrugged one elegant shoulder, smirking slightly. Poppy went pale. Oh, God, Poppy had been *cheating* on him with this Klaus person. Livie had been frozen, mortified to be caught in the middle of their confrontation once again. Now, as much as she didn't want to, she forced herself to move, crossing to Nick and touching his arm. "Let's get out of here."

"Nick—" Poppy tried again, but he threw up a hand to silence her.

"Save it, Poppy. There's not a damned thing you could say to me right now that I have any interest in hearing."

He turned on his heel and stormed out the front door. As she hurried after him, Livie glanced over her shoulder at Poppy and Klaus. Despite what had gone down, despite what she'd done to him, Poppy looked genuinely stricken, as if she hadn't realized the consequences of her actions until everything collided and blew up in her face. Well, Livie hoped she felt sufficiently miserable. She deserved it for what she'd done to Nick.

She rode down in the elevator with Nick in total silence. He stared at the brushed steel elevator door like he was about to burn a hole in it. That muscle in his jaw was still twitching. All of his usual irrepressible energy seemed to have converted to explosives being held under extreme pressure, as if at any moment a spark would cause him to go up in flames.

Out on the sidewalk, he stopped and closed his eyes, his head falling back as he exhaled heavily.

"Nick—" she began cautiously. "I'm so sorry."

"Nope. No." He lifted his head and looked her straight in the eye. "Fuck her. And fuck him. I'm not going to go cry into my pillow over her, because she doesn't deserve it."

Without thinking, Livie grabbed his hand in both of hers, squeezing hard. "You didn't deserve to be taken advantage of like that. By either of them. I can't believe she did that to you."

"Gotta hand it to her. She's an ambitious girl."

"Do you think that's why she—"

He dropped his head forward. "No. That was a shitty thing to say. I think she was just looking for something that wasn't me."

"That doesn't make it okay to cheat on you."

"Fuck, no, it doesn't. Livie, you know what I need right now?"

"What?"

"I need a good stiff drink to erase the visual of Klaus naked and fucking my ex, because that's what's in my head right now."

"I know how to fix that."

"Let's get out of here. Do you think Gemma cooked anything tonight?"

"Gemma always cooks something."

"I could really use a good meal and a drink."

Well, she couldn't heal his broken heart, or fix his fractured family, but she could provide him with a meal, a drink, and companionship. Maybe tonight that was enough.

Chapter Eighteen

Nick dropped his fork onto his plate with a clatter. "Gemma, another knockout."

Gemma smirked as she swept his empty plate away. Turning to Livie, she murmured, "What brought tonight on?"

Nick wasn't nearly as drunk as he'd been the first night she'd brought him to Romano's, but he was on his third vodka tonic, and definitely feeling at peace with the world.

"We went to pack up the rest of his stuff and Poppy was there."

"The ex? So? She still lives there, right?"

"Yeah, except she wasn't alone. And there was every indication that it wasn't a recent development, if you know what I mean."

Gemma's expression softened into sympathy as she looked over at Nick. Frank was commiserating with him about faithless women, probably telling Nick all about his ex-wife. "Ah, poor bastard. That sucks."

"I can't believe she would do that to him." Livie watched Nick for a moment, trying to gauge his mood. He seemed in good spirits, all things considered, but that might have been the vodka.

"You like him, don't you?"

"Of course. He's great." Kind of a mess, but he tried.

"No, you *like* him."

Livie met Gemma's concerned gaze as alarm rattled through her system. Was she that easy to read? "Gemma—"

Gemma laid a hand over hers to stop her. "Just be careful, okay? He's an okay guy, but he's got about a hundred issues he's dealing with right now. You could get hurt."

Gemma's mothering could be really annoying, especially when she was right. "Gem, I know that. I'm not dumb. I got this. We're friends. That's all."

Gemma paused, watching her steadily. "Sure. Friends. Be careful with your *friend.*"

"Gem—"

But Gemma had turned away to get Dennis his refill. Nick was still talking to Frank.

"You gotta be careful with that online stuff, Frank. You could get catfished."

"But I don't fish," Frank protested.

"No, *catfished.* Like, you think you're talking to some attractive divorcee from Bay Ridge and you don't find out she's some dude from Moldova until you've given him access to your checking account."

Frank's mouth dropped open in disbelief. "That happens?"

Nick clapped him on the shoulder. "Frank, you have no idea. Promise me you won't chat with anybody online until you talk to me. I got your back."

"Thanks, buddy."

"Anytime, Frank." He looked back over his shoulder at Livie. "You ready to head out?"

"Um, yeah, sure." She was still unsteady, thrown by the way Gemma had seen right through her. She'd thought she'd been handling these feelings well enough, burying them where they couldn't do her any harm. Maybe not.

They left the bar and stepped out into the quiet coolness of an early fall evening. Farther up the street, there were more lights, more people, but the block Romano's occupied was quieter, nearly empty of pedestrians at this late hour.

Nick fell into step beside her as they headed home. *Home.* Oh, why had she ever asked him to stay? It had muddied up everything, and now she was tangled up in these feelings for a guy who was about as bad for her as it was possible for someone to be.

"You're quiet," Nick said. "What are you thinking about?"

How I'm pretty sure you're going to end up breaking my heart, no matter what I do.

"Um, thinking about you, actually."

"Me?"

"And Poppy. I'm wondering how you're doing with that."

Nick tipped his head back, staring at the flat, starless night sky as he thought. "To be honest, I have no idea how I fucking feel. Is that weird?" His question seemed rhetorical, as he didn't wait for her reply. "It feels like I should be more hurt. Or maybe pissed? And don't get me wrong, I'm fucking furious at that asshole, Klaus. I always hated that prick. I mean, his name is *Klaus*, like some character in an *SNL* skit. Did you see his hair? Fucking ridiculous. Now I know what that condescending sneer of his was really about."

"You sound angrier with Klaus than with Poppy," she pointed out.

"Eh. Too much vodka and good people and good

food, I guess. I don't feel like being mad at Poppy to-night. Maybe I'll be mad at her tomorrow. Or maybe I'll just let it go. What's it matter now anyway?"

"She didn't deserve you, you know."

He slung his arm across her shoulders, pulling her into his side in a one-armed hug. "Maybe she didn't. But maybe I didn't deserve her either. She was right about a lot of stuff. I would get wrapped up in a project and be lost for days."

"Because you're passionate about what you do."

"Yeah, but maybe if I'd been a little less passion-ate about work, she'd have been a little less passionate about *Klaus*."

"You can't blame yourself, Nick. What she did, that was all her. And it was terrible."

"True. Cheating is always a dick move. What about you, Liv?"

"What about me?"

"Did you ever get your heart broken?"

Not until now. "I'd had to have had a relationship for that to happen."

He looked down at her in surprise. "Seriously? Never?"

Ugh, why was it suddenly embarrassing to admit it to him when she'd never cared before? She shook her head, ducking her chin until her hair slid forward. "Never."

"I don't believe that."

"Why is it so unbelievable?"

"Because you're attractive? And brilliant? Somebody must have been into you."

For a second, she couldn't speak, still stuck on what he'd said. *Because you're attractive.* Nick thought she was attractive? Her face flushed as she processed that piece of information.

Finally, she said, "Yes, but *I* wasn't into anybody, and I wasn't going to do it just because society thinks I should."

"You are really something, Liv."

Something? A good something or a bad something? "What does that mean?"

"You're just… You're not afraid of who you are."

"Are *you*?"

He shrugged, and it pulled her in tighter against his side. "I have a pretty shitty track record of hurting people, whether I mean to or not."

"But I've seen you help people, too." He liked to deny that altruistic streak of his, but it was in there.

"Leave it to you to point out all my positives."

"Yeah, yeah. I know. I'm too nice."

"Never stop being nice, Liv. It's the best thing about you."

She kept her eyes on her feet and her warm face hidden behind her hair. If she tried to talk right now, she wasn't sure what would come out.

They reached the house and Livie gratefully slipped out from under his arm, needing to put a little space between herself and Nick, who found her *attractive*. She jogged up the front stoop, but when she paused to unlock the front door, Nick was right behind her, closer than she'd expected. So close she could feel the heat of his body on her back. His breath ruffled the tendrils of hair in front of her ear. Fumbling, she turned the key in the lock and let them both in.

Spudge was right inside the door, his tail thumping loudly on the wood floor, his droopy doggy face lit up with happiness at the sight of them.

"Hey, my man." Nick crouched to rub Spudge's ears affectionately. Every time she wanted to strangle him for being late or waking her up at three a.m. to talk coding, he'd turn around and do something great, like making friends with Frank or cuddling Spudge, and her resolve crumbled to dust. Forget what she told Gem earlier tonight. She was a total idiot where Nick was concerned.

"I'm going up to bed," she said. Sometimes she sat up with Nick watching TV until he felt tired enough to sleep, but not tonight. Her emotions were all over the place, and spending hours sitting inches away from him on the couch wasn't going to make it any better.

"Yeah, sleep would be good, I guess," he muttered, straightening up. "What a fucking day."

"Well…okay." She turned and started up the stairs.

Nick started up them, too, one step behind her. Her heart began to pound, which was absolutely ridiculous. He was climbing the stairs behind her because his bedroom was across the hall from hers. He had to climb the same stairs to get there.

It was dark in the upstairs hall. The lightbulb in the wall sconce had burned out ages ago and it was that specialty kind, shaped like a little candle flame, which they never seemed to have on hand, and nobody ever remembered to get them at the drugstore. None of the Romanos had much minded, as they could navigate this hallway in a blindfold. But suddenly, the darkness seemed to press in on her, like walls closing her in.

She reached her bedroom door and turned back to say good-night. There was only a weak, gold glow from the light at the bottom of the stairs, enough to pick out the side of Nick's face, his jawline, the slope of his cheekbone, the sweep of his hair across his forehead, inky in this light.

He was close. A bit too close for ordinary conversation. Of course, the door to his room was right there, a foot behind him. Maybe it was this pressing darkness that made it feel as if he was close enough to reach out and touch her. He made no move to back up and give her more space. Maybe he was going to hug her, or squeeze her shoulders in that friendly way again. But he didn't touch her. He stood still, watching her, the air between them vibrating, like the space between two magnets.

"Thank you for today, Livie," he said. Oh, that low rumble of his voice did terrible things to her, making her heart pound, and her thighs clench, and—most embarrassingly—her nipples tighten.

"Anytime," she whispered, because her throat wouldn't allow her to speak at a normal volume. Her arm was folded behind her, her hand clutching her doorknob, the wood of the door at her back. All she had to do was turn the knob and she could escape to the solitude on the other side, and put an end to this awful, vibrating tension.

But Nick could have easily stepped back and disappeared into his room, and he hadn't yet. Why was he standing so close to her in the dark? Why was he watching her like that, like she was some puzzle he couldn't figure out? Why—?

Every other question in her mind was abruptly silenced when he took a step forward, lowered his head, and kissed her. She froze, completely unprepared for this turn of events. *Nick was kissing her.* Her hand curled around the carved brass doorknob behind her until the curlicues were surely impressed on her palm.

For an endless moment—at least it felt endless—his lips pressed against hers, smooth, dry, and firm. Then his mouth moved against hers and Livie's thoughts scattered like marbles on a polished floor. Any chance there had been of her doing the smart thing, stepping back, putting a stop to this, scattered with them.

His lips parted slightly. A spear of panic lanced through her. She'd never been kissed before. She didn't know how to do it.

But then his lips gently teased hers apart, and her panic ebbed. It was easy then, to relax and let him show her. Then there was warmth, and wetness, and suddenly she just *knew*. No, that wasn't true. She didn't need to know, because her body had already somehow figured it out. She let him urge her mouth open further, feeling herself dissolve into the luxurious, intimate heat of the moment. Then his tongue touched hers.

Theoretically, she knew how it all worked. But nothing she knew, nothing she'd seen in movies, had prepared her for what it would feel like to have another person's tongue invade her mouth this way. To have *Nick* invade her this way. She melted back against the door, distantly aware of his hands on her hips, his body moving in closer. She finally relinquished her hold on the doorknob, and despite her complete inexperience, her hands knew to reach for him. They knew how to grip his shoulders, how to hang on as he slowly, thoroughly, explored her mouth with his.

Everything tingled, everything ached. His knee slid between hers and suddenly his thigh was between her legs. God, it was embarrassing, how much she wanted him to touch her there, how badly she wanted to grind herself against the long, hard length of his leg.

His fingers curled into her hips, dragging them closer to his own. His teeth scraped across her lower lip, and somewhere low in her throat, she let out a sound, a needy little moan that would have made her blush in daylight.

It was becoming hard to draw a full breath, and then Nick paused. He drew back. In the darkness, she could feel his eyes on her face. She waited for the rest, for him to kiss her again, for him to take her by the hand and lead her to his bed. She'd go, without hesitation. She wanted it more than she'd ever wanted anything in her life.

Instead, she watched as his eyebrows furrowed. He shifted his weight—not much, but enough to put some space between them. Enough space. Somehow his leg was no longer between her thighs. His hands were no longer gripping her hips quite as desperately.

"Ah, fuck," he whispered.

Then his hands slid away entirely, and he took a full step back. She went cold all over. Her nipples still ached, her thighs still tingled, even as the rest of her body slowly began to flood with mortification.

"I'm sorry, Livie."

Her heart thumped painfully. She tried to swallow, to say something—anything—but her throat refused to cooperate.

But now he'd started talking and he couldn't seem to stop. "Today was a nightmare, and my head is a mess, and I don't know what the fuck I was thinking."

She thanked God—who she didn't even believe in— for that blown-out lightbulb, because now he couldn't see the humiliation heating her cheeks, or the tears welling in her eyes. "It's okay," she muttered, her voice choked and rusty.

"You're a good friend and I had no right to take advantage—"

Friend.

Stupid girl. They hadn't been *starting* anything. This was Nick—chaotic, disastrous Nick—being impulsive and thoughtless once again. She knew better. Hadn't he *just* told her he hurt people without meaning to? She *knew* he could hurt her if she let him, and she'd invited him right in to do it with that kiss.

"It's okay," she said again, with considerably more strength.

"It's… I've been drinking, and—"

"You don't have to apologize." She swallowed hard around the lump in her throat, trying to sound confident and unconcerned, and every single thing she was absolutely not feeling right now. "It happens, right?"

Did it? How would she know? It had never, *ever* happened to her, but Nick probably kissed his friends all the time and it meant nothing at all.

Nick hesitated. She couldn't read his expression in the dark. "Right."

"I'd better get to bed."

"Sure. Livie, again, I'm so sorry."

If he apologized for making the colossal mistake of kissing her one more time, she was going to burst into big, ugly sobs, right here in front of him. They were fighting to get out as it was. "You don't need to feel sorry," she said, as firmly as she could manage. "I understand completely."

She absolutely did not. She'd never been more confused in her life, but that was the last thing she'd ever say to Nick. She had to save face, and that meant pulling herself together and pretending this never happened. If she let it be awkward, it would ruin everything between them, so she'd fake a smile and pretend it meant as little to her as it meant to him.

"You sure?" he said quietly.

"Absolutely." She'd never told a bigger lie in her life.

"Livie, you know you're the best, right? I don't know what I'd have done without you the last few weeks."

He didn't have a clue how dangerous he was to her. Fine, let him stay oblivious. They were friends before, they were friends now. "Good night, Nick."

"Night, Livie."

Finally, her hand found the doorknob, turned it, and she let herself into her room. If only she'd managed that ten minutes ago, this whole horrible, humiliating scene never would have happened.

The door clicked shut behind her. She stood still in the darkness, and her fingers drifted up to touch her mouth. Humiliating, yes. God, she'd never get over the humiliation. But the rest…that kiss had been a revelation. Despite the awful way it had ended, she couldn't bring herself to regret it.

Chapter Nineteen

Nick was already awake when the first gray hints of dawn made it into his room. He'd been lying there, staring at the ceiling for hours, terrified he'd ruined everything.

He'd kissed Livie. He'd *kissed* her.

Over the years, he'd kissed plenty of girls. Sometimes because he was into her. Sometimes because he was into her for the night. Sometimes he wasn't into her at all, but everybody was drunk and why not? Kissing was harmless, all in good fun, and no big deal, as long as everybody was on the same page.

Last night was a very big deal. Livie wasn't some random girl to share a casual lip-lock with. First, she was his friend, and as she'd so accurately pointed out the night he first came here, he didn't have too many of those.

Second—*yesterday.* No one was ever going to accuse him of being deeply introspective. Examining his own motivations and emotions wasn't something he regularly did. But even he was aware that yesterday he'd been processing a lot of shit, and grabbing his nearest female friend and sticking his tongue down her throat was perhaps not a wise move. He was a roiling ball of pain and anger, and he'd been drinking. Taking it out on Livie was unfair as hell.

Third, considering what she'd told him last night, he was pretty sure Livie had never been backed up against a door and kissed like that. When it finally happened, it shouldn't have been with some fucked-up hot mess who'd just found out his fiancée had been cheating on him with a guy named *Klaus*. She was great, and she deserved someone great who would treat her great. Even if he was in his right mind right now—which he most certainly was not—he was not that guy.

Last night, she'd seemed okay. She'd accepted his apology and told him not to worry about it. But was that true? Had he done something impossible to undo? Would things be forever awkward between them now? It would really suck if that were the case, because—as he'd realized as he'd laid in the dark all night castigating himself—he'd come to value her friendship. More than value it, he needed it. If he'd fucked things up and lost her, he'd never forgive himself.

Looking for any excuse to stall, he checked his phone. There was a new text sent in the middle of the night. From Poppy.

I'm sorry.

She was *sorry*? About which part? Breaking up with him? Cheating on him? Getting caught at it? A week ago, he'd been desperate for a word from her, but now her vague apology for something so monumental made him mad. *Go have a nice fucking life with Klaus, Poppy.* He no longer gave a shit. Whatever he thought they'd been doing together for the past year, looking back on it now, it all seemed like a colossal waste of time. He tossed the phone back on the nightstand in disgust.

How long could he hang out in bed before he'd be considered hiding? This long, he decided, forcing himself up. Time to face the music.

There weren't even any other Romanos around to offer distraction. Last night was Saturday, and he'd spent long enough with this family to know that Gemma and John would have gotten home late and would sleep away the morning. Jess was over at Alex's place, as she was most nights. There would be just him and Livie.

Spudge was waiting right outside his door, tail thumping against the floor.

"Hey, buddy. We're still good, right?"

Spudge groaned in assent, then heaved himself to his feet to follow Nick downstairs. He was still arguing with himself about how best to play it off when he reached the kitchen and found Livie already there, making coffee. He froze as she glanced over her shoulder.

"Perfect timing. Coffee's ready."

"Um, good." She seemed to be willing to move on as if nothing happened, and part of him was sorely tempted to do the same. But he wasn't a socially awkward sixteen-year-old anymore. Livie was his friend, and last night, he'd fucked up with his friend. She deserved a decent apology from him, not whatever pathetic garbage he'd mumbled in a panic last night before he'd fled.

"Look, Livie, about what happened last night—"

She spun around, smiling brightly. "Don't worry about it, Nick." That damned smile of hers caught him right between the ribs every time, even when she was patently faking it, like now.

"I feel like I should apologize—"

"There's really no need." She was facing him, but her

eyes weren't meeting his. They were focused on a spot somewhere over his left shoulder. "You were drinking, you were upset, you weren't thinking straight. It's fine."

When she laid it all out like that, it sounded like a bunch of clichéd lines, even to his own ears. But what part wasn't true? He'd just found out his fiancée had been cheating on him. He'd been drinking. He was definitely not thinking clearly last night. But he wished he'd reacted in just about any other way than *that* one.

"I want to make sure you're okay. That I didn't—" He stopped and blew out a breath. "You're a good friend, and I really hope I didn't screw that up last night."

Livie exhaled, too, then finally looked him in the eye. "You didn't. I promise."

That should have been reassuring, but he didn't quite believe her. He didn't believe that smile and he didn't believe that suspicious brightness in her eyes. But he wasn't going to push. After what he'd done, she was allowed to play this any way she wanted.

"Okay," he finally conceded. "Thank you."

"I gotta go." She moved to the table to close up her messenger bag. "I've got a meeting at school."

"It's Sunday."

"With Michiko. About some research."

Livie was a terrible liar. He felt awful, knowing she was trying to escape him. But maybe she needed some space. He'd give that to her. It was the least he could do. "Okay. I'm going to spend some time on the program tonight, if you're around."

"Sure. Yes. I'll be here. See you then."

"Yeah, see you." She squeezed past him on her way out of the kitchen. Her hair brushed his arm and he caught a whiff of that soft flowery scent of hers.

Then she was gone, leaving him alone to face another really inconvenient truth, one he'd been desperately trying to avoid all night long.

Kissing Livie had been fucking amazing, and forgetting it was going to be hard as hell.

Chapter Twenty

Livie stared at Langley's office door, summoning the courage to lift her hand and knock.

The email had come through on Monday morning, a short, official missive from the university to all the Astronomy undergrads and PhD candidates: Professor Langley had been named Acting Chair while Professor Finch was out.

For Livie, it was a terrible blow. First, Janet was going to be out long enough that an Acting Chair needed to be named. Second, that the Acting Chair would be Langley. She still hadn't gotten over that fight she'd walked in on. In her heart, she blamed him for what happened. And in her gut, she didn't trust him.

Still, he was in charge now, and when his email had come a few hours after the official announcement, telling her to come in for a meeting to discuss her dissertation, she couldn't exactly refuse.

Taking a deep breath, she raised her hand and knocked.

"Come in," Langley called from inside. His voice was different than his usual speaking voice—lower, more resonant. If she didn't know any better, she'd suspect he'd been practicing that "come in" for maximum effect. It would be so like him.

Langley's office—unlike Janet's—looked like a photo in a brochure of what a fancy British professor's office would look like. Janet's office was littered with a mish-mash of battered, university-issued furniture. Langley had brought in his own, a large mahogany desk and several matching bookshelves. He had a rug on the floor and his desk chair was a huge padded leather thing. There were a few astronomy texts on the bookshelves, all of them in pristine condition, but there was also open space, artfully filled in with sculptures and awards. Which awards, she had no idea. She found the idea of anyone awarding Langley anything for his research astonishing.

He was behind his desk, peering at his laptop, a stupidly small silver thing. It was the only piece of computer equipment in the room. How did he do his job without a bank of computers? There had to be some other office where his actual work happened and this one was just for show, to impress students and university administration.

Although he was roughly the same age as Janet, somewhere in his late fifties or early sixties, he looked a decade younger—or at least he was *trying* to look a decade younger. Like some kind of European movie star, he wore blazers over cashmere sweaters and weird, tight pants. And loafers. He wore loafers with no socks, even in the winter. His dark hair was thick and very carefully styled, not a hint of gray. She could almost hear Gemma in her head, snarking about male hair dye, and she wouldn't put it past him. He probably spent more on his hair than she got in her graduate student stipend.

He didn't look up as she came in, still reading something on his laptop, peering through his glasses—arty, titanium half-rims perched on the end of his nose. As

Livie approached his desk, she thought she spotted the blue band of Facebook across the top of his screen. Of course.

"Professor Langley? You wanted to see me?"

Langley glanced up, looking surprised to see her there, even though he'd requested the meeting himself a few hours earlier. "Olivia! Have a seat. And you know you can call me William."

"Okay," she murmured as she sat. She was never, ever going to call him William.

The two chairs facing his desk were significantly shorter than the one he sat in. They were too short for his desk, even, making her feel like a little kid trying to peer over the top. He turned to face her, lacing his fingers together on the leather blotter on his desk and leaning forward on his elbows. In the few moments since she'd entered the room until now, his distracted smile had shifted, his face transforming to a picture of concern and sympathy.

"Olivia, this business with Dr. Finch is terribly unfortunate."

Livie didn't respond, since he didn't seem to be asking a question, only making an observation. She'd use a stronger word than "unfortunate" to describe what happened to Janet, but then again, Langley was the jerk who'd caused it, so she didn't expect him to be overflowing with genuine grief.

"With her situation still a mystery—"

"It's not a mystery, Professor Langley. I talk to her son every day."

Langley's mask slipped slightly. "Ah. I didn't realize. That's very kind of you, Olivia. I'm sure the family appreciates your concern—"

"I care about Janet very much."

He paused, his eyes taking her in briefly. "I'm sure you do. That being said, we don't have any indication that she'll return to work."

"Of course she will! She's awake. It's only a matter of time." Which was casting Andy's updates in the most optimistic light imaginable. While she was *technically* awake, Janet was still largely unresponsive, not talking or interacting in any way.

"Yes. Well." Langley forged ahead. "The point is, we don't know when she'll return, and as acting head of the department, I thought we should discuss your dissertation."

The change in direction caught her off guard. "My dissertation?"

"With your advising professor absent for the foreseeable future, we'll have to give some thought to how you'll complete your PhD."

"I'm going to complete it with Janet. I'll work without her until she's back, and then we'll get on with it."

"I understood you were working as her research assistant. How will you do that without her here to perform her research?"

"Parts of the project are mine to head up."

"Such as?"

"We're working on a new program to analyze Hubble data. I'm overseeing that project."

That gave him pause. Really, what did he think she did all day? Peter Hockman might be nothing more than Langley's errand boy, but Janet gave Livie serious assignments and expected professional work from her.

"I see. That's quite impressive. That said, I still have reservations about allowing you to continue working on your thesis without your advisor present."

"But—"

He held up a hand to silence her. "For the moment, however, since we don't know how long that will be the case, I'll let you proceed. But if Professor Finch doesn't return to work in a reasonable amount of time, we may need to reconsider."

"I'm sure that won't be necessary." Livie's heart was pounding and her palms were sweating. Could Langley really yank her off Janet's research?

"I'm sure you're right." Langley's falsely sympathetic smile was back. "But we need to keep an eye on your academic and research progress. We'd hate for this unfortunate incident to hinder you earning your PhD, right?"

Livie dropped her eyes to the carpet, unwilling to look at his fake sad eyes for another second. "Of course not."

There was a pause before Langley spoke again, his voice shifting into a new register. "Olivia, you know I'd love to have you working on my research."

She lifted her head and gaped at him, not sure she'd understood correctly. "What?"

He smiled again, but this one wasn't full of fake sympathy. "You're a very bright young woman. I'm sure I could make full use of your talents."

With a clumsy shove, she pushed her chair back and scrambled to her feet. "That's very kind of you, Professor Langley, but I'm sure Janet will be back soon and I'll be hard at work on her research."

"I hope so, Olivia. I hope so. For your sake, if for nothing else."

She didn't buy his concern for a second. He was jealous of Janet's research, of her success, and here he was, looking to torpedo her work the second she wasn't there to defend it. Well, he'd have to go through Livie first.

"Is there anything else, Professor?"

"Not right now. Have a good day, Olivia."

She turned and left without another word.

Chapter Twenty-One

"He said *what*?" Nick looked up from his laptop.

"He wants me to move over to his research group."

Livie was pacing slowly around the guest room, head down, eyes on the floor—what she did when she was trying to work out a thorny problem. He was on the bed, leaning against the headboard, computer in his lap. They'd been wrestling with the Hubble program but had gotten sidetracked as she told him about her meeting with the new department head.

"That's not what you said. You said he could make use of your talents."

Livie waved a hand in the air. "What he meant was that I'm a good student and he wants me on his project."

This Langley guy sounded like a total asshole, and something about the meeting made Nick's hackles rise.

"Are you sure about that? Sounds like the guy was coming on to you."

Livie scoffed. "Oh, please. Why on earth would he even think about me that way?"

Against his will, his eyes roamed down Livie's body as she paced back and forth in front of him.

That damned kiss. Since that stupid kiss last week, he found himself noticing all sorts of new things about Livie. Like how small her waist was when he caught a glimpse of it under those old flannel shirts of her father's, or how long her legs were, and how perfectly curved her ass was, even in those shapeless jeans she wore. He'd been aware that Livie was attractive before, but he hadn't been aware that *he* found her attractive. And now that he did, he didn't have a clue what to do about it.

"No idea whatsoever," he muttered to himself.

"Whatever. For now, Langley's going to let me move forward on the Hubble project on my own. I'm not going to worry about it."

He hesitated before he asked the obvious question, the one Livie didn't want to face. "What happens if she doesn't come back?"

It wasn't an unreasonable conjecture when you were dealing with a woman Finch's age, suffering a massive heart attack and then a stroke, too, left with damage so severe she was still hospitalized and largely unresponsive. None of it was good. Every day that passed made it more unlikely that Finch—the Finch Livie knew and loved—was going to make it back from this as she'd been before.

"She will."

"Livie—"

"She *will*. And when she does, we're going to have this code figured out."

Okay, Livie didn't want to deal with the possibility right now. Fine. Maybe that was better. After all, she seemed more than capable of carrying on Finch's research without her. What better way to care for the woman than by making sure her life's work continued in her absence?

And for that to happen, they were going to need to crack the nut on this program. This was turning out to be one of the biggest challenges he'd ever faced. Hacking was easy. Every computer network or security system, no matter how complex, was nothing more than a puzzle, one with boundaries and rules. All you needed to do was figure out those boundaries and rules and eventually, you'd figure out the solution to the puzzle. Here, the puzzle didn't exist yet. They had to conceive of the puzzle and figure out how to build it, before they could begin to figure out the solution.

He rubbed his face and attempted to refocus. "Okay, the problem is, we can't begin to tell Hubble what to look for without giving it some defining characteristics. But we won't know the defining characteristics until we record them."

"Right," Livie said slowly, still pacing. "It's like trying to focus on something without looking directly at it. How do you see it when you can't look at it?"

He chuckled softly.

She looked over at him. "What?"

"Nothing. I was just thinking... I mean, how dangerous is this stuff Finch is looking for anyway? Like, are we going to spend all this time teaching Hubble how to see it and the second it does, it blasts Hubble out of the sky? Like getting hit by a car you didn't see coming around a blind corner."

"It doesn't work like that. At least, we don't think it does." Livie started to laugh, but then she froze and her eyes went wide.

"What's wrong?"

She threw her hands up and spun away, pacing more urgently. "It's like a car crash. It's the...impact...the damage...you can reconstruct what happened..."

"Livie?"

"Shhh!" She covered her face with her hands. "I'm almost there."

"Where?" What had he said? What was she trying to figure out?

"That's it!" She grabbed her laptop at the foot of the bed and scrambled up to sit next to him, shoving aside the papers and clothes littering the bedspread to make space for herself. She began rapidly clicking through files on her hard drive, looking for something. "It's the mirror shift! I am such an idiot. I've been combing through these numbers for months and—"

"The what?"

Livie paused long enough to look at him. "It's the observation that sparked Janet's entire theory. While she was examining past Hubble imaging of primordial black holes, she noticed some instances of minute red shifts that perfectly mirrored minute blue shifts."

A blindingly complex program opened up on her laptop. He wasn't even sure what program she was running. It wasn't anything he'd seen before.

"And?"

"If we're right, and those are streams of particles and anti-particles coming untethered from the primordial black hole that birthed them as it died, then this mirrored red and blue shift *is* the evidence of their existence."

"Like one went one way and one went the other the second there was nothing holding them in the same place?"

Her face lit up. "Yes! And they left a trail behind as the black hole winked out. *That* is what we're going to look at. The mirror shift."

"The particles speak the language we're looking for."

"Exactly!" Her eyes were sparkling with the thrill of

her revelation. He hadn't thought dark eyes could sparkle, but that was before he saw hers, dancing with delight as she teased apart the mysteries of the universe. A peachy flush suffused her cheeks. Her chest rose and fell with each rapid breath as her lightning-fast mind put the pieces together. She was—in a word—stunning.

Which was not at all a helpful thought when they were in the middle of a potential breakthrough.

He cleared his throat. "How are we going to observe these particles?"

"We don't need to!" She was practically crowing in triumph. "Because Hubble already has, but it didn't know it. It's all in the archives. They go back to nineteen ninety."

"Are you kidding? You have a record of everything Hubble's ever observed?"

"Well, MAST does." She bit her lip as she opened up a browser window and navigated to a website.

"What's MAST?"

"It's a searchable archive of Hubble's observations. Now I'll have to figure out some search parameters, something to narrow the field of what we're going through."

"You're going to have to explain this to me, Liv, because I have no idea what any of that says."

"You don't need to understand, because I do. The point is, if I can figure out how to search for this data and analyze it, how to reverse engineer it, I think we'll find enough mirror shifts, or even partial ones, to reconstruct the profile and hopefully point us in the right direction."

"At least enough to let us build its language." Finally, he'd managed to grasp the tail end of what she was talking about.

She flashed a dazzling smile over her shoulder. "Exactly."

That smile was potent. It was probably a good thing she didn't unleash it too often. Livie could slay the world with that smile if she tried.

The room suddenly felt too small and too warm, and Livie felt entirely too close. *Settle the fuck down, DeSantis.*

Or maybe the room really was too warm, because a moment later, Livie, still scanning Finch's data and muttering to herself, absently stripped off the oversized flannel shirt she'd been wearing and tossed it to the floor.

His mouth abruptly went dry. She was still dressed. Underneath, she wore a thin white tank. A tight one. But *holy Jesus*, her breasts.

How had he not noticed those before now? Larger than he ever would have guessed under those clothes—high and full and lush and…

He blinked. He swallowed hard. Tried to look away, then couldn't.

"Um…" He stopped, cleared his throat, tried again. "Okay, what am I looking at here?"

"It's essentially a search function, but I'll have to give it coordinates of something we already know first. Janet's documented every mirror shift she's observed, so I can start there."

He lost every single word she said after that as she lifted her bare arms, twisted that long, thick fall of hair into a knot, fashioned it into a sloppy bun on the top of her head, and speared it with a pen. Long tendrils slipped free, floating around her face, brushing the back of her bare neck. Her surprisingly swanlike neck. And her pale, slim, shoulders, and the feminine curve of her back, and that tiny waist…

And he was staring again.

She shifted, moving his laptop to the side and setting hers in its place, so he could see the document she had open. Which was pointless at the moment, as he'd lost the ability to do math, along with his power of speech. "This is the location on the sky, the exposure time, the wavelength—"

He stopped listening the second she leaned into him, pointing at the columns of numbers on the screen. The outside curve of her left breast was nearly touching his biceps. His eyes flicked to the side and down, watching that gorgeous swell, wondering, in spite of himself, what they looked like underneath that tight tank top and insubstantial bra. What color were her nipples? Were they big and pointed or small and tight? Would he be able to see them, barely poking through the long curtain of her hair, as she rode his dick?

Shit.

A powerful urge rose up inside him. He wanted to reach for her. He wanted to take her face in his hands and kiss her hard. He wanted to roll that newly discovered lush body under his and rip off every shred of her clothing until he could touch every part of her.

"And this, this is the real key. If we can extrapolate all of that and compare it to this one, we should get some idea of what we're after." She pointed again, and for a brief, white-hot moment, he felt it, the press of her breast against his arm.

Christ. Focus, DeSantis. She's just a girl in a tank top and you're about to spring a boner like a horny thirteen-year-old.

Ugh, too late. The boner was a firm reality—and getting firmer by the second.

"Here, I'm going to highlight this column so it's easier to see."

She leaned across his body to reach the keyboard. He tried to keep his eyes up, he really did. But it was a losing battle. Against his will, his eyes drifted down and…*cleavage.* A deep shadow of perfect cleavage that looked pearly and soft and…

Nick held absolutely still, because if he moved at all, she might notice the embarrassing hard-on he'd developed basically right under her nose. Or maybe not. She couldn't see past her spreadsheet right now. She'd be completely oblivious unless he put her hand directly on it.

Shit. Wrong thing to imagine at this particular moment.

"Here's what I'm thinking—" She turned her head to look at him and trailed off. His eyes, which had been fixed on a patch of silky smooth skin on her neck, right behind her ear, snapped up to hers.

"What?"

Her eyebrows furrowed. "Are you okay?"

"Um, sure. Yeah, I'm fine."

"You don't seem all here tonight."

"Nothing. I'm just thinking about some things." *Your breasts, your legs, your ass.*

Livie's eyes dimmed slightly. "Right. I'm sure you've got a lot of stuff on your mind right now. Poppy and everything."

Poppy? Poppy who? Right now, he could barely recall what she looked like. But he said nothing as Livie dragged her laptop across the bed. "Let's pick this up tomorrow."

"No, you don't need to go." Although maybe it was for the best if she did. If she stayed, he might end up acting on this sudden rush of lust, and that would be a recipe for disaster.

"I've got some emails I have to send for school anyway. I got distracted by all this and forgot."

"Hey, it's pretty exciting, right?"

She looked up at him with cautious eyes. "What is?"

"This. You might have cracked the code, Livie."

"We have a long way to go before we know if that's the case."

"Nah, you did it. I'm sure of it." Like the cleavage wasn't deadly enough, she had that brilliant brain of hers, too. No wonder he was such a mess right now.

She climbed off his bed. "Thanks. We'll see, I guess."

His eyes had drifted down to her ass as she made her way to the door, but they snapped back to hers when she turned to look back at him. "Good night, Nick."

Licking his lips, he forced himself to look her straight in the eye. Not at her bare arms, or that long graceful neck, not at the curve of her ass, and *definitely* not at her spectacular breasts. "Good night, Livie."

Chapter Twenty-Two

Livie clambered up off her knees, a stack of old catalogs in one hand and a phone charger in the other, all of it unearthed from under the coffee table. She'd been wondering what had happened to that charger.

"What's going on in here?"

Letting out a startled yelp, she spun around. Nick was standing in the entryway, looking in at the unusually tidy living room suspiciously. Her pulse fluttered unsteadily at the sight of him. She'd been bad enough before, but ever since that night—that *kiss*—it was like a switch had been flipped in her head and no matter what she did, she couldn't flip it back off.

Something had been awakened in her when Nick had kissed her, something new and eager and yearning. Okay, it was hormones, and what she was yearning for was sex, she knew that, but knowing didn't make the stupid hormones go back to sleep. Every time she looked at him, she flashed back to the feel of his mouth on hers, his body pressing hers into the door, imagining what else might have happened if he hadn't gotten spooked...

Oh hell, she was doing it again.

Ducking her head to let her hair slide forward, she

turned away. "Um, Dad's bringing someone to dinner tonight. We're straightening up."

Jess passed through the room with an armload of clean laundry, heading for the stairs. "He's bringing his *girlfriend* to dinner. Hi, Nick."

"Hi, Jess." He came a little closer, but stopped right inside the living room, eyeing the freshly fluffed throw pillows. "John's got a girlfriend? I've never met her."

"Neither have we. Well, Gemma has, but not *as* his girlfriend."

"How long have they been going out?"

"Um, since last December? But he only told us in May." *That* had been an awkward conversation, Dad sitting them down for a serious talk, ready to ease them into the subject, when all three of them had known about Teresa for months.

Dad's announcement that he'd like them all to get to know each other better was a clear signal that this was serious—Teresa was sticking around. Livie had known that, of course, but knowing was different than confronting it face-to-face. And that was turning out to be harder than she expected. A *lot* harder.

"John was sneaking around with someone? Who knew? John Romano's a horndog."

"That's my *father* you're talking about."

He sobered at once. "Sorry, bad joke. How are you doing?"

She glanced around the living room. She'd done the dusting and run the vacuum. Fresh flowers would have been nice, but there wasn't time to run up to the Kims' green grocery and buy some. "I've got to get the good place mats out of the hutch and set the table, but—"

"No, Liv, I meant, are you nervous?"

"I don't know. I can't tell what I'm feeling. I'm either nervous or I have the stomach flu."

"Well, let's hope for everyone's sake that it's the former. I'll get out of the way so you can finish setting up—"

The words were out of her mouth before she'd even realized they were in her head. "Do you want to stay?" Suddenly, she desperately wanted him there. He wasn't one of her sisters or cousins, or any other family member. He was *her* person, *her* friend. Having him in her corner tonight would make her feel a lot more secure. And someone outside the family being here meant the conversation couldn't wander into weird, uncomfortable, personal places.

Nick froze. "Stay for dinner?"

"Yeah."

"It seems like a family thing."

"You're practically family," she said with a laugh. "I mean, you *do* live here."

He reached up to run a hand across the back of his neck. "I wouldn't want to impose. Besides, I have a thing I gotta do tonight."

"A thing?"

"A meeting. With a new client."

"Oh. Right. Sure." He was lying. She could see the terror in his eyes from across the room. He was fine hanging out at the bar with her dad and her sister, or chatting with Jess over coffee in the morning. He was okay sitting up with her, watching TV in the middle of the night until one of them got tired enough to sleep. But kissing her had freaked him out and sent him fleeing. And being included in an actual family event practically had him chewing off his own foot to free himself.

As if she needed any more reminders that Nick

wasn't meant for her. Whatever had happened with his family had really done a number on him, and he was flat-out refusing to become any more entangled with the Romanos—with *her*—than absolutely necessary. Well, she knew his time here had an expiration date. He was not the kind to stick around. And she wasn't the kind to leave.

"No problem," she said, forcing herself to sound light and unconcerned. "I guess I'll see you later, then."

He stood a moment longer in the doorway, seemingly torn about staying or going. Then he lifted a hand and waved. "Yep. See you around, Liv."

She held on to her fake smile until she heard the door close behind him and she was certain he was gone. Then she straightened her shoulders and prepared to face the night without him.

"They're here." Gemma turned from the stove, where dinner was nearing completion, at the rattle of the front door lock. Livie and Jess exchanged a brief glance as Spudge lumbered out to greet their father and Teresa.

Jess pushed up from the kitchen table. "We should go say hello. Come on, Alex."

Alex, who'd been loitering by the back door trying to look invisible, followed Jess out of the room.

Teresa, to the best of Livie's knowledge, had never been over to their house. They'd been dating openly since the summer, but Dad *always* went to her place. This definitely felt like the beginning of some new era in the Romano family, and while intellectually, Livie was okay with that, emotionally, she was still struggling, for reasons she couldn't precisely put a name to.

When she reached the living room, Dad was shutting the door and Gemma was nervously greeting Teresa. Gemma knew her already, since Teresa sometimes came into the bar. That was how she and Dad had reconnected, years after they'd gone to high school together.

John Romano moved to Teresa's side and set his hand on the small of her back. Such a tiny gesture, yet it jarred Livie to her bones. This was real. They were *together*. As long as she hadn't met Teresa—as long as she hadn't seen it with her own eyes—it hadn't seemed quite real. But now she was here in their house, and her father was gazing down at her with that weird expression on his face that she'd never seen before and this was *real*.

To Livie at that moment, it didn't much matter what Teresa was like, or how this dinner would go. She only wished she could turn back time, to scramble away from this edge, because now that they were going over it, everything would change. The last thirteen years of their family life would end, and she couldn't begin to imagine what the future would look like.

"Teresa, you know Gemma, of course. These are my other daughters, Jessica and Olivia. And this is Jess's fiancé, Alex."

Teresa turned to Jess and Livie, standing side by side. She was pretty. Not as pretty as their mother had been, but Angela Romano was frozen in time at thirty-five. Still, Teresa was attractive—with a small, delicate build and fine features. Her hair was blond, which for some reason surprised Livie. Mom had had the same dark brown hair and eyes as her three daughters. Teresa looked different, not at all who she'd have imagined Dad with.

Jess, always the most socially sophisticated, was naturally the first one to greet her.

"Hi, Teresa. It's nice to finally meet you."

"It's great to finally meet you girls. John talks about you all the time."

John. That was his name, of course, but there was something intimate about the way Teresa said it, the way she casually referred to all these private conversations she had with their father.

Alex, ever the perfect, charming one, was the next to greet her. "Welcome, Teresa. It's a pleasure to meet you." He sounded like he was greeting the British ambassador.

"Can I get you something to drink?" Gemma said. "It's white wine, right? Or we've got beer, soda, whatever."

"Wine would be great. Thanks, Gemma."

"Something sure smells fantastic, Gem," Dad said.

"Dinner's ready. Why don't we all sit down? I'll be right back." Gemma had on her very best company manners, and so did Jess and Alex. Livie vowed to herself, no matter how strange this felt, that she would try, too.

Dinner was not unpleasant. Just stiff. It was new, Livie told herself, having a stranger join what had been their intimate little family for over a decade. The family had easily expanded to embrace Alex, and even Nick, who had no real connection to them at all and didn't seem to want one. Of course, it would expand to embrace Teresa, too. Logically, Livie knew that. Then why did she feel like there was a cement block sitting on her chest? Why did this all feel so hard?

Livie watched her chat with Gemma about people they both knew from the neighborhood and tried her best to imagine it—this woman—this stranger— joining their family. She couldn't. She could envision sub-atomic particles dancing on the edge of an event horizon, but she couldn't picture Teresa becoming part of this family.

"Livie—is it alright if I call you Livie? John says that's what you go by."

"Sure. I mean, yes, I go by Livie." Although literally everybody called her that except Professor Langley, it still felt weirdly intimate to let Teresa do it.

"Your dad says you're getting your master's degree in astronomy?"

"PhD. I'm getting a doctorate."

"Oh, my mistake. A doctorate in astronomy." Teresa's light brown eyes widened. She had kind eyes. And a nice face. It was just an unfamiliar face. "Isn't that something? Well, your dad said you were a genius."

"I'm not a genius. Genius is just a level of IQ results and IQ tests aren't an accurate measure of mental abilities. They fail to measure several aspects of intellect, and these days they're not widely relied on as an indicator of intelligence." Under the table, Jess nudged her with her foot, and she shut her mouth so fast her teeth clicked. *Nice, Livie.* That's exactly what this dinner needed—a lecture about the unreliability of IQ tests. *This* was why she avoided talking to strangers. She opened her mouth and a bunch of irrelevant nonsense poured out.

Teresa seemed unfazed. "Sure are smarter than me. Nobody we grew up with even went to college, right, John?" She elbowed Dad, who chuckled along with her as they shared some memory from their past.

Except he wasn't supposed to have a past with this woman. Their mother was his past. That's how it had always been. What would happen to Angela Romano now that Teresa was here? How was this going to work? Would they have to pack up all her pictures? Would everybody slowly stop mentioning her? Would Teresa step into the spot their mother had once inhabited so fully that it would be like Angela Romano had never even existed? How was she going to ever get used to having this stranger in their house? This person she couldn't hold a normal conversation with to save her life?

When Livie clammed up, Teresa switched her attention to Jess. Jess was much better at this, chatting animatedly with Teresa about her job, the latest story she was pursuing at the paper, her recent engagement, anything and everything. Alex swung in after that. Alex was used to chatting up Fortune 500 execs and senators. Making conversation with Teresa came as easy as breathing to him.

Livie watched her sisters closely, wondering if this was hard for them, too. It didn't seem to be. Jess was much better at adapting to new things. She was probably fine. And Gem had spent her whole life wearing a brave face. You could never tell if something upset her. Livie was terrible at pretending to feel things she didn't feel, and just as terrible at hiding what she *did* feel.

Somehow, dinner was eaten. Conversation was managed. Maybe it wasn't one of the free-wheeling family dinners the Romano table usually witnessed, but they got through it. As soon as Gemma started clearing the table, Teresa leapt to her feet, offering to help. Gemma firmly shut her down, and Dad led her to the living room, where they turned on the TV to catch the end of the Jets game. Well, at least she was a Jets fan. Dad never would have dated her if she rooted for the Giants.

"Well, what do you think?" Gemma whispered as she covered leftovers in plastic wrap and stowed them in the fridge.

Livie turned on the hot water and squirted some dish soap into the sink. "She seems nice."

"I like her," Jess declared as she scraped plates into the trash. "And she makes Dad happy, that's obvious."

"They make each other happy. Teresa's had a rough time of it, too," Gemma said, turning to take an empty serving bowl from Alex. He cast one brief look around the kitchen, realized the girls were having a post-mortem, and headed back out to the dining room.

"What happened to Teresa?" Jess asked.

"You know when she was married, she lived out in Jersey? Her husband was pretty high up in some construction company. Did well for himself. They had a nice house, Teresa didn't have to work, all that. Then he up and left her for her best friend. She never saw it coming. Completely broadsided her."

"That's awful."

"And," Gemma continued, "he got some shark of a lawyer to hide all their assets. Somehow he shafted her out of everything in the divorce."

"Bastard," Jess growled.

"Typical," Gemma concurred. "Anyway, on top of all that, her mother got diagnosed with cancer. She had to move back home to take care of her, but it wasn't like she had a lot of options in her situation."

"Poor Teresa."

"I'm glad she found Dad. He's a good guy, and she deserves a prince."

"I guess," Livie conceded. "She's…"

"What?" Jess pressed.

"She's different than Mom. That's all."

Gemma shrugged. "Maybe that makes it easier for Dad."

"What do you mean?"

"Maybe if he was dating someone exactly like Mom, he'd always be reminded of her, or feel like he was trying to replace her. With Teresa, he won't compare, you know?"

"Do you think…?"

Jess handed Livie a stack of plates. "What?"

"Do you think it's serious? Do you think Dad's really serious about her?"

Gemma paused for a moment before answering. "I think, after all these years, Dad wouldn't have brought her home if he wasn't thinking about marrying her."

Marry her? Dad was going to *marry* Teresa? For a second, Livie couldn't breathe. She was silent as she washed and passed the dishes to Jess to dry, tuning out Jess and Gemma's quiet chatter about the dinner and Teresa.

When they'd finished cleaning up, they moved out to the living room. Livie stopped cold, arrested by the sight of Teresa and Dad, side by side on the couch, his arm around her shoulders, her body tucked into his side. The intimacy of it took her breath away. It occurred to her in a flash that maybe Teresa was spending the night.

"I'm going to go to the bar," she announced, not realizing what she was saying until the words came flying out of her mouth. "To check in with Clyde and see if he needs a hand."

Everybody turned to look at her. "I'm sure he'd text if he needed help," Gemma said slowly.

"It's Monday night. There's a game. You never know."

Without waiting for anyone else to speak, she turned and left the house.

Chapter Twenty-Three

For the entirety of the short walk to the bar, Livie berated herself. She'd been childish and stupid. So what if Dad's girlfriend was spending the night? So what if they got married? It shouldn't matter to her. Why did it?

The crowd at Romano's was a little bigger than an ordinary Monday, owing to the Jets game, but that wasn't what surprised Livie when she entered. It was the sight of Nick sitting at the bar.

"What happened to your meeting?"

He swung around to face her, guilt flashing in his eyes. "They cancelled."

"You don't need to keep lying. I know you didn't have a meeting."

His shoulders slumped. "I'm sorry, Liv, I just—"

She waved away his apology. "It's fine. You were right. It was a family thing and you don't do families, right?"

"Um, yeah, I guess. Is dinner over?"

"Yeah. Except Teresa's still there."

"Then why are you here?" Nick asked.

"I think she's staying over." Saying it out loud felt so weird.

"Ah, I see. You escaped."

"I didn't *escape*, exactly," she lied. "I came to see

if Clyde needed a hand." At the moment, Clyde was watching the Jets game along with everybody else. He was hardly being run off his feet.

"Hey." When she looked back at Nick, he leaned in closer. "You don't need to keep lying to me."

She scoffed softly and looked away.

He patted the stool next to his. "Sit."

She sighed and climbed up on the stool. "It's nothing."

"Liar." He only grinned when she flashed him an annoyed look. "How was dinner?"

"It was fine."

"How was Teresa?"

"She's nice."

"*Fine. Nice.* Wow, you're the master of exposition tonight. Now the truth, please."

"That *is* the truth. She's very nice."

"So what's the problem?"

"She's the first person Dad's dated since Mom died."

"Really? No one? Thirteen years is a long time to stay on the shelf."

"No one," Livie confirmed. "Not a single date in all these years. And now, out of nowhere, he's really serious about Teresa."

"I guess it would be hard, when you've had him to yourself for so long, to see someone new come into his life."

"I'm not jealous," she said defensively. "It's more like… You know how I told you people don't like me?"

"Hold up. Nobody dislikes you. They're intimidated by you. But they don't dislike you."

"Whatever. None of that mattered, because my dad always did. He doesn't understand any of my research or my work, but he asks questions, and he listens to me, even when he doesn't know what I'm talking about. He cares, you know?"

"Ah. And no one else did."

"I didn't really care about not having friends as long as I had my sisters and my dad." As soon as she said it out loud, though, something clicked in her brain, a revelation that had never before been apparent to her. She thought of Michiko, asking her to the departmental potluck, and Teresa, patiently trying to tease out any information at all about her as Livie repeatedly shut her down. People *did* reach out to her. *She* was the one backing away.

The realization left her with an unpleasant sensation clawing at her insides, something that felt like a muddle of guilt, shame, and fear. Because realizing that about herself didn't mean she knew how to fix it, or that she was brave enough to try.

Livie was clearly upset. Nick could see it in the hard set of her lips and her flat, expressionless eyes. When Liv was upset about something, she closed down, like steel gates lowering at Fort Knox. He nudged her elbow with his. "I can always tell when you're thinking big thoughts. You get that look on your face."

"It's nothing."

That was a lie if he'd ever heard one. She didn't want to tell him what she was thinking, so he hazarded a guess. "You won't lose him, you know."

"What?"

"Your dad. I mean, obviously I have my own complicated relationship with my parents—"

Livie snorted a laugh. "You mean the ones you haven't seen since you were eighteen?"

"Shut up. We're talking about your hang-ups, not mine."

"Sorry. Go on."

"Livie," he began, lowering his voice and leaning into her until she raised her eyes and met his. "I've only been hanging around here for a few weeks, but I can see how much your father loves you. All of you. That won't change, no matter who he hooks up with."

"I know that." She looked down at the bar. "But everything else will change."

"Well, yes, I guess so. Maybe that's a good thing?"

"I don't do well with change. I mean, look at me."

He'd been doing his best *not* to look at Livie, since every time he did, his mind unhelpfully wandered down the same path it had a week ago, noticing breasts and lips and skin, and how hot she was when she was puzzling out a difficult problem. But he was trying *very* hard to be a good friend who did *not* notice those kinds of things.

"I don't know what you're talking about," he said.

"My only friends are my sisters."

"Hey, am I imaginary?"

"I look exactly the same as I did at sixteen."

"Think how handy that'll be when you're forty."

"I'm twenty-five and I still live at home."

"Just because you're going to Adams and it's in Brooklyn."

"But I didn't have to," she said, before quickly cutting herself off.

"What do you mean? Did you have other offers?"

She looked away and shrugged. She was hiding behind her hair again. "Sure."

He reached out and carefully tucked it behind her ear, until he could see the side of her face. "Like?"

Another shrug. "MIT. Berkeley. McArthur."

"McArthur has some of the best science programs in the country." He knew because they'd been courting him along with DeWitt.

Her eyes stayed fixed on the bottles lining the shelves behind the bar. "I know. And they offered me a full tuition waiver, plus a stipend for teaching, and a fellowship."

That was one hell of an offer, better than the one they'd made him. And while he was reasonably sure Adams had coughed up a decent financial aid package, Adams was no McArthur. Not by a long shot.

"And you said *no* to that?"

"I picked Adams because of Janet."

Okay, yes, Finch was doing exciting work, but there was something else hiding in Livie's reasoning, he knew it in his gut. She hadn't picked Adams just for Finch. Adams was right here in Brooklyn, and McArthur was all the way out in Colorado. He'd bet his best laptop that she'd also picked it because Adams was here, close to home. She'd picked it because she didn't want to leave.

It had been different for him. He'd been so eager at sixteen to get away from a family that didn't understand him, from always being compared and found wanting, that he'd have moved to the moon if that's where the offer took him. And in one way or another, he'd been running away from them ever since.

But Livie's life was different. Her family was different. There was no judgment here, only love and unconditional acceptance. He couldn't really blame her. He probably wouldn't have wanted to run away from that either, if he'd had it.

"Do you ever wish you'd said yes to McArthur?"

She shook her head. "I wanted to work with Janet. Her research is exactly what I want to do."

"But there might have been great research happening at McArthur, too," he said carefully.

"What are you saying?"

"Okay, I have no life plan, right?"

She hiked one eyebrow at him, and for a second he forgot where he was going with this. "Did you just figure that out?"

"*No*, I'm trying to make a point. You've seen how I work. I say yes to whatever sounds interesting, because you never know where it might lead."

"I can't work like that."

"I know you can't. That's not what I meant. I mean, sometimes I'm wrong and the job sucks. But sometimes I'm right and I get to do something amazing. Like this project with you."

"I get it. You're saying I should try more new things. You sound like Gemma trying to get me to try beets when I was seven. I still don't like beets, by the way."

"I'm *saying* that playing it safe might not always make you happy. Or as happy as you could be. Shaking things up can sometimes lead to great things. Maybe your dad being with Teresa is one of those things."

She heaved a sigh. "Yeah, maybe you're right. I should give her a chance."

As she stared unseeing at the liquor bottles against the mirrored wall, her expression was impossible to decipher. Had he helped her at all? He wasn't sure. It was laughable, anyone coming to him for advice. Sure, he'd had some success in life, but in retrospect, only by accident. His past seemed to be nothing but a string of reckless self-destructive acts that somehow led to success instead of abject failure.

"Ready to head back into the lion's den?"

She hopped off her bar stool. "Clyde, you sure you don't need help with closing?"

"Nah, I got this. Night, Livie."

Outside, the night air was almost balmy for mid-October, which was good, because in her panicked dash from the house, Livie hadn't bothered to grab a jacket. It was late on a Monday, and the sidewalks were nearly empty.

"You really think Teresa's staying over tonight?" Nick asked her.

"When I left, they looked pretty cozy together on the couch." That was the last thing she wanted to think about right now. What if she ran into Teresa outside the bathroom in the middle of the night? Oh God, what if she could *hear* them?

Nick chuckled. "You get it, John Romano."

She shoved his arm. "Eeew. Come on. That's my dad. My previously *celibate* dad."

"Um, Livie, the man has three daughters. I hate to break it to you, but he's had sex before."

"That may be, but I still don't want to know about it."

"Come on, let your dad have a little fun." He slung an arm across her shoulders. His friendly affection was a blessing and a curse. The closer he got, the harder it was to think clearly. Her body got all flushed and she had to duck her head to hide the heat in her cheeks. "His idea of fun used to be fishing with Uncle Richie," she muttered.

"Trust me, he's having a *lot* more fun with Teresa tonight."

Right. Sex. The sex literally everybody seemed to be having except her. And here she was next to the one guy she was desperate to climb on top of, his arm wrapped around her like they were…like they were *something,* dammit! And yet, when they got home, he'd tell her good-night and she'd spend the rest of the night lying in bed, fantasizing about him, imagining doing all kinds of things with him, too afraid of messing up what they had to push for anything more.

But what did they have, really? A working relationship and a friendship, both probably with an expiration date, because she knew he wasn't sticking around for the long term.

So what was she protecting? If he was going to cut and run eventually anyway, why should she be content with this tepid, friendly affection when she wanted a lot more? When she was pretty sure he wanted more, too. He wouldn't have kissed her that way if he didn't want her at least a little.

As they passed in front of Vinelli's Meats, she stopped walking. Nick turned back to look at her. "What is it, Liv?"

When she said nothing, he took a step toward her. "Is everything okay?"

Inhaling deeply, she licked her lips and prepared to jump off a very high cliff without any idea what was waiting at the bottom. "I want to try something."

Livie took a step closer to him, close enough that, if he wanted to, Nick could touch her hand with his without even lifting his arm. Close enough that he could feel the warmth of her body. Her eyes glimmered, fixed on his face. "Hold still. And tell me to stop if you don't want this."

His mind lurched to a halt, like a needle dragging across a record. His blood began to pound in his veins as the air between them crackled with an awareness he was all too familiar with. He knew what came next. And some part of his brain—the nice, honorable, smart part of his brain—thought maybe he *should* stop this before something happened they couldn't undo.

But he didn't stop her. He didn't move at all as she moved even closer, as she set one hand on his shoulder and laid one hand along his jaw, as light as a whisper. He didn't stop her as she looked into his eyes, her own dark and glittering in the reflected streetlight. And he didn't stop her as she pushed to her toes and pressed her lips to his.

Oh, Christ—soft and sweet and warm and every damned thing he'd been trying so hard to forget. Now it all came rushing back, and his hands curled into fists as he resisted grabbing hold of her.

Slowly, she leaned back and opened her eyes, looking at him expectantly. She was waiting, because she was a good and decent person, for him to sort out what he wanted, if he wanted her.

He drew in a deep breath. Blew it out slowly. Waited for the right words to assemble themselves in his brain. "Livie…"

"I know what you're going to say. I know Poppy messed with your head and you're in a bad place. I know you're not looking for forever or even next month. I know all that. And I don't care."

"This is, um, unexpected." He was stalling for time and he knew it, scrambling to figure out which response was the right one.

"But is it really, though? Nick, you kissed me."

"I did."

"So?" She lifted one eyebrow, that same challenging, knowing look she'd given him back at the bar, the one that had totally scrambled his brain cells. It was so fucking hot.

Fuck it. He wasn't spending one more second stalling, trying to talk himself out of what he really wanted to do. He reached out with both hands, took her face between his palms, pulled her in, and kissed her hard.

Part of him knew she had a point about all of this—his life was a mess. *He* was a mess. He was about as bad for a girl like Livie as it was possible to be, but he didn't care either. Right now, he was practically howling at the moon, fucking delighted to have this chance to do the thing he hadn't been able to stop thinking about for two weeks.

Her hands found their way to his shoulders and she melted into him. He teased her lips apart and she opened for him, letting his tongue invade her mouth. He slipped an arm around her waist, pulling her firmly up against his body. Last time—that impulsive fumble in the hallway—his head had been such a mess and blurry with alcohol, that he missed what it truly felt like to kiss Livie. He wasn't making that mistake tonight.

She was all softness in his arms, those amazing breasts pressed against his chest, her thighs brushing his, her silky hair tickling the back of his hand. Her kiss was totally unstudied, which was—surprisingly—hot as hell. It had been a long time since he'd kissed someone inexperienced. She wasn't trying to seduce him with her sophisticated technique, or trying to bring him to his knees with some erotic trick she'd read about online. She just kissed him, let herself be kissed by him, let him explore her mouth with his tongue, slowly, thoroughly, and for a very long time. And that was enough, all by itself, to nearly bring him to his knees.

Somehow he'd managed to back her up against the

steel rolling security gate of the butcher shop. Livie's hands gripped his shoulders, then slowly slid up into his hair. The feeling of her fingernails scraping the base of his neck sent a tremor of desire shafting through his body.

He kissed across to her ear, tonguing her earlobe. She sighed, a shaky little exhale that made his dick twitch. The skin of her neck was silky, smooth, and warm under his lips, exactly the way he'd been imagining. Her head fell back, making the metal gate behind her rattle. His hand was drifting north from her waist, and she was doing nothing to stop him. When he cupped the magnificent fullness of her breast with his palm, she sighed again, and this time, his dick did more than twitch. With his other hand, he pulled her hips tighter to his, pressing against the rapidly increasing swell of his cock.

Who knew how long he'd have pinned her to the gate, grinding against her? But a couple of pedestrians passed behind them on the sidewalk, one chuckling and whispering to the other. Okay, this definitely wasn't the place.

He drew back enough to make out Livie's face. Her lips were slightly swollen, sheened with moisture, parted and ready for him to kiss again. And God, he wanted to. Kissing, touching, and a whole lot more. But there was something he needed to say, a niggling of guilt that needed to be dispelled. The last thing he'd ever want to do was hurt her, but she deserved to know there was every possibility he'd wind up doing it anyway.

"You're not wrong, you know."

"About what?" she whispered. He could feel her words on his lips more than he could hear them.

"I'm a mess right now. You deserve better, Livie. You—"

She reached up and pressed two fingers to his mouth. "I told you, I don't care. I want you." Those words sparked a warm glow in his chest, something more than lust, but something he was happy not to examine too closely tonight.

Maybe tomorrow, in the cold light of day, he'd have second thoughts, reservations. Right now, there was nothing but the pure satisfaction of her declaration humming through his blood. He didn't care about the rest of it either. Tonight, all he wanted was her.

Chapter Twenty-Four

"Nick, this is amazing," Livie said as she sat cross-legged on his bed, scrolling through the first set of data he'd produced on her laptop. "I can't believe you processed this much data this quickly."

He'd had to do *something* to keep himself busy for the past week. Since that night outside the bar, they'd done plenty of kissing, but not much more than that. Clothes had stayed on, they'd stayed vertical, and usually, it happened downstairs in the living room or the kitchen—where, in theory—someone could walk in at any moment. All of that had been intentional on Nick's part. He was trying to be a decent guy and take this easy, even though he was going slowly mad imagining everything they weren't doing. Nothing like throwing yourself into a complex batch of coding as a distraction.

"*I* didn't process anything. The program did."

"But this is incredibly complex data."

He shrugged, swelling slightly with pride. His achievements always felt better when Livie was the one he was impressing, because blowing *her* mind wasn't easy. "Nothing's all that complex if you write the right algorithm."

"I thought it would take weeks to crunch these numbers."

"Not if you've got me, it doesn't." He leaned across the bed, laid his hand against the back of her neck, and kissed her. "Now tell me how brilliant I am."

"You're brilliant," she muttered against his mouth before looking back to the screen. "I need to analyze these for patterns. If I find a pattern, we can identify an area of the sky where we have a good shot at predicting an event."

"Tell me what you're looking for and I'll build a machine learning algorithm."

"In some instances, human beings are better at recognizing repeating patterns than computers, you know."

"That cannot be true."

"It is! A lot of astronomy researchers recruit people to analyze data for exactly that reason. They call them citizen astronomers."

"I'm going to build an algorithm anyway. Then you can tell me who's faster."

She smiled at him, hiking one eyebrow in that way that drove him crazy. "Is it so impossible to believe that humans could be better at something than a computer?" Damn, she was cute when she was teasing him.

His eyes dropped to her cleavage, exposed tonight since she'd left off her baggy flannel shirt and was wearing only a tank top. "Humans are a *lot* better at some things," he murmured.

She wasn't paying attention anymore, her eyes back on her screen. "When I find repeating patterns, it will let us begin to build a profile—"

Nick cut her off with another kiss. She let out a muffled yelp of surprise, but then relaxed against him, letting him tease her lips apart and stroke her tongue with his own. Without breaking the kiss, he slid her laptop out of her hands and closed it. Analysis could wait.

Tearing her lips away from his, she tried to retrieve her computer. "But—"

He set it on the nightstand by the bed. "Later. Coding turns me on."

She laughed before he kissed her again. That wasn't entirely a joke. Cracking a thorny problem always left him buzzing with adrenaline needing an outlet. And here was Livie, sitting on his bed next to him, getting all excited about science. How was he supposed to resist that? She had no idea how hot she was when she was obsessing over data.

She let him tumble her onto her back and deepen the kiss. Her hands slid up into his hair. His knee insinuated itself between hers. The kiss went from playful to hot. He nipped at her bottom lip, and dragged his tongue across the roof of her mouth. His hand curled into her waist, his thumb sweeping back and forth, right under the hem of her shirt.

Livie bent her right leg and suddenly his hips slid right in between her thighs. Ah, Jesus, that felt good. He fought down the urge to grind himself against her, keeping some small distance between them.

Then, slowly and deliberately, she hooked her calf behind his hips and hauled him in flush against herself.

His breathing stalled in his chest.

"Shit," he groaned, pressing his forehead to her shoulder. This was why he'd been trying to go slow.

Livie had never done this before, and he had no idea how he was supposed to handle that. He'd never been with a virgin, not even when he was one himself. His first time, when he was fifteen, had been with a seventeen-year-old high school senior at computer camp. As much as he wanted Livie, as much as she seemed to want him, he couldn't help but wonder if it would be a mistake, her throwing it away on someone as unworthy as him. He was a mess—no good for anyone. But that eminently responsible voice was continually being drowned out by his libido, and Livie wasn't helping.

And now here they were, tangled together on his bed, the door closed, and the house silent. Jess was at Alex's, Gemma was at the bar, and John had taken Teresa to his brother's place on City Island for the weekend. No one would put a stop to this, unless he did.

He shifted his weight, intending to regain some distance and, hopefully, a little sanity, but somehow their hips collided again. He was hard as a goddamned rock, straining against the fly of his jeans, and incredibly sensitive. Again, he groaned.

"Livie—"

Her hand was on his hip, and now she slid it up under his shirt, over his ribs. Her palm felt like fire, branding his skin.

"I think you should take this off," she murmured, tugging on his T-shirt.

He lifted his head, looking down into her face. Ah, hell. Her eyes were heavy-lidded and sexy, her thick lashes casting shadows on her cheekbones. Her lips were flushed pink and parted. Her chest rose and fell underneath him as she dragged in a breath. Why couldn't he do this again? There was a good reason he'd been avoiding it, right? But what was it? Why couldn't he strip off his shirt as she asked, and then strip off hers, and then strip off everything else and bury himself in her? She wanted him to. It was right there, all over her face. *He* wanted to—so bad that it literally hurt.

Then she reached up a hand to touch his face, laying her palm on his cheek, running the pad of her thumb along his bottom lip, and the tenderness of her expression brought it all back. This wouldn't just be sex for Livie. He wasn't sure it would just be sex for him either. And this was a colossally bad time for him to be starting something when he had no idea if he could finish it.

"Livie, I'm not sure this is a good idea."

"I want to."

"I know. So do I." God, he wanted to. Every molecule of his body wanted to.

"Then let's do it."

"But—"

She brought her other hand to his face, holding him still and silencing him. "It's okay, Nick. It won't change anything."

A greater lie had never been told, and he opened his mouth to say so, to tell her that sex would most definitely change things, but then she leaned up and kissed him with such luxurious thoroughness that for a minute, he forgot his own name, never mind all those imminently rational arguments against this. She was shifting her hips against his, torturing his swollen cock at the same time she teased his tongue with hers.

He was going to lose this fight. He realized that even before she reached for his hand and placed it over her breast. But once that glorious warm flesh was in his hand, it was all over.

"I want this, Nick. I want you. I want it to be you."

Her words finished him off. He might have been able to do the right thing if it only entailed reining in his own desire. *Maybe.* But there was no way he could fight hers, too.

So he kissed her back, and he squeezed her breast, and she moaned into his mouth, and his cock swelled. Now that he'd given in, now that he knew he was going to do this, his body was practically shaking with anticipation. It felt like he might explode with the slightest provocation. But...

This was her first time.

Just because he'd crossed his own line and decided to do this, that didn't mean he had leave to tear her clothes off and take her. He was determined to make this good for her. That was the very least he could do.

Livie's entire body vibrated with desire. She'd never in her life wanted something as much as she wanted this with Nick. She wanted him on top of her, inside of her—she wanted everything with him, everything there was to feel, everything there was to know.

But to her endless frustration, instead of getting on with it, he slowed down. She managed to get him out of his shirt, but he made no move to take off hers. His hand left her breast, coming up to gently cradle her face instead. He rolled them both to their sides and kissed her—just kissed—which was nice. Nick's kisses usually made her weak in the knees. But right now, parts of her besides her lips were desperate to be touched and he wasn't making a move.

Finally, she pushed him away and sat up.

"Livie, what's wrong—?"

His words trailed away as she lifted her arms and stripped off her shirt. It was gratifying, the way his eyes zeroed in on her breasts and stayed there, like he couldn't look away. She'd thought she'd feel embarrassed, undressing in front of a man, but there was none of that now. She felt beautiful and sexy and turned on. As he stared at her, she reached behind herself and slowly unhooked her bra. Nick swallowed so hard she could see his throat move.

She reached for the straps, about to shrug out of it, but he held up a hand to stop her.

"Wait. Can I?"

She dropped her hands to her sides, holding still, trembling only a little bit as he reached up and slid the straps down her arms. He bit his lip and his eyes practically devoured her as her bare breasts came into view. Tossing her bra to the floor, he lifted a hand and slowly placed it over her right breast and squeezed gently.

Oh. She hadn't expected—hadn't known—it could feel so good, that it could make her heart pound and her sex ache. And that was before he slowly swept his thumb across her hardened nipple. She couldn't help the involuntary little gasp of pleasure she let out.

With a sound somewhere between a groan and a growl, Nick slid his free hand up under her hair, grasping her by the back of the neck and pulling her forward into a hard kiss. Without breaking their kiss, he reared up, leaned over her, and laid her on her back. Then he pulled back to look down at her, and sucked in a breath.

"Jesus, your breasts are fantastic," he breathed.

"They are?"

"Oh, yeah."

She'd never thought of them as anything particularly exceptional, but the way Nick was looking at her said otherwise. Before she could figure out how to respond to that, he set one hand on her right breast and lowered his head to the left, drawing her nipple into his mouth and sucking gently.

The sound that left her throat was barely human, and she arched up underneath him. God. She'd had no idea…the heat, the wet, the incredible sensation of his tongue on her nipple.

Without realizing it, her hands sank into his hair, fisting tight. Oh, yes, more of this.

His fingertips traced shivery little trails across her other breast, brushing her nipple, teasing it until she was practically panting. Then his fingers closed around it and pinched, squeezing hard enough to almost hurt. Once again, she couldn't control the needy little moan she made.

He shifted over her, his mouth closing over her other nipple, while his hand slipped down her stomach, tickling and teasing as he skated across her skin. Her breathing stalled when he flipped open the button of her jeans and lowered the zipper. She couldn't breathe at all as his hand slipped inside, under the waistband of her panties, and then lower.

"Nick," she gasped, alarmed at the sudden, unfamiliar sensation.

He lifted his head, looking down at her. "Are you okay? Do we need to stop?"

Just knowing he would was enough to dispel her attack of nerves. The last thing she wanted now was to stop. "No, I'm fine. I promise."

"Tell me if—"

She put her fingers over his lips to silence him. "I will. I don't want to stop."

He kissed her again, slow and gentle, his hand cradling her face with such tenderness that it was easy to let go, to let her body sink into his. Then he was there again, sliding through her wetness, dancing past the most sensitive part of her, teasing at her entrance. This time she wasn't nervous at all.

Oh, God. Her thighs began to tremble as his fingers kept up their gentle assault, first teasing, then rubbing, and finally touching that perfect, aching spot. Suddenly it was happening, she was falling and flying, tumbling down deep into pleasure. She stiffened and cried out, her head falling back and her body going rigid.

As she floated down from her orgasm, her eyes fluttered open. Nick was leaning over her, smiling down at her.

"That was amazing."

He grinned. "We're only getting started, sweetheart."

"Show me the rest?" Because she was ready, so, *so* ready.

His smile faded. "This is crazy, but I'm actually nervous."

"Why are you nervous?" He was the one with loads of experience. Why was it different with her?

"Because it's your first time. You're the one who gets to feel nervous."

He was taking the whole thing much more seriously than she was, which was very sweet, but totally unnecessary. She took his face in her hands and kissed him. "I'm not nervous at all. I trust you."

"I don't want to mess this up."

"You won't."

"Please tell me if I do anything you don't like, okay?"

"I will, but so far I've liked every single thing you've done."

He grinned again. "Okay, let's see if I can top myself. You know I love a challenge."

Slowly, he stripped her out of her clothes, kissing his way down her thighs as he slid her jeans down and off.

"You have great legs," he murmured, his hands tracing their shape as he moved back up her body. Then he kissed her right at the top of her sex, over her panties, and she gasped. "Shhh, just getting ready to take these off."

Then he did, taking away the last garment between his eyes and her body. His eyes roamed over her, from her toes to her face. She resisted the urge to cover herself, as he seemed to really like what he saw.

"You still have a lot of clothes on," she observed.

"Well, let me take care of that."

He rolled away from her long enough to strip efficiently out of his jeans and boxers before rolling back to face her, propped up on one elbow.

Suddenly, she had a hard time lifting her eyes to his. Maybe Nick was inured to it, but she found the experience unspeakably intimate, being this bare and vulnerable in front of each other.

She didn't make herself meet his gaze yet. Instead, she looked at all the rest of him, the sculpted planes of his chest, the scattering of dark hair between his pectoral muscles, and another line of hair low on his abdomen. That one led straight down to…

Oh, wow. She hadn't expected it to be quite that large or prominent, hard and curving up toward his stomach.

Nick slanted a grin at her. "Have you ever…?"

"You know I haven't," she said, unable to tear her eyes away from it. "Can I?"

"Touch me? Absolutely."

Tentatively, she reached out for him. She wasn't exactly sure what she was doing, but she figured he wouldn't mind letting her figure it out on him. She wrapped her fingers around the hard length of him and looked up to gauge his reaction. He was watching her intently, breathing heavily, holding himself very still.

She squeezed once, tentatively, and he sucked in a breath. She did it again, this time stroking him from the base to the tip. He groaned, a sound she felt in her stomach.

This time her hand tightened on its own, and she took her time with the stroke, watching Nick's lips fall open, watching his breathing hitch.

"You can go harder," he bit out through clenched teeth.

She leaned in, until her lips were close to his ear. "Show me?"

He closed his hand over hers and squeezed. Oh, better. She liked them doing it together, watching him slowly come apart as he showed her how he liked it. When she had the tightness and the rhythm of it, he let go, his hands fisting into the pillow on either side of his head. Without thinking, she sped up, loving the feel of it, knowing she was making him feel good. He threw his head back, the tendons in his neck straining.

Abruptly, he put his hand on her wrist, stilling her. "What's wrong?"

"Nothing at all. But this is going to be over really soon if we keep doing that. Besides, tonight's your night."

"Yours, too."

"Trust me, I'll enjoy everything."

He took her face and drew her in until he could kiss her, gentle and easy, slowly rolling her onto her back. She felt his weight as he shifted over her and it filled her with anticipation and arousal. She was a little nervous, but not worried. Never worried. He'd never hurt her.

When his hand closed around the back of her thigh, urging her legs apart, she spread them for him, letting him slide between. The hard length of him was pressed against the inside of her thigh, but he made no move to go further, just kissing her, stroking her, toying with her breasts, until she was nearly desperate for more.

"Nick…"

"What? Did I hurt—?"

"No, you didn't. I'm ready."

He touched the side of her face with infinite gentleness. "Are you sure?"

If she hadn't been, that would have made her certain. She touched her fingertips to his bottom lip. "I've never been surer."

After a moment's hesitation, he licked his lips and pushed himself away. "Hang on." He fumbled over the side of the bed, retrieving his wallet out of his pants pocket and pulling out a condom. She watched, fascinated, as he broke open the package and rolled it onto himself.

"It might hurt," he murmured as he came back over her.

"I don't care." Whatever discomfort was to come, she was sure he'd make it as good as he possibly could. And that, more than anything, was what really mattered. She trusted him to take care of her. How could she possibly be afraid?

Slowly, he began to push in.

First there was an unfamiliar pressure. Then a stretching, uncomfortable and getting worse, sharpening into pain as he kept going. She sucked in a breath.

He stopped moving entirely. "Livie?"

"It's okay," she whispered. It was that, his willingness to stop, that made her not want to. "Keep going."

He did as she asked, not stopping, pushing forward. Then the pain faded away as quickly as it had come and he was in, fully sheathed by her body, holding himself still as she breathed deep, adjusting to him.

"It's okay," she said.

"You sure?"

"Yes, I'm sure."

"Open your eyes and look at me when you say that."
She still had them squeezed tightly shut, which she
hadn't realized. She opened them and looked up into
Nick's eyes. He was staring down at her with such concern and gentleness. He was inches away, arms caging
in her head—over her, inside of her, hard and pulsing.
He was *everywhere*. There wasn't a single part of her,
inside or out, that Nick wasn't touching in some way,
and looking into those gentle dark eyes, too…it was
too much.

Suddenly she wasn't so sure. No, that wasn't right.
She was sure she wanted to have sex with him. But she
hadn't expected this part, this unbearable closeness,
the feeling that she'd bared much more to him than her
body, that she'd let him into much more than her va-
gina. She'd been naive and foolish, she realized, when
she'd assured him a few minutes ago that nothing would
change. Everything had.

Nick felt like he might die if he didn't move soon, but
not until he was sure Livie was okay. He waited, barely
breathing, for her to tell him to keep going.

Something passed in her dark eyes as she looked up
at him, something bleak and sad, and for a moment,
he'd worried he'd fucked this all up, hurt her in some
way he'd never be able to undo.

"Livie," he whispered. Reaching up, he touched her
cheek, ran his fingers down the side of her face. "What
is it? Did I hurt you?"

She blinked and that terrible expression on her face
cleared. She slid her palms up his biceps and over his
shoulders, linking her fingers behind his neck. "A little
nerves. I'm okay."

He wasn't entirely sure he believed her. "You're beautiful, you know that?"

"You're just saying that because I'm naked and underneath you right now."

Despite being in the middle of such a momentous event, he laughed. She did, too, which helped the steel band of anxiety around his chest ease a little.

"You sure you're okay?"

"Positive."

"Okay. Because I promise, it gets much better."

"It's already great."

"What did I tell you about me and challenges?"

That made her laugh again. This was more like it, easy and fun. He could do this without hurting her—her body or her heart.

"Tell me to stop if I hurt you again."

"You won't."

He wouldn't, he swore. That was the last pain he'd cause her tonight. The rest would be pure pleasure.

Finally, he let himself move, slowly at first, and then a little faster when Livie began to move with him, when he could tell she was enjoying it. He'd intended to control himself and make this experience entirely about her, but his body couldn't do it. Without meaning to, his tempo picked up, his hips snapping against hers faster and faster.

Her breathing grew ragged under him, her hips moving in tandem with his. Her eyelids fluttered. Her lips parted. He felt like she might be close.

Without pausing, he rolled them, bringing her on top of him. Her eyes went wide as she braced her palms on his chest and stared down at him.

"I don't know how—"

"You don't have to," he told her. "Do whatever feels good and I'll take care of the rest."

She began to move over him, tentatively at first, but gradually with more confidence as she found her pace again. He'd told her he'd do all the work, but the scientist in her wasn't satisfied, trying first one thing, then another, until she found her groove. Her eyes were closed, her teeth digging into her bottom lip, when he reached between them and found her clit with his thumb. She moaned, her head tipping back.

God, she was gorgeous—exactly like he'd been imagining. All that long dark hair, spread around her shoulders like a curtain, her full breasts bobbing with his every thrust, her eyes closed and her expression clouded with lust. He closed a hand over her breast, teasing her nipple as his thumb teased her sex.

In moments, she was falling apart, letting out breathy little pants as her fingers clutched at his chest, and he loved it, watching Livie, so solemn and self-possessed, lose herself with him.

"That was amazing," he told her, his voice ragged with emotion.

She opened her eyes, smiling dreamily at him.

"What about you?"

"Oh, I'll take care of that."

Gently he rolled her onto her back again, pulling her knees up, urging her to wrap her legs around his hips. It didn't take him long after that. He'd been so close for what felt like hours now, and the memory of Livie's gasping cry as she came was enough to drive him right up to the edge. Now he gave himself over to it fully, his whole body growing taut as his orgasm bore down on him.

When it finally crashed over him, the pleasure

rushed through his body like a wave, almost painful in its intensity. He gasped, his spine arching and his thighs clenching. It felt like it lasted forever, stripping him down to his bones.

In the quiet aftermath, the only sounds in the room were their mingled pants. He felt wrung out, slicked with sweat, weak with his release. Livie was warm and pliant underneath him, her body still holding on to him.

Usually right about now, he'd be getting twitchy, ready to make for the door or to roll over and go to sleep, but neither option so much as crossed his mind in the moment. He wanted to drag out this blissful moment as long as he could. Only the need to deal with the condom was enough to make him move away from her. Afterward, he lay back on his back and slipped his arm underneath her shoulders, rolling her body into his side.

"Thank you," Livie murmured.

"Uh, I'm the one who should be saying thank you, Liv."

"I had no idea what I was doing. I'm sure it was—"

He shut her up by rolling over on top of her. Smoothing her tangled hair out of her face, he looked down into her eyes with all the sincerity he could muster. "That was fucking amazing. You were so sexy and sweet. Thank you. For sharing that with me."

Her cheeks flushed with color. "I can't imagine it ever being better."

He couldn't help the self-satisfied grin that took over his face. "Oh, Livie, you know I can't resist a challenge."

"What—"

"Hold still," he murmured. Then he began kissing his way down her body.

Livie let out a low, slow sigh. "That feels good."

"I can make it feel even better."

"You can?"

"I promise."

"Then I think you should."

He spread her thighs apart and pressed a lingering kiss to the inside of one, feeling her tremble, feeling her breath hitch. "With pleasure."

Chapter Twenty-Five

Livie kept her eyes closed for a long time after she woke up. When she opened her eyes, the night would truly be over, and she didn't ever want last night to end. It almost hadn't. She and Nick had had sex two more times. It was nearly three a.m. when they finally fell asleep, and for once, sleep came easy.

This morning, her body was reminding her of everything they'd done as she lay still and took stock of herself. The insides of her thighs ached. Between her legs she felt a little sore, and her nipples were tender. Her body felt gloriously used and tingly. Every bit of last night had been perfect. Well, except for that one moment of fear, when she'd realized she might be in much deeper than she thought. But this morning, it was just as clear as it had been last night that it was too late to protect herself. And as good as he made her feel, she didn't really want to.

Eyes still closed, she rolled her face into the pillow and smiled so hard her cheeks hurt. The pillow smelled like Nick. She hadn't been aware that Nick had a smell, but after last night, if felt like her body might forever be attuned to it, some Pavlovian response she couldn't control.

She could feel him behind her, his body warming the

length of her back. He wasn't touching her now, but she had a hazy memory of falling asleep spooned against him, his arm slung across her waist.

When she rolled over to look at him, her breath caught in her chest. He was on his stomach, his face turned toward her on the pillow, his dark hair falling across his forehead. His lips were slightly parted as he slowly breathed in and out. His expression was clear and untroubled in sleep. He looked years younger and utterly carefree.

She wanted to run her fingers over his face, to trace the slashes of his heavy eyebrows with her fingers, to touch the fullness of his bottom lip. Instead, she curled her fingers into her palm and studied him. She'd promised him when this started that nothing between them would change. Last night might have rocked her world, but she would do her very best to hold to that promise, and that meant no mooning over him while he slept.

As quietly as possible, she slid out of bed and retrieved her clothes from the floor. Nick slept too little as it was. She didn't want to wake him unnecessarily. He shifted, let out a sexy little groan, and rolled over onto his back, but he stayed asleep.

Pausing at the door, she took one more look at him. The sheet had ridden down to his hips. Even relaxed in sleep, his upper body was a wonderland. The broad shoulders, the muscles of his upper arms, the hills and valleys of his rib cage, the flat expanse of his stomach, that little dusting of hair starting low on his abdomen and disappearing under the sheet. Now she knew exactly where it led, which lent it a crazy, sexy appeal it hadn't had before.

Before this day, her appreciation of male beauty had always been theoretical, removed. A handsome guy in a movie was nice to look at, but she rarely felt stirred by any particular one—well, aside from her brief fascination with Tony Stark in the first *Iron Man* movie.

Nick was different. Looking at him made her heart pound and her palms sweat. Looking didn't feel like enough. She wanted to touch him, to learn every inch of him. Last night, the focus had all been on her, but maybe next time—because she was determined there would be a next time—it would be different. Next time, she'd be the one to touch. There was so much more of him to be explored.

Downstairs, she could hear Gemma up and about. She slipped out of his room and quietly shut the door behind her. Spudge, waiting patiently in the hall, hesitated for a moment, looking mournfully at Nick's closed door. In the end, he left his post near Nick and followed Livie down the stairs. She found Gemma in the kitchen, of course, puttering at the stove, grating something over a pan full of eggs.

Livie got a mug down from the cupboard and poured herself a cup of coffee. "Morning."

Gemma flashed her a brief look over her shoulder. "Morning."

"How was last night?"

"I could ask you the same thing," Gemma replied.

"I wasn't at the bar last—"

"I meant here." Gemma kept her eyes on the pan. "I noticed when I got home that your door was open and your room was empty. And Nick's door was closed."

Livie could *feel* the heat flooding her cheeks. "Gemma—"

But Gemma held up a hand to silence her. "Look, Livie, it's none of my business. You're an adult and you're going to make your own choices. But be careful."

"You don't like him."

"I like him! But he's a mess."

"I know he is."

"He doesn't strike me as a happy-family kind of guy," Gemma said carefully.

"He's not. He hasn't spoken to his family in eight years."

"Why?"

"He won't talk about it."

"That's not a good sign, Livie. Because you're a happy-family kind of girl."

She sighed. "Yeah, I know."

"I know you don't have a lot of field experience yet, but I don't think damaged bad boys are quite your speed."

She sighed again. "They're not."

"Maybe—"

"Gemma, I know. I know him better than he thinks I do. I know at some point he's going to freak out and run."

Gemma stopped stirring the eggs and turned to look at her. "Yes, he will. So?"

Livie dropped her eyes to the scuffed linoleum floor. Now that she'd crossed the line and done the dumb thing she'd been trying to avoid, it was too late to go back to how it was before. She didn't want to. He was here for now, and she was going to enjoy as much of him as she could get. "I want to enjoy him for as long as he's around. That's all."

"And what happens to you when he's gone?"

Livie didn't want to think about that. It was like a giant black hole straight ahead in her future, one that would suck her in and crush her into nonexistence. But not yet. That event horizon was still, hopefully, a long way off. "I'll be fine," she lied, keeping her eyes on the floor.

"Really?"

"Sure. I know what I'm doing. We're friends, and now we're friends with benefits. People do that all the time, right?"

Gemma let out a chuckle and shook her head. "Oh, sweetie, not you, though."

"Gem, it'll be okay. Don't worry about me."

"Yeah, that's not gonna happen. Worrying about you is part of my DNA. But promise me you'll try to protect yourself? Go ahead and give him your body if you want. Lord knows you waited long enough. Have fun. Knock yourself out. But hang on to your heart."

They were in perfect agreement on that one. She might have given in to this thing with Nick against all her better judgment, but that was the last mistake she planned on making. He wasn't looking to win her heart, so she had to make sure she didn't accidentally give it to him.

Chapter Twenty-Six

Livie's phone alarm went off and she groaned as she flailed a hand to silence it. After a week of nights spent in Nick's bed, it was harder than ever to pry herself out every morning.

"Where are you going?" Nick's voice was a low, rough grumble behind her. The arm he'd draped across her waist tightened as he pulled her back against his chest.

"I have to teach class this morning."

He took her by the shoulder and rolled her onto her back, smiling down into her face. That smile made her heart thump painfully in her chest, every single time. "I can't imagine having a teacher who looked like you when I was in college. I might have tried harder to stay in DeWitt."

Livie rolled her eyes. "Come on. You don't have to say stuff like that to me because we're...you know."

A wicked smirk unfurled across Nick's face. Oh, she knew what was coming next. Nick was going to *tease* her. He loved doing that, saying anything and everything he could to get her to blush. He didn't have to work hard to do it. "We're what, Livie?"

"Come on."

"You mean because we're hitting it? Tapping that? Netflix and chilling?"

She shoved ineffectually at his shoulders. "You know what I mean."

"Yeah, but I want to hear you say it." He captured her wrists in his hands and pinned them to the pillow on either side of her head. Her body began to hum with arousal.

"Why?" She'd suddenly gone all breathless.

"Because it's hot. I wanna hear you say it."

Of course she knew what he was getting at, but she played dumb to drag the moment out. Two could play at this game. "Say what?"

Nick leaned down until his lips were right next to her hear. "Tell me what we did last night, Livie. Tell me what we were doing when I put you on your knees and made you hold on to the headboard, and grabbed hold of your hips. What did we do, Livie? What did I say to you while I was doing it? Say the word."

Her eyes fluttered closed and her sex was suddenly aching and wet. Her voice came out as a breathy whisper. She rarely cursed, but for Nick, right now, she'd make an exception. "Fucked. We fucked."

Nick let out a sound that was little more than a growl. "Damned right we did," he muttered, as his teeth closed over her earlobe. "And we're gonna do it again."

She hooked her heels over his calves, pulling his hips tight against hers. "If you say so."

Oh well. She hoped the subway was on time today, because she was definitely going to be running late.

Half an hour later, she scrambled out of his arms. "I really do have to go this time."

Nick fell back on the bed, exhaling dramatically.

"Fine. When are you back? I finally finished that stupid security system job. We could work on the program this afternoon, if you want."

"Sure," Livie muttered distractedly, hunting for her bra in the clothes scattered across Nick's floor. Last night Nick had started undressing her seconds after he'd closed the door behind her, flinging garments everywhere in his haste to tumble her into bed.

The bra emerged from underneath Nick's inside-out jeans. As she clipped it closed and twisted it around her body, Nick propped himself up on one elbow and reached out to drag his knuckles along the side of her breast. "Bye, friends."

She swatted his hand away. "You're obsessed."

"With your breasts? I am absolutely obsessed. I will not apologize for that. I'm literally going to be counting the minutes until I can see them again."

She pretended to frown, but secretly his words warmed her already heated body. She loved that he loved touching her—that he wanted her so much. It made her feel beautiful, desirable, sexy. Never in her life had she ever thought to apply any *one* of those three words to herself.

He toyed with her bra strap as she turned her T-shirt right side out. "You sure you can't stay?"

"Class."

"Right. You stand up front while half the class fantasizes about you."

She burst out laughing. "You're deluded. They don't even know I exist. I'm just a boring grad student telling them a bunch of stuff they have no interest in hearing."

He ran a hand down the length of her thigh as she reached for her phone on the bedside table. "Trust me, they know you exist. I promise you, you're starring in a dozen sexual fantasies during class." He sat up behind her, brushing her hair away from the back of her neck before dropping kisses down the length of it. "If you'd been my teacher, it would have been all I could think about."

But she barely heard him, frozen into disbelief as she stared at the latest message to show up in her university email account, reading it and re-reading it, trying to understand.

"I can't believe this!"

"What?"

"I've been yanked off my lab assignment!"

"What lab assignment?"

"I teach the lecture class three times a week, and one night a week I oversee the undergrad lab hours. Janet assigned me to the Tuesday night slot at the beginning of the year, but for some reason I've been moved to Friday nights."

"Nobody talked to you about it?"

She shook her head. "Not a word."

"Can they do that? Change an assignment Finch gave you?"

"Janet gave it to me when she was chair of the department."

"And now the chair is…"

With a sinking sensation, the realization hit home. "Langley."

Chapter Twenty-Seven

"Professor Langley?" Livie stopped right inside his office door. "Can I speak to you for a moment?"

Langley looked up at her. "Did we have an appointment, Olivia?"

"No. Sorry. I'll just be a minute. My lab assignment has been changed."

"Ah, yes." He leaned back in his chair. "It was unavoidable, I'm afraid. I needed Peter's assistance with my research. We had to shuffle the lab assignments to free him up."

His smile was fake and brittle, entirely at odds with the hostility he was silently emanating. A few months ago, she'd have slunk out of his office without another word, too intimidated and scared to question him. But if Nick was inspiring a whole lot of pleasant new emotions in her, Langley was inspiring a host of less pleasant ones. She let all those unpleasant emotions power her next question.

"You need Peter's help with your research on Friday nights?"

Langley's smile didn't shift, but it turned ice cold as he stared at her in silence. Adrenaline flooded her body, but she refused to back down or apologize.

"Precisely," Langley finally said, his voice tight with

anger. "Now, if there's nothing else, Miss Romano? I've got work to do."

Work. He was staring at that useless little laptop, as usual. Probably posting selfies from that trip he'd just taken to London.

Livie stood her ground for another moment, but Langley was still acting chair of the department, as unjust as that was, and in the end, he could do what he wanted. But at least she'd called him out on his bullshit. This had nothing to do with needing Peter's help and everything to do with punishing her because she wouldn't abandon Janet's research to work on his. Now he knew she knew.

"No. Nothing else."

"Enjoy your Friday nights," he murmured as the door closed behind her.

Some unfamiliar emotion exploded in her chest. *Rage*. She'd never been so angry in her life. Her hands were shaking with it as she forced herself to walk away. She was still shaking as she entered the departmental office.

Michiko was there, leaning on Anita's desk as they chatted. They both looked up as Livie entered.

"Hey, Livie," Anita called.

Behind her glasses, Michiko's eyes quickly assessed Livie from head to toe. "What happened to you? You look totally freaked out."

"Nothing." Livie shook her head, trying to rein in this feeling, to get herself back under control. Her anger wasn't going to help anything. "Just asking Langley about something."

Anita huffed. "It's the lab assignment, right?"

Michiko looked back at her. "What about the lab assignment?"

"I got bounced to the Friday night lab." She couldn't keep the bitterness out of her voice.

"What?" Michiko bounded to her feet. "In the middle of the semester?"

"He said he needed Peter's help with his research, so he had to shuffle the schedule."

There was a beat of silence as Michiko and Anita absorbed that. Finally, Anita snorted in disgust. "That's some stone-cold bullshit, right there."

"*Total* bullshit," Michiko said. "What are you going to do?"

"What can I do? He's the department chair."

"*Acting* chair," Anita growled.

Which was true, but what were the chances Janet was coming back anytime soon? And until she did, Livie was at Langley's mercy, and that was starting to feel like a very bad place to be.

Chapter Twenty-Eight

When Livie arrived home, both Gemma and Jess were in the kitchen. Gemma was making a pot of something to take to the bar when she started her shift later in the evening, while Jess chatted to her about her latest story. Spudge was crashed out on her feet, snoring loudly.

Gemma glanced at Livie over her shoulder. "You okay? You look rattled."

Livie sank into a chair and dropped her head into her hands. "I've had better days."

"Problems with that feral hacker you dragged home?"

"I'm going to ignore most of that, and no, it's not about him."

"Are we talking about Nick?" Jess interjected. "Did something happen?"

"I told you, it's not about him," Livie said, at the same moment Gemma said, "Oh, yes, something happened."

Jess's eyes went wide. "Livie, tell me everything."

"It's personal."

"Um, I distinctly recall the two of you grilling me like CIA interrogators the first time I stayed over at Alex's."

"We're sort of…" Livie waved her hands in front of her, searching for the right word to use. Without other relationships to compare it to, she had no idea how to classify this one. How did people describe these things?

"Are you sleeping with him?" Jess pressed.

Livie felt her face heat. "God, Jess."

"She is," Gemma said.

"Gem!"

"Holy shit, Livie. This is big! I can't believe I had to hear it from *Gem*."

"Are you going to tell me you don't like him, too?"

"I like him!" Gemma protested.

"I like him, too," Jess said. "But he seems like trouble."

"Ha!" Gemma thrust her spoon in Jess's direction. "See? That's exactly what I said."

"Be careful, Livie," Jess said, reaching out to cover Livie's hand with her own.

"Can everybody quit worrying about it? I promise, I have it under control." She wasn't quite as confident about that as she sounded, but right now, she had bigger problems to focus on. "Nick's not even the problem."

Gemma tipped her head to the side. "Then what's wrong?"

"I'm pretty sure Dr. Langley has it out for me."

"Is he that douchebag with the Italian loafers I met when I went to that lecture thingy with you last year?" Jess asked.

"That's him." Briefly she outlined how Langley had been promoted to Acting Chair and had abruptly changed her lab assignment on the flimsiest of pretexts.

"It's not fair that he's playing favorites with his own research assistant," Jess said. "But unfortunately there's probably not a lot you can do about it. The power imbalance in the university system is huge."

"I don't think he did it to play favorites with Peter Hockman. Honestly, I don't think he even likes Peter."

"Then what's it really about?"

"He wanted me to drop Janet's research and work on his. I said no."

"And you think he's doing this to punish you?" Jess pressed.

"A few months ago, I'd have said it was impossible. Nobody in science could be that petty and underhanded."

Jess snorted in disgust. "Dream on."

"But now? I don't know."

"What are you going to do about it?" Gemma asked.

"I don't know that either. Like Jess said, there isn't a lot I can do. I guess I have to keep working on the research as best I can and hope Janet recovers soon."

Jess and Gemma exchanged a dubious look, which Livie pretended not to see. She was fully aware that she was clinging to a very thin hope, but she wasn't ready to let go of it yet. Because if she let go of that hope, then she'd be facing a problem she had no good solution for.

Spudge lifted his head from the linoleum floor and let out a soft woof before scrambling to his feet and lurching away toward the front door.

"That's got to be Nick," Gemma said. "He's the only person besides Dad Spudge is psychically attuned to like that."

Sure enough, Nick strolled into the kitchen a moment later, Spudge fast on his heels. He was smiling, brimming over with that contagious energy Livie found so infuriatingly irresistible.

"You're all here," he said.

"Been out mining bitcoin from a payphone?" Jess teased.

"Very funny. Actually, I've been out apartment-hunting."

The words hit Livie like a blow to the chest.

"Apartment-hunting? You're moving out?"

She should have known. She should have expected this. Once they'd crossed this line, he was sure to get antsy and run. But she'd gotten lulled by his kisses and his body and the crazy things he did to her. What was that phrase Jess's friend Lina used to describe it? Right—*dickmatized.* So drugged by the good dick that you stopped paying attention to the problematic guy attached to it. He'd dickmatized her and she'd never seen him inching toward the door.

"I can't hang out in your spare bedroom for the rest of my life," Nick said, dropping into the chair to Livie's left. "Don't get me wrong, you've all been great. But I *am* a grown-up. Time to get back out there."

Gemma nodded approvingly. "Good for you, Nick."

"And you found a place? In New York?" Jess asked. "That fast?"

Nick shrugged. "When you're willing to throw a bunch of money at a problem, you can solve most things fast."

Jess rolled her eyes. "Yeah, I've seen that in action. You should see Alex's dad operate."

"Tell us about your new place," Gemma said.

Livie listened in silence as Nick described it, the square footage, the amenities, all the work he'd have to do to get the internet up to scratch, and she tried not to feel stung. She had no right to be hurt. She'd gone into this with her eyes wide open. She wasn't allowed to be angry at him for doing exactly what she'd known he was going to do—if she hadn't been so dickmatized she quit paying attention.

Okay, so he'd be living somewhere else. Their coding wasn't done yet, so she'd still see him, right? Although maybe that would go back to a purely work arrangement, which might be more terrible than not seeing him at all. She couldn't imagine being friends again after this, but wasn't that what she'd signed on for?

Gemma went down into the basement to find a tote bag strong enough to hold her full stockpot, and Jess went upstairs to grab a change of clothes before heading to Alex's apartment. When they were alone, Nick twisted in his chair until he was facing her, dropping his arm across the back of her chair.

"I'm not ditching you, Liv."

Great, now he could read her mind, too. "No, I know."

He leaned closer, tucking her hair behind her ear. "It's a little weird, knowing your dad is sleeping down the hall while I'm doing a dozen filthy things to you in bed."

She didn't believe him. Once he was living somewhere else, it seemed inevitable that this—whatever it is they were doing—would eventually draw to a close. "I'm sure you'll appreciate having your privacy again."

Dipping his head to the side, he kissed her neck, slowly and softly. "I'll appreciate having room to lay you out and have my way with you without worrying about disturbing the neighbors."

Livie's eyes slid closed as his tongue flicked out to taste her skin. "Why do you always talk like that?"

He chuckled, the vibration racing through her body, making her nipples tighten. The hand that had been on her knee slid to the inside of her thigh, stroking upward. "Because I like watching you squirm. I like making you wet."

She sucked in a breath.

"Are you getting wet, Livie?"

"Um. I mean, yes." How could the filthy things he said to her make her this unbelievably turned on? Even now, when she *knew* he was setting up his exit strategy, her mind was telling her no while her body was begging for him.

Another chuckle, and now she ached between her legs. "I want to feel it." His fingertips brushed against the seam of her jeans.

She moaned softly.

"Let's go upstairs before another family member shows up to cock block us."

Whatever he said about it, his moving out was definitely the beginning of the end. But it wasn't over yet, which meant she might as well enjoy every second she had left with him. She let him take her by the hand and pull her out of her chair, up the stairs, and into his room. She let herself get so lost in his arms she forgot all about the future.

Chapter Twenty-Nine

"It's great, right?"

Livie turned in a slow circle, taking in Nick's new place in Greenpoint. It was very big. Very clean. Very white. And totally and completely empty. Just endless expanses of pristine white walls and glossy pale wood floors.

The place was in a brand-new development, and it had everything—an on-site gym, a roof deck with a pool, and sweeping views of Manhattan from most of the units' balconies. What Nick's unit didn't have was a single stick of furniture.

"It's empty," she said, her voice echoing slightly in the sterile void. "When are you moving your stuff in?"

Nick looked around at the vast, blank space. "I don't really have a lot of stuff."

"But you must have some stuff."

"My equipment, of course."

"Nick, you have to own more than that."

"I have clothes," he said defensively.

"But all that stuff in your old apartment—"

"Was Poppy's."

"Oh. But what about before that? In California?"

He rubbed his hand across the top of his head as he looked around at all the blank whiteness. "Palo Alto,

Mountain View, San Jose, Santa Clara... I bounced around a lot. Sublets, mostly. And I didn't plan on moving here. I met Poppy and didn't go back."

How could someone be this completely rootless? Eight years since he'd left home and he hadn't once planted himself anywhere. It gave her a cold, hollow feeling in her stomach, imagining all that wandering, with nowhere to call home, no safe place to go. She remembered Poppy's apartment—its impersonal coldness, not a hint Nick had even lived there. At the time, she'd blamed Poppy, thinking she kept it that way on purpose. Now she suspected it was Nick's doing. Engagement or not, he'd never seriously committed to that situation, not even enough to properly move in with her. It was no wonder he was already chafing at living with the Romanos. All that family and togetherness—their roots that stretched so far and went so deep—must be absolutely terrifying to him.

"What's your plan? Are you going to sleep on the floor?"

"I've done it before."

Seeing the irritated look she aimed at him, he relented. "Okay, obviously I need to buy some stuff. What do I need first?"

She'd spent her whole life living in a house continually inhabited by her family for four generations. Their problem had always been too much stuff. Layers upon layers of it, each new generation adding more while rarely getting rid of what was already there. Faced with such an empty void, Livie was at a loss. How did you turn this into a living space?

"You need everything. Furniture, lamps, rugs, kitchen stuff."

"I don't suppose you'd want to—"

She threw up her hands. "Don't look at me. I'm terrible at shopping."

"Do you think I can hire someone?"

"I guess you'll have to."

He sighed again, running his hands over his face. "I don't suppose you know where I should look for someone?"

"Not a chance. I could help you out writing a paper about sub-atomic particles in space, but interior decorators? Sorry, you're way outside my area of expertise."

They were both silent for a moment as they looked around at the endless yawning expanse of empty apartment.

"Except…"

Nick looked up at her expectantly.

Once again, Livie had something Nick needed. This time it was two women with a passion for HGTV and no homes of their own to tinker with. "I could ask my family."

"Gemma and Jess?"

The idea of Jess picking out sofas and wall art made her laugh out loud. She'd hate that as much as Livie would. But Gemma wouldn't. And neither would Kendra. "Gemma and my cousin Kendra. They're both really into this stuff. They might be willing to help."

"Seriously? I'll hand over my Amex Black. Take it. They can buy whatever they think I need. I don't care."

Gemma and Kendra set loose to shop without a limit? Even if they were doing it for someone else, it would be like Christmas coming early.

"I'll ask."

His relief was palpable. He walked toward her, arms outstretched, then he pulled her into a tight hug. "You're a lifesaver, Livie."

She wrapped her arms around his waist and rested her cheek on his shoulder. Such a warm, perfect place to be. But perfect things were always fleeting.

"Nick?" she murmured into his shoulder. He was going to run soon, she knew that. It might be easier for her to handle if she knew he wasn't running back out into his rootless existence, and there was a way she might be able to make that happen.

"Yeah."

"I'm happy to loan you my family when you need them, but you know you have your own, right?"

He pulled back to look at her. "What?"

"You have family. Maybe they'd want to help you out, if they knew you needed help."

His eyebrows furrowed into a furious frown. "No, they wouldn't."

"How do you know? You haven't spoken to them in years."

He turned away, running a hand roughly through his hair. "I know them, Livie. You don't. Trust me, they're happy I'm out of their lives."

Surely he was mistaken. At least, she hoped he was. It was horrible to imagine, your own family not wanting you. But Nick had closed up tight, unwilling to discuss it, or even look at her. She wasn't sure how long she might have with him. The last thing she wanted to do was hasten the end by fighting.

"Okay, fine. Forget I said anything. Let's go talk to Gemma."

"You really think she'll help?"

"Um, a chance to spend somebody else's money without a limit? Yeah, she'll help."

Chapter Thirty

"Nick, sand or taupe?"

Nick looked up at Gemma in confusion. "What?"

She shoved her phone in his face. "The couch. Sand or taupe?"

There were two identical couches on the website on her screen. "They're the same."

"One is sand and one is taupe. Which one do you like better?"

He cast a pleading glance at Livie, who ducked her head to hide her smile. Traitor.

"Seriously, Gemma, they look exactly the same to me. Get whichever one you like."

Gemma sighed in exasperation.

"Sand," Livie said suddenly.

He and Gemma both turned to look at her in surprise.

She shrugged. "The sand one looks like your couch. The taupe one doesn't."

Gemma considered that a moment, then tapped her phone to resume her phone call. "We're going with sand, Kendra. Of course, that means we need to get the rug in sage, not moss. Right."

Nick watched her running through the myriad purchases with a gnawing sense of panic. Not about the money. Gemma had yet to put a serious dent in his spending limit. It was the permanence of it all. He hadn't thought much of it when Livie suggested letting Gemma and Kendra furnish the place for him. He needed stuff if he was going to live there, and this solved that problem quickly and efficiently, like moving in with the Romanos had solved his homeless problem without a lot of fuss.

But like that situation, simple things never really were. Living with the Romanos, especially once he and Livie had started this thing, was thorny and complicated. They were a family, tightly knit and tribal, and he constantly felt himself being drawn in by the sheer gravity of them. Which wasn't bad…he genuinely liked them. But the deeper he fell into their world, the worse it would be for everyone when he eventually screwed it up and it ended.

Moving out had seemed like a good solution. A little distance would be good, and that empty, raw space had felt right for him the minute he saw it. A blank slate—the perfect place to hit restart. Now Gemma and Kendra were filling it up with stuff—stuff that was supposed to be his—and every choice she presented him with—sand or taupe—felt much more significant than which color he liked better. He was being asked to describe what *home* would feel like to him—and that was something he didn't have a clue about.

He knew he was supposed to be excited to see the finished product, but secretly, it filled him with dread. He'd have a home of his own for the first time, crafted just for him. What if he didn't recognize himself when he saw it?

"Thanks for doing all this, Gemma," he said when she'd ended the call with Kendra—after negotiating the purchase of half a dozen other things. They'd both refused him when he offered to pay them for all this, which would have at least turned it into a straightforward business transaction. Now it felt like family pitching in to help. And families made him itchy.

"Are you kidding? I'm living in a house my grandmother decorated. I never get to do stuff like this. This is a blast."

"See?" Livie slid off her bar stool and retrieved her coat from the coat rack in the corner. "Told you she'd have fun. I gotta go."

"Go where?" he asked.

Livie was going *out*? It was eight p.m. Usually Livie was holed up in her room with her laptop and a stack of research by this time of night. And it was a Friday night. Where was she going? And with who?

"It's my new lab assignment, remember?"

"Right. It's your class." For reasons he didn't want to examine too closely, that was a relief. *School.* She was going to school.

"It's not really teaching. The students have to do a lab as part of their class. I keep an eye on the equipment, help them calibrate the telescopes, that sort of thing."

"Hold up. Like, actual telescopes? Looking at the sky?"

"That's what astronomers do, you know," she said with a smirk. "We look at the sky."

"Very funny. Where is the lab? At Adams?"

"No, it's off campus, all the way out in Mill Basin."

"How do you get out there?"

"A subway and two buses, which is why I have to go."

"Why don't you drive? John has a car, doesn't he?"

"Yeah, but I don't drive."

Nick burst into laughter. "You don't drive?"

She prickled defensively. "Tons of New Yorkers don't know how to drive."

"*I* know how to drive," Gemma interjected as she poured a beer at the taps. "*Jess* knows how to drive."

"Nobody asked you, Gem."

"You seriously never learned?" Nick pressed.

Livie shrugged and Gemma answered for her. "Dad tried to teach her, but she chickened out."

"Hey!"

"Livie, were you scared?"

"No, I wasn't *scared*. There was a lot to keep track of. And other New Yorkers drive like crazy people."

"Well, *I* know how to drive, too. Want me to drive you out there?"

Livie turned her big brown eyes back to him. "You'd do that?"

He shrugged, reaching for her hand. "For you? I'm willing to do a couple of special favors."

"It's this way," she said, heading across the street to a ramshackle wooden shed.

Nick locked John Romano's car and followed her. The streets, lined with well-kept single-family homes, were empty in this quiet little far-flung residential neighborhood of Brooklyn. A wooden construction fence lined a small lot on the corner, the door to the shed seemingly the only access.

"Adams leases the lot from the city," Livie explained as she wrestled with the stubborn lock on the door. "It's the darkest spot we can find in the borough, since we're this close to the water."

"We are?"

"Mm-hmm. On the other side of the lot. It's still too light for serious stargazing, but they're undergrads in an intro class. It's more about learning to use the equipment and finding their way around the night sky."

The door gave way, screeching open on rusty hinges. Livie flipped on a light and a weak, red glow from a single bare bulb washed the small room with an eerie half-light.

"Cozy. Is this where you dismember the bodies?"

"Funny. The light has to be dim so it doesn't interfere with the telescopes in the field. And red light is least intrusive."

The room was spartan, a university-issued steel desk and chair in the corner, and a huge whiteboard on one wall. On the other side of the room, a dozen battered telescopes on tripods stood along the wall like a line of soldiers.

Livie set her bag down but didn't remove her coat. Neither did Nick, since it was cold as hell in here. There was no sign of anything like a heater. He watched as she got out her paperwork, checked something on her phone, and wrote out a bunch of stuff on the whiteboard.

"What's that?"

"We give them the coordinates of one object in tonight's sky, so they can calibrate their telescopes based on that. Then they have to find other objects on the worksheets and answer questions. It's pretty basic stuff. Can you grab a telescope?"

He did as he was told, following her through a door in the wall opposite the entrance. It opened onto a field. No, that was too kind. It opened onto an empty lot, bare of vegetation, the ground lumpy and uneven. Beyond the wooden fence on the far side, he could see the inky darkness of the water, reflected lights shimmering off the surface. Across the water, a strip of land, dotted with low buildings, cut across the horizon.

"That's Jamaica Bay out there," Livie said as she set down her telescope and deftly kicked the legs open. "Across the bay is the Rockaways, and past that is the harbor."

Nick wrestled with his telescope, far less proficient with it than Livie had been with hers. As soon as he got one leg out and tried to move the other, the first would swing back. "This is like wrestling with an eel. What the hell am I doing wrong?"

Livie came to help. She swung her hair over one shoulder as she bent down to straighten the legs. "There. You can set it down now. They're pretty crummy, but Adams doesn't have the money for anything better."

"How many more should we set up?"

"That's it. And chances are, nobody will show up to use those two."

"Are you serious?"

"If you were an undergrad and you had your choice of lab times, would you choose to come all the way out to Mill Basin to stand around in the cold and dark on a Friday night?"

"Point taken. This is why the Friday night slot sucks."

"Yep. It's a waste of time."

This was her punishment from that asshole Langley, being shunted to this crummy babysitting assignment. It made him want to punch something, preferably Langley's face. If he wasn't a responsible, reformed, law-abiding citizen, he'd be seriously tempted to electronically fuck up the dude's life in some subtle and awe-inspiring ways. But sadly, he didn't do that stuff anymore.

"Any update from Andy about Finch?"

She shook her head. "No improvement."

Not good. Not good at all. "What are you going to do?"

"What can I do? I'm going to keep working on the program with you, and keep working on the application for time on Hubble. That way, everything's in place for Janet when she gets back." He didn't point out the obvious—that it was becoming increasingly likely that Finch wouldn't come back. He'd tried that once before and Livie hadn't taken it well.

"You know this research as well as Finch. Can't you keep moving forward without her?"

"It's her work. I wouldn't feel right doing it without her. And besides, it's not that easy."

Taking her hand, he ran his thumb over the back of her knuckles. "Explain it to me. I've been told I'm pretty smart. I bet I can keep up."

"Janet didn't get the purchasing requests submitted for approval before her heart attack."

"Can you submit them?"

"No. And even if I could, it wouldn't matter. Janet has to personally sign off on all expenses before Skylight will release the funds to the university's account."

"Isn't that dickwad Langley head of the department now? Surely he's got the authority to do it."

Livie's eyes flashed up to his then away again, and she caught her bottom lip with her teeth. Something was eating at her.

"What is it?"

"Nothing. I'm sure it's nothing."

"Obviously it's not nothing. What are you thinking?"

"I don't want to ask Langley for anything to do with Janet's grant."

"Why?"

Again, she paused. "Remember I told you about the

fight she was having with Langley right before she collapsed? He wanted her to purchase some stuff for him with it."

"Right. You don't want him getting his filthy hands anywhere near her grant money."

"Pretty much." Then she shook her head. "Ugh. Forget I said anything. I'm just being paranoid."

"Maybe you're not. What's happening to Skylight's money while Finch is out?"

She shrugged. "Nothing, I guess? It's sitting in their account."

"You sure about that? Langley sounds like he thinks he's entitled to it."

"Well, he's not. It's Janet's grant."

"But she's not here to defend it."

Livie turned her wide brown eyes to his. "What's he going to do? *Steal* it?"

"Maybe." He knew plenty of people who wouldn't think twice about doing just that.

Livie let out a shocked huff of laughter. "Come on, Nick. This isn't the movies. There's no espionage at work here. This is *academia*. There are rules. Langley's a jerk, but he's not a criminal. He can grumble all he wants, but I'm sure the money is safe."

"I'm serious, Liv. I can totally see that guy trying something shady. You need to watch your back."

"And you need to stop imagining everybody is as morally flexible as you."

"I don't need to imagine it, because most people are, or they're worse."

She was flustered now, breathing faster and twisting her hands together. He reached out for her, taking her face in his hands. "Hey, I'm only warning you because I'm worried about you. I don't want to see you get hurt."

He knew what she was scared of, even if she didn't. If she admitted to herself that Finch wasn't coming back, that Langley was an irredeemable asshole bent on sabotaging her—then she would need to do something about it, make some sort of life-altering change. And he'd already figured out she did not like her life altered. She wouldn't be at Adams otherwise.

Now here she was, still stumbling along the path she'd set for herself even after the road had disappeared beneath her feet. If it were him, he'd have lit a match, burned it all down, and started fresh. But she wasn't him. All he could do was keep nudging her in the right direction when she'd let him, press her with the uncomfortable questions until she shut him down. He hoped it worked, because otherwise she was in for a world of hurt, and he did not want to see that happen to her.

Which, he supposed, meant he'd begun to care. He cared about her, of course. They were friends. But this was different. He'd begun to feel stuff you didn't feel about someone who was just a friend or even a friend with benefits. He wasn't supposed to get serious about Livie—wanting to take care of her, to protect her, like he was her boyfriend or something. He was not in a good place to be anybody's boyfriend. Not now and probably not for a long time. And considering his dark view of life, he was a terrible candidate to be *Livie's* boyfriend even under the best of circumstances. She needed someone as decent and honest as she was. Someone who saw all the best in the world instead of wallowing around in its dark corners.

But when she was looking up at him with those dark eyes full of that warm light, and her lips looked soft, and her hair felt so silky under his fingers, it was hard to remember to keep his feet firmly on the ground. It was tempting to be selfish, and pull her closer, because that light in Livie's eyes was pretty good at warming up his cold heart.

"Nick, I can handle this," she said.

Since she'd shut him down, he wouldn't try again, at least not tonight. "I know, I know. You can take care of yourself."

Finally, she relented, smiling up at him. "But thank you for worrying."

He kissed her gently, tempted, as he always was when his mouth was on hers, to go further. Their physical chemistry had taken him completely by surprise. He'd fully expected to enjoy sleeping with her. But he hadn't been ready for this, the way his brain short-circuited every time he touched her, the way thoughts of her consumed his every waking minute. But they were outside and it was cold, so he firmly told his dick to stand down. This wasn't the time or place.

Clearing his throat, he stepped away from her. "Tell me what you can see with one of these things."

She moved to one of the telescopes. "With these? Here in Brooklyn? Not much. Venus and Mars, depending on the time of year. The Pleiades, if there's no moon, like tonight. Come here."

He joined her, watching as she leaned forward and pressed her eye to the eyepiece. Her hair fell around her face as she fiddled with the knobs and shifted the telescope's aim.

"Here, look."

He did. "What am I supposed to be seeing? Is it that fuzzy blue patch?"

"That's the Pleiades, a star cluster. Can you see some bright spots inside the cloud? Those are individual stars in it. There's Merope, Electra, Alcyone, Atlas."

"Can you name everything up there?"

She laughed, that bright sound that always sent a little shiver down the back of his neck. "You know there are an infinite number of objects in space, right? Knowing them all is impossible."

He straightened up and looked at her. Her head was tipped back, face turned to the night sky.

"What do you like about it?"

"Space?"

"Yeah. Is it that thing everybody says, about space making them feel small and insignificant?"

Livie shook her head, eyes still on the stars. "No. Space doesn't make me feel small. It makes me feel bigger. More than I am."

"How so?"

"Space doesn't welcome human beings. It's not our place. We're too small, too fragile. But when I'm working, when I see something new come back from a telescope, something no one else has ever observed before, I feel like I've figured out a way around our human fragility. Maybe space doesn't welcome most humans, but I've found a way to walk up there amongst the stars, to look back through time. I mean, primordial black holes! You're looking at the birth of the universe. And I can do that. *Me*. And that makes me bigger, stronger, than anybody else. I'm alone out there with space and all its mysteries."

He stared at her pale, perfect profile against the dark of the night around them. This girl was destined for greatness. What a waste that she was here, killing time in a grimy, empty lot, waiting around for a bunch of unappreciative undergrads, being hassled by a blowhard professor who wasn't worth a tenth of her. One day, she'd break free of her orbit around Adams and their insignificant little Brooklyn neighborhood, and when she did, she'd light up like a comet, streaking away to parts unknown to change the world, to crack the code of time and space.

He rubbed the heel of his palm across his chest, trying to ease the ache that image caused him somewhere deep inside, somewhere in the vicinity of where his heart would be. If he still had one. It would be a good thing, Livie getting out there and blazing a trail of brilliance across the world. And he'd be out there on his own trajectory again, too. This little interlude—when she was biding her time in this academic backwater and he was biding his time until the next opportunity reached out to grab him—would be over. And he absolutely refused to feel sad about that.

"You're beautiful, you know that?" His voice sounded rough with everything he was holding back.

She startled, looking at him with those big dark eyes. "I told you, you don't have to say that kind of stuff to me."

"I'm not saying it to flatter you. I'm saying it because it's true." He reached for her hand and she turned to face him fully. She was back, returned from her momentary trip to the stars, back on earth, and back with him. For now.

He ran his hands up her arms, over her shoulders, and up her neck, under the warm fall of her hair. "I'm saying it because I think it every time I look at you."

She said nothing as he leaned in and kissed her, only released a long, slow breath.

"I'm saying it because when I'm not looking at you, I'm thinking about what you look like, your hair, your lips, your breasts."

"You're obsessed," she murmured against his lips.

"I told you I was," he said back.

He kissed her again, less sweet and soft this time, urging her lips apart, finding her tongue with his. One step brought their bodies flush. Arousal pulsed through his veins, even though there were layers of coats and sweaters and shirts between his body and hers.

"How much longer did you say you have to stay out here?" he whispered against her mouth.

"As long as there are students here working."

"Livie. I don't see any students."

A small smile tugged at the corner of her mouth as she gazed up at him, her fingers toying with his hair. "Then I guess I don't have to stay."

Chapter Thirty-One

Vinelli's Meats was a madhouse. It always was on the afternoon before a major holiday, as everyone crowded in to pick up their custom orders.

Thanksgiving was tomorrow, and Gemma had tasked Livie with picking up the turkey she'd ordered weeks before. Everybody knew Vinelli's had the best birds in Brooklyn, so everyone else ordered from them, too. People came all the way from Bay Ridge and Marine Park to get a Vinelli turkey.

Vinelli's was already decorated for Christmas, which she loved. They always started well before all the other businesses on the block. The faded light-up Santa in the front window and the dusty plastic holly swags overhead were older than she was. Boxed panettones imported from Italy lined the wall behind the meat cases. Vinelli's had already put out the Christmas booze, too. In the corner, a silver tray held a little forest of open bottles—some scotch, vodka, whiskey, rum, and a bottle of Baileys—along with a stack of disposable plastic cups. For the next month, customers would help themselves to a drink while they waited on their orders and chatted with their neighbors. While Livie didn't drink or chat easily with neighbors, she liked watching other people do it. It was one of the things that made this neighborhood great, and gave her that warm feeling of belonging someplace.

On the other side of those glass cases, featuring meat products in every permutation imaginable, three harried guys in white butchers' coats ran back and forth, retrieving turkeys from the walk-in cooler in the back and calling out names out front. Livie patiently waited her turn, pickup ticket clutched in her hand. She stepped up to the counter and handed it over to one of the butchers when another butcher held a giant turkey aloft and called out the last name of its new owner.

"DeSantis! Twenty pounds!"

Spinning around, she skimmed the crowd, looking to see who replied. She'd have known the woman anywhere, because her face was Nick's face. She was somewhere in her fifties, with Nick's dark brown hair, peppered with gray and pulled back in a ponytail, and Nick's dark eyes, framed at the corners with tiny lines. With a tight, harried smile, she edged through the crush of bodies to reach the counter and retrieve her turkey.

Nick's mother.

People swept in in her wake, like the tide coming in on the beach, and Livie lost sight of her. Elbowing her way through the crowd, all her warm, fuzzy thoughts of holidays and communities vanished, Livie fought her way to where the woman had been a moment ago. When she got there, she was gone, but then she spotted her accepting the hefty bagged turkey from the cashier. She'd nearly reached the door when Livie finally caught up to her.

"Mrs. DeSantis?"

She turned, looking at Livie with polite curiosity. "Yes?"

Now that she was face-to-face with her, Livie had

no idea why she'd pursued her. What had she meant to say? Mrs. DeSantis had the strained smile of a busy New Yorker wondering why a strange woman had run her down in the middle of the butcher shop.

"I know your son."

Her smile brightened slightly. "Oh, you know Christopher?"

"No, Nick. I know Nick."

The blood drained from Mrs. DeSantis's face, and her smile vanished.

"You've seen Nicky?" Livie could barely hear her hoarse whisper over the chatter in the shop.

"Yes, he's staying at our place right now."

"Is he okay? Is he in trouble? Does he need help?" Mrs. DeSantis's anxiety was palpable. Why on earth did Nick think she didn't care about him. She was nearly frantic as she begged for news about her son.

"He's fine. He needed a place to crash while he was between apartments. He's moving to a new place soon." It didn't seem right to share Nick's recent romantic history, not even with his mother, not even if she was desperate for any news of him.

"Can you tell me—"

At that moment, a butcher shouted out her last name across the shop. "Can you wait a second? I need to pay for our turkey."

"Your name is Romano?"

"Romano's Bar? That's us."

"Romano's," she echoed faintly. "Of course."

Livie fought her way back to the counter to retrieve her turkey and pay for it. When she returned, Mrs. DeSantis was hurriedly scribbling something on the torn-off corner of her shopping list. "Here." She thrust it in Livie's direction. "It's my cell number and my husband's. Please, give it to Nicky and ask him to call. I just want to hear from him. I want to know he's all right."

Part of her wanted to reassure Mrs. DeSantis that Nick was doing fine. He was wildly successful and wealthy. But she held back, because the other part of her knew it wasn't true. He was alone, bouncing from one temporary situation to another, steadfastly refusing to let himself put down roots. He was not okay. Whatever happened years ago between Nick and his family obviously affected him to this day.

Livie took the paper. "I will, Mrs. DeSantis," she promised, even though she had no idea how she'd accomplish that. If she simply handed it over and told him to call his parents, he'd just throw it away and refuse outright. Somehow she'd have to explain this encounter, convince him that his mother genuinely missed him.

"Please, it's Laura. And you…?"

"Olivia. Livie, I mean. You can call me Livie."

"Livie." She absolutely beamed at Livie, like she was Santa Claus and the Pope all rolled into one. Reaching out, she grasped Livie's hand tightly. "Thank you, Livie."

Livie's heart ached for her. She clearly loved and missed him and wanted him back. Nick was the one staying away. But maybe she could figure out how to reconnect them. If she could somehow fix this thing with Nick's family, then maybe, for once, he wouldn't run. Maybe he'd stay.

"Happy Thanksgiving."

"You, too, Livie. Tell him…" She paused, squeezed her eyes shut briefly, and took a deep breath. "Tell him I'm sorry."

And with that cryptic postscript, she turned and left the butcher shop. She was sorry? What for? What had happened eight years ago to send Nick out into the world totally alone? And how the hell was she going to convince Nick to forgive his mother and give his family another chance?

Chapter Thirty-Two

Since Thanksgiving was the next day and Gemma was up to her neck with meal prep, Livie offered to cover her at the bar, as she had in previous years. Ordinarily a Wednesday night would be slow, but the night before Thanksgiving always defied that rule of thumb. Most people were looking at a four-day weekend, which meant Thanksgiving Wednesdays were always fairly crowded and celebratory.

Tonight, all the regulars were there, plus a few old-timers who showed up less frequently. Teresa was there, too, chatting with Livie's father whenever he had a minute to breathe. He smiled with Teresa—more than Livie had seen him smile in years. There was a...well, a lightness about him that hadn't been there before. Her own feelings about Teresa were still pretty mixed, but she couldn't deny Teresa made her father happy.

A bunch of pressed-shirt college guys wandered in and took up residence at one of the tables. Romano's didn't see many of their type in the bar, and Livie got the impression that maybe they'd come in to slum it at someplace so obviously uncool. But they weren't being assholes. They were watching the game on the flat-screen, and occasionally got a little loud, but not enough to drive everyone else away. Her dad was grateful for them, since they were drinking solidly and leaving hefty tips for every refill.

The college boys made things busy enough that Livie texted Jess to see if she could come pitch in, which she did, along with Alex. And when Nick found out Alex was going to be there, he walked over, too. Now the two of them held down one end of the bar, watching the game.

Laura DeSantis's phone number was burning a hole in her pocket. Every time she thought about it, a knot of anxiety formed in her stomach. She hadn't been alone with Nick since she'd gotten back from the butcher shop, so there'd been no chance to tell him about the encounter. The truth was, she hadn't looked very hard for a chance, since she had no idea how to broach the subject. He was going to be angry, she was sure of that. And he'd probably flat-out refuse to contact Laura. What could she possibly say to convince him? Nothing had come to her yet.

She finished refilling the college boys' pitcher and set it on a tray just as Nick reached for her arm across the bar.

"Hey, gorgeous, two more for me and Alex when you get a chance?"

"As soon as I drop this at their table," she promised him.

"Thanks, Liv." As he sat back, he dragged his fingers down the length of her forearm, sending a pleasurable little shiver down her spine.

She was still smiling distractedly as she set the pitcher of beer down in the middle of the rowdy college boys.

At that moment, the front door of the bar opened and Laura DeSantis stepped inside. Livie stopped cold, staring at Laura, who was looking around the bar with painful hopefulness.

"I couldn't wait," she said with a shrug. "I wanted to see if he was here—"

Nick's voice cut through the chatter of the bar. "Mom?"

As he strode across the bar, his eyes were dark with anger. Laura's face lit up with a tremulous smile. "Nicky," she breathed.

Nick stopped a few feet short of her. "What are you doing here, Mom?"

Laura flicked a glance at Livie. "Livie said you were staying in the neighborhood."

Nick crossed his arms over his chest, turning that angry glare on her. "Oh, she did, did she?"

"I ran into your mother at the butcher shop," Livie explained lamely. More like ran her down and tackled her. "I was going to tell you later."

"You were going to tell me." His voice was flat and emotionless, and the look in his eyes scared her.

Everything seemed to slow down around her. Alex had swiveled around to watch as soon as Nick left his stool. Her father and Jess had stopped what they were doing to see what was happening. Dennis and Frank had interrupted their conversation for the drama. Even the table full of college boys seemed to be paying more attention to the standoff than to the game on TV.

"Yes, I—I was going to tell you," Livie stammered. "But now she's here, so..."

His gaze swung back to his mother. "Yes, she is. I don't know why you came here, Mom."

"I wanted to see you, Nick." She was twisting her hands together anxiously. "Can we go somewhere and talk?"

A muscle twitched in Nick's jaw as he stared her down. Livie held her breath, praying he'd give her a chance, and dreading the scene that would erupt if he didn't.

After a pause that felt like it lasted a year, he exhaled heavily and dragged a hand through his hair. "Outside," he muttered.

He brushed past Livie without a word as he followed his mother outside. Livie stared at the door after it closed behind him. It felt like the right thing to do at the time, reaching out to Laura DeSantis about her son. At least he *had* a mother, one who was alive and well and obviously desperate to heal the breach with her son. Yes, she didn't know what had caused it, but whatever it was, surely some small attempt to repair their relationship wasn't too out of line?

She hoped Nick eventually felt that way, too, or he might never forgive her for what she'd done.

Outside on the sidewalk, Nick stopped and faced his mother for the first time in eight years. What the fuck was he supposed to say to her? What could she possibly have to say to him?

"There's a little coffee shop up the street," she said tentatively, pointing over her shoulder. "Can I buy you a cup of coffee?"

Nick thought longingly of his beer back at the bar, back with Alex. A game to watch, Frank and Dennis talking his ear off about a whole lot of nothing. Simple and uncomplicated, the very opposite of what he was about to face. But he didn't suppose there was any getting out of it at this point. He might as well let her have her say and get it over with.

A few minutes later, they were seated at a tiny table

for two in the front window of Brooklyn Coffee Roasters, a sleek, modern coffee joint that was packed, even at this hour, with twentysomethings on laptops.

His mother turned her coffee cup in circles nervously. "You look good," she said at last.

Nick said nothing. The last time he'd seen her, he'd been eighteen. He sure as hell *hoped* he looked better.

"Are you doing okay? Do you need money?"

That startled a huff of laughter out of him. "No, I don't need money. I've got plenty."

"You do?" she asked, surprised.

Of course. Still shocked he could succeed at anything. "My computer work pays pretty well."

She dropped her eyes to the table, everything in her sagging slightly. Which made him—inexplicably—feel bad. He shouldn't feel sorry for her. They were the ones who'd all but disowned him for something that wasn't even his fault. At least, not *entirely* his fault. They didn't deserve his pity.

She looked older—surprisingly so. More than the eight years that had passed. And there was this air of nervousness around her that he didn't remember, along with a kind of pervasive sadness. As much as he was trying to harden his heart against her, she was getting to him.

"Livie said you were staying with her, so I thought…" His mother trailed off helplessly.

"It's temporary. I signed a lease on a new place a couple of weeks ago. I'm moving in as soon as the furniture gets sorted out." Although right now, Greenpoint didn't feel nearly far enough away. The moon wouldn't be far enough to make him feel comfortable.

"She's nice." When he looked up at her, she shrugged.

"Livie. She seems very nice. Comes from a good family. The Romanos, everybody knows them."

"Yep, the Romanos are great." He was absolutely *not* discussing his relationship with Livie with his mother.

"Chris is married now," she said after a moment, to fill the silence.

"Is he? Good for Chris." Perfect Chris, keeping it on-brand.

"Kate. She's lovely. And they have a little boy. He's about to turn two. Anthony."

That was like a fist to the chest. Chris had a *kid*? One he'd never even seen? Anthony was *his* middle name. Had to be a coincidence. Right? There was no way Chris would have named his kid after Nick.

"He's exactly like you were at that age. Afraid of nothing. You used to scare the life out of me with the things you'd get into. And no matter how many times I explained to you how dangerous something was, how you could get hurt, you just wouldn't believe me. It was like you thought bad things could only happen to other people."

His gut twisted with guilt and anger. All right, enough with this bullshit chitchat over coffee, reminiscing and catching up on family news. That wasn't why she'd come, not after all these years.

"Why'd you come track me down, Mom? Didn't you say it all eight years ago?"

He'd expected her to get angry, like she had eight years ago, to shout back at him, and tell him it was all his fault, once again, reckless Nick bringing disaster everywhere he went. But to his shock, her eyes filled with tears and her face collapsed.

"I can't bear to think about what I said eight years ago."

She let out a ragged little sob, dabbing at her eyes with a wadded-up napkin. Nick said nothing, frozen, watching as she pulled herself back together. Finally, she took a deep shuddering breath and looked up at him—reluctantly, it seemed, because there was something like shame in her eyes.

"You have to understand, as a parent, when your child is in danger, there's nothing worse. I was out of my mind with panic. That's no excuse for anything I said, I know, but you have to believe me, Nicky, I've regretted those words every day for eight years. Your father and I both have. I wanted so badly to talk to you, to make it better somehow, but you were just gone." She lifted her hands and dropped them again. Tears slid down her cheeks unchecked. "The not knowing was the hardest. We'd heard you went to California, but then nothing. I worried that you were on drugs, or homeless. Every night, when I went to bed, the last thing I thought about was you. I wondered where you were, how you were doing. I prayed to St. Anthony to protect you and take care of you."

She didn't finish, her words lost as she was consumed with weeping. His mother, always so tough and no-nonsense in his memories, had vanished, leaving this broken woman in her place. She collapsed in on herself, curled over, shoulders jerking with each soul-wrenching sob.

It turned out his heart wasn't as hardened as he thought, because he couldn't handle watching her beat herself up anymore.

He stood and reached for her, taking her by the shoulders, pulling her to her feet and into his chest. "Come on, Mom. It's okay. Stop crying."

Her arms came around him, her hands twisting into

his shirt, and she sobbed even harder against him. Murmuring a bunch of soothing nonsense, he patted her on the back as she cried, her whole body shaking with the force of it.

He'd have to be a cold bastard to ignore her pain, to refuse to accept her apology, which she obviously meant with every fiber of her being. Had she'd been torturing herself like this all this time? Imagining him drug-addicted and homeless, for God's sake? Guilt twisted in his gut again, but this time it wasn't guilt about his actions eight years ago, it was guilt about what he'd done—or hadn't done—all the years since.

Chapter Thirty-Three

As the night stretched on, Livie found herself looking toward the door every five minutes, then every two minutes, torturing herself with thoughts about what might be happening between Nick and his mother, and what he was going to say to her when he came back. If he came back.

It was after midnight when the door opened and this time, Nick was the one who stepped through it. Livie had been drying a rack of glasses, but froze, her towel-covered hand still stuffed down inside a pint glass.

He stopped right inside the door, not making a move to come any closer, watching her from across the room. Her stomach erupted in butterflies.

Her dad looked up from his conversation with Teresa at the end of the bar, his eyes cutting back and forth between them. When Teresa gave him a very unsubtle nudge, he cleared his throat and straightened, coming to take the half-dried glass out of her hands.

"It's slowing down. Why don't you head home, Livie?"

Jolted out of her frozen state, she looked up at her father. "Are you sure?"

"Yeah," Jess chimed in behind her. "We got this. You go on home."

She wasn't exactly looking forward to this conversation with Nick, but putting it off wasn't going to make it any easier. Might as well get it over with.

She ducked under the pass-through and walked over to Nick, tucking her hands in her back pockets to keep from fidgeting. He watched her approach without reaction, closed up like a vault, every thought and feeling locked inside.

"I'm heading home," she said as brightly as she could manage. She was so terrible at pretending. "Want to walk with me?"

He gave her one tight nod and moved to the side to let her walk out ahead of him.

Outside on the sidewalk, he fell into step beside her, hands stuffed into his jacket pockets, head down, eyes on the sidewalk.

Livie had intended to let him do the talking, but when he made no attempt to break the silence for several endless minutes, she couldn't take it any longer. "Nick, I'm so sorry. I didn't plan it, I swear. I saw her at the butcher shop and I acted on impulse. I didn't know she was going to come here tonight."

"It's okay."

"I have no idea what your relationship with them was like, and it wasn't my place to insert myself or try to fix things. I'm so sorry you were ambushed that way. I had no right to put you in that position."

He blew out a long breath and tilted his head back to look at the dark sky overhead. "Liv, it's fine."

She almost missed a step in her surprise. "Really? I mean, it is? You seemed really angry earlier."

"I was. But not at you. Not much anyway." He trailed off, turning his head away. "It's a long story."

"You can tell me. If you want." She hesitated, then

charged on. "I mean, I know we're not...this is not... But I'm your friend."

Finally, he looked at her, turning his head enough to give her a slight smile, and to brush his elbow against hers. "Yeah, you are."

Taking a deep breath, she asked the question that had been eating at her since she met him. "Nick, what happened with your family? Was it about getting kicked out of DeWitt?"

"No. I mean, not directly. But it started there." He took a deep breath of his own. "After I got kicked out, I moved back home." He shook his head ruefully. "Things were tense. Things had *always* been tense, but DeWitt made it all a thousand times worse."

"You didn't get along with your parents?"

"Without trying to sound like a whiny teenager, they never understood me. The computer thing started early. I got my first desktop when I was six. Built another one out of spare parts and instructions I found online when I was seven. By the time I was eight, I was writing code, building websites. And this was twenty years ago. There were plenty of grown adults who couldn't even turn on a computer back then, including my parents. They didn't understand it, so they didn't trust it. They were sure everything I was doing was illegal, that I'd get into trouble for it."

"*Was* it illegal?" Considering adult Nick's attitude toward legality, Livie wasn't so sure his mother was wrong to question him.

"Nobody'd even written the laws yet. The internet back then..." He stared up at the sky, smiling at the memory. "It was like the Wild West. Anything was possible. People were doing amazing new stuff every day. Things that would have seemed like science fiction just five years earlier were happening right in front of my eyes. I knew the people doing it. *I* was doing it. It felt like we were making the future happen, you know?"

Hearing him talk about those days, it was easy to understand why he loved it. It was no different than what she did, really. The thirst for answers, the giddy high you got when you puzzled out something no one else had yet.

"All the rules and laws about what you could and couldn't do," he continued. "All that came later. Some of us got caught, some of us didn't."

"You didn't."

"Oh, there were one or two cease and desist letters."

"Nick!"

"Relax. Nothing serious. Corporate blowhards protecting their turf. But yeah, my parents were pretty freaked out. I was nothing like Chris. Straight As, on track to graduate with honors, already had a job offer from a major brokerage waiting for him when he graduated. To my parents, that's what success looked like. What I was doing? That was just goofing around on the internet and getting into trouble. They changed their tune a little when I got the full ride to DeWitt, but they never really trusted me, you know?"

It must have sucked, to be constantly compared to his brother and found wanting. As different as she and her sisters were, never once had her father set one against the other.

"Anyway, when my little run-in with the Department of Defense happened, and I got kicked out of DeWitt, they were furious. I mean, I get it. They didn't even go to college. They had to scrimp and save to put Chris through City College. I landed a full ride to an Ivy at sixteen and then I *blew* it. I didn't see it that way, but I can see how they did."

"How *did* you see it?" Livie couldn't imagine screwing up so bad as to get kicked out of college and not seeing it as a life-altering disaster. It would have destroyed her, but Nick shrugged it off as some minor inconvenience.

"Honestly, college was boring. Two years in and I already knew what I was going to do with my life, and it had nothing to do with what was happening in class. I was never going to graduate and get a job writing code for Microsoft or running an IT department for some corporation. The crazy thing is, I was already working from my desktop in my dorm room. People were already paying me to do stuff. *Interesting* stuff. College seemed like a waste of my time."

She wanted to tell him that education was *never* a waste of time, but she suspected this was yet another way in which she and Nick would forever differ. "So hacking the Department of Defense."

He let out a soft chuckle. "Okay, I admit it. It was a stupid thing to do. But I was young and dumb, despite my brains, if you know what I mean."

Of course she did. Nick was a genius when it came to figuring out a computer program, but sometimes he couldn't figure out the right thing to do when it was staring him in the face. Livie was brilliant at making connections inside reams of complex data, but sometimes it felt like she couldn't connect to a human being she wasn't related to if her life depended on it.

"Why'd you do it?"

"I had a lot of friends online. Other specialized computer experts."

"Hackers."

"Yeah, I was running with a pack of hackers. The elite, if there was such a thing. Anyway, we talked a lot about the ultimate hack, what would be the hardest system to crack. It was all theoretical, really. A game we played. This one guy said the Department of Defense would be impossible. He was being kind of a dick about it, actually, so I decided to prove him wrong."

"You're right, that was really dumb, Nick."

"I told you."

"You hacked the Department of Defense on a *dare*."

"Okay, I get it. Believe me, I heard more than enough about it from my parents, back when it all went down."

He was quiet for a bit, lost in his memories. She left him alone with his own thoughts as they wandered down Court Street, waiting until they'd reached the relative solitude of her block before she tried again.

"You were living back at home?"

"Right. And working. See, I got into trouble for what I did, but in certain circles, it made me kind of famous."

"Famous?"

"Infamous. Legendary. I was picking up a lot of free-lance work from people looking to utilize my specific brand of genius."

"You were hacking."

He shook his head. "Nope. No way. I told you I didn't get indicted, but that doesn't mean the government let me walk away scot free. I cleaned up their system for them so they didn't prosecute, but they kept me on a pretty tight leash. I skirted the line of legality sometimes, but I could *not* afford to cross it, or our deal would be off."

He paused again, dropping his eyes to the pavement. "I had offers, of course. People who wanted me to do what I did to the DoD, but to other government agencies…to other *governments*. There are a lot of seriously shady characters out there looking for guys like me to do their dirty work."

"But you said no."

"Right. There was no amount of money these guys could offer me that would make me risk going to prison for the rest of my life. I might have been dumb back then, but I wasn't an idiot."

"Prison for life?" Cold dread filled her stomach. What he'd done was *that* serious?

He shot her another small smile, a faint echo of his usual cocky grin. "Don't worry. My government friends and I are on good terms these days. I don't cross the big red lines and they leave me alone to do my thing. I wouldn't work for any of the really bad guys, but guys like that, they don't like to take no for an answer."

Livie's skin prickled with apprehension. "What do you mean?"

"These guys, they were, I guess you'd classify them as terrorists? It depends on which government you ask. Anyway, they approached me to do some work, some highly *illegal* work, which I refused. But they thought they could convince me it was in my own best interest to do their job."

"How were they going to do that?"

"By kidnapping me."

Livie stopped moving, her feet frozen as she stared at Nick. He paused and turned back to face her.

Her heart was pounding with horror. "What did they do to you?" She was terrified that whatever he told her next would be indelibly seared on her brain for life. She needed to know and she never wanted to know.

"Not me," he answered. His eyes were dead and his voice had gone flat. "Christopher. We look a lot alike, and we were both living at home. He went out for a run one morning and he didn't come back. For two days, we didn't know what had happened to him. These guys figured out pretty quick that they had the wrong De-Santis brother, so they changed the rules. A couple of days later, they contacted me with their demands. I did the job or they'd kill him. Slowly."

Livie covered her mouth with her hand. Her eyes stung and her throat ached. "What happened? Did they hurt him?"

Nick scoffed as he turned to the front and started walking again. Livie had no choice but to walk with him, although her body was still frozen with dread.

"These fucking idiots. They tried to extort me because I'm one of the few people on the planet who could do what they wanted. I'm good enough to bring down a fucking government but it never occurred to them I was also good enough to track them down?"

"You found them?"

"I found them in an *hour*." He rolled his eyes, disgusted with their incompetence. "My government friends took care of the rest. They got Chris back for me and arrested a tidy little bundle of Interpol's most wanted as a bonus."

Livie exhaled for the first time in many minutes. "Chris was okay."

"Chris was okay," he echoed, but there was a bitterness to those words that hadn't been there before, and Livie could begin to guess at what had gone wrong between Nick and his family.

"Your parents must have been terrified," she said cautiously.

His cheek twitched as he ground his teeth together, his jaw going tight with anger. "Terrified until we knew he was safe. Then they were enraged. It was all my fault, of course." The words came faster now that he'd finally let them out, tumbling out of him in an angry rush. "My mother couldn't say enough. I was so reckless, so irresponsible, so selfish. I couldn't leave well enough alone. I had to push and push, and look what happened as a result. I got myself kicked out of college, I got myself arrested. I nearly got my brother killed."

"I'm sure she was upset—"

"She said she was sorry they'd failed, that they hadn't gotten me like they'd planned."

The words hit her heart like a fist. "Oh, Nick, I'm sure she didn't mean it—"

"Oh, she meant it—" But he stopped, the anger suddenly draining out of him. "I don't know. Maybe she didn't. But at the time, it really felt like she did. So I left."

"You what?"

"As soon as we got word that the cops had Chris, I packed up my computer and I left. I walked out, threw away my phone, and I disappeared. That was the last time I saw or spoke to any of them. Until tonight."

"Your mother must have been a wreck." She remembered Laura DeSantis's face when she'd mentioned Nick's name. It was like he'd just come back from the dead. Because for Laura DeSantis, he had.

"Yeah, I get that now." He shook his head. "She was a mess tonight. Eight years." He sighed. "She's been killing herself over this for eight years. I don't think I was wrong to be pissed, but maybe I shouldn't have disappeared like that. I should have at least let them know where I was. But honestly, I didn't think they'd want to know. I didn't think they'd care."

"You know they do."

He looked down at his feet. "Yeah, they do. Chris got married and had a kid. Can you believe that? All this shit happened while I've been out there hiding from them."

"I'm sure they don't blame you." They'd reached her house by now, but she paused on the front stoop. Nick didn't seem in any hurry to go inside and end this conversation. She wondered if he'd ever told anyone what had happened. The way it rushed out of him once he started, she was guessing not.

"No, they don't blame me for disappearing, they blame themselves. How the hell does that feel even worse? My mother is so fucking grateful that I didn't spit on her. I mean, what the hell is that? I shouldn't have been such a dick about it."

Earlier, she'd told him it wasn't her place to insert herself into his family, but it seemed like he might be looking for *someone* to, for someone to tell him it was okay to forgive them. "It's not too late to fix it, Nick."

"No, it's not. I'm…" He paused, drew a deep breath, continued. "I'm going to their place for Thanksgiving tomorrow."

"You're going home for Thanksgiving?" That was a better outcome than she could have hoped for.

"To my *parents'* place. That's not really home for me anymore."

"Nick, it's your home. It'll always be your home. That's the point, right?"

"Yeah, I guess." He didn't sound happy about it, but he did sound determined to go through with it. His family was going to welcome him back in with open arms, she knew it. He might not see that now, but tomorrow, he would. He'd be glad he did this.

"You're not mad at me?"

"For telling my mother you knew me? Liv, I might have been a self-absorbed dick when I was eighteen, but I'd like to think I've evolved a little by now." He reached out and snagged her hand, his thumb running across her knuckles. "No, I'm not mad at you."

Her breath left her in an unsteady huff. She'd been half-convinced tonight was it—that he'd come back just long enough to tell her it was all over. Instead, everything had changed. He was patching things up with his family. He was going home tomorrow. He was *staying*.

For the first time since she'd met him, she had hope. It was nothing more than a tiny little flicker, but it was there. Maybe he'd figure out how to quit running away. Maybe he'd stay. Maybe there was a chance they'd exist beyond the next five minutes.

She reached for his hand. "Come upstairs?"

He let her lead him inside.

Chapter Thirty-Four

Upstairs, in his room, things felt different. Usually when they had sex, Nick was excited and playful, pulling her clothes off her in an eager tumble toward the bed, alternating between kisses and filthy whispers that made her blush.

Tonight, he was quiet. In fact, he made no move to touch her right away, looking around the room as if he wasn't really seeing it, as if he was lost somewhere else.

Livie went to him instead.

"Hey," she murmured, taking his face in her hands. His hands found her hips, and he looked back at her. "It'll be okay."

He nodded, closing his eyes. She kissed him—a brief press of the lips at first, but then again, slower and longer. Eventually, he began to kiss her back, his hands curling into her hips. Still, he made no move to take things further. Summoning her courage, Livie took the initiative, something she'd never done before.

Slowly, she unbuttoned his shirt, leaving off kissing his mouth to drop kisses down his neck, and still farther down to his chest. Nick drew in a ragged breath, lifting a hand to cradle the back of her head. When he made no move to undress her, she straightened up, looked him in the eye, and began to unbutton her shirt.

He watched as each button slipped free of the fabric. When it was hanging loose, she shrugged it off, letting it fall to the floor.

He didn't reach for her tonight the way he usually did. He just looked, his eyes roaming over her bare shoulders, the swells of her breasts above the scooped edge of her tank top.

So she didn't stop. She stripped off the tank, too, shaking her hair free as he watched with hungry eyes. After only a moment of hesitation, she reached around and unhooked her bra, tossing it away. His eyes locked on her breasts but still, he didn't touch her.

This felt different. She was jumpy with nerves. Usually, by the time she was naked, they were already in bed, he was naked, too, and they were seconds away from coming together. It was easy to get lost in the rush of physical sensation. She'd forget about her own body entirely, completely focused on what was happening between them. Now, there was just him, standing there fully clothed, watching her, half-naked. Her nipples hardened into tight buds under his relentless gaze.

"Take off the rest?" he murmured. "Please?"

It never crossed her mind to refuse him. As Nick stood still and watched her, she kicked off her shoes, then slid her jeans down her legs. His heavy-lidded dark eyes never left her. There was nothing left but her underwear. Her eyes flicked up to his. He stared back in question. Before she could lose her nerve, she hooked her thumbs into the sides and slid them down her legs, too.

His eyes raked over her slowly, from head to toe. She stood still, still trembling, and let him look. Finally— it felt like a year—he reached out and laid a hand over her breast. Her eyes slid closed and she let out a trembling sigh.

"I'm being selfish," he said. "Just taking."

"Not if I want to give it. Maybe you need it." He seemed rattled tonight, more uncertain of himself than she'd ever seen him. This time, maybe she could take the lead, and make it all about him.

"I don't deserve you, Liv."

She covered his hand where he was touching her. "You've got me anyway. Tonight, you can have all of me, any way you want me."

Slowly, when she'd worked up her courage, she stepped forward, lifted her hands, and began undressing him, too. He let her, watching her intently as she unbuttoned his shirt and stripped it off, then unzipped his jeans and nudged them down. He moved only enough to toe off his shoes. She did the rest, sliding his jeans down his legs and urging him to step out of them.

While she was down there, on her knees, she glanced up and there he was, right in front of her face, hard and ready. She'd never done this before. The very idea had struck fear into her heart. There seemed to be a lot of ways to screw it up, and it was definitely not an organ you wanted to make a mistake on. But now, when he seemed so lost, when all she wanted was to make him feel good again, it felt right to take him in her hand, to lean forward, then to take him into her mouth.

Nick let out a moan that made her shudder, then he muttered a stream of expletives. "Jesus, Liv. Jesus. Goddamn."

Jesus and God were the last thing on her mind at the moment. She focused all her considerable mental abilities on what she was doing, trying hard to keep her teeth out of it, to use her hands for the significant part of him that wouldn't fit in her mouth.

She still had no idea what she was doing, but Nick didn't seem to care. His hand had moved to the back of her head, caressing her, tangling in her hair. The surprising thing about the whole experience was how hot she found it. It was patently all about him, right? He was the only one receiving any stimulation. Then why were her nipples tight? Why was she wet and achy between her legs? She didn't want to stop. She wanted to keep going until she'd made him fall apart. It was a heady rush, knowing she had this kind of power over his pleasure.

"Oh, shit," he hissed. His hands closed around her upper arms, and she found herself hauled roughly to her feet. "You are fucking magnificent," he muttered, right before he took her mouth in a hungry kiss.

Now he was everywhere, his hands on her breasts, skimming down her body, dipping in between her legs to tease her until she was gasping and trembling. Still kissing her, he backed her toward the bed. When her calves hit it, he paused and drew back, taking her face in his hands and looking at her.

"Liv, you are just…" When she looked in his eyes, that hole in him, the one that she thought might have started to heal tonight, seemed more vast than ever. It was a dark emptiness that sent a cold shaft of fear into her heart.

She reached out to touch his face. "Nick, what is it?"

But he didn't answer. He shook his head and kissed her again. Whatever else she might have said was lost in that kiss, lost in his body coming down over hers.

Chapter Thirty-Five

His parents had moved, which had surprised Nick last night. His family had been in the Carroll Gardens house since his grandparents' days. But his mother said that after the "incident"—which is how she referred to Chris's kidnapping and his disappearing act—there were too many bad memories in the house. Plus, with Chris married and moved out, and Nick gone, it was too big for the two of them. They'd sold up and bought a smaller place in Sheepshead Bay.

Their new place was on a quiet block lined with identical brick houses, one pressed up against the other. The tiny landscaped front yard looked tidy and well cared for. Even this late in November, it was the nicest yard on the block. His dad had always had a green thumb.

Neither of the cars parked in the tiny driveway was familiar. Of course, why would his parents have the same car he remembered? That old Honda they'd driven probably met its maker years ago. The other car had a car seat in back. There was also a tricycle parked on the front porch. More signs of all the changes he'd missed.

Taking a deep breath, he forced his feet up the three steps to the porch. From inside, he could hear the faint sounds of a TV. His dad and Chris were probably already watching football. Did they still do that on Thanksgiving? Or would it be all Barney and cartoons now?

He stared at the door, willing himself to lift his hand and knock. While part of him wanted to—wanted to put an end to eight years of bitterness and anger—another part of him wanted to run away. It was safe back there in his isolation. Once he did this, rejoined his family, they'd be back in his life again, and change, even good change, was a little scary.

He wished Livie was with him. She was good at this part. Not change. She was terrible at facing changes. But she was great at needling him to face the thing he didn't really want to face. This wouldn't even be happening if not for her.

It surprised him, his need for her in this moment. And made him a little uneasy. Relying on her too much was a mistake, because someday soon she was going to wise up and get the fuck out of here. But for today, she was back in Carroll Gardens with her own family. And he was here with his. If he could make himself knock on the door.

He was still standing there, at war with himself, when he heard a voice from inside, approaching the front door.

"It's in the car seat, babe. I'll get it."

Suddenly the door opened and he was face-to-face with his brother.

It wasn't quite that eerie looking-in-a-mirror feeling he'd had when they were younger. In eight years, their looks had diverged a bit. Chris's face was a little leaner, more angular. His hair was shorter than Nick's, clipped neat and conservative. There were a few fine lines around his eyes.

The eyes were the same, though. Chris had his eyes,

and now they widened in surprise. His mouth fell open, and a second later, a wide smile spread across his face.

"Nick. Goddamn, you're really here."

"I—" He didn't get to finish that sentence, as he found himself yanked forward, into a ferocious, crushing hug. Chris drew in a shaky breath that Nick felt against his shoulder. A rush of emotion so powerful it almost hurt welled up in his chest. For all the bullshit rivalries and squabbles over the years, he'd missed this perfect, infuriating jerk. He'd missed his brother.

From inside the house, he heard his mother's voice, high-pitched and painfully eager. "Is that him?"

Chris leaned back to look at him, still hanging on to his shoulders. "Get your ass in here, man. We have eight years of family bonding to make up for."

And somehow, after eight years of silence and bitterness and recriminations, it was that easy. He showed up, and they invited him right back in.

As Chris dragged him over the threshold and shut the door behind him, his mother appeared from the back of the house, wiping her hands on a dish towel.

"Nicky!" she cried, crossing the tiny living room and throwing her arms around his shoulders. He submitted to another crushing embrace, patting his mother on the back when it seemed she might start crying again. Over her shoulder, he saw his father come in, still straight-backed and broad-shouldered, although with a lot more wrinkles and silver in his hair than had been there last time Nick saw him.

A tremor of nerves, the kind he hadn't felt since he was a kid, raced through his body. Neither of his parents had ever really understood what made Nick tick, but his father had been particularly flummoxed and frustrated by his younger son. In Dad's world, sons followed in their father's footsteps, or they built upon what their old man started. Dad's dad was an MTA mechanic and Dad was an MTA supervisor. Chris took what they'd built, got himself a degree, and went into banking. Nick had ignored everything that came before him and forged a wholly new path. Dad had accused him more than once of being an ungrateful little shit. But how could he be grateful for something he'd never wanted?

As his mother released him, gazing up at him with glassy eyes and a delighted smile, Nick braced himself for a scene with his father. Surely now was when he'd get called out for his disappearing act. If anyone was going to get mad, it would be Dad.

But Michael DeSantis didn't do anything Nick expected him to do. He ducked his chin, cleared his throat, and shook his head. If Nick didn't know better, he'd have thought he was fighting back tears. Then he crossed the living room in a few long strides, reached for him, and hauled him into yet another hug.

"Jesus, Nick, we've been so worried," he murmured, his voice tight with emotion. "Thank God," he whispered, thumping him hard on the back. "Thank God you're okay."

Once again, a surge of emotion caught Nick by surprise. He hadn't expected, he hadn't realized… Jesus, he'd *missed* them. All this time, under the anger and the hurt, there was this gaping chasm of loss, and he hadn't even known it was there. Livie had sensed it, though. All this time, something had been missing in him and she'd seen it, she'd recognized the shape of that hole in his heart. He'd needed his family. And Livie gave them back to him.

His father released him, gripping him by the back of the neck as he looked him over. "You look good."

Nick had to clear his throat to speak. "I am good. I mean, I'm fine."

"Good, good. That's good," Dad said gruffly, releasing him and stepping back. All that emotion had clearly made him uncomfortable.

Chris stepped into the moment of awkward silence that followed. "There's somebody you should meet, Nick. A couple of somebodies, actually."

Looking past his father, he spotted them across the room, the woman who must be Chris's wife, and on her hip, Chris's son. His nephew.

"Hi, I'm Kate," she said, coming toward him with her free hand extended. She was small and slim, with long light brown hair, a dusting of freckles across her nose, and blue eyes that scrunched up when she smiled, like she was doing now.

"Nice to meet you."

She didn't stop with a handshake, leaning up on tiptoe to kiss his cheek. "Welcome home, Nick," she said near his ear. "You've made everybody so happy."

He felt a flush of embarrassment, a tinge of shame. All he'd done was show up, after hiding for eight years. He didn't deserve this kind of gratitude.

Chris hoisted the wiggling toddler out of her arms. "And this," he said, his eyes full of pride, "is Anthony."

"Hey, man." How were you supposed to greet a baby? Shake his hand? Pat him on the head?

Anthony looked him over with big dark eyes—the same as Chris's, the same as his own. Then his face lit up and he flailed one chubby fist at Nick. Guess that's how you said hello to a toddler.

"Nicky's still standing here in his coat," his mother said, snapping to attention and bustling around him.

"Michael, take his coat. Chris, get your brother a drink. Come in and sit down, Nicky."

And just like that, Nick was home again.

It was a little weird. For one thing, the house was different. It was all the same stuff—the furniture he remembered, the pictures that had always hung on the walls—but all rearranged in a new setting. It felt like a dream, where you think you know where you are, but it's all different in a million little ways. He had to ask where the bathroom was. The spare bedroom wasn't full of his stuff or Chris's. It held a crib and a shelf full of toys. Instead of football on the TV, there was some show on called *PAW Patrol*, and little Anthony watched it like it contained the mysteries of the universe.

"I'm going to start him on *Star Trek* next year," Chris told him with a grin.

Right. *Star Trek.* He and Chris had watched hours and hours of old VHS tapes of *Star Trek* when they were kids. It was their thing. That's where he'd developed his love of space movies.

There were other familiar things waiting to jump out and swamp him with nostalgia. His mother still wore that ratty red plaid apron when she cooked, the one that had belonged to her mother and grandmother. She busted the thing out of storage every Thanksgiving and Christmas. The smell that permeated the house when she took her sausage stuffing out of the oven made his mouth water and his heart clench.

Dinner was a little awkward, if he was being honest. So much time had passed, so much had been missed, that they ended up asking polite questions of each other like a bunch of strangers stuck at the same table at a wedding.

"What's your business called, Nick?" his father asked.

"My business?"

Dad shot a brief look at Mom. "Your mother said you own your own business? For the computer stuff?"

"Oh. It's not really a business. I freelance."

"Can't get health insurance as a freelancer," his father grunted.

"You can if you pay for it." Which he totally intended to do, one of these days. It just kept slipping his mind.

"And what'll you do about retirement? No pension or 401K when you work for yourself."

"I have retirement covered, Dad." Not that he ever expected to give up his work, but if and when he decided to, there was plenty of money to take care of it.

"So you're doing well, then?" That was Chris, trying to shut down their father's prodding.

"Yeah. Really well."

Chris shook his head. "I always knew you'd end up owning the world, Nick. The next Bill Gates."

He had? He'd always assumed Chris thought he was a waste of space, like his parents did. But here he was, looking at him with eyes full of pride and respect.

"That's not my scene. Way too many corporate types ruining the fun. I like being my own boss."

"You got investments?"

Nick shot a teasing grin at his brother. "Why? You want to handle my portfolio?"

"I'd love to," Chris said, full of sincerity. "All you have to do is ask, buddy."

"Thanks," he replied, genuinely humbled. "I appreciate that."

"I can't believe you *have* a portfolio. That doesn't sound like you."

Nick chose to make a joke out of his totally truthful reply, to keep the conversation from getting too heavy. "Well, after you make the first million, it's pretty hard to store that many small bills in your mattress. Gotta put it someplace."

His mother passed the basket of dinner rolls around the table again. "You said you're moving again soon, Nick?"

"Yeah, I've been crashing at the Romanos' while I found a new place." Explaining about Poppy, his engagement, the fight, getting thrown out of their apartment, felt too daunting so he skipped it. What did it all matter at this point anyway? It was in the past. "I'll be moving in as soon as…" How was he supposed to explain handing his credit card over to Livie's sister and her cousin and begging them to sort his shit out? "As soon as the decorators finish up."

Her eyebrows lifted. "Decorators? Fancy."

"I didn't have time to deal with it myself."

"She's very nice."

"Who?"

"Livie." His mother turned to Chris. "Olivia Romano. She's how I found your brother. Her family owns Romano's Bar. Remember?"

"Yeah, I remember. You guys dating?"

Were they? He and Livie had never really labeled what they were doing. He'd pointedly avoided labeling it, because then it would start to feel real. Permanent. And they both knew it wasn't. Right?

"Um, we're sort of—"

"You should bring her to dinner," his mother said, turning her bright, hopeful smile on him.

"What?"

"Livie. We should have her over for dinner. Maybe her parents, too?"

"Her mother's dead."

"Oh. Poor thing. Her father, then."

Sweat prickled across the back of his neck. His heart was starting to pound. They hadn't just welcomed him back, they were clearing out a Nick-sized space for him in their lives, ready to slot Livie in at his side, exactly like Chris, with a goddamned wife and kid and a 401K he did not need. The old resentment flared up again, hot and bright. He wasn't Chris, goddammit. He never would be.

"I don't think—"

"Relax, Mom." Chris laughed. "He just came back home. Give him a little space."

She turned back to him with that awful, guilt-inducing, grateful smile. "I'm just happy to have you home, Nicky. Back where you belong."

But did he? Did he really belong here? Had he ever? Maybe the past eight years were really how it should have always been. Perfect Chris with his perfect wife and kid, here making his parents proud, and Nick the disappointment, out there on his own. If he stayed here, would it all go back to how it had been before, him forever beating against the walls, trying to break out of the too-tight mold they'd stuck him in, and them, forever disappointed that he couldn't just make himself smaller?

"Hey, Mom, pass the gravy?" Chris said, once again defusing what was rapidly turning into an awkward situation.

"Make sure you leave room," Mom said, passing the gravy boat down the table. "There's pie for dessert!"

After dinner, Kate went upstairs with Anthony to put him down for a nap. His father and brother gratefully popped open a couple of beers and turned the channel to the football game. Nick accepted a beer from his brother and did his best to relax. They were trying. He would try, too. Maybe he'd never truly fit in here the way they wanted him to, but that didn't have to mean the complete exile he'd lived in for eight years. Still, he felt defensive, braced for judgment, ready for the whole fragile house of cards to collapse the second he breathed wrong.

When his phone buzzed in his pocket, he lunged for it, desperate for a distraction. It was a text from his friend Luke in Palo Alto. They'd worked on a couple of start-ups together back in the day, and crossed paths on dozens of other freelance gigs since then. The text was short and abrupt, like all communications from Luke, who didn't understand the concept of casual conversation. He was abrupt as fuck, but a decent guy. Good coder.

Hey. Call me. Urgent.

He hadn't been back to Palo Alto in a year. Hadn't spoken to Luke outside of a few random emails and texts in months. What the hell could be urgent now? He was about to ignore it and pocket his phone again when another text came through.

I'm serious. Need to talk to you.

With a frisson of unease, he excused himself from his father and Chris and slipped his coat on, stepping outside on the porch to make the call. Had some mutual friend of theirs died? Was Apple going bankrupt?

Nothing else he could think of would account for Luke's urgency.

He dialed and Luke picked up on the first ring.

"Hey, what're you doing?"

"Uh, hey, Luke, nice to talk to you, too."

"Cut the shit. When are you coming back to the South Bay?"

He laughed. "I moved back to Brooklyn a year ago. Remember?"

Luke let out an impatient huff. "Right. Forgot. What are you doing right now?"

"Um, Luke, it's Thanksgiving."

"I know, but you never really cared about holidays and shit."

He was right. Back in California, he'd worked through all of them. It wasn't like he had a family waiting on him.

"Well, I'm at my parents' today."

"Look, I got hired onto this start-up. These guys tried to cheap out the tech department and now they're paying for it. Soft launch is supposed to be in a week, and the whole system is a goddamned mess. If the site doesn't go live next week, they lose their VC. Shit is about to get very real. They brought me on to fix it, but it's a two-man job. I need you. Today."

Nick exhaled in surprise, his breath making a cloud in the cold air. "I can't fly back today."

"Why not?"

"Because…" Why not? In the past, he wouldn't have thought twice about it before heading to the airport. But that was before, back when he hadn't been beholden to anybody, when nobody cared where he went or why. Now he had his family back inside, so abjectly grateful he'd come to dinner he could barely stand it. Their happiness itched at his skin, leaving him twisting in a mess of guilt, resentment, and shame.

And once he escaped his own family, he'd be going home to face the Romano extended clan—all those aunts, uncles, and cousins, assembled for the holiday and curious as hell about who he was. They'd ask questions, just like his own family. They'd want answers about him and Livie, answers he didn't have.

He imagined that flight back to Sacramento and just like that, his chest unclenched and he drew in what felt like his first full breath in hours. And on the other side of the flight—nothing. Nothing but days of coding, a tough but finite problem to solve, with a predictable, reliable outcome. His brain went very quiet.

"Come on, man. There's nobody else who can clean up this disaster. You can name your price to these guys."

"It's not about the money," he said by rote. It was never about the money. It was about the project, what opportunities the project presented to him.

"Please tell me you'll do it."

Nick heard his own voice from far away. "Yeah, I'll do it."

Chapter Thirty-Six

Thanksgiving felt endless this year.

Things got off to a bad start when Livie texted Andy Finch, wishing him and his parents a happy Thanksgiving. She'd hoped Andy would have responded with a cheerful message from Janet herself, some sign that she was finally on the mend. But Andy's reply had been short, sad, and made no mention of his mother.

Nick wasn't there, although for the best possible reason this time. He was with his family today, exactly where he should be. She hoped it was going well, that today could be the start of a new era in their family. If Nick had them…well, she didn't want to get too far ahead of herself.

Then Gemma mentioned, almost as an afterthought, that she'd invited Teresa and her mother to Thanksgiving dinner. Which was fine. Livie wasn't nearly as hostile to the idea of Teresa as she'd been when Dad first brought her home. But inviting Teresa and her elderly mother to a holiday dinner felt an awful lot like the start of blending their families, which made this no ordinary Thanksgiving dinner.

Of course, it was already the oddest Thanksgiving the Romanos had ever hosted, since Jess had invited Alex, Alex's father, and Alex's father's girlfriend.

Which would have been fine, if Alex's father wasn't a world-famous media tycoon and his girlfriend wasn't Jess's boss at the newspaper. Jess, usually Livie's steady rock in tense family situations, had been a jumpy mess herself, even though the whole thing had been her idea. Dan Drake was going to be Jess's father-in-law, she reasoned. Mariel Kemper, her boss, seemed to be holding strong as Dan's steady girlfriend, much to everyone's shock, since in the past, Dan had gone through women like tissues. Jess was therefore determined to start working Dan—and, by extension, Mariel—into the Romano clan.

The house was full of the usual collection of aunts, uncles, and cousins, with the addition of Teresa, who everyone was curious about, and Dan and Mariel, who everybody was slightly scared of. It made for interesting dinner table conversation, to say the least. Livie had thought Dan Drake's presence would stifle her usually boisterous family into silence, but Dan had a crazy ability to charm nearly anyone he met, and by the end of dinner, the Romanos had casually accepted him as one of their own.

After dinner, Livie had expected that Dan and Mariel would take off, but to her shock—and Jess's—Dad invited him out to the living room to watch the football game with them and Dan *went*.

Gemma had been up at three a.m. getting their monster turkey into the oven and now she looked ready to fall asleep on her feet. Jess and Livie chased her out of the kitchen for cleanup, and sent her up to bed for a nap. With a bemused smile Mariel watched Dan cheering along with their dad, Uncle Richie, and the rest of the relatives when the Jets made a touchdown. Then she turned to Jess and Livie. "Well, it looks like we'll be here for a while. You might as well put me to work."

"Oh, no," Jess protested. "You're a guest."

And her boss, but Mariel waved her away. "Nonsense. I want to help. Why don't I bring in the leftovers from the table?"

Jess sighed in defeat before she and Livie got to work scraping plates and starting the dishes.

There was no sign of Nick, but Livie told herself not to expect him. Maybe he'd even stay over with his parents tonight. They had a lot of catching up to do, right? It would be only natural, she told herself. She absolutely wasn't allowed to miss him.

But when she closed the fridge after stowing the leftover turkey carcass, she nearly jumped out of her skin to find Nick standing in the doorway to the kitchen.

He hooked a thumb over his shoulder. "You guys know Dan Drake is watching the Jets game in your living room right now?"

"Please tell me Uncle Richie isn't telling the shark story again," Jess groaned.

"No mention of sharks," Nick assured her. "But they are talking about fishing. Apparently Dan's going fishing with your uncle Richie next spring?"

Jess and Livie exchanged a nervous glance. "Oh, no," Jess murmured.

"Liv," Nick said, motioning back over his shoulder toward the front door. "You got a second?"

She glanced around the kitchen. "We're still cleaning up."

"Go on," Jess said. "Mariel can dry dishes until you get back."

"Okay, I'll be back in a minute."

She followed him through the crowded living room,

wincing when the Jets made another touchdown and the entire room erupted in screams. Dan Drake was high-fiving her cousin Paulie. When she stopped to grab her coat in the front hall, she noticed Nick's backpack, stuffed full and sitting on the floor by the door. Where had that come from?

Outside, Nick walked to the edge of the stoop, looking out at the street and not at her.

"I have to go out of town for a couple of days."

The words were innocuous enough, but there was something off about him. He seemed jumpy, distracted, a little guilty. "Okay. Where are you going?"

"San Jose."

"California? Why?"

"A friend's working on a start-up and they've run into major trouble. I'm going to go sort it out for them."

The explanation was simple enough, but she couldn't believe he was dropping everything to fly to California for some random internet start-up he had no real connection to—today of all days, when he'd just reconnected with—

"What did your family say?" she asked, as the pieces clicked into place.

"About what?"

"About you leaving before dessert was even served. Because that's what you did, right?"

"What are you talking about?"

"They just got you back and now you're leaving again." It was easier, asking about his family's feelings than asking about hers. She wasn't supposed to have any feelings for him. It had been the deal from the start. She'd foolishly begun to think maybe she could, maybe it would be safe to love him, but it wasn't. It never had been. Oh, how it sucked that it was too late now, and she did. She'd been side-stepping these emotions for weeks, but now she'd tripped right over them and face-planted. She'd gone and fallen in love with him. The one thing she'd promised herself she wouldn't do.

"Liv, it's no big deal. Look, why don't you come with me?"

She startled. "What?"

"Throw some shit in a bag and let's go. Come on, the flight leaves in an hour."

"You're…it's… I can't just *leave*."

"Why not?"

"I have to teach next Tuesday. I have research. We're in the middle of our *project*."

He scoffed. "Of course you can't leave. Figures."

"Don't you care about *anything*? It's *Thanksgiving*. We've still got a house full of guests. You might feel fine running out on your family, but I can't do that."

"What's that supposed to mean?"

"You think I don't know what's going on here? You're running away again."

"What?"

"It's not just some job. Running away is easier than staying and fixing things, isn't it?"

He took a step toward her, eyes flashing with anger. "Don't start telling me what I'm thinking and feeling, Livie. You don't understand."

"Don't I? One afternoon with them and you're hopping a plane, going backward, not forward. It's because you're scared. You'd rather go back to hiding from them instead of fixing everything that went wrong."

"Scared? You want to talk scared, Livie? You're the one who's scared."

"Me? What am I scared of?"

"You tell me."

"Tell you what?"

"Why did someone so brilliant pass up MIT and McArthur to take a spot at a backwater school like Adams? Why are you wasting yourself in that place?"

"I told you, I came here for Janet's research."

"She's gone, Livie, and she's not coming back."

Panic flared up, hot and bright. "Shut up."

"She's not," he said, his voice gentling. "You've got to face it and make a new plan."

Her face flushed and she felt nauseous. "You don't know what you're talking about."

"Oh, I do. You say you came here, that you're staying here, for Finch, but she's nothing but your excuse. You couldn't bear to leave this place, because the thought of leaving terrified you. It still terrifies you. I ask you to leave for a week and you come up with a dozen bullshit reasons why you can't. If I'm the one always running away, Livie, you're the one too scared to leave in the first place."

"Stop it," she snapped, but without heat, because she had a terrible, sinking feeling that he was right. There was an uncomfortable kernel of truth at the heart of every justification she ever came up with for choosing Adams, one she'd very diligently avoided ever putting a label on. But Nick had reached right in and stuck his finger on the truth, and it hurt like he'd touched a raw nerve.

He blew out a breath and dragged his hand through his hair. "Fuck. Livie, I'm sorry. I shouldn't have said that."

He reached out to touch her arm and she stumbled in her haste to get away from him. "Don't."

The last thing she could bear right now was his pity, his well-meaning and devastating sympathy. Not when none of it meant anything. Not when none of it was enough to make him stay.

Nick drew back his hand, looking like she'd struck him.

Finally, he drew a deep breath and spoke. "I gotta go. I'm on the last flight out tonight."

She grit her teeth, keeping her eyes on her toes.

"I'll call you when I get back."

"No." The word sprang from her lips before she'd even thought it. Nick looked as surprised as she was.

"No?"

"No, don't call me." She had to stop and swallow down the lump in her throat before she could continue. "Your place is almost ready, and the coding is almost done. There's nothing you need to call me for."

She didn't mention their relationship, or whatever it was they'd been doing all this time, but she didn't need to. It pulsed between them like a dark, living thing, impossible to ignore. Nick watched her, waiting.

"You're sure?" he asked at last.

That breathless pressure was back in her chest, making her feel light-headed. This was going to happen sooner or later, and Livie didn't want to wait around for later. She didn't want to wait as she fell a little more in love with him every day, holding her breath and bracing for the moment when he said goodbye for good. This was an act of self-preservation, she knew it, but still, every word felt like coughing up glass.

She nodded, still not looking at him. "I'm sure."

The moment of silence felt endless, brittle and raw. She didn't breathe, didn't move. Her body felt frozen. In a minute, this would hurt worse than she could possibly imagine, but not yet. If she didn't breathe, maybe she wouldn't move forward into the future without Nick.

"Okay, if that's what you want," he finally said, every word landing like a tiny bomb in her heart.

No, she wanted to scream. *It's not what I want. I want you, but all of you, the way you'd never intended to give yourself to me.*

But the words only echoed in her head, never to be spoken out loud. Wordlessly, Nick retrieved his backpack from inside the front door and hefted it onto his shoulder.

"I'll…" He stopped, tipped his head forward, exhaled, and continued. "I'll see you around, Livie."

Then he descended the concrete steps, walked down the path through the front yard, and was gone.

Livie stayed where she was, her breaths coming in short, shallow rasps. How was she supposed to move from this spot? How was she supposed to move forward into the next minute, the next hour, tomorrow, the day after, when it felt like some vital part of her had just been cut out of her?

She lost track of how much time had passed since he left. Suddenly someone was there, coming up the steps to the house. She lifted her head. Teresa.

"Hi there, Livie. Getting cold out here, isn't it?"

She opened her mouth to reply, but couldn't. Instead, she gasped, a desperate, panicky sound. Now that she'd moved, she was shaking. Her whole body was trembling so hard her teeth clattered together.

Teresa peered into her face, concern etched into her features. "Honey? Is something wrong?"

Frantically, she shook her head, but hot tears broke free, streaking down her face and making a liar of her.

"Was it Nick?" Teresa asked, with a note of resignation in her voice. "Did something happen?"

This shouldn't be Teresa, Livie thought wildly. She

shouldn't fall apart in front of this total stranger. It should be Jess, or Gemma, or even her father. But they were all inside, with a house full of guests. Teresa was here, and now she'd taken Livie by the shoulders and somehow moved her until she was sitting on the edge of the stoop. Teresa sat down next to her, one arm around her shoulders.

"He's gone," she choked out, her breath shuddering as she inhaled.

"I know it doesn't feel like it right now, but you really will survive it," Teresa said kindly.

How could that possibly be true? How did anybody get through this devastation and come out fine on the other side?

"When my husband left me," Teresa continued, "I thought my life was over. There didn't seem any reason to get out of bed, or even to keep breathing. But I had to. My mother was sick. So I got up. I kept breathing. I kept getting out of bed. And one day, it hurt a little less. And then a little less the day after that. Then I met your father again, and I realized somewhere along the way, I'd gotten over him. It happened when I wasn't even looking, when I was trying to get through all those days, one after the other. It'll happen for you, too, honey."

Her tenderness, her kindness, finally punctured the fragile membrane that had been holding Livie's misery at bay. She opened her mouth to breathe and instead she wailed, an ugly, inhuman sound. Teresa didn't flinch away. She only tightened her grip on Livie, raising one hand to stroke her hair out of her face.

"Eventually isn't right now, though," Teresa said quietly. "And right now, it's really going to hurt, sweetheart. I'm sorry."

Livie let Teresa fold her into her warm embrace and

she let the hurt come. It rushed in like a tidal wave and nearly drowned her. It was only Teresa, holding on tight and refusing to let go, that kept her head above water.

Chapter Thirty-Seven

It was nearly noon when Livie woke the next day. Not surprising, as she hadn't slept all night, alternately staring into the darkness like a zombie, or breaking down into fresh onslaughts of tears. Sometime near dawn, she'd drifted into restless sleep, and when she opened her eyes to her bedroom, awash in midday sunshine, she felt gritty and utterly wrung out.

She sat up in bed and took stock.

Nick was gone, and he wasn't coming back because she'd told him not to. Her tender, aching heart—the part that had broken apart over and over all night long—wanted to reach out to him, to tell him she was wrong. *Come back.* She'd take him, however she could have him.

But during that long, dark night she'd endured, some other part of Livie had been awoken. And that part was absolutely sure she'd done the right thing. She was tired of performing this delicate balancing act between friendship and love, terrified of tipping too far over the line and scaring him away. If he was so easily scared, let him go.

Actually, in the harsh light of a spent morning, Livie found herself tired of a lot of things about her life. What the hell had she been doing for the past several months?

Being with Nick had been the only bright spot. When she assessed everything else... Well, her life was a fucking mess.

Her mentor, the woman she'd constructed her entire academic career around, was sidelined. She'd spent an entire semester spinning her wheels fruitlessly, accomplishing absolutely nothing. And her PhD was being systematically sabotaged by that *asshole*, Langley, while she'd stood by anxiously wringing her hands and doing nothing. She was ashamed of herself.

On the nightstand next to her bed, her phone buzzed with a text. Hesitantly, she picked it up, half-hopeful and half-dreading who it might be from and what it might say. It wasn't Nick, though. It was from Teresa.

How are you doing this morning?

How bizarre that it had been Teresa, of all people, who'd held her hand through that miserable time last night—Teresa, who she'd seen before this as an outsider, an interloper who could never truly understand the Romano family. But last night, she'd understood perfectly, and she'd said exactly the right things. Another thing Livie had been wrong about, another person she'd been pushing away for no good reason.

She typed out a response.

Better. Ready to move on.

Not entirely true, but wasn't that what Teresa told her last night? Get out of bed. Keep living your life. Eventually, it would get easier.

Good girl. Call me if you want to talk.

Livie read the text over. Actually, she might call Teresa. Teresa would understand.

Thanks.

Anytime, Livie.

If she stopped to think about Nick, it hurt so bad she couldn't breathe. Teresa promised her it would get better if she kept moving forward, and that's what she was going to do. Each day further into the future would be a day further away from this day, when her heart was in pieces. She was done with this day.

Lying in bed feeling sorry for herself wasn't going to get her anywhere. Her life was a mess and she needed to do something about it, Nick and her broken heart be damned.

Scrambling out of bed, she marched to the bathroom to clean up. After splashing some water on her face, she grabbed a towel and straightened up to dry off.

Who was that girl looking back at her? She was the exact same Livie Romano from the family portraits downstairs, the same Livie Romano she'd been all her life. Why did she look like such a stranger?

Because inside, she was no longer the same. These past few months had changed her, and as much as losing Nick had hurt—was still hurting—she wouldn't have taken them back for the world. She was smarter, wiser. And yet, here she was, exactly as she'd been at thirteen, with her stupid curtain of hair, hiding in her father's hand-me-down flannel shirts.

It was time, Livie resolved, to grow the fuck up.

But first, she had work to do.

Janet was still out for the foreseeable future, but that

didn't mean there was nothing she could do. She and Nick had nearly finished the Hubble program. The application for time on Hubble was nearly done, too. She'd put off actually finishing it, hoping Janet would come back soon to put her own stamp on the work. Why couldn't she finish it up and submit it herself? She could claim time on Hubble and record the black hole data for Janet herself. She understood what they were doing as well as Janet did. What was she waiting for?

Twisting her ridiculous rope of hair into a knot on her head, she headed back to her room, sat down at her desk, and got to it.

Chapter Thirty-Eight

"Jesus, what a fucking mess." Nick's eyes were burning and bloodshot from another sleepless night and unrelenting hours of staring at a glowing blue screen full of coding.

"You said that twenty minutes ago. And twenty minutes before that." Luke's voice rose up, disembodied, from behind a wall of monitors on the other side of the table. He and Nick had been hunched here behind their respective phalanx of screens for days, unpicking this knot of coding.

"Because I still can't believe these guys were this inept."

"Well, you get what you pay for. They paid for shit and they got shit. I think we're almost there, though. When you're finished backing up to the server, we should give it another test run."

"I still have to sort out the security back door and a hundred other things."

This whole fucking website was a nightmare, so badly conceived and executed that starting from scratch would have been easier than fixing what was already here. He hated this kind of mind-numbing work, scanning thousands of lines of coding looking for tiny mistakes that needed correcting. There was nothing new or interesting about it, nothing to be learned, no creativity he could bring to bear to solve a problem. Nothing but tedium and sleep-deprivation. Why exactly had he said yes to this project? He'd been asking himself that all week.

Twelve hours of sleep in four days, never more than an hour at a stretch, on the hard, scratchy couch in the corner, shitty takeout food, enough coffee to make his nerves vibrate. And for the privilege of enjoying this miserable experience, he'd blown up everything with—

He couldn't even think of Livie's name without feeling like he'd been punched in the gut.

It had been days and he wasn't getting any better. Every time he thought about her—and she was in his head constantly, despite the never-ending lines of code—he couldn't breathe.

When she'd ended things between them on her front porch, he'd been too stunned to fight her on it, or even respond much. How had a quick job in California turned into a fight that vicious? How had they ended up saying such ugly, hurtful things to each other? While he'd been standing there trying to figure out a way to back down off that cliff, she'd ended everything between them with a few brief, brutal, dismissive words.

It was undoubtedly all his fault. He'd gotten angry and said things he shouldn't have said. Sure Livie was hiding out at home because she was scared, but who was she hurting, outside of herself? If that's what she wanted from her life, who was he to judge her?

Before his plane had even landed in San Jose, he'd figured out she'd been right about his motivations. Yes, Luke was a friend in a bind, but he doubted he'd have acquiesced so quickly if he wasn't standing in the midst of his newly recovered family, feeling shaky and volatile, conflicted and still a little angry, when he'd called.

Emotionally stunted moron that he'd always been, he'd jumped at the first opportunity to escape, no matter who it hurt. His family, looking at him with wounded eyes as he made his excuses and split—Livie, hurling her fury at him as he picked up and left her for some crummy job. He'd left a lot of carnage behind him when he'd boarded that plane at JFK.

Livie had said things in anger, too, but she hadn't bolted for the airport like he had. When he'd lashed out, he'd hurt everyone around him, starting with her. Maybe they'd never spelled out what they were to each other, but he owed her better than this. Unfortunately, it seemed he might never get the chance to make it up to her. And the thought of that was beginning to make him feel a whole new kind of panic. Ending a casual fling wasn't supposed to feel this way. He wasn't supposed to feel this lost. Confused. Devastated.

"Hey, man." Luke's voice startled him out of the hazy fog of exhaustion and guilt he'd been sinking into. "Since you're back, I got a million gigs I could use your help on."

"I'm not back, Luke. I still live in Brooklyn."

Luke scoffed. "You only moved there for that chick, the model. And you told me you guys broke up."

"But I'm still not moving back to California."

"Why not? All the work is here."

"I pick up plenty of work in New York."

"All the big *money* is here."

"I have plenty of money."

"But, Brooklyn, man. What the hell is keeping you *there?*"

"I'm with someone. It's important." That first part

was a lie, since Livie had just chucked him out of her life. But the second part was the absolute truth, he suddenly realized. Livie was important. She was fucking vital. *That* was the reason for this feeling he couldn't shake. That's why he felt panicky at the thought of never seeing her again. He hadn't just left Livie behind on her front stoop, he'd left a big, important part of himself behind, too. The better part of himself that Livie seemed to bring out—the unselfish part, the dependable part, the part of him who won over her family, who forgave his own.

And no matter what he did, no matter how far he ran, he wasn't ever going to feel whole again until he got them both back—Livie and that better version of himself.

"She's important?" Luke echoed.

Nick jerked, like he'd been scalded, and blinked at the monitors in front of him. What the hell was he doing here again?

"I'm in love with her." He heard the words from a distance, like somebody else had spoken them. *In love with her?* Where had that come from? Was he in love with her?

"You said that a year ago, when you met the flower chick."

"Poppy. I was wrong. I didn't know the first fucking thing about love."

"And now you do?" Luke sounded dubious.

"Now I do." Yes, he realized, now he knew exactly what love felt like. It felt like this.

Love. All this time, he'd been bending himself into knots trying to figure out if Poppy had ever loved him, whether he'd ever loved her. He'd been asking himself the wrong question. It didn't matter how he might have once felt about Poppy. All that mattered was how he now felt about Livie. And now, sitting here on the other side of the country, half-blind and punch-drunk with exhaustion, he knew the answer, without a shadow of a doubt. He *loved* Livie. And he'd just lost her. Fuck.

"Is this the space chick?"

"The what?"

"You said you were doing that Hubble telescope project with some science chick."

"Livie. Her name is Livie. I'm in love with Livie." Every time he said it, he was more certain. The feeling was expanding inside of him, flowing into all the dusty, unused corners of his heart. He'd never been as certain of anything as he was of this emotion—he was in love with Livie. And somehow, he was going to prove it to her and get her back.

Chapter Thirty-Nine

Outside of Langley's office on Monday morning, Livie steeled herself for the meeting, suppressing every unpleasant feeling she had about the man. This was business. The application for time on Hubble was finished. She'd spent the whole weekend polishing it to perfection. But she needed one critical thing before she could submit it—Janet's signature. And since that was impossible to get at the moment, she was going to suck it up and do something she really didn't want to do—she was going to ask Langley to sign off on it instead.

Taking a deep breath, she rapped smartly on his door. That was a confident knock. That was a knock that said, "I mean business."

"Come in," he called.

As always, his office was spotless, without a sign of his work anywhere. In fact, the place looked even more like something out of a movie. The thick Persian rug on the floor was new, as was the framed abstract painting on the wall behind Langley's desk. While he still didn't have a computer that looked capable of producing any serious scientific work, his laptop was new—tiny, sleek, and silver. Music was playing, something weird and instrumental, piped in from invisible speakers he must have recently had installed. There was a new brass nameplate on the edge of his desk. "Department Chair, Dr. William Langley." He certainly seemed to be settling in for the duration. Presumptuous jerk.

"Hi, Professor Langley. Can I have a minute?"

"What can I do for you, Miss Romano?"

She wasn't "Olivia" anymore, she was Miss Romano? Fine. She'd always hated the way he said her name anyway. "I'd like to talk to you about the situation with Dr. Finch."

He frowned slightly, his eyes still on his laptop. "Very unfortunate. Any update from her family?"

"Andy—that's her son—said she's still recovering."

"Terrible," he said, not sounding at all sorry.

"That's why I'm here. I've been doing the best I can to move the research forward without her, but there's only so much I can do with our current resources. It was our plan to apply for time on Hubble, but she didn't get a chance to complete the request before her heart attack."

"That's too bad." He still hadn't lifted his eyes from his laptop screen. Livie was about to reach out and slam the damned thing shut. But she still needed something from this useless asshole, as much as she hated it.

"Well, I've gone ahead and completed the application."

That did get his attention. His eyes snapped up to hers. "That's very industrious of you."

"I spoke to someone at NASA's outreach program for guidance. They've been very helpful. The problem is, I need Janet's signature on the application before I can submit it."

"That is a problem."

Now she was to the tough part. She absolutely hated asking this man for anything, but she had no choice if she wanted to keep working. And right now, she wanted—no, she *needed*—to keep working. "I was hoping you could sign off for her."

Langley frowned and leaned back in his chair, weaving his fingers together. "I'm afraid I can't do that."

Disappointment surged through her, but she wasn't backing down yet. This was too important. "Why not?"

"It's university policy, I'm afraid. No one other than the head of the research project may sign off on work related to that project."

"Not even the acting head of the department?"

"No, not even the head of the department." He left off the "acting" in his job description. That was no mistake. "It has to do with keeping the researchers accountable every step of the way. I'm sure you understand. If Finch had listed you as a research partner, it might be different. But as it is, you're just one of her students."

She wasn't just any student. She was Janet's *star* student. He was trying to put her in her place, to rub her nose in her powerlessness. Fury bubbled up in her chest. White-hot, impotent fury. Because no matter how much of a jerk Langley was, in this one way, he was right. She was powerless.

"What if I submit the request on my own? Not as part of Janet's research?"

"Without a comprehensive research proposal, it's doubtful a graduate student would get approved for a spot on Hubble. And since you can't use Finch's work, I'm afraid you don't have enough on your own to justify the spot."

He smiled then, a thin, slightly smug smile, as he leaned back in his chair. Livie clenched her back teeth together so hard it hurt. He could sign off on her application if he wanted to, she knew it. The bastard was perfectly willing to bend the rules when he wanted Janet to pay for his equipment with her grant money, but suddenly he was all about the rules if it meant screwing her over.

"You're telling me I can't move forward until Janet is back?"

He made a show of frowning, like he was actually sympathetic with her plight. "You're a bright student, Miss Romano. One of our best. I'm sure you'll think of something."

The best. She was the department's best student and he knew it. Maybe she'd been too self-effacing in the past to admit that, but not anymore. She *knew* how good she was. Langley had all but admitted it himself when he tried to get her to abandon Janet's research for his.

In a flash, it all became so clear. It had nothing to do with rules, or even Janet, really. This was about her. She'd turned him down and now he was punishing her. He was *enjoying* watching her PhD go down in flames, almost as much as he was enjoying his power over the whole department. For once, he was the king around here, and he was loving the hell out of it.

"I'm sure I will," Livie bit out from between clenched teeth.

"Good luck, Miss Romano. And give Professor Finch's family my best when you speak to them again."

He could pick up the phone and call them himself, but she knew he wouldn't. "Sure. Thanks for your time."

"My door is always open for you," he said magnanimously as she stood.

She had no intention of ever willingly stepping foot in his office again. Never in her life had she had an urge to commit physical violence. Maybe it was her frustration at this injustice. Maybe it was leftover anger and grief over Nick. But right now she wanted to plant her fist square in Langley's face. The urge was so strong that she was practically shaking with it. But her position in this department was precarious and getting worse by the day. Violence—even a well-earned display of temper—wouldn't help, and would only make things worse for her.

Even though it felt like swallowing glass, she smiled at Langley as she left his office.

She was still in a daze as she walked down the hall.

Everything was for nothing. Months of working with Nick on a program that they'd never be able to use, for research that was never going to happen. Maybe it would have been better if she'd never met him, if none of this had ever happened, if this was how it was going to turn out.

No. As terrible as she felt—and if she allowed herself to think about him for even a second, the grief punched her so hard she could barely breathe—but she still couldn't regret having met him, having loved him. He'd changed her life. Yes, in an awful way, by breaking her heart. But also in a million good ways. Maybe Teresa was right, and one day she'd be able to look back without pain and appreciate that.

She was barely aware of what she did as she entered the departmental office and made her way to her mail cubby.

"Hi, Livie," Anita called from behind her desk in the corner.

"Hi, Anita."

Michiko was riffling through a stack of flyers by her mail cubby. She paused, looking up at Livie. "Hey, you okay? You look like your dog died."

Spudge had not died this week. That was about the

only piece of good news Livie could come up with at present.

"Um, it's been kind of a crappy week."

Michiko's lips quirked to the side as she considered that. "Is it school or life? Or should I not ask?"

Once, Livie would have made some polite demurral and escaped. She was not one to share herself with strangers. But that was once, and she wasn't the same as she used to be. Besides, Michiko wasn't exactly a stranger, was she?

"Both. But right now, school is the major problem. Langley won't sign off on my application for time on Hubble. Without that, Janet's research is dead in the water. And so am I."

"Why won't he sign off on it? I mean, I know she's supposed to, but under the circumstances, I'm sure he could make an exception."

Livie's anger flared anew. "He *could*. I *know* he could. But he won't, because he's an asshole and he's punishing me because I won't work on his stupid research."

Michiko blinked in shock at her sudden outburst. Anita chuckled.

Livie squeezed her eyes shut as she rubbed a hand across her forehead. "Sorry, you guys. It's been a bad few days."

"That's okay. You really think this is personal? That Langley has it out for you?"

"He's got it out for me *and* Janet."

"Professor Finch? Why?"

A few months ago, Livie never would have shared what she'd heard between Janet and Langley. There would have been no one to tell, for one. And she would have felt obligated to protect their privacy, to not insert herself in a conflict that didn't involve her. But that was a few months ago. It clearly involved her now, and it wasn't right. Fuck Langley's privacy. Why should she keep his secrets?

She told Michiko the gist of the fight she'd walked in on the day Janet collapsed.

"Daaamn," Michiko said when she'd finished. "I knew I didn't trust that son of a bitch."

"I never liked him," Anita chimed in. "Never trust a man who wears loafers without socks in the middle of winter."

"It's just a departmental rivalry," Livie said. "I'm caught up in the middle of it."

"I'm not so sure about that," Michiko said, casting a glance over her shoulder at Anita.

Livie looked between the two of them. "What are you talking about?"

Anita made a huge show of turning her attention to her computer monitor. "I'm busy going over this office supply request. I'm sure I'd never notice if that master key on the edge of my desk disappeared for a few minutes."

Livie watched, wide-eyed, as Michiko scampered across the room and snatched the key off Anita's desk.

"Come with me." Michiko grabbed her by the elbow and steered her out of the office.

"Where are we going?"

"Peter Hockman's office."

"Why the hell are we going there?" In the last twenty-four hours, Livie seemed to have lost both her filter and her aversion to cursing. She didn't miss either one.

They'd reached the hallway that led to Peter's office. It also led to the men's room, so Michiko hung back, watching casually from the corner until a freshman kid carrying a huge backpack wandered out of the men's room and around the corner.

"Come on. We'll be quick."

"What are we doing?"

Michiko unlocked Peter's door and flipped the lights on. "Take a look."

Well, it was a mess, for starters. And not simply the clutter that sometimes accompanied the mind of a genius. It was *dirty*. There were empty takeout containers, soda bottles, and candy wrappers littering the floor.

"Did you bring me here to show me Peter's a slob? Because I already knew that."

"No, Livie, *look*." Michiko pointed to his desk.

Sitting on the corner was a brand new high-end color printer. It was a specialized model, used for printing out the kind of images generated by deep space telescopes. It retailed for thousands of dollars. There was also a new thirty-inch high resolution monitor. That clocked in at four thousand dollars. Livie knew what they cost because she'd priced them out and included them in the budget for Janet's research. They'd never been able to buy any of the equipment, though, because Janet had gotten sick before she'd signed off on the purchases.

"Where did he get this equipment?"

"That's a very good question, don't you think?"

"Do you think—"

"That Langley is skimming off Finch's grant money? What do you think, Livie?"

A few months ago, she'd have said absolutely not. She didn't like the guy, but there was no way he'd do something so underhanded, so flat-out wrong. But she wasn't that I anymore. And she wouldn't put a goddamned thing past Langley.

"I think I need to figure out how to play hardball."

Chapter Forty

For all the time Livie had spent at school with Janet, she'd never been to her house. She hadn't even known where she'd lived. How had she worked so closely with someone and been this disconnected personally? It was no different than Michiko. She'd spent two years alongside Michiko, but hadn't exchanged more than a couple of words with her until this year. It turned out Michiko was great. Brilliant, funny, and definitely a person you wanted in your corner.

Janet lived in a pretty two-story house in Ditmas Park. The neighborhood was a suburban oasis in the middle of Brooklyn, with quiet, tree-lined streets and large, well-tended Victorian houses. The Finch house was white, with a wide front porch and leaded glass windows.

Yesterday, after her terrible meeting with Langley and Michiko's subsequent revelations, she'd texted Andy Finch, telling him she really needed to speak to his mother. His response had been to invite her over the next day. And now here she was, about to see Janet and tell her everything that was happening in the department. Maybe she wasn't yet well enough to come back and fight the battle herself, but hopefully she could tell Livie what to do, give her some insight into how to handle it.

Andy opened the door, smiling, but tired.

"Hi, Livie, come on in. Dad had to be at a thesis defense today. He's sorry to miss you."

"Oh, that's okay. What about you? Don't you have work?"

"I've taken a leave of absence to help with Mom."

A tremor of unease trickled down her spine. Janet still needed that much help?

Janet's house was a typical academic's house, overstuffed bookshelves everywhere, mostly classics and literature, which Livie assumed belonged to her husband. Janet had always generated clutter, so it didn't surprise Livie that her house was the same explosion of stuff as her office. But there was something different about this clutter. It wasn't the product of a brilliant mind racing far ahead of any human's ability to keep up. This felt like lives in chaos.

Papers were stacked high on the dining room table, sharing space with empty takeout containers. Unopened mail littered the table inside the front door. Random pieces of medical equipment—plastic bags of tubing and syringes, sharps containers, pill bottles—were scattered over numerous surfaces. Andy and his father were barely hanging on.

"Thanks for coming, Livie. I know Mom will be happy to see you. It's this way."

She followed Andy up the stairs and down the hall to a bedroom.

He stopped at the closed door and turned back. "Livie, you should know, she's not herself."

"I'm sure. It was a serious heart attack."

"I just don't want you to be shocked. After the stroke, there were deficits."

Deficits? "What kind of deficits? Will she get better?"

"It's hard to say. With the brain, there's never any predicting."

Brain deficits. Dr. Janet Finch. The most brilliant woman Livie had ever met. Before she'd fully grasped the implications of that, Andy opened the door and ushered her inside. "Hi, Mom. Look who's come to see you. It's Livie."

A hospital bed dominated the room, along with a forest of medical equipment crowding the edges. In the middle of the massive bed, propped up, was Janet. She'd always been small, but now she was a shadow of her former self. Her face was all cheekbones and hollow eyes, and her hands, withered and gnarled, rested on the blanket. Her body barely made a lump under the covers. Her hair had been salt and pepper the last time Livie had seen her, more brown than gray. It was almost all gray now, thin and wispy.

A flare of her old panic resurfaced, Livie's terror of hospitals, of people lying helplessly in beds. That dread of looking death in the face. But she couldn't give in to it this time. Nick wasn't going to come hold her hand and help her through it. She had to do it on her own.

Tentatively, she took a step closer to the bed. Janet looked decades older. How long would it take for her to come back from this? *Could* she?

"Hi, Janet," she said.

Andy pointed to a chair placed near the head of the bed, so she sat. Janet's eyes tracked her across the room, like she was trying to place her. That wasn't immediately alarming. Janet had always operated on another plane. She was easily distracted and hard to bring back to earth.

Suddenly, her expression brightened. *This is it*, Livie thought. *She's back.* But then she opened her mouth and no words came out. Instead, it was sound, garbled, half-formed. It might have been her name, but it was impossible to tell. Livie's blood ran cold.

"She's still having a hard time with speech," Andy said. That was putting it very, very mildly. She couldn't speak at all. Andy patted his mother's hand. "Yes, Mom, Livie came to visit. You're glad to see her, right?"

She was still trying to talk and failing, her mouth opening and closing helplessly, a string of gurgling and moans the only sound she was able to produce. Her hands were twitching on the blanket. It was horrible to watch. Livie started talking, to end the terrible tension. "Don't worry about the research. I'm keeping up with everything until you get back. Everything is fine."

That was a total lie, she realized now. It hit her like a physical blow. Everything everyone had been trying to warn her about was true. Janet was never coming back. Her research would remain forever unfinished.

Janet raised a hand and gestured at Andy. Her fingers were cramped up sideways into claws. Something like a word came out of her mouth, but Livie couldn't understand it. Andy did, though. He grasped his mother's hand and squeezed.

"Yes, Mom, it's Livie."

She looked at Livie, and for a second, there was a flash of recognition, of the warmth that had been there before, but it was trapped inside this unwilling shell of her body, like something in a frozen lake, unable to reach the surface.

Livie felt her eyes prick with tears, and she reached

for Janet's free hand. Her withered fingers clutched helplessly at Livie's. "It's so good to see you, Janet," she whispered. Then she forced herself to talk, about anything and everything—the approaching holidays, the weather—anything except what was really important. She didn't mention school again, or the Skylight grant, or their research, or Professor Langley. Because it no longer mattered, at least to Janet. That was all part of her past. This was her life now, and it would be for as long as she lived. Everything else was now Livie's problem to solve.

When her eyes began to drift closed, Andy tapped Livie on the shoulder. "We're going to let you rest, Mom."

Livie gave her hand one last squeeze before setting it gently back on the blanket. Then she followed Andy outside. He closed the door behind them. They stood in silence for a moment, Livie stunned, Andy exhausted and sad.

"Come downstairs and have a cup of coffee," he said eventually.

Ten minutes later, they were sitting at the cluttered dining room table, Livie's hands curled around a cup of coffee she couldn't bring herself to drink.

"I came to see if she was ready to wade into some departmental stuff that's been happening. But I can see that's not going to happen."

Andy looked up with tired eyes. "What's going on?"

Livie gave him a brief rundown of the situation—how she hadn't been able to move forward on Janet's research without her there to sign off on major proposals and purchases. She also told him about Langley being made Acting Chair in Janet's absence, and her suspicions that he was somehow skimming from her grant money.

"That fucking Langley," Andy said. "He's always been such a dick."

"Agreed."

Andy was quiet for a moment, thinking. Then he sat back in his chair and reached up under his glasses to rub his bloodshot eyes. "She's not coming back, Livie."

She swallowed thickly. Her throat felt raw with unshed tears. "I've pretty much figured that out."

He looked so tired and grief-stricken, and suddenly Livie felt unbearably selfish. "I'm sorry, Andy. None of that stuff at school is important. Her health is all that matters now."

Andy smiled sadly. "Her work was the most important thing in her life. I can't tell how much she remembers, but if she remembers that black hole research, then it's killing her that she can't follow through on it now."

"I know. It's killing me, too. It's not fair."

Andy sat forward, folding his hands together on the table. "Livie, you should know, she thought the world of you."

Livie's eyes burned as she fought back tears. Janet was alive upstairs, but it felt like they were sharing condolences at her funeral. "It's nice to hear that. Thanks."

"I didn't tell you to make you feel better. You know how much this research meant to her. She was so excited when you decided to come to Adams, because she wanted you to work on it with her. Livie, it shouldn't just die. Dad and I have been discussing it and we're in full agreement. We want you to take her research and move forward with it. We'd thought you could do it at Adams, but it doesn't seem like Langley's going to let that happen. So use it to get yourself into a new program. Take the work she's done and run with it. We'll give you our full endorsement on Mom's behalf. With her work, any program in the country would want you. MIT, McArthur."

The two programs she'd turned down to stay in Brooklyn, to go to Adams and work with Janet.

In a flash of clarity, of miserable self-awareness, Nick's words from their fight came back to her. She'd chosen Adams for Janet, it was true. But he was *right*— she'd also chosen it out of fear. All this time, she'd been convincing herself that she was getting what she wanted, when really, she was just settling for what was safe. She was passing up amazing opportunities because the prospect of change of any kind terrified her. She was such a coward.

All her life, she'd been erecting invisible barricades for herself out of fear. And if she didn't figure out a way to break through them, then Janet's research would die here with her. Livie's future would wither and die, too.

"What if she improves and wants to be a part of it later?"

"That's not going to happen. We'll be lucky if she ever gets out of that bed again. And between you and me? Langley's going to torpedo that research any way he can, because it was Mom's. He's always resented her."

The enormity of what Andy was suggesting finally began to sink in. He wanted her to take Janet's research to another school and carry on without her. Suddenly it felt hard to breathe.

"But the grant money. It was hers. It was for the work."

He shook his head. "I can't help you there. It's up to Skylight if they'll let you keep her grant. But I can tell you one thing. If Langley's figured out a way to tap into it, he'll make sure you never see a dime for this project as long as you're at Adams and under his thumb."

Livie knew he was right. Langley would block the research at every turn. He'd make sure she never had a chance.

"Mom would want you to move on without her, Livie. The work was always the most important thing to her, not this departmental political bullshit. Take her work and finish it. Make a name for yourself. You're the only one who can. It would make her so proud."

"It's not right that Langley is doing this."

Andy sighed. "No, it's not. And if you can figure out a way to bust him for it before you go, I wouldn't complain. She's always hated the little shit. But I can't waste time worrying about him now. And neither can you. Get out of here, Livie. Take care of your own future. Make something of Mom's work, since she can't."

Chapter Forty-One

When Livie arrived home after her miserable visit with Janet, the house was quiet and empty. Dad and Gemma were at the bar and Jess was at work. There was only Spudge, crashed out in his favorite sunny spot by the back door.

She sat down at the kitchen table, trying to process everything that had happened. Could she do it? Could she really take Janet's research and start over someplace else? Logistically, it was probably an option. She'd been on very good terms with the dean of the Astronomy department at McArthur while she'd been applying. He still emailed her now and then, to see how her work was coming along. She was a strong candidate all on her own, but if she would be bringing Janet's research with her? If she reached out to him and explained her situation, she suspected she'd be enrolled at McArthur and back to work when the new semester started in January.

But was that what she wanted? To leave? To move to Colorado and start a whole new life? It was a terrifying prospect. A year ago, she'd have said absolutely not. Even considering it would have been impossible. But as she'd discovered lately, a lot had changed in the past year. She wasn't content anymore to hide herself away where she was safe—where she'd always been safe.

Safe had gotten her here—living at home, right where she'd started, academic career in shambles. But taking chances...she'd taken exactly one chance. She reached out for Nick instead of playing it safe. And sure, she hadn't held on to him—that was never in the cards. But for a little while, he'd been hers, and it had changed everything. What else might happen if she quit playing it so goddamned safe all the time and took a chance?

The daylight faded and night fell. She didn't move to turn on any lights. She sat in the darkness and thought about her life, all the choices she'd made—and hadn't made—that had led her to this point.

She was still there, sitting in the dark, hours later, when Gemma and Jess returned together. They were laughing about something, some funny incident that had happened at the bar when Jess had stopped in after work.

Gemma flipped on the kitchen light and yelped when she spotted Livie at the table.

"Jesus Christ, Livie, you took ten years off my life. Why the hell are you sitting here in the dark?"

"I've been doing some thinking."

Jess sat down next to her, reaching for her hand. "Is it about Nick?"

"Ugh," Gemma growled. "Don't even mention that asshole's name."

"It's not about him," Livie said. "And what happened wasn't his fault."

Gemma stomped over to the counter and retrieved wineglasses. "Excuse me? He ditched you and ran out of here so fast, you'd have thought the house was on fire. Didn't even say goodbye. And all for some dumb job. I knew that guy was trouble. I knew he'd break your heart."

When she set one down in front of Livie, she didn't bother to remind her sister that she didn't drink. Maybe tonight she did? Why not? New Livie might do all kinds of things Old Livie would never have considered. Actually, she was looking forward to finding out all about New Livie. She took a sip of wine. It sort of sucked. Okay, New Livie still didn't drink.

"Gemma, I went into it with my eyes wide open. I knew exactly who he was. I knew what he was capable of and what he wasn't. And guess what? I was right. If I got my heart broken, that's on me. I'm not spending another minute crying over him anyway." Would she ever feel as confident as she sounded? Teresa had told her it would happen. If she kept moving forward, focusing on her own life, her own work, her heart would eventually take care of itself, right? God, she hoped so.

"Good for you," Jess said fiercely.

"I have bigger problems than some guy."

Gemma set her wine down. "Like what?"

Livie filled her sisters in on everything that had been happening at school, finishing with Andy Finch's extraordinary offer this afternoon.

"Oh, Livie, I can't believe this. You really think Langley's taking the grant money?" Jess's eyes were lit up with a familiar spark. She smelled injustice and she was ready to tear down the world to right it.

"I can't prove it. And if I accuse him, I doubt it'll go anywhere. He's now the head of the department and I'm just a grad student. He'll probably turn it around and make me out to be some jealous underling." Now that she'd figured him out, Langley's actions were so clear to her. How had she ever given that asshole the benefit of the doubt?

"This isn't fair," Gemma fumed. "You shouldn't have to change schools because of him."

Livie took a deep breath and looked at both of her sisters. Leaving them would be the hardest part of all. "It's not just about Langley. It's about me, too."

"What do you mean?"

"You know I had other choices for graduate school."

"Yeah," Jess said. "MIT accepted you, right?"

"And McArthur."

"But you picked Adams because of Finch," Gemma pointed out.

"That's true." She swallowed hard. Admitting it to herself had been hard enough. Admitting it to her sisters? Brutal. "But I also picked it because I was scared. Because I didn't want to leave."

Jess and Gemma both looked back at her in silence. Then Gemma's eyes filled with tears. "Oh, babe, why would you do that to yourself?"

"I didn't realize I was." She didn't want to tell her sisters that it was Nick's accusations that sparked her revelation. They hated him enough already. "We lost Mom so quickly. And our whole family changed overnight."

Gemma swiped at her nose and Jess sniffed loudly.

"But once we were past the worst, and we were still standing, Dad and the three of us, I didn't want it to change any more. I was *afraid* of it changing again."

Jess reached for her hand, squeezing hard. "Livie, you're too smart to hold yourself back this way."

"I know. I know that now. Janet gave me the reason I was looking for to stay. But she's…well, she's gone now. And I need to do what's best for me."

Jess and Gemma exchanged a glance. It hung there,

unspoken in the quiet kitchen. Livie missed them so much already, and she hadn't even left yet.

Then Gemma set a hand on her shoulder. "Then that means you have to go, babe."

Chapter Forty-Two

Nick ended up staying three more days in San Jose. He wanted to leave the instant his feelings had flattened him like a bulldozer, but as much as he hated it, he'd committed to getting the stupid site up, and bailing on Luke would have been a dick move. The minute they launched their first successful test, though, he packed up and left, leaving Luke to clean up the rest of the little details.

In the cab at JFK, he gave the driver the Romanos' address first, forgetting for a second that he didn't live there anymore. He had to retrieve the address of his new place from his email.

Once he arrived, he dumped his backpack and surveyed it. He didn't know shit about interior design, but the place looked amazing—transformed. The furniture was all neutral and plush, with colorful rugs and throw pillows to keep it from looking too sterile. Unlike that hard leather couch in his old place—the one Poppy was in love with—this one looked actually comfortable to sit on. He still couldn't tell if it was taupe or sand, but he liked it.

The thing he liked best was that it undeniably looked like his place, even though he'd had no idea what his home would look like. *He* couldn't figure out what that looked like, but somehow those Romanos had. There was a time perceptiveness like that would have had him frantically searching for an exit, desperate to put some distance between him and anybody who might get close enough to really know him. But he was done with running.

Only one thing gave him pause. When he opened the door to what would be his office, expecting it to be empty, all his computer equipment was already there and set up. He'd left it all at the Romanos'. And apparently, they'd brought it back, severing his last tie with them. It was a punch to the gut, another reminder that he might have broken things beyond repair, on many fronts.

Well, the beautifully decorated apartment gave him exactly the opening he needed. He'd been trying to call Livie for three days to no avail. Either she was ignoring his calls or she'd blocked him.

But if he couldn't reach one Romano sister, he'd try another, and now he had a perfect excuse.

Gemma didn't pick up right away, and for a second, he was afraid she might have blocked him, too, but right before it rolled to voice mail, she spoke.

"What the hell do you want?"

"The apartment looks great, Gemma. Thank you."

She snorted in disgust. "How's California?"

"Over. I'm back. That's why I called. I'm looking for Livie, but I think she blocked my number."

Gemma's voice was steely with fury. "Oh, that's just great. You ditch my sister and fly away to California without a second thought and think you can sail back in and pick right back up where you left off. Meanwhile Livie's been here handling all this shit on her own—"

"Handling what shit? What's happened?"

"Nothing that has anything to do with you."

"Gemma, come on. Is she okay?"

"The professor she was building her career around is never coming back, her entire PhD is hanging in the balance, and some jackass who's got it out for her is stealing the grant money she busted her ass off to get. But it's nothing you need to worry about. Her *family* has her back."

"Are you talking about Langley? He's *stealing* the grant money?"

She huffed, muttering, "Not that she can prove it."

"Look, is she there? Let me talk to her. Please."

"No!" she snapped, with an awful finality. "Don't come near her. She's doing okay. Better than I thought she'd be after you ditched her." Nick was tempted to point out that Livie had actually been the one to do the breaking up, but he was pretty sure Gemma would bite his head off if he did. "The last thing Livie needs is you messing with her head again. Not when she's got so many other problems to deal with."

"Gemma, I'm sorry. You have to believe me. I never meant to hurt her."

"Well, you did."

"I know I made a mistake, but…" Somehow he didn't expect that he'd be making this confession to Luke and then to Gemma before he ever said it to Livie, but life was funny that way. "I love her. I'll do whatever it takes to convince her of that."

Gemma was silent for so long he was afraid she'd ended the call. "You love her."

"Yeah. I didn't realize that until I was gone, until we were over. I know, I know, I'm an idiot."

"I'm not arguing with you on that one."

"I want to make it up to her. I will, I promise."

She sighed, the anger draining out of her voice. "I'm not sure you're going to get that chance, Nick. She's leaving."

"What? Where is she going?"

"She hasn't made up her mind yet, but it's all over for her at Adams. It's time for her to start over somewhere else."

The wheels started turning in his mind. He needed to do something to prove to Livie how much he cared. He'd just figured out what that was. And he was going to relish doing it.

"Fuck that. If she *wants* to leave, fine. But no puffed up, loafer-wearing asshole is going to force her out. Not if I have anything to say about it."

"What are you talking about, Nick?"

"I'm fixing this. I'm in. All in. With you, too. I'm gonna win you over, Gem. You watch."

"But—"

"Look, you tell her I'm coming for her as soon as I figure this out."

Gemma sighed again. "I have no idea what you're planning, Evil Genius, but good luck, I guess. Don't do anything stupid."

"Oh, Gem, doing something stupid is about all that's going to work."

Chapter Forty-Three

"Thanks for coming to help, Michiko."

Michiko, crouched on the floor in front of Janet's bookshelves, flashed a bright smile over her shoulder. "Any time, Livie. I'm happy to help out a friend."

She hefted another stack of books into the box beside her.

Another revelation from the past few days—Michiko was her *friend*. She had a friend who wasn't related to her by blood. At least this revelation was a good one.

All this time, she'd been happy to hide in the safe cocoon of her family, convinced that was all she needed or wanted. It turned out, family wasn't always enough, and there were other people out there willing to give you a hand, if you let them. Like Michiko. Like Teresa.

The semester was ending in a couple of weeks, and Livie had things to do before it was done. The first was packing up Janet's office for Andy. He had his hands full with his mother. The last thing he needed was to have to come in and deal with the chaos of her books and papers.

The second was sorting through her research files, which she was doing now, while Michiko tackled the bookshelves.

And when she was done here, she had one more stop to make—at the dean's office.

Michiko sat back on her heels holding a book on particle physics in one hand and a book on planetary geology in the other. "Is there, like, a system to this I should be preserving?"

"Chaos. Janet's shelving system was always 'chaos.'" She missed her with an ache that felt physical. But Janet wasn't coming back. She'd finally faced it. The best she could do for Janet now was to preserve her legacy.

After she'd dumped another armful of books into the box and taped it shut, Michiko stood, dusting off her hands. "Okay, I'm dragging this last load of books down to Anita's office then I'll be back to start on the file cabinets."

"Thanks, Michiko."

Livie turned her attention back to the computer screen, clicking through Janet's research files, saving to her flash drive anything she'd need to carry on the research. There was a lot to wade through. Janet had been working on her theory for nearly a decade.

"What are you doing in here?"

Livie looked up to find Peter Hockman's bulky form filling up the doorway. A few months ago, Livie might have flushed and started babbling, apologizing for existing, even though she had every right to be here. But that was a few months ago. Now she barely spared a glance for Peter as she turned back to her work.

"What does it look like I'm doing? I'm packing up Janet's office."

"You're on her office computer?"

"Peter, your powers of observation are staggering. Has anyone ever told you that?" She had no idea where all this snark had suddenly come from, but she wasn't complaining. It felt great to say exactly what she was thinking for once, instead of having the words finally come to her half an hour later. Maybe it was because she knew she was leaving. She'd already lost everything here. Nothing that happened, nothing that anyone could say or do, mattered anymore. She was free.

Peter's eyes went wide as she leaned down to swap out the flash drive for a new empty one. "Are you downloading her files?"

"Will your brilliance never end?" Baiting Peter Hockman was a blast. Why hadn't she ever done this before? Oh, right. Fear. Well, she was all done with fear.

"You shouldn't be doing that. Professor Langley should be the only one accessing her files. You know, as the department head."

"*Acting* department head. Janet isn't dead yet, no matter how hard Langley wishes she were."

"He's not going to like you in here pawing through her stuff."

"Then he can take it up with Janet's husband, since he gave me her office keys, her passwords, and his blessing to take whatever the hell I want."

"He did?"

"He did." She took a moment to lean back in the chair and grin smugly at Peter. Being a cocky asshole was *fun*. No wonder Nick was so good at it.

"What do you need all that for anyway? It's not like you can keep working on her research without her."

"You're right," she conceded. "I can't keep working on her research *here*."

"Then what are you going to do with it?"

She locked eyes with Peter, because she *really* didn't want to miss Peter's reaction when she dropped her bombshell on him. "I'm taking Janet's research with me to McArthur, and I'm going to work on it there."

Livie reveled in the shock spreading across his face. "What?"

"I'll go slow and use small words, so you can follow me. I'm transferring to McArthur. And I'm taking Janet's research with me. They can't wait to have me. They've offered me the full and unflagging support of the entire department. So you and Langley can take your interstellar medium bullshit and shove it up your asses where it belongs."

Oh that felt *amazing*. She should have tried being a bitch years ago.

"Y-you can't do that!" Peter sputtered.

Livie looked around herself with exaggerated surprise. "Really? Because it's already done. I'm starting in January."

"What about Adams?"

"Adams, and Langley, can kiss my ass."

"You can't take her work, though! Langley was going to—"

He cut himself off abruptly and Livie sat back, staring at him as it clicked in her mind. Oh, why was she so slow to pick up on other peoples' shitty motivations? But she was getting better, thanks to Nick. Her days of naively believing in people who didn't deserve it were over.

"Langley was going to publish her research himself, wasn't he?"

Peter swallowed hard. His skin had gone pasty. Well, pastier. Peter looked like a raw potato under the best of circumstances.

Livie scoffed, turning back to the computer screen and copying a few more files. "Like that intellectual featherweight could even *dream* of completing her research. Well, he's not getting the chance to try, because it's going with me."

Peter found his voice again. "I'm sure there are university regulations about Finch's work."

"I checked those university regulations, and actually, with her approval, I can take whatever I want. Which I have, through her husband, who now has power of attorney over all her affairs. Husband. Keys. Passwords. Blessing. Remember? Keep up, Peter."

Peter lifted his hands and dropped them again helplessly. "I can't believe you're doing this."

"You can't believe I'm not sticking around here to watch Langley torpedo my career? That's very unimaginative of you."

"Well, Peter is pretty slow, you know."

Peter spun around to face Michiko, who'd slipped up behind him at some point.

"Figures you'd be in on this, too, Satsuma."

She sneered up at him. "Move aside, Hock-a-Loogey. We've got work to do."

"Langley's not going to be happy when he hears about this."

"Probably not," Livie replied. "Why don't you be a good boy and run and tell him?"

Michiko snorted in laughter. "That's all he's good for anyway."

"Langley's in Paris," Peter muttered angrily.

Livie looked at Michiko and raised her eyebrows. "Paris, huh? That sounds like a pretty fancy trip."

Michiko tapped her chin. "And wasn't he skiing in Switzerland two weeks ago?"

Livie clicked on a few more files. "Guess he's doing pretty well for himself these days, what with the new laptop, and the fancy painting in his office. He seems to be *really* good at stretching that professor's salary."

Peter's cheeks went ruddy as he realized that he'd inadvertently said too much again. He really was colossally stupid. It was criminal he'd ever been admitted to the program.

"I'm telling him about all of this as soon as he gets back."

"I'm sure you will, Peter. Now do you mind? We're busy."

Michiko peered around the door frame, watching Peter stomp off down the hall, before she collapsed into giggles. "Oh my God, that was so awesome. His face!"

"You should have seen him when I told him I was transferring to McArthur."

"I bet it was epic!" Michiko crowed. Then she sobered. "This sucks. I mean, I'm really happy for you, Livie. You're going to do amazing things at McArthur. But I'm going to miss you."

And Livie realized she was going to miss Michiko, too. Scrambling out of her chair, she rounded the desk and pulled Michiko into a hug. She'd wasted *so* much time, missed so many opportunities, because she held herself back, never looking up, never connecting to the people around her. When she got to McArthur, she wasn't making the same mistake. "I'm going to miss you, too."

Chapter Forty-Four

The adrenaline rush from facing down Peter Hockman had all but evaporated by the time she reached the dean's office that afternoon. But her courage hadn't, and that was all she needed.

She didn't harbor any naive belief that talking to the dean was going to help. Sometimes the good guys won, but not always. Sometimes the bad guys had more power and knew how to rig the game. She understood that now. Langley was a tenured professor, and even though she thought he was a slimy kiss-up, lots of other powerful people at Adams had been fooled by him. He'd already shown he was willing to tank her academic career as punishment when she wouldn't work for him. She didn't doubt he'd make up any number of lies to discredit her and anything she had to say about him.

So, yeah, she might not be able to stop Langley, but there was no way she'd go quietly.

The outer office was empty when she came in, aside from the dean's secretary, sitting behind a desk. She was a slight woman in her fifties with a salt-and-pepper pixie haircut. She looked up as Livie came in. "Can I help you with something?"

Livie shut the door behind her. "Yes, I have an appointment with Dean Haverman at 3:30. Olivia Romano."

She checked the schedule on her computer monitor. "Here you are. Have a seat, Miss Romano. He had to take an unexpected meeting and it's running a little late."

But before Livie could take a seat in one of the chairs the secretary motioned to, the door behind her—the one that presumably led to the dean's office—opened.

And Nick walked out.

He was looking back over his shoulder at the dean, who was still talking to him.

"Thank you for the information, Mr. DeSantis. We're going to take steps immediately."

"Looks like they're done after all," the secretary said brightly. "You can go on in, Miss Romano."

Livie's mind spun as she tried to understand what was happening. Nick was back? And taking a meeting with the dean of Adams U? What the hell was going on here?

"Nick? What are you doing here?"

He turned back, and his face lit up with a smile. "There you are."

Then, as she stood there gaping at him in confusion, he closed the distance between them, took her face in his hands, and kissed her.

For a minute, she forgot they didn't do this anymore. Or maybe it was more accurate to say she didn't care. Since he'd left, she didn't let herself think about him. She refused to remember. If she'd started thinking back on their time together, she'd have crumpled up in a ball of misery and grief. She'd ruthlessly shoved every thought of Nick into a mental strongbox and hidden it deep in her brain.

But this kiss brought it all back. That box was dragged back up into the light and the padlock was blown clear off, allowing Nick, and every intoxicating thing about him, to surge back in and drown her. It had only been a week but she'd missed every single thing— the feel of his mouth on hers, his hands on her body. She'd missed the way his hair felt under her fingers, and the rasp of his breathing when he kissed her, and his smell. It had been less than a week since he'd left, but it felt like she'd been missing him for a thousand years.

This was what she'd been desperately trying to out-run. It had caught up to her, and she was left devastated by it, this longing for him.

With a gasp, she pushed him away, but Nick didn't let her go. His fingertips were massaging the base of her skull through her hair, and sending little zips of pleasure shooting through her body. Stupid body, not even caring that he'd left her and probably would again.

"What are you doing, Nick?"

"I thought that was obvious. I'm kissing you."

"Why?"

"Because I love you."

Surely this is when she would wake up. Or she'd snap out of whatever delusional daydream she'd fallen into and find herself sitting in one of those waiting room chairs, alone.

But Nick was still there, still holding her face in his hands, still looking into her eyes with an intensity that made it hard to breathe.

"I don't understand."

"I didn't either, and for that, I'm sorry. I'm so sorry, Livie. As soon as I realized I'd lost you, I also realized I loved you. You know me, I'm a genius, but sometimes I'm really dumb."

"You love me," she repeated, the words not feeling any more real from her own lips than they had from his.

"I love you." His expression was so earnest, so sincere. Somewhere deep inside the concrete and steel bunker she'd hidden it in for safekeeping, her heart cracked wide open. When she tried to breathe, her throat closed up, and she let out a tiny, strangled sound, somewhere between a gasp and a sob.

Nick's eyes softened as he drew her closer again, kissing her forehead, then her cheek, then the corner of her mouth. "I love you," he whispered. "I love you so much, Livie."

Her fingers fisted in his shirt as he kissed her again. This time she let it drag her under, opening her mouth to him when he urged her lips apart, and meeting his tongue with her own. He moaned into her mouth, releasing her face, wrapping his arms around her, and hauling her in close.

She might have happily lived out the rest of her life in that one spot, kissing Nick, if someone clearing their throat nearby hadn't shocked her back to reality. The dean was still standing in the doorway to his office, the expression on his craggy face somewhere between exasperated and amused. His secretary had her hands clutched to her chest as she stared up at Livie and Nick with hearts in her eyes.

"Why did you come here, Nick?"

"Because I love you."

"No, really."

"Really. I love you and I wasn't about to let anyone get away with hurting you if there was something I could do about it. And it turned out, there was something I could do about it." He glanced back at the dean, who nodded.

"I don't understand."

"Well—"

But before he could say more, there was a knock on the outer office door.

Nick's eyes cut toward the door. "That's probably my ride. I gotta go."

The door opened and two men in dark suits stepped in. One held up a badge in a billfold. "FBI. We're looking for Nicholas DeSantis?"

Livie turned back to Nick, who didn't look the least bit surprised to see them there.

"Nick, what's going on? Why are they looking for you?"

"Right here, guys. One second." He took her face in his hands again. "Livie, I'm sorry. The last thing I want to do right now is to disappear again, but it can't be helped."

What the hell was he talking about? All she knew was that the FBI wouldn't be here looking for him just to say hello. She was nearly light-headed with panic. "Nick, what—"

"I don't know how long I'm going to be gone, and I don't know if I'll be able to contact you. I know I can't ask you to wait for me, and I'm not going to. It wouldn't be fair. But know this—I love you and I'm coming back for you, no matter how long it takes me. The rest, well, it's all up to you."

Then he kissed her again. Hard, like he was trying to imprint himself on her that way. He didn't need to worry. Nick's kiss was pressed into her soul, along with the rest of him. Long before she was ready to let him go, he released her and stepped back.

The two FBI guys were advancing toward him. He

turned to face them. "You don't need to cuff me or anything. I'll come."

Cuff him? "Nick, what have you done?"

She reached for his arm, but the agents were already moving him toward the door. Politely, but firmly. He looked back at her one more time, his eyes overflowing with emotion. "I did exactly what I had to do. This is your choice to make. Nobody's got the right to force it on you. And now you can. I love you, Livie. I'll see you around."

And then he was gone, ushered out the door between two FBI agents. Livie stood frozen, staring after him, desperately trying to understand what had happened.

"Miss Romano?"

She spun around. The dean was still there, still watching the whole thing play out. Except she had no idea what that "thing" was.

"What just happened here?"

"Perhaps you should come in so I can explain the situation."

"Please."

He looked at his secretary and sighed heavily. "Vicky, clear my schedule for the rest of the day and all day tomorrow. I'm going to have my hands full."

In his office, after she'd sat in one of the two leather chairs facing his desk, the dean fell heavily into his own chair and threaded his fingers together. On his desk, under his hands, there was a scatter of paper, computer printouts, lists of numbers. She couldn't read any of them from where she sat.

"Earlier this afternoon, your friend Mr. DeSantis came to me with a rather explosive allegation. He claimed Professor Langley, the Acting Chair of your department, has been skimming funds from a grant awarded to the Chair, Professor Finch, who's indisposed with an illness. I'm guessing that's what you intended to tell me during your appointment today?"

"Yes." Livie nervously ran her fingers down the line of upholstery tacks in the arm of her chair. "I can't prove it, but he is, I'm sure of it."

"Well, Mr. DeSantis proved it." He leaned back and waved his hands at the papers strewn across his desk. "He presented me with a fairly incontrovertible chain of evidence, including banking records from Skylight Telecommunications listing withdrawals by the university and deposits in those same amounts to Langley's personal checking account. He also produced electronic copies of the university fund request forms with Professor Finch's signature on them. Since he's informed me Professor Finch can't yet walk or talk, I'm guessing these signatures are forged."

He lifted a printout and skimmed the page. "I'm not sure I want to know how he acquired these records."

Livie stared at the printouts. Skylight's internal banking records, the forged request forms from the university's internal system, Langley's personal bank account activity, and the "how" was crystal clear to her in an instant.

"No!" Livie covered her face with her hands. "Oh, *no*! He couldn't have been so stupid, could he?"

But she already knew the answer to that question. He'd hacked into Skylight's financial records, and the university's databases, and Langley's personal bank account. He hadn't *left* with those FBI agents, he'd been *arrested* by those FBI agents. He'd crossed the one line he wasn't supposed to cross. And he'd done it for her.

"He also seemed to think Langley had it out for you personally?" The dean was obviously upset about the scandal that had just exploded in the middle of the university, but his voice was kind, as were his eyes, as he examined her across the piles of evidence that might send Nick to jail.

"He did. When Janet had her heart attack and didn't recover right away, Langley tried to get me to work on his project instead. He wasn't happy when I said no."

"Is there anything else about Professor Langley I should know before I take steps to resolve this matter?"

So she told him everything—about getting shunted to Peter's lab assignment, about his refusal to sign off on her Hubble application, knowing it would imperil her PhD, about the new stuff in Langley's office, the new equipment in Peter's—by the time she'd finished, Dean Haverman was wearily pinching the bridge of his nose.

"You have my apologies on behalf of the university, Miss Romano. Whatever we can do to facilitate you advancing your work on your thesis, please don't hesitate to ask."

"I want Langley held accountable for what he's done. That's all. I don't need any help." She paused to draw a deep breath. It felt like she was about to jump off a very tall cliff into very cold water far below. "Because I'm transferring to McArthur to finish my PhD. I start in January."

Haverman looked utterly defeated. "I'm very sorry to hear that. Your records indicate you're an exceptional student. Is there anything I can do to get you to reconsider?"

She shook her head. "It's not about this. It's about me. This is something I should have done a long time ago."

Haverman pushed himself to his feet and extended a hand toward her. "Then I wish you good luck with your future studies, Miss Romano."

Chapter Forty-Five

All things considered, Nick was treated quite decently by the guys who arrested him. It might have been that he called them up as soon as he'd gotten the information he'd needed and told them exactly what he'd done and when and where they could come and arrest him for it.

He didn't see much point in trying to hide. They kept pretty close tabs on him. They were bound to figure it out sooner or later. Why not save the taxpayers a few bucks and make everybody's job a little easier?

He was mildly surprised that they'd hauled him all the way to DC instead of interviewing him at a field office in the city. But then again, he was a sensitive asset, and they liked to keep those pretty close to the nest.

He'd been cooling his heels in an interrogation room for the better part of an hour, but it wasn't some break-your-will-to-live kind of place like he'd seen on TV, or like he'd experienced firsthand back when they'd picked him up eight years ago. No glaring bare bulbs overhead, no one-way mirror, he wasn't cuffed to a steel table. This looked more like the office of some low-level bureaucrat who hadn't had the time to decorate yet. He sat in one battered office chair—not even handcuffed to it—and on the other side of the desk an empty chair awaited his interrogator. They'd even brought him a cup of terrible coffee and some chips from the vending machine while he waited.

Finally, the door opened and a familiar face entered the room. Nick knew him as Agent Smith, but he was pretty sure that was not his name. He was carrying a fat file in one hand—all of it no doubt about one Nicholas DeSantis—and a coffee mug emblazoned with the FBI logo in the other. Smith circled around the desk and took a seat, leaning forward on his elbows to examine Nick.

"You look good, Agent Smith. You been working out?"

Smith cracked a small, sarcastic smile. "I figured I'd see you here again one of these days, Nick. A guy like you can't resist the lure his whole life. Eventually he's gonna get back in the game, and sooner or later, he's bound to shoot himself in the foot."

Nick shrugged. No point in explaining himself. They already knew it all. All that remained to be seen was how he'd be made to pay for what he'd done.

"But I gotta admit," Smith continued, flipping through the file. "I'm a little confused about how you chose to do it. You finally go rogue, but you don't in-filtrate a Vegas casino or sell your services to one of those Russian outfits. Skylight Telecom is admittedly a little interesting, but you didn't even break into their research and development division. You broke into their *financial* database. And the rest of this? Bureaucratic records at a mid-level city college? One single personal checking account at Chase Bank? I'm not seeing a crim-inal mastermind hacker at work. Mind letting me in on your genius plans here? After all this time, why'd you cross the line for *this*?"

Nick bit back a smile. "Would you believe me if I said I did it for a girl?"

Agent Smith threw his head back and laughed. "Honestly? That's the only explanation that makes sense." Sobering, he folded his hands in front of him on the table. "But while I find that terribly romantic, you understand you fucked up?"

"I do."

"And you understand our previous arrangement no longer applies?"

"I do."

"This isn't something we can overlook. There will be consequences."

Nick lifted his head and looked Smith straight in the eye. "Whatever they are, it was totally worth it."

"She must be one hell of a girl."

Nick thought back to Livie's face in that last moment, right after he'd kissed her senseless and right before he'd vanished without a trace. That memory might have to last him quite a while. How long remained to be seen.

"She *is* a hell of a girl." He smiled, a small, private smile. "She walks amongst the stars."

"Stop it. You're gonna make me cry." Smith sat back and took a sip of his coffee. "Okay, then. Let's talk about what happens next."

Chapter Forty-Six

"This is so cool!"

"Hang on," Livie said, leaning over and punching a few buttons on the telescope. The huge metal tube slowly swung to the left and oriented itself to the new coordinates. "Take a look now."

The sullen fifteen-year-old boy, who'd been dragged along to the community outreach event by his mother, peered into the eyepiece again. "Holy shit, what is that?"

"Cameron!" his mother wailed. "Language!"

"It's okay, I'm from New York. I've heard much worse. That is the Horsehead Nebula."

"What is it?" Cameron breathed, never lifting his eye from the eyepiece. Nearly everyone else from the evening stargazing event had gone home. There was only Cameron and his mother left. She'd been urging her son to wrap it up for fifteen minutes, but the kid was hooked. From someone who hadn't wanted to step foot in the observatory earlier this evening, now he'd become someone she couldn't tear away.

"It's a star nursery."

"What's that mean?"

"It's made up of interstellar dust and gasses that come together to create new stars. See those little bright spots inside of it?"

"Yeah?"

"Those are stars being formed."

"Wow."

"I know, right? It's pretty cool."

"So cool."

"Okay, Cameron," his mother interjected. "The stargazing ended fifteen minutes ago. We're keeping Dr. Romano from getting home. I'm so sorry."

"It's okay. I really don't mind. And I'm not a doctor yet."

Cameron finally looked up from the telescope. "You're not? But you know so much stuff."

"I'm still in school, I've got another year to go and when I've finished, I'll submit something called a dissertation. It's a paper, about the research I'm doing here at McArthur. After that, I'll graduate and become a doctor."

"What will you do then?"

"Even when I finish my dissertation, I'll still have a lot of research to do on my subject," she explained. "My dissertation will only describe a tiny part of it. Hopefully I'll get hired to teach at a college somewhere that will let me keep working on it."

"They should definitely give you a job, because you're a great teacher."

"Thanks," Livie said. To her surprise, she agreed with Cameron. She'd become a great teacher since she'd arrived at McArthur. She'd never have believed it when she'd stepped in front of her first Intro to Astronomy class back at Adams. A lot had changed since then. Most importantly, her.

"McArthur opens the observatory to the public once a month," Livie told Cameron. "Be sure you come back."

"Oh, absolutely," his mother assured her. "I haven't seen him this excited since they released a new edition of *Fortnite*. Thank you so much for your time."

"It was no problem at all. Drive safe. The road down the mountain is a little scary at night."

It was scary even in broad daylight, when she'd only had her license for a few months. At night, it was absolutely terrifying. But she was working on that. A little fear wasn't going to keep her away from McArthur's mountaintop observatory.

"See you next month!" Cameron called as he trailed his mother out of the observatory. Livie waved them off, pausing for a moment at the door to breathe in the night air.

This high up, it was cool at night, even now, in late spring. The pine-scented air was so crisp and clean here in western Colorado, like taking a drink of freezing cold, crystal-clear water. Down the mountain, in the valley below, the mid-sized college town of Greenvale, and the McArthur campus would still be busy and lit up, but up here on the mountain, it was pure darkness. The only sound was the whistle of the wind through the thick pine forest around the McArthur Observatory.

Overhead, the sky was carpeted with stars, something she'd never really been able to see back home in Brooklyn. Tonight, a new moon night, the Milky Way was visible, too. Occasionally, you could even see it down in Greenvale, if you got far enough away from the lights.

She held her hand out in front of her, pale gray-blue against the inky darkness. Without a moon, the stars provided the only light. *Starlight.* Here, she could actually *see* the starlight, another thing she loved about McArthur.

There was quite a bit she liked about McArthur. They'd bent over backward to accommodate her, showering her with resources and attention. The state-of-the-art labs and computer equipment had taken her breath away the first time she'd toured the Astronomy building. The academic staff was littered with the best and brightest of the astronomy world, all of them eager to help her puzzle out her research. All along, all she'd wanted was the chance to work on this research, and now she had that chance.

All the other grad students bitched about their tiny campus apartments, but Livie loved hers. After living her whole life in the Romano house, surrounded by other people and generations' worth of stuff, her own place felt miraculously uncluttered and serene. She hadn't even known what she valued in her own space until she had it. She might have never figured that out about herself if she hadn't left home.

She'd worried her fellow students might view her as an oddball, turning up with her old professor's research in the middle of her third year, and trailing rumors of an academic scandal in her wake. Instead they'd been interested and welcoming. They'd started inviting her to departmental get-togethers before she'd even unpacked her bags, and this time, Livie said yes. Maybe she'd never be the life of any party, but she now had a handful of people she considered friends, people who were happy to tell her how to find the grocery store, or where to find the best coffee on campus. Everywhere she looked, people were willing to help her out. All she had to do was let them.

Not that she didn't miss home. At least once a week, she'd be hit with a painful bout of homesickness, missing her family so much she could cry. But it never lasted long and there were a million other things she loved about being at McArthur—things she never would have had back in Brooklyn—that it made it worth it.

Although she'd been planning to go back home for the whole summer, she'd just heard from the Very Large Array radio telescope observatory in New Mexico that she'd been granted a research slot this summer. That meant all she'd get would be a quick visit to Brooklyn before she headed to New Mexico, which made her sad and excited at the same time.

With one last glance at the Milky Way, she went back inside to shut the observatory down for the night. The sliding doors on the dome were sticky, as usual. She was still wrestling with the controls when the sound of gravel crunching underfoot outside sent her heartbeat into overdrive.

This quiet mountainside was safer, by anyone's estimation, than the New York City streets, but it was all about what you were used to. In New York, being surrounded by people twenty-four hours a day made Livie feel safe. These dark, empty parking lots made her jumpy as hell.

"I always knew you'd be a good teacher."

She spun around, hand clapped to her chest, already scrambling for her cell.

Nick was standing in the open doorway.

"Nick! Jesus, you scared me."

He grinned, and her heart began pounding for an entirely different reason. It had been *months*, and not a single word from him. She'd have assumed he'd been sent off to jail, but Google searches turned up nothing on him. Well, Nick had never been findable online, but there were no indictments, no court cases, no sentencing—none of the official information you'd expect to see if he went to jail. It was like he'd just vanished.

And now here he was, looking too good to be true, in jeans and a leather jacket, his hair windblown from the breezy night outside, and his dark eyes watching her like she was the most precious thing he'd ever seen.

"You just created a new astronomer."

"What?"

He jerked his chin toward the parking lot down the hill behind him. "That kid. I'm not sure what he was into more, the Horsehead Nebula or you."

"Oh, come on."

"I'm serious. That kid had stars in his eyes."

His sudden appearance had shocked her senseless, but now her brain was coming back online, asking all sorts of questions.

"How did you find me here?"

"Come on, Liv. I found Interpol's most wanted in an hour. You think *you* were much of a challenge?"

She laughed nervously. "I guess that's true."

Nick's answering smile faded and his eyes grew serious. "How have you been, Livie?"

"I should be asking you that question. *Where* have you been? You *vanished.*"

He made a face, then pushed off the doorway and wandered into the dark gloom of the observatory. She could barely pick out his features in the low light. "I told you, I didn't have a lot of control over my situation."

"Which was?"

"Going into lockdown for a while? They didn't let me out much. Like, not at all."

She swallowed hard. "You've been in jail."

"No, I'm much more valuable to them out of prison than in."

"Then where—"

"The government has all kinds of hidey holes where they can keep people who are proving useful to them."

"Nick, just tell me what happened to you."

He circled around the telescope. "I'm trying. There's a lot I can't tell you about. Most of it, in fact."

Then he stopped, now only a few feet away from her. "But there's one thing I *can* tell you. I thought about you every day. A dozen times a day. More. And as soon as they let me travel, I came straight to you. I missed you, Livie."

She'd been trying so hard to keep her emotions in check since she'd turned around to find him standing there. Sure he'd told her he loved her that day last year in Dean Haverman's office, but then he'd walked out the door and disappeared. For *four months*. Half the time she suspected she'd dreamed the whole thing. The only proof it had all really happened was when Langley's indictment had come down a couple of months ago.

Throughout all these months, as she'd navigated her move, as she'd built her new life in Colorado, as she'd gotten down to doing the work she'd come here to do, she'd done her very best not to think of Nick, not to pin her hopes on that declaration, not to sit around waiting for him to show up. He'd told her not to. She hadn't. She'd gotten on with her life like Nick DeSantis had never been a part of it and never would be again.

But here he was, back again, and in an instant, she knew he'd never left her, not for a second. He'd been right here, hiding in her heart, and with the slightest encouragement, she could fall just as much in love with him as she'd ever been.

"I missed you, too," she finally admitted to him.

A slow grin unfurled across his face. He slid one

hand along the length of the telescope as he took a step closer. "You cut your hair."

Automatically, she reached up to touch it. It was a little past her shoulders now, and slightly thinned into long layers. She'd done it right before she'd moved to McArthur, part of her quest to become a new and improved version of herself. Gone were the oversized flannel shirts and shapeless jeans she'd lived in back home. Gone was that curtain of hair she hid behind.

Nick seemed to like this new version of Livie. His eyes roamed down her body, slowly taking in her skinny jeans and the thin V-neck sweater she wore under her lightweight leather jacket. He raised his eyes to hers again, and the intensity of his gaze sent a shock of awareness through her. "You look really good."

"So…so do you." Apparently there was enough of the old Livie still hanging around to leave her tongue-tied the minute Nick so much as glanced at her.

"Are you happy?"

His question took her aback. "Happy?"

"Here. McArthur. Are you happy here?"

"Oh. Yes. I mean, how could I not be? The facilities are amazing. The faculty is totally supportive of my work. I have all the time I need. I only have to teach one lecture class, and no lab."

"What was this then?"

"This is just community outreach. I volunteered."

He chuckled. "*You* volunteered to deal with people?"

"I know, I know. But it's fun, you know? Showing people all the cool stuff out there. Like that kid tonight. He'll never forget this."

Nick scoffed softly. "He'll never forget *you*, that's for sure. How about Colorado? Do you miss home?"

Sometimes she missed it so much she couldn't

breathe. But that was getting easier. She was proud of her life here, because it was *hers*. She'd gone out and worked for every part of it. Nothing had happened by default, because she was too afraid to try for more.

"Yes," she finally answered. "I miss my family. But I'm happy here, too. What about your family?"

"I told you, I came straight to you. They're next on my list."

"Nick, you should at least call them. They've had to go years not knowing where you were. Don't do that to them again."

"Relax, I called before I went away and called again on my way out here. I promise, I'm not hiding from them anymore. I'm all done with that. But the reunion will have to wait until later."

"Later?"

"After. Look, Livie." He took a deep breath and ran a hand through his hair, looking uncharacteristically unsure of himself. She'd never seen Nick this nervous. "I know I didn't ask you to wait, and if you didn't, I'll understand."

"What do you mean?"

He waved a hand at her. "You look different, with the haircut and the clothes. And you're starting this amazing new life out here. If you decided to leave your old life behind, leave *me* behind, I'd understand. It's no more than I deserve."

She still wasn't great with men and relationships, but she had a tiny inkling of what he was trying and failing to say. It made her oddly feel better, seeing him so unsure of himself, no charm to fall back on. Anything he was saying this badly had to be one hundred percent genuine. "Are you asking me if I'm seeing anybody?"

He exhaled and looked at her with pure desperation. "Yeah, that's what I'm asking."

"No, I'm not."

"You're not?" His eyes lit up with a cautious hope, but he held still, not assuming anything, waiting for her to tell him what she wanted.

She shook her head and took a step toward him, reaching up to run her finger down the length of the telescope. "See, a lot changed for me when I moved out to McArthur, but there's this one thing that didn't change, even though sometimes I wished that it would."

Nick tracked her slow approach with hungry eyes, every inch of him tense and unmoving. "What's that?"

"The problem is, I fell in love with you the minute I laid eyes on you, and no matter how hard I tried, I couldn't seem to fall back out again."

He let out a shaky huff of laughter. "Livie, will you do me a favor?"

She stopped, no more than a foot away from him. "What's that?"

He moved suddenly, planting his hands on the telescope on either side of her head. "Stop trying to fall out of love with me, okay? Fall all the way fucking in. Because I promise, I'm here, too, waiting for you."

Her eyes began to burn and her throat felt tight. "I think I'm already all the way in," she whispered.

He leaned in, until his lips were just a breath away from hers. "And see? Here I am."

He closed the distance, kissing her with a slow, thorough tenderness that made her knees go weak and her body catch fire. His hands roamed everywhere as he explored her mouth, as if he couldn't get enough of touching her—her face, her hair, her neck, then down her back to her hips, and back up to cradle her face again.

"I love you, Livie," he murmured between kisses.

"I love you, too. God, I've wanted to say that for so long."

"Keep saying it." He kissed her again. "I want to hear it every day for the rest of my life."

The implication of "forever" made her heart leap with joy, until she remembered that there might be an expiration date on this interlude.

She pulled back enough to look into his eyes. "And will you be here to hear it?"

He flashed that crooked grin that had first made her go weak for him. It still did. "Are you asking if I'm going to cut and run again?"

"Yes. And also if armed agents are going to show up to disappear you again."

He chuckled, rubbing the pad of his thumb over her cheekbone. "No, we're all square again. Although my job situation has changed a little bit."

"What do you mean?"

"I work for them now. No more fun freelance gigs. I'm exclusively on the government's payroll."

What did that mean? Was he leaving again to disappear into one of their oubliettes?

"It's got its pros and cons," he continued, leaning in to nip at her bottom lip.

"Like?" The feel of his teeth scraping across her tender skin was making her go tight in all kinds of interesting places, and she was dangerously close to tossing aside her need for answers in favor of her need for sex.

"Well, the pay isn't great. I'm a civil servant now, with a civil servant's salary."

His hand skimmed up her rib cage, stopping just shy of her breast. Her nipples ached to feel his touch. She was practically panting with it. "That's rough."

"It is," he conceded, sweeping his thumb back and forth across her midsection. With each pass, the tip of his thumb barely brushed the underside of her breast. She clenched her thighs together against the sharp ache of desire. "Although I do get to keep all the money I already have, and there's loads of that. Plus, there's a perk."

"There is?" What were they talking about again? All she could think of was getting his hands on her bare skin as quickly as possible.

"Yep." He pressed another soft kiss to her lips, licked her bottom lip briefly before drawing back. She shivered in his arms. "I can work from home. And home can be anywhere I choose to make it. I want to make it wherever you are."

Finally some part of what he was telling her sank in. "You're not leaving again?"

He looked down at her, all teasing gone from his expression. "I'm not leaving, as long as you tell me I can stay. Livie, can I stay?"

Her fingers curled into the back of his neck, drawing his face down to hers. "Please stay," she whispered, just before she kissed him.

* * * * *

Watch for Love Around the Corner, *the third book in the Romano Sisters series, coming from Amanda Weaver and Carina Press in spring 2020.*

Reviews are an invaluable tool when it comes to spreading the word about great reads.
Please consider leaving an honest review for this or any of Carina Press's other titles that you've read on your favorite retailer or review site.

To purchase and read more books by Amanda Weaver, please visit the author's website at www.amandaweavernovels.com/books.

Acknowledgments

Every book takes a village to produce, but I've never felt the truth of that as much as I have during the writing of this book. So many people helped me shape it, refine it, and perfect it, and I owe them everything.

At one point in the history of The Romano Sisters, there was no book here. The book I'd intended to write in the middle fell apart and I had to come up with an entirely new story for Livie that would fit in between Jessica's story and Gemma's story. My agent, Rebecca Strauss, listened to me bounce ideas off the wall, trying to come up with something. With her guidance, I came up with a whole new story and a whole new Livie, and this one is so much better than what was there before.

I owe a huge thanks to my husband, Matthew Ragsdale. Well, I always owe him a huge thanks, but for this particular book, he gamely read countless scientific articles and brainstormed Dr. Janet Finch's entirely fictitious astronomical theory.

Here's the thing about this book. I decided to write a book featuring an astrophysicist heroine when I don't really know a thing about astrophysics. Thankfully Dr. Ashley Pagnotta was willing to make sure the mess I'd written had some basic scientific accuracy. I could not have gotten this far without her, and any remaining scientific errors are entirely my own.

All science aside, many thanks to Anne Forlines for invaluable feedback about these characters and their relationship. I couldn't do it without her.

And this book owes everything to my editor at Carina Press, Alissa Davis. Her insights are always spot-on, but this time, her comments led me to a dozen revelations about these characters and their story that I'd never have reached on my own.

About the Author

Amanda has loved romance since she read that very first Kathleen E. Woodiwiss novel at fifteen. After a long detour into a career as a costume designer in theatre, she's found her way back to romance, this time as a writer.

A native Floridian, Amanda transplanted to New York City many years ago and now considers Brooklyn home, along with her husband, daughter, two cats, and nowhere near enough space.

You can find her online at:
http://www.amandaweavernovels.com

You can find out all about her next release here:
http://eepurl.com/bvgkEv

She's on Facebook here: http://on.fb.me/1W6LnGS

And she's on Twitter here: http://bit.ly/1Zkf6MF

She's on Goodreads here: http://bit.ly/1KcRpPu

As a former visual artist, Amanda adores Pinterest.